PRESIDENTIAL POWER

Also by John Ford Clayton

Manipulated

PRESIDENTIAL POWER

JOHN FORD CLAYTON

Library of Congress Number: 2021907924

ISBN: 978-0-9995482-4-0

John Ford Clayton, Harriman, TN

ACKNOWLEDGEMENTS

Presidential Power is a fictional account of crime, corruption, and collusion among some of America's most sacred institutions. Thank you to those real institutions for providing such rich source material from which to create this story.

To my editor Linda, thank you for your thorough review and wonderful counsel.

To my cover designer Barbie, thank you for your persistence and patience with my many revisions.

To my friends Art, Bob, Jeff, Tanya, and Tyler; thank you for reading early versions of Presidential Power and providing great suggestions and consistent encouragement.

To my granddaughter Zoey, thank you for bringing joy, laughter, and hugs in a challenging year.

To my beautiful wife Kara, thank you for your support, encouragement, and patience. To the moon and back!

And always Galatians 1:3-5.

PROLOGUE

"Looks like it is about time to check on our high-profile prisoner again."

The deputy exhaled a long sigh and asked, "Where does the sheriff think he's gonna go?"

"That's not our concern. We're just supposed to check on him every hour on the hour. It's 4:59 a.m., and it is your turn to check."

"Fine, I'll go!"

The protocol was not normal, but Victor Youngblood was no normal prisoner. Twelve hours ago, Victor was the guest of honor in Rock Springs, Wyoming (population 23,350), visiting as the Republican vice-presidential candidate in an election that was less than a month away. Having never hosted such a high-profile guest, Rock Springs and the greater Sweetwater County area were aflutter with excitement.

They didn't know that Victor's vice-presidential candidacy credentials paled in comparison to those for his primary job as the founder and head of Mouse Trap, the world's most powerful and dangerous clandestine criminal enterprise. His role in Mouse Trap had landed him, not in front of a cheering crowd, but inside the holding cell at the Sweetwater County Sheriff's Department under arrest for the murder of Wyoming Senator Grant Wembley, who was also the previous Republican vice-presidential candidate and whose death paved the way for Victor's ascension.

"Just like every other hour, he was sitting in a chair in the middle of the cell, wide awake, staring into space."

"I'm not gonna lie; the guy creeps me out. He's been here for 12 hours, and he hasn't said a word. Every once in a while, he writes in that notebook."

"What's going to happen to him?"

"Great question. I've got no answer."

Circumstances outside the sheriff's office were equally uncertain and chaotic. The two dozen media members who came to Rock Springs to cover Youngblood's campaign appearance had stumbled on one of the biggest stories of the century—a vice-presidential candidate arrested for the murder of the previous vice-presidential candidate. Those first few media members had remained in place waiting for any nugget of news. They had been joined by over 100 more from around the country who, on short notice, came to Rock Springs, Wyoming, by planes, helicopters, trains, buses, and automobiles.

Joining the media outside the sheriff's office were the four aides who had accompanied Youngblood on the trip and who had been on the phone trying to determine what to do next.

The two Secret Service agents assigned to guard Youngblood had similar late-night calls with their superiors in Washington, who eventually told the agents to position themselves outside the building and wait for further instructions.

The fact that the murder involved a sitting U.S. senator raised jurisdictional questions, causing the FBI to send agents from field offices in Cheyenne and Casper to the now buzzing Sweetwater County Sheriff's Department. Although the sheriff had briefly talked with the Feds, he told them to wait outside like every other interested stakeholder, a command that was not well received but nonetheless heeded.

The circus outside was capped off by four deputies posted at the front and back entrances to ensure peace was maintained, a task that was about to become even more challenging.

"What's going on outside?" one deputy asked the other.

"I can't tell, but there seems to be a commotion."

Two black SUVs had navigated their way down Highway 30 and onto West Flaming Gorge Way. Escorted by two Wyoming Highway Patrol cars, they weaved through the media and other onlookers before finally stopping in front of the sheriff's department in an area deputies had kept empty as a buffer zone between the crowd and the department.

"Go wake the sheriff."

"Why do I have to wake him?"

"OK, let's both go wake him."

Sweetwater County Sheriff Buck Earnest had been at his office for close to 24 hours. After 18 hours, he had decided to take a short nap on his office couch, after giving his deputies strict instructions to wake him if anything unusual happened.

"State troopers? That's just great! We have the FBI, Secret Service, and city police; we might as well bring some more guys to the party. Let's go see what they want."

Sheriff Earnest put on his boots and hat and ambled to the front door just in time to see the procession approaching the building. The assembly included two state troopers followed closely by six men dressed in high-priced suits and $250 ties.

"Sheriff Earnest?"

"That's me."

"Sheriff, these gentlemen would like to speak with Mr. Youngblood. They are his lawyers."

"OK, but why is the Wyoming Highway Patrol escorting Youngblood's lawyers?"

Before the troopers could respond, a gentleman who was obviously the lead lawyer pushed past the troopers to engage the sheriff.

"That's none of your concern. I'd like to see my client. Please take me to him immediately," the lawyer demanded.

"Now just a second, I'm not—"

"Are you obstructing my client's right to representation, Sheriff Earnest?"

"Well, no, I'm just—"

"I'd like to see my client now," the lawyer insisted.

The sheriff threw his hands up in defeat. "OK, right this way."

Sheriff Earnest started down the hall; as he looked back over his shoulder, he was surprised to see that only the lead attorney was following.

"When will bail be set?" the lawyer asked while following closely behind.

"I'm not sure. That's not my department."

"I want to see everything you have on this case," the lawyer demanded.

Ignoring the lawyer, the sheriff rounded the last corner and gestured for him to enter the door to his left where he finally saw Victor Youngblood.

"Don't worry, Victor; you'll be out of here in less than an hour," the lawyer promised.

After opening the cell door and allowing the lawyer to enter, the sheriff relocked the cell.

"Just push that button when you're done, and a deputy will be back to let you out," the sheriff instructed as he left the two men alone.

"Victor, I'm terribly sorry about all of this. We got here as soon as we could, but this is quite a remote location. Now, tell me everything that has happened."

Finally breaking his stare, Victor locked eyes with his lawyer, shook his head, and said, "No."

Taken aback by the response, the lawyer muttered, "*No? I'm not sure what you mean. I want to get you out of here immediately, but I need some information. I—"

"No," Victor interrupted.

"Victor, you don't deserve to be in here. They don't understand who you are."

"I am going to stay here," Victor insisted.

"But I don't understand."

"I know you don't, but I do."

"Victor, I—"

"Go back to Washington," Victor insisted as he handed a sealed envelope to the lawyer. "Give this to Zeke and no one else. Do you understand?"

Having trusted Victor Youngblood for over 20 years, the lawyer finally conceded, "I understand."

Victor nodded. The lawyer took that as his cue to leave. He pushed the button, and a deputy immediately returned to let him out of the cell. Victor never looked up as the lawyer glanced back at his client before leaving.

The lawyer walked back through the office, passing the sheriff along the way. He motioned for the other five men to return to the SUVs. The state troopers escorted them out of town and onto Interstate 80, where they disappeared into the still dark morning.

"What was that all about?" a deputy asked.

"I'm not sure," Sheriff Earnest replied.

The sheriff walked to the cell door, peered in at the prominent prisoner, and mumbled to himself, "What are you up to?"

Turning to the sheriff, Youngblood, for the first time since his incarceration, dropped his stoic demeaner and from the pit of his soul conjured a wry, knowing smile.

The game was on.

1

"See Jeremy Prince."

"Excuse me?" Chip, the front desk clerk was first startled by the harsh tone, then by the speaker's menacing look.

"See Jeremy Prince."

"Oh, you want to see Jeremy?"

There was no response.

"I'll take that as a *yes*. Can I tell him who's asking?"

"Nyet."

"Umm…give me just a second to find him, OK?"

There was no response.

The visitor stood at the desk, arms crossed, emotionless.

"Hey, Dad, I've been doing some research on an app to help us manage inventory. It would be a small investment, but I really think it would pay off in the long run. Come take a look." Jeremy Prince gestured to the monitor.

"An app, huh? You know, I've been using these spread-sheets for years, and they work fine." Not moving from his chair, Walter Prince stroked his chin.

"But just come and look, Dad."

Walter sighed and walked slowly to his son's desk.

"You can tie this in with all our suppliers, and the app actually tells them when we need more product. We don't even have to place an order; the app would do it for us."

"Really? I spend half my day filling out orders." Walter took a couple of steps away from the computer and then looked back at Jeremy, his head cocked. "Jeremy, I want you to know how happy I am that you're here at the store work-ing with your mom and me. This is...well...this is good."

Chip approached the entrance to the Prince's Hardware business office. "Hey, Jeremy, there's a guy out front to see you."

"Who is it?"

"I don't know, but he's a stocky older guy. He's got a weird accent; and get this—he's wearing an eyepatch."

A short stocky guy with an accent and an eye patch? Jeremy knew that could only be one man—Andrei Ovchen-ko, the head of Blackforce, the enforcement arm of Mouse Trap—the deadliest department in the world's deadliest or-ganization, which Jeremy thought had been disbanded and scattered to the winds and which was Jeremy's former em-ployer.

"Umm...did he say what he wanted?" Jeremy asked

pensively.

"Nope, he just asked—well, actually demanded—to speak to you."

Jeremy tried to process the possible reasons Ovchenko had traveled to the small town of Abingdon, Virginia, just to see him. He was surprised at how many possible reasons his mind could conceive. The logical answer was revenge. Jeremy helped authorities arrest Mouse Trap's founder and leader, Victor Youngblood, whose demise was the lead domino in a long line that had affected Ovchenko and his Blackforce team. But if it were revenge, why would Ovchenko enter the hardware store in broad daylight? No, Ovchenko would have sent three of his Blackforce assets in the dark of night to do whatever it was they were ordered to do.

Maybe he was there to thank Jeremy for freeing him from working for Victor, who was a demanding boss. Maybe Jeremy's efforts allowed Ovchenko to finally get away from Victor. No, that's crazy. Ovchenko loved what he did with Blackforce.

Jeremy shook his head as if trying to awaken from a bad dream. He knew the only way to know why Ovchenko had come was to face him head-on. He strode confidently from the office to the front of the store.

"Yes sir, welcome to Prince's Hardware. How may I help you today?" Jeremy asked in his most helpful tone.

"Thirty-two million seven hundred fifty-thousand dollars," the man said in a thick Russian accent.

Ovchenko's brusque approach caught Jeremy off guard. "Excuse me, sir?"

"Thirty-two million seven hundred fifty-thousand dollars," Ovchenko repeated.

"I'm…not following."

It was a complicated situation. Jeremy had never actually met the man standing in front of him, but he knew all he needed to know about the lethal Andrei Ovchenko and Blackforce. Manned almost exclusively by former Soviet and Russian military personnel, Blackforce was called upon whenever Jeremy's former boss, Victor Youngblood, needed to handle a messy situation. Jeremy knew a Blackforce engagement always meant one thing—death.

"You sent email." As Ovchenko spoke, he slapped a piece of paper on the counter, the only thing standing between Jeremy and certain peril.

"An *email?*" Jeremy was still confused.

Ovchenko grabbed the paper and read.

"*Mr. Ovchenko, Victor Youngblood has been arrested. Mouse Trap is closed for good. The services of Blackforce are no longer needed. Thanks to Mr. Youngblood's meticulous documentation of Blackforce activities, each mission your organization undertook is recorded on video. You and the members of Blackforce should consider leaving the country.*"

"*Your* email," Ovchenko stated bluntly pointing a cracked and grease-covered stubby finger at Jeremy.

Although it was true that Jeremy had written the email as one of his last acts as a Mouse Trap team member, he had used an unattributed email address hoping it couldn't be connected to him. Jeremy's hopes obviously hadn't been realized. Not knowing how to respond, Jeremy was silent but knew he needed to remain steely-eyed or Ovchenko would sense fear and pounce.

"Thirty-two million seven hundred fifty-thousand dollars. Victor owes me. Victor in jail; you were number two; so, now *YOU* owe me."

Jeremy's well-planned scheme had landed Victor in jail in Sweetwater County, Wyoming, for the murder of a U.S. senator. The scheme also caused the downfall of Victor's Mouse Trap empire—at least that's what Jeremy had hoped.

"I don't have—," Jeremy started.

"Thirty-two million seven hundred fifty-thousand dollars," Ovchenko stubbornly repeated, this time in a booming voice.

As Jeremy searched for a response, Ovchenko's increased volume prompted his father, Walter, to enter the conversation.

"Is there a problem, Jeremy?"

"No, Dad, everything is good. This gentleman was just asking for directions. Let's go outside, and I'll show you the road you need to take." As Jeremy spoke, he attempted to nudge Ovchenko toward the door. He could have more easily pushed a 100-year-old oak tree; the Russian didn't budge. Almost 70, Ovchenko was well beyond his prime but was still a hulk of a man, albeit a short one.

"Thirty-two—"

Before Ovchenko could finish, Jeremy interrupted, "Yes, it is about 32 miles. Come on out, and I'll show you the road." Jeremy was at the front door holding it open for his unwelcome guest. After a scowl that would terrify a pit bull, Ovchenko reluctantly followed Jeremy out the door.

Jeremy walked briskly toward the parking lot trying to distance himself from the store. Finally reaching the back corner of the lot, he said, "Look, I don't know what you think—"

Before Jeremy could finish, Ovchenko put a hand over Jeremy's mouth and snarled, "We complete seven missions for Victor that we receive no pay for."

The contrast in the two men couldn't have been starker. Although Jeremy had caught Victor's eye and experienced an inconceivable meteoric rise to be the second-in-command at Mouse Trap, he was only 24 years old and not even three years out of college. Ovchenko, on the other hand, had been a general in the Soviet army. He had navigated the shark-infested waters of the Soviet Communist Party, fought in Afghanistan, lived through the Soviet Union's hellacious fall, and then moved to the United States to lead a team of battle-hardened mercenaries who had executed hundreds of American citizens. This conflict was truly a David vs. Goliath battle of wills.

"OK, here's the deal; yes, I worked for Victor and Mouse Trap, but I don't any longer. There is no Mouse Trap; and, as you said, Victor is in jail. I'm here working in this small town with my parents. I don't have any money or any access to money. I am sorry if Victor didn't pay you, but I'm not the guy you are looking for. I can't help you."

Jeremy's boldness caught Ovchenko off guard. He was unaccustomed to being told "no." In the brief moment he tried to formulate a response, Jeremy decided to fully embrace the role of victorious 'David.'

"So, we're done talking! Don't come back here and bother me or my family again!"

Before the stunned Ovchenko could respond, Jeremy had wheeled around and was walking briskly back to the store. Although he tried to stride with boldness, he was thinking, "I hope he's not following me." Shockingly, he wasn't. The 24-year-old had won this round against his formidable opponent, but it was only the first round in what would be a long and difficult fight.

2

After a restless night thinking about the prior day's hardware store encounter, Jeremy grabbed his cell phone from the nightstand and began to text.

Han, this is Luke, R U OK?

Hey, Luke, yeah, I'm good. Is something wrong?

No, not really. I had an interesting visitor yesterday. I think it was a false alarm. Just wanted to make sure everything was good with U.

Was it a storm trooper?

Yeah, but like I said, everything is OK.

OK. Keep me posted if you have any more visitors.

Will do.

"Yesterday was the culmination of countless hours of work by everyone in this room. You should be proud of yourselves; your hard work finally paid off. I am honored and humbled that the American people selected me to be the 45th president of the United States."

In addressing his campaign staff, Mitch McCoy was technically correct. American people did select him to be president; however, it was only a few dozen—specifically, a few members of the U.S. House of Representatives. Eight weeks earlier on Election Day, McCoy garnered only 39% of the popular vote and 41% of the electoral votes. In an election unlike any other, the traditional Democrat and Republican candidates were challenged by an independent candidate named Elijah Mustang.

Although his campaign as an independent candidate started too late, had too little money, and had no political party infrastructure to rely on, Mustang still won both the popular and the electoral votes. However, the campaign fell two electoral votes short of the magic 270 required to be elected president. The electoral stalemate sent the decision to the House of Representatives, who eschewed the voice of the voters and just yesterday selected Senator Mitch McCoy, Democrat from Connecticut, to be the 45th president of the United States.

"Of course, I would be remiss if I didn't welcome to the

stage the next vice president of the United States, my trusted confidante and running mate, Sally Naughton!"

The staff cheered as Naughton greeted McCoy with an embrace. The only problem was that in an electoral situation as in 2016, the vice president is selected by the Senate and is not the de facto running mate of the president selected by the House of Representatives. McCoy would soon discover that his presidency would face an unexpected challenge.

A lush snow covered the majestic summits just a few miles south of Walland, Tennessee's Blackberry Farm. The magnificent retreat, located in the foothills of the Great Smoky Mountains, hosted the gathered dignitaries. The team had reserved Bramble Hall, named for the prickly vine upon which grew the farm's namesake fruit. Designed after timber-framed barns of a simpler time, the hall boasted equal parts luxury and comfort. Its massive stone fireplace was roaring, providing comfort from the sub-freezing temperatures just outside the door. It was debatable whether the fire or the intensifying discussion was supplying the most heat.

"Somebody needs to explain why we're here because I sure don't know."

"As soon as you figure it out, please let me know," another disgruntled attendee echoed.

"I know we're all still disappointed with the election's outcome, but we must press on to bring this chapter to a close. We owe it to those who supported this campaign to end this the right way." Admiral (ret) Jackson Adair had ascended through a series of campaign roles, including an initial position as volunteer, then member of the leadership team, then leader of the leadership team, culminating in being selected as Elijah Mustang's running mate. On this day, Admiral Adair was doing his best to quell the leadership team's simmering frustration with the requisite responsibility of closing out the failed presidential campaign.

"I just don't understand why we have to handle this. Can't we just hire someone to tie up the loose ends?" One leadership team member's sentiment was shared by many in the room.

Another team member responded, "I agree; the voters had their say, and they said 'no.' I invested my time in the campaign, but it didn't work out. Now I need to get back to running my business." The leadership team was comprised of successful men and women from all walks of life, who put their professional and personal pursuits on hold to serve in this most unusual campaign.

"Leadership doesn't just walk away after a loss. Leadership shakes the victor's hands, puts the shoulder pads and helmet on the shelf, cleans up the locker room, and turns off the lights on the way out. That's what we're here to do."

Although Adair could still sense resistance in the room, he pressed on. "One of our first agenda items is to ensure we thank the many people who sacrificed their time, talent, and finances for this campaign. That acknowledgement starts with the people in this room."

Comprised of nine men and six women, the leadership

team included former congressmen, CEOs, a retired federal judge, a former secretary of agriculture, the bass player for a 70's rock band, a professional fisherman, an electrician, and a talk-radio host. Adair walked around the room announcing each member's contribution. "I've never seen such a diverse group of individuals mesh so well in such a short period of time. I know each of you backed Elijah 100%."

"Speaking of Elijah, has anyone heard from him recently?" a team member asked.

It was a question everyone was thinking, but no one had found a way to work into the conversation. Shortly after the election, just over two months before this meeting, Elijah left the country to serve with Promise Ministries, a non-profit he started to serve the neediest in Central America with a recent expansion to South America. Reports had surfaced of Elijah sightings in Honduras, El Salvador, and Brazil; but he had not appeared publicly since the election.

As Adair continued pacing, he nodded in agreement that it was a question that needed to be addressed. "I spoke with one of Elijah's daughters last week; she hears from him every few days. As we all witnessed firsthand, the campaign took a toll on Elijah. He deserves some time away from the limelight."

The team agreed with Admiral Adair; Elijah had put everything he had into the campaign, which he never really wanted to enter. The team accepted that he was now due some solace from the chaos.

"One of our primary agenda items is campaign finance. As you know, we've secured the services of Taylor and Blue out of Nashville to manage campaign funding. I've asked Brett Taylor to give us a report of where things stand. Brett, the floor is yours."

With Elijah's campaign having unfolded so rapidly, finances were one facet that the team outsourced to an experienced firm. Taylor and Blue had managed the campaign finances of two presidential hopefuls, over a dozen senate and congressional candidates, and close to 100 state-level contenders.

"Thank you, Admiral. I must start by saying what an honor it has been to be part of this historic campaign. What you have done will rewrite political science textbooks for years to come."

Taylor clicked the remote to start the presentation.

"Let's talk about timing first. Most presidential campaigns begin planning up to three years in advance. They are supported by major political parties that are in perpetual campaign mode with hundreds of staffers. You started from zero, six months before the election. You had no party backing you, yet you won the popular vote by a wide margin and came within two electoral votes of winning the presidency. I sense you're all dejected, but you need to understand that what you did doesn't normally happen in American politics."

Although Taylor was hired to be the numbers guy, he embraced the Mustang for President campaign's channeling of the nation's frustration with the two mainstream parties' gotcha politics. He wanted to instill a sense of accomplishment in the Mustang team.

"Let's talk numbers. In six short months, your campaign

raised $90 million by Election Day. With no organization and no party, that's impressive. Let's compare that to the two major party candidates. Ireland, the Republican, raised $875 million, almost ten times what you spent. McCoy, the Democrat, raised $985 million. And yet you got more votes than either of them!

"Here's an impressive stat for you. Ireland raised $27 for every vote he won. McCoy raised $19 per vote. Elijah Mustang—your guy—spent $1.38. A BUCK THIRTY-EIGHT!! Like I said earlier, you guys are rewriting the political history books!

"And here's what's really exciting. I said that you had raised $90 million by Election Day, which was over two months ago. Since then, you've raised another $40 million. People are continuing to give. They are expecting you to keep this movement going. You all seem to think this gathering is the end of something, but the people are telling you it is the beginning of a movement. The people rose up and spoke on Election Day, and now they are calling on you to keep the movement going."

One of the leaders responded, "The election is over. It is great that people are contributing, but what are we supposed to do with the money? We have no power. Exactly *what* are we supposed to keep going?"

It was a question that would have an unexpected answer within minutes.

"Hear ye! Hear ye! Hear ye! All persons are commanded to keep silent, on pain of imprisonment, while the Senate of the United States is sitting for the election of the Vice President of the United States." The Sergeant at Arms, Reginald Z. Honeycutt, made the proclamation as the sitting Vice President ascended to the podium.

"Per agreement from the leadership of both parties, today's vote will be held without debate or discussion. A roll-call vote is required. The clerk will call the roll." The Vice President promptly began the proceedings.

On December 9, 1803, Congress passed the 12th Amendment to the U.S. Constitution. That amendment provides the remedy for a situation, such as the 2016 presidential election, in which no candidate garnered the majority of Electoral Votes. While this Amendment guided the process whereby the House of Representatives elected Mitch McCoy to be the 45th president, it decrees that the Senate must elect the vice president.

In 2016, the Republicans held the Senate majority 54-46. According to the 12th Amendment, the Senate may only select between the two candidates receiving the most votes. This situation complicated the selection process because the Republican candidate came in third. The Republicans in the majority had the unenviable task of choosing between the Democrat candidate, their bitter rival, and a completely unknown outsider. It was a historic selection.

"Mr. Abernathy, how do you vote?" The clerk began.

"Because this team chose to spend only the money you had raised, you avoided going into debt; therefore, you finished the campaign with over $5 million in reserve. Adding that to the $40 million raised since the election, this movement now has $45 million." Brett Taylor's voice raised an octave, revealing his genuine enthusiasm.

"So, what are we supposed to do with $45 million?" a team member asked.

Taylor continued, "You're supposed to find a way to keep this movement going. The House probably thought selecting McCoy would quell the voice of the people, but it had just the opposite effect. The National News Service just released a poll showing a 74% approval rating for Elijah Mustang. As I said earlier, this is *historic*."

"Look, I understand that the people are behind this movement. They're donating money; approval ratings are up. I get it, but what are they supposed to rally behind? Elijah isn't even here. We have no power. We have no voice." Noticing Taylor with his head down looking at his cell phone, the team member's aggravation was piqued. "Come on, Brett; you're not even paying attention! Get off your phone!"

Taylor slowly looked up from his phone; a huge smile engulfed his face. "So, you have no power?" Taylor sauntered toward the head of the large oak table. "You have no voice?" He then put his arm around Admiral Adair, smiled at him, then back at the team. "Ladies and gentlemen, I've just received some interesting news. You want power and a voice? OK, I give you the next Vice President of the United States, Admiral Jackson Adair."

3

Three months later…

"You are not going through with this interview!" President McCoy demanded, pacing frantically, stopping only to point a finger in the Vice President's face.

"Yes sir, I am," Vice President Adair insisted professionally but forcefully.

Losing control, McCoy spoke in an awkward, high-pitched tone with his arms flailing, "No you're not! I forbid it! I demand that you cancel it right now!"

The meeting's location, the Oval Office, was selected intentionally to convey an air of ultimate authority. The audience was hand-picked from President McCoy's closest advisors including the chief of staff, secretary of state, communications director, press secretary, and a smattering of other advisors, clearly sending a message that the Vice President was outnumbered.

The message was not having its intended effect. "Mr. President, I intend to conduct the interview as planned." As a three-star vice admiral (ret), Jackson Carter Adair had encountered intimidating circumstances on many occasions. This gathering wouldn't crack his top-100 fiercest conflicts.

The tandem of McCoy and Adair at the helm of the Federal Government was historic on many levels. It was the first time in over 150 years that the President and Vice President were from different political parties. It was the first time in almost 200 years that no candidate had garnered a majority of electoral votes. These circumstances are a testament to the wild and wooly presidential election of 2016.

The Republican ticket was led by Lionel Ireland, former CEO of Diversified Communications, or Di-Com as it was commonly known. Ireland was a business icon but a political newcomer. His brash, bombastic style caused friction among many party loyalists. His running mate, Grant Wembley, was killed during a hunting trip in what was thought to be an accident. However, it was later learned that Wembley was murdered by Ireland's campaign manager, and second running mate, Victor Youngblood. These tawdry circumstances led to Ireland winning only a handful of states and 49 electoral votes.

On the Democrat side, 38-year-old Senator Mitch McCoy from Connecticut was the nominee. He was a legacy politician whose father was a four–term congressman and three-term senator. McCoy was by all accounts a despicable person. Although married to the same woman for 15 years, his philandering was among Washington's worst-kept secrets.

McCoy scratched the itch of his progressive base, winning many coastal states and all the New England states, garnering 221 electoral votes, which were well shy of the 270 needed to win.

Elijah Mustang was the 2016 wild card, an independent candidate who rode the wave of dissatisfaction with the traditional parties. Mustang quickly gained traction with American voters. The founder and CEO of a large trucking company, Mustang personified integrity, character, and humility; his faith guided his core values. He almost pulled off the biggest upset in American history, but his 268 electoral votes left him two votes short.

"What is so hard for you to understand? You're a naval officer. You're used to obeying orders. I'm the President of the United States, the leader of the free world, the Commander-in-Chief! I'm telling you to cancel the interview." McCoy was mostly speaking to the ceiling, unable to look Adair in the eye.

"I do follow the chain-of-command. You're just not in my chain. You didn't select me, and you do not have the authority to fire me. I was constitutionally selected by the U.S. Senate."

McCoy mockingly repeated, "I was constitutionally selected by the U.S. Senate. How could I forget?!"

The two-party dynamic was threatening to the insecure McCoy. The day after inauguration he demanded that all questions and issues from major policy decisions down to mundane protocol matters flow through his office. He gave no duties or responsibilities to Adair.

This marginalization was quickly recognized by the media, who wanted to know more about Vice President Adair. Over the course of the first several weeks of the McCoy presidency, requests to interview Adair were declined, having the opposite effect than McCoy had intended as interest in Adair was now volcanic. #FreeAdmiralAdair was the highest trending hashtag on social media for the previous ten days.

Seventy-five days into the McCoy presidency, Adair decided to bypass McCoy and his staff to schedule his own interview with National News Service anchor Laurie Delgado. The interview was scheduled for the following night.

McCoy walked behind the Resolute Desk and slumped in his chair. Without looking up, he waved an arm and muttered, "Fine, give it to him."

The White House communications director handed Adair a folder.

"What's this?" Adair asked.

"It's a list of what you can and cannot say. It's also a list of the McCoy presidency's policy positions. We expect you to align your remarks with them." The communications director stated bluntly.

"No thank you. I'll be fine." Adair handed the folder back.

McCoy rose from his desk again and approached Adair. "You have two options: cancel the friggin' interview or follow these talking points. Got it?!"

Adair then rose from his chair, and at 6' 5" almost a foot taller than 5' 8" McCoy, placed the unopened folder in the chair and stated, "You gentlemen have a good day," and left.

"I'm serious. Follow these talking points! Don't stray off the script!" McCoy screamed as he heard the door to the Oval Office shut.

"I don't think he's going to follow the script," the communications director stated flatly.

"Oh, shut up." The flustered President again plopped down into his chair.

In the six months between the day Elijah Mustang declared his candidacy and Election Day, many unprecedented events took place. Among the most stunning was the grass-roots organization that emerged to build enthusiastic momentum for Elijah's campaign. Every state in the U.S. and thousands of individual communities organized in support of this unorthodox campaign. With no vast headquarters or centralized party apparatus, supporters knocked on countless doors to encourage their fellow citizens to vote for Elijah.

As Election Day drew closer, a palpable excitement was growing among Elijah's supporters. With each passing week, Elijah's poll numbers continued to grow. The enthusiasm led many Americans to become actively involved in politics for the first time in their lives, feeling like they were part of a historic movement. However, as high as the buildup to the election was, the Mustang for President alliance felt an excruciating low when the results left Elijah agonizingly short of victory.

In this disappointment's aftermath, one of two paths was

destined to prevail. One path was paved with frustration, alienation, and resignation. That path would send supporters running away from politics and, more importantly, from any civic responsibility to correct the ills the country was suffering.

A second path was marked by determination, a sense of unfinished business, and a healthy dose of patriotism. Elijah Mustang tried to nourish this second path, even before the results were in. In an election eve speech to 100,000 supporters, Elijah had a clear message:

"I don't know how the vote is going to go tomorrow; but it almost doesn't matter, at least it shouldn't matter. Tomorrow isn't the end of the process; it's the beginning. It's the beginning of your taking back control of your country. Wednesday morning when the voting machines are returned to their closets, the pollsters put away their computers, and the networks convert their studios back to normal, you are just getting started.

"Stay engaged. Run for school board or city council. Run for statewide office. Write your congressman. Be your congressman! Make a difference!

"Beyond the emotion you are feeling tonight, there's something more lasting going on inside you. A feeling of inspiration that you know things not only need to be different but WILL BE different. Take that feeling and inspire others. Keep this going! Because YOU'RE NOT DONE!"

Elijah could never have dreamed how his words would

inspire his supporters to continue the movement, even after the disappointing election results. The speed at which events were moving in the three months since the House of Representatives selected McCoy as president left political pundits speechless.

As the movement worked to better organize after the election, one of the first decisions to be made was their name. A few suggestions were offered, but supporters never moved beyond the name *Mustangs*. They weren't the Mustang Party; they were simply *Mustangs*. The name was derived from their candidate's surname, but it had a deeper meaning. In the West, the mustang was a horse that was free to roam where it wished. It was unbridled but not wild. Originating from many breeds, Mustangs came in all shapes, sizes, and colors. Even the U.S. Congress recognized in 1971 the Mustang horse's uniqueness, passing an act that stated, "Wild free-roaming horses are living symbols of the historic and pioneer spirit of the West, which continue to contribute to the diversity of life forms within the Nation and enrich the lives of the American people."

With the name Mustangs settled, the next order of business was to add substance to what it meant to be a Mustang. This pursuit revealed the need establish a process for reaching consensus among the far-reaching supporters.

A meeting among Mustang leaders was quickly organized just two weeks after McCoy's election. Over 3,000 Mustangs assembled in Knoxville, Tennessee's Convention Center to establish rules of engagement. After dozens of breakout sessions, several general meetings, and countless hallway conversations, a decision-making structure was established.

Mustangs would be organized in geographic teams at the state and local levels. An equal voice for each state would be a central tenet of the Mustang movement; thus, each state would get one vote for each decision. State votes would be determined at the local level with each state establishing a process for reaching consensus. The national headquarters would be located in Knoxville, Tennessee. The national organization would be limited in power and would serve in primarily organizational and administrative roles. All of the Mustangs' proposed core beliefs would originate at the local level and would be submitted to the respective state organizations, who would forward all approved ideas to the national level for organizing a vote.

While this process made sense during a group planning session, its implementation proved challenging. Mustangs left the Knoxville meeting full of enthusiasm and hundreds of ideas. Quickly overwhelmed, the small HQ staff were unable to process the numerous proposals and also found duplication, overlap, and contradictions as they reviewed the submissions.

The leadership team—who remained intact except for the loss of their leader, Admiral Adair—knew they needed to find a quick solution involving minimal bureaucracy. They hired a firm to build a simple app to process ideas and tally votes. Via the app, any local Mustang team could submit a proposal to the state for consideration. Proposals adopted at the state level would then go to the HQ staff for a brief review to combine similar proposals. Then they would be loaded onto the app for all Mustangs to see. In this formative stage, there was virtually no limit to what could be considered. Proposals could include a platform in the Mustangs' core belief, a candidate they wanted to support, or an event they wanted to organize.

Every Wednesday night, each local Mustang team would vote on that week's proposals. The app would tally votes at the local and state levels. Strong support was sought before a proposal was adopted; therefore, to obtain a "yes" vote at the state level, 75% of the local votes had to be in favor. To obtain a "yes" vote at the national level and to be adopted by the Mustang movement, 75% of the states had to be in favor, the same margin required to amend the U.S. Constitution.

Although the Mustangs were united in support of their presidential candidate and in their frustration with the country's political direction, they found it difficult to be united on other matters. Only a handful of proposals had garnered the necessary 75% local/75% state vote. Items passed included the following: the U.S. Constitution would be the guiding document; the movement would not be a political party; no elected official identifying as a Mustang could serve more than two terms on any level (local, state, or federal); and that they supported the selection of Admiral Adair as vice president.

An important vote was pending on this night that could play a pivotal role in sustaining enthusiasm for the movement.

"What time does the voting window open?"

"6 p.m. We'll have the usual 24 hours to get everyone's

input although this vote should be easy. Everyone is excited. I'm expecting the tally to be at least 45-5. May 6th can't get here soon enough!"

While this discussion was happening at the Paducah, Kentucky Mustang team meeting, similar discussions were happening throughout the country. The Knoxville HQ staff had received proposals from five states recommending a national gathering of Mustangs. The HQ staff took the best of all proposals and put the following up for a national Mustang vote:

Mustangs shall gather on Washington, D.C.'s National Mall on Saturday, May 6, 2017, from noon to 8 p.m. to encourage one another, make our voices heard, publicize our beliefs, and serve as a clarion call that WE'RE NOT DONE!

May 6 was selected because it was the date that Elijah Mustang had formally declared his candidacy for president in 2016. Washington D.C. was selected because it was supposed to represent the people of the United States; however, many Mustangs believed it had become home to the entrenched political elites with the American people's representation far down on the priority list. They felt that showing up *en masse* would serve as a wakeup call that the Mustangs were leading the charge for wrestling their government away from those who had held it tightly for too long.

Undertaking such an event in less than a month would have been ambitious. There was no agenda, no speakers, no coordination with the Capitol Police or the National Park Service. Trying to pull this off in such a short time was far from normal. However, if Mustangs had shown anything consistently, it was that they were redefining *normal*.

Although states were given 24 hours to debate and reach consensus on each proposal, by 6:30 p.m. the Paducah, Kentucky team had voted unanimously to support the proposal for the May 6th gathering. By 7:30 p.m., every other local Kentucky team had also voted affirmatively. By 9 p.m., all 50 states had joined with Kentucky in supporting the proposed event.

The 50-0 vote had put wind in the movement's sails. Mustangs throughout the country were exuberant about gathering in the nation's capital. It was an exciting time to be a Mustang.

4

66 M r. Vice President, thank you for agreeing to this interview. I think you know you've been in high demand." Laurie Delgado was the National News Service's senior White House correspondent. She had worked for weeks to secure the interview with Vice President Jackson Adair.

"I am happy to do it. This is long overdue. I'd like for you to meet my wife, Janell."

Admiral Jackson Adair was a natural leader, not loud but supremely confident. He had that certain something that inspired people to follow him. Janell, his wife of 37 years, was just the opposite. She was quiet, some would even say meek. A homemaker for most of their marriage, she was content to be in the background. However, her husband and her two grown children knew she was the true backbone of the family. Jackson never made an important decision without first seeking her wise counsel.

"It is nice to meet you, Mrs. Adair," Delgado responded graciously.

"It is wonderful to meet you, Ms. Delgado. Welcome to our home."

The interview was to be conducted in the sitting room at Number One Observatory Circle, the Vice President's official residence. The 9,150-square-foot, three-story brick structure was built in 1894 for the Superintendent of the U.S. Naval Observatory. It was home to the Chief of Naval Operations from 1923 until 1974, when the Queen Anne style mansion became the vice president's home.

Delgado was known for her professional tenacity in pursuing interview subjects. She knew that all reporters were trying to score an interview with the Vice President. Half of America and a large percentage of the world would be tuning in. She wanted to assure Adair that everything was going according to plan.

"The crew should have everything set up shortly. They are just going through the final tech checks. We really appreciate your graciously giving us two hours to conduct this interview. We're recording so we can take a break at any time, but we would like to get as much on-camera time as possible. The interview will be airing on Friday night in the 9 p.m. prime time slot."

"I understand. Thank you." Adair was as excited to be speaking to the country as Delgado was in scoring the interview.

"Audrey, what time is the car picking me up?"

"Noon. The plane is fueled and ready to go at Teterboro."

Teterboro, New Jersey, a greater New York City general aviation airport catering to corporate jets, was always the choice for Scott Foster, CEO of Dominion Media Corporation, as it was a 35-minute limo ride from his Manhattan office suite.

"You'll be in the air by 12:45 and on the ground in London just before midnight London time. A limo will be waiting for you on the tarmac."

"Am I staying at the Dorchester again?"

"Yes sir, you are." Audrey raised her hand as she felt the buzz of her phone. "One moment sir, you have a call on the priority line." As always, Audrey had a headset ready to field a call at any moment. Only a select few had access to Audrey's almost-direct line to the CEO. "Mr. Foster's office, how may I help you? Oh, really? Yes, we'll hold."

The normally composed assistant had an uncharacteristic, stunned look on her face. "Sir, it's the President."

"The president of what?"

"The President of the United States."

Dominion Media was a highly diversified media and entertainment conglomerate. Its holdings included a movie studio; 17 newspapers; 27 local TV stations; three cable TV networks; a record label; and the subject of this call, a major cable news outlet named the National News Service.

A curious Foster picked up his phone. "This is Scott Foster."

"Mr. Foster, hold for the President."

Foster shushed away his assistant as he awaited the President's joining the call.

"Scott, thank you for taking my call. I know you are a busy man."

"Mr. President, I'm honored that you would call. What can I do for you?"

"Scott, as a CEO, I'm sure you understand the difficult financial circumstances our country finds itself in. So many pressing needs, yet our government just doesn't have the resources to deal with everything."

Foster remained confused about the purpose of this unusual call. He decided to keep his responses vanilla.

"Yes sir, we certainly have some national challenges."

"*Challenges*—that's a great term. While we have these collective challenges, we have individuals sitting on over $50 trillion in so-called wealth. $50 trillion!! You probably know that the centerpiece of my campaign was a wealth tax to try to restore some balance between the individual and the collective."

"Yes...I... uh—"

"Don't worry, Scott, I'm not going to ask for your support on this initiative. That's not the purpose of my call. What I'm looking for is an honest news outlet that embraces everything the First Amendment is designed to protect. I'd like to find an outlet that we can share early information with as we float various trial balloons for this ambitious initiative. We know Dominion has assets in print, radio, cable, and network news. We'd like to know if you'd be interested in this type of early information sharing. You have my word that we'll provide the facts and leave it up to Dominion how they should be reported. We'll give you access to anyone in my administration that can help answer any questions you might have."

Understanding that the primary currency in 2017 journalism was being "first" to any story, Foster knew he was being offered a gold mine. He had to at least pretend to protect the integrity of his news assets although his answer was already settled.

"Mr. President, this is a very generous offer. I just want to make sure I understand. We would be under no pressure to report stories friendly to the administration's initiatives or to shelve stories that might be at odds with your initiatives. We would still be able to maintain our journalistic integrity."

"Absolutely, Scott! Freedom of the press is one of our nation's pillars. Undermining that pillar undermines everything my administration stands for."

"Mr. President, I think we have an agreement."

"Outstanding, Scott. I believe this partnership will support both of our interests; but more importantly, it will be in the country's best interest."

"Yes sir, I concur."

"Scott, there is one more urgent matter I'd like to discuss."

"I'm told our techs are finalizing the lighting; we should be able to get started in the next few minutes." Laurie Delgado glanced into a small mirror and made a final makeup adjustment.

"That's fine. There's no hurry." Adair worked to clear his mind for the long-awaited interview. He knew this was as important for the country as it was for him. As Adair spoke, an assistant stepped in and whispered in Delgado's ear. The confused and concerned reporter nodded in understanding, then turned to address Adair.

"Mr. Vice President, I apologize; but I'm going to have to take a quick call." Clearly agitated by the interruption, Delgado hurried into an adjoining room before Adair could respond. She was still visible to the Vice President; and from her body language, he could tell the conversation was not going well. The brief call concluded with Delgado reentering the sitting room, her face ashen from the news she had to deliver.

"Mr. Vice President, I'm terribly sorry and tremendously embarrassed to tell you that I'm not going to be able to conduct this interview. I...I can't begin to express my disappointment."

"Is there something wrong?" the confused Adair asked.

"Yes, Mr. Vice President, a lot is wrong. I...I'm so sorry."

The producer had received the news as well and had instructed the techs to hurriedly pack up the lights, rigging, sound, and video equipment.

"Ms. Delgado, I'm very confused," the Vice President declared.

"I'm sorry. I hope someday we have the opportunity to

conduct the interview, but today is not the day."

As the news crew packed the final items, Adair had time to reflect on what was happening. It didn't take him long to put the pieces together.

Janell entered the room, surprised by the activity. "Jack, where's everyone going? Surely the interview's not already done."

"It was done before it ever started," Adair blurted.

"I don't understand."

Adair responded with a single word, "McCoy."

5

Twenty-five miles north of Asheville, North Carolina, up the Blue Ridge Parkway and down Ox Creek Road, a thickly forested area known as Bull Gap contained the remains of a 4H camp closed more than a decade earlier. The property is among thousands acquired through the years by subsidiaries of the clandestine organization known as Mouse Trap. These properties were threads in an intricate financial web used to accumulate unimaginable wealth. Although the camp was abandoned, according to IRS records it housed the Pisgah Camp for Disadvantaged Children with 2016 donations totaling over $9 million.

The camp's neglected structures included four bunkhouses, a dozen cabins, two barns, a cafeteria, and an 11,000-square-foot activity center. The center was structurally intact, making it the perfect locale for an ambitious resurgence.

"I'm sorry I am late. The drive took longer than I had

planned. I didn't realize this meeting was going to be in such a secluded location." As she took off her coat, Penny Butcher noticed the sparsely populated room. "I *am* late, right? Where is everyone?"

"So far, this is it." Zeke Gibson tried to hide his disappointment but was failing.

"Oh, I thought this was going to be a meeting of the whole management team."

"I tried to contact 60. So far six are here, including you and me. Maybe more will show up later."

For over 40 years, Zeke Gibson served Mouse Trap faithfully, ultimately reaching the leadership's upper echelon. Mouse Trap had tentacles extending beyond comprehension. A force that was as powerful as it was secretive, it had hundreds of billions of dollars in assets, control of significant portions of American institutions, such as print and broadcast media, Hollywood, the music industry, professional sports, and politicians from both parties. Just six months earlier, its founder and leader, Victor Youngblood, was poised for his ultimate payoff. He had devised a scheme to use the 2016 presidential election to put himself at the top of the U.S. government. To Victor's shock, the scheme—involving a vice presidential candidate's murder—came crashing down when he trusted a young apprentice named Jeremy Prince. Focusing on the election, Victor surprisingly named Jeremy as Mouse Trap's new head. Turning the tables, Jeremy lured him into a trap, which ultimately led to arrest for Victor's role in the homicide. With Victor in a small-town Wyoming jail, Jeremy sent an email to all members of Mouse

Trap informing them that the organization was closing its doors immediately. Jeremy also had collected records of Mouse Trap's carnage that included involvement in over 3,000 murders. In a final step, Jeremy sent the FBI a treasure trove of information documenting 40 years of Mouse Trap's nefarious acts. He hoped this step would end any remaining remnant of Mouse Trap; the opposite of what today's gathering sought to accomplish.

"I think you know everyone here." Zeke ushered Penny around the room for the reacquaintances. Third in command in Mouse Trap's financial division, Penny was responsible for accumulating the significant portion of corporate equity that Mouse Trap had acquired over 40 years.

The attendees also included Easton Brummett, who worked as one of the IT executives responsible for Omnia, Mouse Trap's computer hub. Omnia, derived from the Latin word meaning *everything*, was the engine that made Mouse Trap work. It included a messaging app through which all Mouse Trap communications were conducted. Mouse Trap's financial app provided employees access to their bonus accounts, in which even the most junior members had more than a million dollars, with most team members accumulating many millions. It was also the portal through which Mouse Trap's team members could access almost any computer system in the world. It was the repository for all of Mouse Trap's records as Victor invoked a strict no-paper policy, ensuring employees wouldn't inadvertently—or intentionally—leave work with Top Secret information. To the dismay of those assembled, Omnia was powered down when

Victor was arrested and had not been brought back online in the six months since. During that time, those assembled had no income, no access to Mouse Trap savings, and no way to interact.

Neal Campano and Shelby Wolf, two of Mouse Trap's 20 project managers, were present. Alyson Phillips, manager of the Cable and Network News Division, was the only one of 20 functional managers attending.

Zeke had arranged the meeting in the camp's activity center with 60 chairs, hoping most invitees would attend. The six people occupying the large space only served to accentuate the low turnout. At 8 p.m., two hours past the scheduled meeting time, Zeke decided to press on.

"I want to thank everyone for being here. I obviously had hoped for more attendees, but we'll start with what we have and go from here." As always, the 78-year-old Zeke had the energy of a man half his age.

"I want us to focus on a few key subjects this evening that will help identify a path forward for Mouse Trap. Let's start with the elephant in the room, the low attendance. Any theories as to why so few of our team showed up?"

Neal Campano was the first to speak. "To be honest, I think some were scared. Jeremy's email was very blunt: "Mouse Trap is closed." While not many of us knew everything that Mouse Trap did, we knew that we'd all be in trouble if the truth ever got out."

"That's a fair assessment, Neal. Anyone else?" Zeke prodded.

It was Penny's turn. "To build on Neal's theory, I think

some were relieved to have a way out. We all know once you're in Mouse Trap you don't get to leave. Most of us didn't know until we were in too deep. The six-month shutdown gave us…well…them a chance at a new start."

"Good thought, Penny," Zeke continued. "I'll add my own theory into the mix; it is a little more mundane. As you know, we normally communicate through Omnia. Since it is no longer available, I had to use personal email addresses for the meeting invitations; and some may not have been up to date. Some people simply may have not received the invitation. At least that's what I choose to believe." Zeke spoke that last sentence almost under his breath. "OK, let's move on; we have some important topics to discuss.

"I want to give you an update on Victor. The judge in Wyoming has denied bail, so Victor is stuck in the Sweetwater County jail for now. His lawyers have filed many motions, including a change of venue; but so far nothing is moving. We hope that he can join us, but we should assume we are going to be on our own for the foreseeable future. Easton, tell us what you know about Omnia. We can't do much without it."

Easton shook his head before he spoke. "Honestly, there's not much to tell. I've tried every address I can, but I can't even access the logon screen. The system is obviously powered down. For all we know, it could be destroyed."

"I'm guessing our best bet to awaken Omnia is Leonard Applebaum," Zeke interjected.

"Leonard would be my first option. He is really the primary Omnia architect, and it is rumored that he was working with Jeremy to bring down Victor."

"That is a rumor I can confirm," Zeke exclaimed. "Leonard was indeed working with Jeremy. If we want to find Leonard, we must find Jeremy and—"

Zeke was interrupted by the sounds of the front door bursting open, heavy footsteps entering the room, and a voice booming, "Jeremy is in Virginia. I have seen him. He is working with parents. I am looking for my thirty-two million seven hundred fifty- thousand dollars."

Of everyone in the room, only Zeke had personally met Andrei Ovchenko, the head of Blackforce. The attendees had heard many stories about the one-eyed man now standing before them, but even the most exaggerated rumor only scratched the surface of everything Ovchenko and his henchmen had done at Victor Youngblood's behest.

Zeke tried to lower the tension that Ovchenko's presence had brought. "Andrei, welcome to the group. Let me introduce you—"

"Thirty-two million seven hundred fifty-thousand dollars." Ovchenko clearly had no interest in lowering the tension.

"Yes, Andrei, we're all owed substantial sums. That's why we're here. We believe the best path is through Omnia. We think that path starts with Leonard Applebaum and Jeremy Prince."

Ovchenko described his encounter with Jeremy at the hardware store. After some debate, it was decided that Ovchenko should visit Jeremy again with a more pointed demand for any information Jeremy could provide about Leonard and Omnia. Ovchenko welcomed the mission.

Zeke issued one last caution. "Andrei, I must remind you that we don't have Victor covering our trail this time. You must tread more lightly and not leave carnage in your wake."

Offering no response, Ovchenko turned and left the cabin as abruptly as he had entered. He was on a mission.

As the meeting drew to a close, Zeke retreated to his personal cabin, reached into his jacket pocket, and pulled out an envelope he had been given six months earlier. It was a to-do list written by Victor and given to Zeke by Victor's lawyer. Zeke had read the list dozens of times and wanted to start checking items off months ago, but item #1 was *Wait six months to start*. Although uncertain why Victor insisted on the delay, Zeke followed orders. The six months' wait made the satisfaction of marking off item #1 as complete even sweeter. He was equally gratified that Mouse Trap's re-start allowed him to also mark off item #2. He folded the list, returned it to the envelope and the envelope to his pocket. Then he prepared for item #3.

6

"**H**ow many of you have read today's *Wall Street Journal*?"

The entire Cabinet—except for one member—looked away, trying to avoid being the first to make eye contact with the President.

McCoy held up the newspaper for everyone to see the front-page headline:

McCoy Presidency Without Direction

"The article states, 'No president in recent history has done less in his first four months in office than President McCoy."

Located in the West Wing adjacent to the Oval Office, the Cabinet Room overlooks the Rose Garden. The well-equipped Georgian-style room boasts a large elliptical mahogany desk, upon which McCoy slammed the offending newspaper. The sturdy desk fought back, causing the embarrassed President to shake his hand, wincing in pain. After regaining both his composure and the feeling in his hand, the most powerful man in the world continued, "You understand this article is not just about me; it's about you too. It says you're a failure. It says everyone sitting around this table is a do-nothing, incompetent clown. Is anyone happy about that because I'm certainly not."

The semi-rhetorical question elicited a few "No sirs" from the less-than-enthusiastic Cabinet members.

"Everything is changing today. We're launching a course of historic action, and we're going to see it through. The American people elected me to this office for a reason."

"The American people didn't elect you to this office; the House of Representatives did."

The bold response was met with gasps and murmurs throughout the room. McCoy craned his neck to confirm the source of the retort, but he already recognized the voice. After quickly glancing at Adair, he sneered at his chief of staff and said, "I thought I told you not to invite him."

Relations between the President and Vice President had continued to deteriorate. The cancelled interview with the National News Service prompted Vice President Adair to move away from a defensive posture, freeing him to speak even more boldly to the President. His 30-year military discipline kept him from being outright insubordinate, but he was determined to let his feelings be known when the situation warranted. Adair realized that this meeting was such a situation.

"Why are you chastising your Cabinet? You've been in office almost four months, and this is your first Cabinet meeting. You haven't proposed a single significant initiative. The *Journal* isn't writing about the people in this room; it is writing about *you*."

The President seethed, stammered, and stuttered, unable to voice a cogent response. After more than a few awkward moments, he was finally rescued by Chief of Staff Riley Indigo.

"Mr. Vice President, that's a great segue as the purpose of this meeting is to discuss an incredibly significant initiative. President McCoy's cornerstone issue during the campaign was overhauling the country's tax system and instituting a historic initiative to level the playing field for America's working class, thus addressing the scourge of economic inequality. Today we are beginning the process of rolling out a wealth tax. With over $60 trillion of wealth in this country, this simple tax of 5% will yield the treasury $3 trillion annually. That's close to what we collect in income taxes from everyone combined in the country. With half the $3 trillion, we will cut taxes for everyone making under $100,000. With the other half, we're going to fix this country's ills. We're going to repair roads, bridges, dams, and levees. We're going to rebuild our suffering inner cities. We're going to take care of our poor and our seniors."

After finally recovering from Adair's broadside, McCoy decided to retake the reins of the meeting from his chief of staff.

"Each person in this room has an assignment. I need

each of you to tell me what you'd do with a 50% increase in your budget. We need to sell American citizens on this historic initiative by letting them know what's in it for them. This is a turning point in my administration, and we're going to seize the mandate the voters have given us." McCoy did his best to close with a dramatic crescendo.

Adair resisted the urge to respond, falling back on his decades as a naval officer. He remained silent for the time being.

"Is this where Jeremy Prince works?" the tall blonde asked frantically.

"Yes, this is Jeremy's family store. It has been in the—"

Before the clerk could finish his sentence, Savannah interrupted, in an even more urgent tone. "I need to speak with him right now."

"OK, I think he's in the back office. Just a moment."

"Please, tell him to hurry."

Savannah paced nervously around the hardware store's front desk, glancing at the displays of Flexsteel, pocketknives, and gutter guards before Jeremy emerged from the office. Jeremy's initial excitement of being told a tall blonde was there to see him quickly devolved to a sick feeling in the pit of his stomach when Savannah turned around to look Jeremy squarely in the eye.

"Oh, it's you," Jeremy said in his most disgusted tone.

"I know, I know, Jeremy. I don't blame you," Savannah

replied apologetically.

Without saying a word, Jeremy pivoted to return to the office.

"Please, Jeremy, just give me a minute."

After a couple of steps, Jeremy paused, looked down at the floor, sighed heavily, then shook his head in disbelief before speaking. "I honestly can't believe you're here."

"I know, Jeremy. Trust me, I understand."

"You understand?" Jeremy turned fully toward Savannah, taking three steps back in her direction. "What exactly do you understand? Do you understand that you are responsible for my being part of the deadliest organization in the world? Having a role in MURDER? Being thrust into the middle of a rigged presidential election? Spending time in jail? Is *that* what you understand?"

Savannah had been an operative for Victor Youngblood, who sent her to pose as a college student in order to convince Jeremy they had been in a class together at Virginia Tech. After gaining his trust, Savannah urged Jeremy to apply for a job with Victor, setting in motion a series of events that neither could have predicted.

"I know, Jeremy; that's all terrible. I promise one day we can discuss all of that, but we don't have time right now." Savannah took a deep breath, collected her thoughts, and then proceeded, "Jeremy, you are in serious danger, not just you, but your entire family."

"*Danger*? What are you talking about?

"There's a remnant of Mouse Trap that's trying to re-start. They are convinced you are the key to getting Leonard to restore Omnia and reclaim their assets. This is serious. Ovchenko is coming."

Jeremy laughed. "Ovchenko? He's already been here, and I told him I didn't know anything and not to come back to my store. I think I sent a pretty clear message."

"No, Jeremy, it doesn't work that way with Ovchenko." Savannah was becoming more frantic. "He doesn't just walk away. He doesn't give up. Jeremy, he's coming back. You gotta get away and take your family with you."

Jeremy raised both hands in protest. "OK, that's it. I've got a business to run. I don't have time for these fantasies. Please leave my store now and don't come back."

"Jeremy, please, this is really serious."

"I said LEAVE." Jeremy pivoted and walked quickly back to the office.

"But, Jeremy, you gotta believe me."

As Savanah was met with the sound of the office door slamming, she turned to walk out of the store, her mood transformed from frantic concern to resignation. She knew the question wasn't *if* something bad was going to happen but *when*. The answer would come sooner than she could imagine.

7

"OK, let's get going. We're down to 20 days until the big event. Let's start with venue logistics this morning." Minnie Carpenter opened the meeting.

The logistics lead responded, "I think things are going as well as they can. We've pushed as much as possible out to the local and state levels. They are responsible for transportation and lodging. At the national level, we have secured every port-o-potty in a 75-mile radius. As of the last count, we have over 500 food trucks committed. Our most significant breakthrough has been with the National Park Service. As I noted in a briefing a few days ago, this sounded like a big challenge with the alphabet soup of regulations for events to be held on the National Mall. But we have an ace in the hole with Admiral Adair, who found many in the Park Service sympathetic to our cause. Having overcome all those hurdles, we're on a clear path to May 6."

"Great job. Glad to hear everything is on track." With

Jackson Adair's ascension to the vice presidency, a vacancy was created at the top of Mustang's leadership team. It didn't take long for the team to select Minnie Carpenter as Adair's successor. As chief operations officer for the second-largest U.S. cell phone provider, Minnie successfully juggled being a strong leader while maintaining a jovial personality and good humor. Her first name was always a conversation starter. Too many times to count, Minnie told the story of how her parents were living in Orlando, Florida, when Walt Disney World opened in 1971. They quickly fell in love with the Magic Kingdom; and in honor of their new favorite hangout, they named their daughter, born in 1972, after the second-most famous mouse in the park. She often joked that she was happy that her parents never had a son; otherwise, she might have had a sibling named Goofy. Throughout the 2016 presidential campaign, Minnie proved to be a fountain of wisdom that Elijah Mustang trusted. It was only natural that she was now leading the team and this morning's daily 7 a.m. status meeting, held in the downtown Knoxville Mustang headquarters.

"OK, Regina, how's the speaking docket coming together?"

"It's coming together. We have a good mix of knowns and soon-to-be-knowns. We have all three members of Congress who align with the movement plus Senator Harmon. We also have a trucker, an electrician, and a fast-food manager. Of course, Admiral Adair will be among our last speakers. We're still holding the keynote slot open in hopes that we find Elijah and can convince him to speak."

"Keep holding, Regina. We hear about Elijah sightings over in Roane County, but nothing has been confirmed. We know this event wouldn't be the same without Elijah. Give us more time to find him."

"Will do, Minnie; but I recommend we start thinking about a backup plan, just in case. As everyone knows, we're just 20 days out now."

Minnie turned to look at the countdown clock positioned prominently on the conference room wall. "Actually, we're only 19 days, 22 hours, 47 minutes, and 33 seconds out. Good advice, Regina. We'll keep the keynote as a standing item on our daily agenda." Minnie walked over to the 12th-story window looking to the west toward Roane County and muttered, "Where are you Elijah? We need you, my friend."

The Oval Office was selected to give the President a home-court advantage. He had invited five prominent fellow Democrats, three senators and two congressmen, to join him and a handful of his trusted advisors in the meeting designed to jump start his flagging presidency.

"Thank you for coming on such short notice. I understand your time is valuable, so I'll get right to the point. As you all know, the centerpiece of my campaign was the initiation of a wealth tax to help level the financial playing field in this country. I'll spare you the statistics and campaign rhetoric, but this is an initiative I'd like for you to get rolling through both houses of Congress sooner rather than later. Advocacy groups have drafted several bills that you can use as a starting point. I want to get your thoughts on how soon we can get them in committee."

An awkward hush filled the room as no one wanted to be the first to speak. Finally, Senator Weinberg broke the silence. "As you know, Mr. President, the country is facing many challenges we are trying to address. The deficit is out of control, unemployment is rising, the economy is—"

McCoy raised a hand to signal his impending interruption. "Yes, Senator, I'm aware of those challenges; but many of them will be addressed by the money a wealth tax will yield. We estimate that a 5% wealth tax could generate $3 trillion next year. Do you think your constituents would like their fair share of $3 trillion?"

Again, a response was delayed until the Democrat whip relayed some unwelcome news. "Mr. President, internal polling on this issue is dismal. Less than 30% of Americans support taxing wealth. It's just not something we can sell right now."

"That's where I come in. Once you get this issue rolling through Congress, I'll use my bully pulpit to promote it to the American people."

"Mr. President, that's one of the problems. Not only do less than 30% of Americans support taxing wealth, less than 30% support you. We must get some wins to enhance your popularity before we introduce something Americans don't support."

As McCoy was wont to do, he turned to berate his staff.

"See? This is on you!" He then turned back to his visitors. "I tell them every day that it is their job to get our approval ratings up, but they do absolutely nothing about it."

Working to get the President back on topic, the Democratic Whip announced, "Mr. President, we wanted to discuss a related topic with you. After the election, we expected the Mustang movement to dissolve; but frankly, it's growing in popularity. Almost 70% of the public views the Mustangs positively. The event they are planning next month is only going to bolster that enthusiasm."

McCoy's head bobbed as his eyebrows rose. "*What* event?"

"You don't know, sir? They are having a big gathering on the National Mall designed to keep the movement going. They are expecting hundreds of thousands, maybe even close to a million people. In fact, the Vice President was just announced as one of the key speakers."

Now the silence belonged to the President. His breathing labored as the anger stewing inside him began to boil over. "Adair! Why is it always Adair?!" Unable to form a coherent sentence, McCoy stormed out of the Oval Office, slamming the door, and mumbling as he left.

Chief of Staff, Riley Indigo, was left to close the meeting. "Thank you for coming today. We know you'll take the President's wealth tax idea under consideration soon." Even Riley didn't believe his own words.

As Jeremy settled in for bed, he reached for his cell phone to make one last text message before calling it a night.

Han, this is Luke, R U OK?

Hey Luke, yeah, I'm good. You?

I had another visitor yesterday.

Was it another storm trooper?

No, more like Princess Leia.

Who?

Princess Leia.

??

It was Savannah; Savannah visited me yesterday.

You know we're not supposed to use real names. What did she want?

She said I was in danger.

What kind of danger?

She said more storm troopers were coming and that I needed to leave.

What are you gonna do?

Nothing. We're probably fine. I just wanted to check in. Stay safe and continue to lay low.

Will do.

8

After his whirlwind year working for Victor Youngblood's Mouse Trap, one of the great joys for Jeremy Prince was being the first to arrive at the hardware store early in the morning as the sun slowly crept above the eastern horizon. In April, a chill was still in the air as spring stubbornly held off the coming summer heat. As he pulled into his parking spot, the Eagle's "Peaceful Easy Feeling" perfectly punctuated his tranquil morning. Unfortunately, a divergent experience was awaiting Jeremy just outside his Jeep Cherokee's door.

"Thirty-two million seven hundred fifty-thousand dollars."

Jeremy gasped as the voice caught him off guard, even eliciting an involuntary squeal. "What...oh...it's you." Jeremy had prayed that his bold response four months earlier was enough to keep Andrei Ovchenko away for good. His prayers hadn't been answered.

"Thirty-two million seven hundred fifty-thousand dollars. You had time to get money. Now, you pay," Ovchenko demanded.

"Look, I uh…" Realizing his voice had risen three octaves, Jeremy paused, cleared his throat, and tried to muster a more authoritative tone. He didn't succeed. "I…uh…told you to stay away; I don't have any money."

Ovchenko let Jeremy's frantic response briefly occupy the silence, leaving Jeremy shuffling nervously.

"No money?" Ovchenko slowly shook his head. "That is problem."

"I…uh…don't…," Jeremy continued to mumble, unable to look Ovchenko in the eye.

"Maybe another way."

"What do you mean, *another* way?" Jeremy muttered, not sure he wanted to hear the response.

"You had computer system. Give back system and computer boy Leonard; debt can be paid." Ovchenko was finally revealing his real reason for the visit.

"Wait, *what?*" Jeremy, now clearly confused, continued, "You mean, Omnia? That system is shut down, destroyed. And I haven't heard from Leonard in months. Look, I don't know what's going on; but I'm going to go open the store, and you're going to turn around and go right back where you came from."

Ovchenko took two steps to close the gap, reaching up to put his hand behind Jeremy's neck. "This is not game. Computer and Leonard. Where are they?"

"I *told* you that Omnia is destroyed and that I don't know

where Leonard is!"

Ovchenko's nose-to-nose proximity had the intended unnerving effect. "You will soon understand how serious this is. Next time you see me, you will talk." Ovchenko looked up to the store and offered an ominous parting word. "You will hear from me soon."

Ovchenko quickly disappeared into the alley as Jeremy attempted to respond.

"Wait a minute. What do you mean—I'll hear from you soon? Wait!"

Ovchenko was gone. Jeremy was baffled by his parting words.

"Jeremy, are you OK?"

For the second time in two minutes, Jeremy was startled, this time pleasantly so. "Oh, Dad, yeah, I'm…uh…fine."

"Are you sure?"

Still looking in the direction where Ovchenko disappeared, Jeremy uttered a faint, "Yeah, I'm sure."

Han, this is Luke. I had another visitor today.

Princess Leia again?

No

Jeremy Prince and Leonard Applebaum were an unlikely duo to be responsible for dismantling the largest clandestine criminal organization ever to exist and for incarcerating its leader, Victor Youngblood. Jeremy's meteoric rise to the #2 position in Mouse Trap and Leonard's role as Omnia's system administrator left them uniquely positioned to inflict the lethal blow.

As Jeremy manipulated circumstances to coax Victor into admitting to murder, Leonard used Omnia's pervasive camera network to catch both the crime and the confession on tape. Through a series of well-planned events, the duo sent the monolithic organization crashing to the ground. One of the final blows to Mouse Trap was the destruction of the computer system, Omnia. Responsibility for Omnia's demise fell to Leonard. Although Leonard knew Omnia was used for nefarious purposes, he also saw this computer system as a beautiful creation he'd spent the better part of two decades creating. He reasoned that, as a system, Omnia was neither good nor bad. However, he also believed that if he could eventually resurrect Omnia, he could use its capabilities to benefit mankind. Leonard knew that Jeremy would never understand this struggle.

Because of the lurking danger of what might be left of Mouse Trap, Jeremy and Leonard agreed they shouldn't be seen together for the foreseeable future. Jeremy was committed to returning to work in his parent's hardware store in Abingdon, Virginia. Leonard sought more anonymity and moved to a suburb of Salt Lake City. They agreed that the only communication would be via burner phone text. Leonard insisted they use pseudonyms. Embracing the full geekhood of a computer nerd in his love for everything Star

Wars, Leonard insisted on being called Han, leaving Jeremy to assume Luke as his alias.

Another storm trooper?

Not really, it was more like…Darth Vader.

??

Ovchenko…I know we're not supposed to use names, but it was Ovchenko.

Oh

Yeah, and I don't want to scare you, but he asked about you.

What did he want?

He wants to turn on Omnia.

Oh

I told him it was destroyed but he wouldn't believe me.

You gotta be careful Luke.

I will, you too Han.

I will.

"We're a bit down on our luck and were hoping that maybe y'all could help a little." Beau Trenton was 23. His wife Meghan, 22, sat beside him, holding his hand. Their four-year-old daughter Destiny, the catalyst for their marriage when Meghan was still in high school, sat on Beau's lap. Trevor, almost a year old, sat in the stained car seat beside their feet.

"I don't like to ask for help, but I'm a carpenter and have had a hard time finding work. We just got kicked out of our apartment, and we don't have anywhere to stay. We don't have any money for food, and Destiny needs some medicine. I just don't know where else to turn."

"Beau, I'm so sorry this has happened to you. You have a beautiful family." Pastor Stephen Roberts of New Hope Church in Kingston, Tennessee, had a heart for the community's hurting and needy. The church set aside a portion of its budget for benevolence, but it was never enough. The needs always outweighed what New Hope could support. Nevertheless, Pastor Roberts was committed to doing what he could.

"Beau, we have a well-stocked food pantry that should provide for your family until you get back on your feet. We have formula for the little one too."

Ashamed of his situation and unable to look Pastor Roberts in the eye, Beau managed a faint 'thank you.' "Do you know anywhere we can stay for a while?"

"Did I hear you say you are a carpenter?" The voice from the Pastor's doorway caught everyone off guard.

"Wait a minute, you're—," Meghan began.

"I could use a good carpenter, but this project needs personal attention. You'd need to stay at the place while you worked."

"You're Elijah Mustang."

"I get that all the time," Elijah chuckled.

"No, you're really him! You're Elijah Mustang!" Beau responded.

Pastor Roberts attempted to rescue his friend from awkwardness. "Elijah, this is Beau and Meghan Trenton and their kids, Destiny and Trevor."

"It really is him. I can't believe this," Meghan said, her mouth agape.

During the 2016 presidential election, Elijah had become among the most recognizable faces in America. Fame and attention were the last things Elijah was seeking; nevertheless, they found him. Elijah had spent much of the last four months traveling in Central and South America on mission trips with his charity, Promise Ministries. He hoped that serving the neediest would rid him of the feeling of self-indulgence that often accompanies fame. On occasional stops at his East Tennessee home, he'd often visit his friend, Pastor Roberts. With Elijah's whereabouts a national mystery, the media kept a close watch on his primary home on Watts Bar Lake, causing him to spend the nights he was back home in a cabin that few people knew he owned, tucked away on

40 wooded acres.

"Here's my situation. I have a cabin a couple of miles off Sugar Grove Valley Road. It has three bedrooms and a couple of baths, but boy does it need some work. How about you, Meghan, and the kids move into the cabin; and I'll let you know what needs to be fixed. Here's the address."

"I don't know what to say," Beau gasped, equally stunned by both the gesture and the source of the generosity.

"OK, sounds like we have a deal. I'll see you folks there tonight." As Elijah turned to leave, he winked at Pastor Roberts.

His voice now restored to full strength, Beau looked into Pastor Roberts' eyes for the first time and declared, "*That was Elijah Mustang.*"

"Is everything OK, Jeremy? You don't seem like yourself today."

There were positives to Jeremy living at home with his parents; among them were the low cost and his mom's home-cooked meals. One of the negatives was the absence of privacy, compounded by spending the day at work with his parents before coming home to spend the evening with them as well.

"Yeah, Mom, I'm fine. I think I may go grab some dinner out tonight. OK?"

"Sure. Who are you going with?"

"I don't know, maybe just me."

"Your dad's working late at the store. Maybe I'll go with you."

Jeremy sighed. "Mom, I think I might just go by myself tonight."

"Oh, OK, that's fine. I'll just warm up some leftovers when Walter gets home."

As his mom spoke, Jeremy's cell phone emitted a curious tone. He looked down to see the source of the sound. "That's odd; it's the alarm at the store."

Just then, sounds of sirens could be heard in the distance as Jeremy's phone rang.

"This is Jeremy."

"Jeremy, it's Steve. I just drove by your store. Did you know it was on fire?"

"On fire?!"

Jeremy hung up the phone, grabbed the keys, and commanded "Mom, let's go, the sirens are from the store. It's on fire."

"Jeremy, your dad's still there!" Rosita screamed as both ran for the car.

9

Jeremy and Rosita made the eight-minute drive in five. The road was barricaded in front of the store, causing them to park three blocks away. Hopping out of the Cherokee, they sprinted the rest of the way to the store. They both stopped in their tracks as they saw four fire trucks on the scene and the three-story brick building engulfed in flames. Jeremy and Rosita saw the ambulance at the same time.

"Dad!" Jeremy screamed.

As Jeremy and Rosita ran closer to the store, they were met by an Abingdon police officer. "Hold on there; you can't go any farther."

"But that's my store!" Rosita shrieked.

"And my dad may be in there!" added Jeremy.

"I'm sorry; it isn't safe to go any farther. Come with me, and we'll take you to a safe place."

"But my dad, has anyone seen my dad?"

"We haven't seen anyone yet."

"Maybe he's left already!" Rosita hoped.

As Rosita finished speaking, the officer's radio carried an ominous message. *"We're bringing out one body. Have the paramedics ready."*

"A body?!" Jeremy cried.

"Walter!" screamed Rosita.

Before the officer could stop them, Jeremy and Rosita rushed to two parked ambulances. As they arrived, breathing heavily, two firemen emerged with a stretcher. There was a body but no movement.

"Walter!"

"Please give us some room, ma'am." Two officers stepped in as paramedics joined the fray.

"He's going to be OK, right?" Rosita pleaded. There was no response. "Jeremy, he's going to be OK, isn't he?"

"Yeah, Mom, he's got to be OK," Jeremy answered, wiping away the tears, knowing his response was based in hope, not fact.

The paramedics worked frantically for several minutes before slumping to the ground, heads down.

"What's happening? Why did they stop?!" Rosita exclaimed.

The captain approached Rosita, his hat under one arm, his face black with soot. "I'm sorry, ma'am. We did everything we could. He was already out when we found him. The smoke in the office was thick. He didn't have a chance."

"*Nooooo!*" Rosita screamed. "You have to keep trying! He's right here. You must try!"

"I'm sorry, ma'am. I'm really sorry."

"Are you sure this is right?"

"This is what he said—go down Sugar Grove Valley, past the church, then take the unmarked gravel driveway exactly two miles on the left."

Beau Trenton navigated his '96 Chevy Astro van up the curvy drive, his tires crunching the gravel. Around the last curve, he began to see lights from the cabin in the distance. Finally pulling into the driveway, Beau exited the van and approached the front door, hopeful he was in the right place. It didn't take long to get his answer.

"So glad to see you guys found me! I know it's a bit off the beaten path, but that sorta works well for my situation," Elijah bellowed. "Come and get those kids into the cabin. It's a chilly night."

As Elijah held the door open, Meghan rushed past, Destiny holding her hand, Trevor in the car seat occupying her other hand. Beau remained outside, seemingly unable to move.

"Well, are you coming in or staying outside?" Elijah asked.

"I...just...don't know how to say—."

"You don't have to say anything; just go in the house. I'm getting cold."

As Beau walked in, he looked around, astounded at the well-furnished cabin. A large stone fireplace was on one wall, large timbers spanned the width of the house, a sturdy staircase curved up to the second floor, and rugged shelves lined with books filled the back wall.

"It's like something out of a magazine," Meghan observed.

"Well, maybe, if the magazine is called *Fixer-Upper*," Elijah protested. "Come on, let me show you to your rooms. Beau and Meghan, this will be your room." He walked them into a large bedroom with a king-size bed. "There's a closet over here. Pastor Roberts sent over some clothes. We guessed at your sizes, so I hope they fit." Beau and Meghan looked stunned at the piles of newly folded clothes.

"Let's walk down the hall to Destiny's room." Destiny sprinted as she saw a large dollhouse well-equipped with furniture and accessories. "I have a buddy who makes these by hand. He happened to have one that he just completed. He owed me a favor, so—"

"I love it!" Destiny uttered, sitting on the floor in awe of her new treasure. The next sounds heard were canine kisses followed shortly by Destiny's enthusiastic giggle.

"Oh, Clyde, leave her alone. Sorry about that folks, Clyde is my best buddy. He's an Aussiedoodle. He keeps me company here at the cabin."

"He's awesome!" Destiny exclaimed.

"There are clothes here for Destiny too. And of course, there are clothes, diapers, and toys for Trevor. There's pizza warming in the oven."

Meghan and Beau simultaneously broke down in tears, unable to speak.

"Now don't do that. I'm a crier too, and I'll just join in," Elijah declared.

"I just don't know what to—," Beau began.

"Beau, you don't have to say anything. All is well."

"Hey, Mr. Elijah, do you want to play with me and Clyde?" Destiny asked.

"Destiny, I can't think of anything I'd rather do."

10

"OK, things seem to be falling into place. We're over the snafus with Washington, right?"

"Yes, Admiral Adair has cleared a path for us. We're good to go."

"Great. Let's talk about the agenda."

As she had done every day over the last several weeks, Minnie Carpenter started the day with a 7 a.m. meeting to ensure the event, named *We're Not Done 2017,* had the best chance for success. Estimates were that close to a half million citizens would be descending on D.C. With an event of this scale, unexpected problems were to be expected; but Minnie Carpenter's leadership was eliminating as many as possible. The remaining major hurdle was being addressed.

"Any word from Elijah?" Minnie asked hopefully.

"Yes *and* no," a staffer began. "Yes, we've had reports of him in El Salvador, Brazil, California, and right here in East Tennessee; but nothing has been confirmed. We've left messages with everyone that he would normally contact—but so far, no luck."

"That's disappointing, but I understand. As you know, we've been holding the keynote slot open in hopes that he would make it. I think it's time to move on without him. What do you think the crowd will say?" Minnie asked anxiously.

"For the last two weeks, we've been sending word through the state and local organizations that Elijah most likely wouldn't attend. I know some folks think we're just trying to lower expectations and then he'll come out and surprise everyone; but I agree, it is time to move on."

"How's the video coming?" When it looked like Elijah wouldn't make it, Minnie had asked the tech team to develop a series of videos comprised of the highlights of Elijah's speeches during the campaign. If he wasn't going to be there in person, she wanted his inspirational words to motivate the crowd in short bumpers to be run between speakers.

"The videos are ready to go. We have over a dozen. It was hard settling on just a few highlights. Even though the campaign ended just five months ago, I forgot what a phenomenon Elijah was."

Minnie echoed the sentiment, "Yes, there's a reason we're expecting such a massive gathering. Elijah started something big. It is our responsibility to keep it going. OK, we'll move Admiral Adair to the keynote. Having the Vice President as a backup plan is not too shabby. Moving a few other speakers around should work. Let's go make this happen."

"Mr. President, I understand that you wanted to speak with me."

"Yes, Jackson, thank you so much for coming. Please have a seat."

The two men atop the U.S. government's executive branch took seats across from one another in the Oval Office, accompanied by Riley Indigo and Secretary of State Barry Woolridge.

"Jackson, I sense that we've gotten off on the wrong foot. It's not healthy for us—or, more importantly, for the country—when the President and Vice President don't see eye-to-eye."

Admiral Adair's internal alarms were at full volume, especially with the President addressing him by his first name. If there was one thing he'd decided about Mitch McCoy, it was that he could not be trusted. For the time being, Adair decided to play along.

"I agree, Mr. President. Although we can have healthy debates in areas where we may disagree, our country is best served when we are aligned."

"Exactly, Jackson. I couldn't have said it better myself. To that end, I'd like to extend an olive branch. That's why I've asked Secretary of State Woolridge to join us. We have a situation brewing in the Pacific where the 7th Fleet is observing some unusual activity from the Chinese. Secretary Woolridge has a meeting with his Chinese counterpart, and I'd like for you to go as a show of strength." He scooted to the edge of his chair, clenched his fist, and tapped Adair on the knee. "With your 30 years in the Navy, I think this is a great opportunity to use your skill and experience."

"Sounds interesting," Adair responded cautiously.

"Secretary Woolridge can fill you in on the details," the President said, sitting back in his chair.

"What are the dates for this meeting?" Adair asked.

The Secretary responded, "We'll leave May 5th and meet with the Chinese delegation on May 6th. We'd like to spend a day in Japan meeting with the 7th Fleet on May 7th. We thought the Navy team would love to hear from one of their own who has made such significant contributions to the nation."

Adair shook his head in understanding, a slight smirk crept into the corner of his mouth. "May 5th to 7th, those are interesting dates."

"We realize it is coming up fairly soon and wanted to give you a few days to plan," the President responded.

"Mr. President, I think you know I have a conflict on May 6th."

"A conflict? What type of conflict?" McCoy wondered.

Adair turned to the Secretary. "Barry, I would expect this from the President, but not from you."

The Secretary lowered his head, unable to make eye contact.

"I'm afraid you've got us all stumped, Jackson. What's the conflict?" McCoy worked to continue the facade.

"Mr. President, you know May 6th is the event on the Mall for the supporters of the Mustang movement."

"That's May 6th?" McCoy responded incredulously.

"And I know *you know* because you've called the Secret Service, the National Park Service, the Capitol Police, and the FBI to cancel the event."

"That's unfortunate that the event conflicts with this assignment. I would certainly understand if you weren't able to accompany the Secretary," McCoy declared, now pacing about the Oval Office.

Realizing he was in a high-stakes game of poker, Adair decided to call the President's bluff. "Absolutely not, Mr. President. Duty always comes before politics. I will be there. Mr. Secretary, send my staff the details. Thank you for this opportunity. I'm happy to serve."

Caught off guard by Adair's response, McCoy sat in stunned silence before finally uttering, "Well, alright then. Sounds like we have a date."

"Is there anything else, Mr. President?"

"No, Jackson. That's it."

The Vice President stood, shook the hands of those assembled, and exited the Oval Office.

The Secretary was the first to break the silence. "Well, that's unfortunate. What are we going to do?"

McCoy stared at the Secretary and commanded, "You're going to get on the phone with China and schedule a meeting!"

"Yes sir."

11

With word spreading among the scattered leadership team that Zeke was getting the Mouse Trap band back together, the once spacious activity center was now starting to feel crowded as the remnant had grown to 40 in the last three weeks.

"It is good to see so many familiar faces joining us." Zeke knew that keeping the team energized was a major task demanding his leadership skills. "I honestly believe we will restore Mouse Trap to even greater than its former glory. Like any noble undertaking, it is going to require work and time; but I am certain we will get there. In fact, a significant step in that direction has recently been taken. Mr. Ovchenko has some important news to share. Andrei, the floor is yours."

Ovchenko, who was already standing, adjusted his eye-patch for effect, interlocked his black-gloved fingers, and peered at the assembly with his one good eye.

"We have attention of Jeremy Prince. He will lead us to

computer boy Leonard. Computer will be back soon. I will have thirty-two million seven hundred fifty-thousand dollars.

On this trip to the camp, Ovchenko brought along a half-dozen members of his team, known as Blackforce. While Mouse Trap had been disbanded and team members had dispersed, Blackforce remained intact. Although there were no missions to complete, the Blackforce team remained in its headquarters in a former auto-parts manufacturing facility on the outskirts of Pittsburgh, ready for whatever was to come next.

Over the previous three weeks, Zeke had crews busy at work on the camp where the decaying activity center was now repaired and freshly painted. IT crews had equipped the building with satellite-based Internet providing download speeds of 100 Mbps. The once-open room was segmented into workstations, each furnished with desks, chairs, and computers. The center space had a large meeting area where the team was assembled.

"OK, Zeke, you want to have the first honor of connecting to the outside world?" the IT lead asked.

Zeke logged in to a computer situated on his makeshift desk. He opened the web browser and typed "Victor Youngblood" in the search window. Over 10,000,000 results were returned in 0.54 seconds. The IT team cheered, sharing awkward high fives.

"Great job!" Victor encouraged. "Thank you for your hard work."

After shaking hands with the IT staff, Zeke reached into his jacket pocket, pulled out the envelope, removed the list, and crossed off item #3.

I just heard about your dad. I'm really sorry. R U OK?

No

What's going on?

This is my fault.

No, it's not, none of this is your fault.

Gotta go.

I'm really sorry, remember, this is not your fault.

"I know we are both excited and nervous about tomorrow, but we must stay focused. We have done all the planning we can do; now we just have to execute the plan. According to the Park Service's reports, 100,000 people are already at the Mall; so, this event is going to be bigger than our most optimistic projections."

Minnie Carpenter maintained her cool leadership throughout the planning of *We're Not Done 2017*.

"We have a special visitor who has stopped by to speak

with the leadership team."

As Minnie spoke, she could hear a whisper of "Is it Elijah?" that she chose to ignore. "I just got word that our keynote speaker, the Vice President of the United States, will be joining us any minute. I hope you all understand how historic this is. Admiral Jackson Adair is the first person elected as Vice President who is not a Democrat or Republican in over 150 years!

"Speaking of long overdue, I'm sorry if I'm late." As Admiral Adair entered the room, everyone stood and applauded for what became an embarrassingly long time.

"Please, please, sit down. You know I'm not into pomp and circumstance. You should be applauding for yourselves. I'm only in this position because of your hard work over the past year. You get all the credit. Of course, if you knew what I had to put up with daily from the gentleman in the White House, I'd say you get all the blame as well." The joke received a disproportionate helping of belly laughs, more out of respect than amusement.

"But in all seriousness, I'm hearing this is going to be a massive gathering. Again, a testament to your leadership and to the hunger our country has developed for something different. One of the clear messages we are going to convey tomorrow is exactly what we are offering this country. Unfortunately, I have to run because I have a meeting with the President."

The word *president* evoked a series of jeers and boos. "Come on, Team; we have to do our best to maintain decorum. After wrapping up some final business with the

President," Adair paused for a response. Hearing none, he continued, "That's better. After meeting with the President, I'll rejoin you in the morning. Do your best to get some sleep; you need to be as sharp as possible. Good evening."

As Adair strode out of the room, the team stood in respect, which he was unaccustomed to receiving at the White House.

"Jeremy, can I make you a grilled cheese? Jeremy? *Jeremy*?!"

"No, thanks."

"Jeremy, you know, it's not—"

"Don't say it, Mom."

"But it's not—"

Jeremy shook his head and raised his arms in protest. "Mom, just stop!"

"But it's not your fault!" Rosita insisted.

It had been 17 days since Walter Prince's tragic death. Jeremy and Rosita had been through the funeral and had spent time with family and friends. Now they were left with each other. While Rosita was seemingly progressing through the grief cycle, Jeremy seemed to be stuck on Step 1, shock. He hadn't left the house in two weeks. He had barely eaten anything. He had little conversation with his mom. His consistent refrain was that his father's death was his fault—a refrain his mom fought to counter.

"Mom, you just don't understand."

"You're right; I don't understand. That's what I'm trying to get you to tell me. How could this possibly be your fault?"

Before Jeremy could offer a response, the doorbell rang, startling both of them.

"I don't want to talk to anyone," Jeremy muttered.

"I'll go," Rosita assured, walking toward the door.

"Yes, can I help you?"

"This is where Jeremy lives, right? I need to talk with him right now."

"Now, hold on, young lady. Who are you?"

"My name is Savannah. I worked with Jeremy. I'm so sorry about your husband. I tried to warn Jeremy, but…but… that's not why I'm here."

As she spoke, Jeremy came to the door. "Then why *are* you here?" Jeremy asked angrily.

"Jeremy, I know this is terrible; and I know you think it can't get any worse, but it can. You gotta warn Leonard."

"*Who's* Leonard?" a confused Rosita asked.

"I can't deal with this!" Jeremy said, walking away from the door.

"Please, Jeremy, you have to listen this time!"

Savannah's words pierced Jeremy's soul, causing him to spin around in anger. "*This* time?! You mean since I didn't listen to you last time it got dad killed?"

"No, Jeremy, that's not what I meant!"

"You two, stop. Young lady, please come in the house and let's talk about this." Rosita grabbed Savannah's hands, pulling her into the house. Savannah offered little resistance. The statuesque blonde, who normally looked as if she walked out of a Ralph Lauren ad, had greasy hair, was without makeup, and was wearing ill-fitting sweats.

"Holy crap, you look awful—and you smell worse!" Jeremy exclaimed.

"Jeremy, that's not nice," Rosita chastised. "Please, Savannah, come and sit down."

Savannah's presence proved to be a godsend for Rosita. She and Jeremy spent the next two hours cycling between argument and revelation. Rosita came to understand just how evil Mouse Trap was, that people were trying to resurrect it, and that her family was caught in the crosshairs.

"We have to warn Leonard," Savannah pleaded.

Rosita raised her hands in objection, walking over to put her arms around Savannah. "What do you say we call it a night. Come with me, Savannah. Let's get you cleaned up and in some decent clothes. We have a spare bedroom, and we can finish this discussion tomorrow."

"You're inviting her to stay HERE?!" Jeremy exclaimed.

"But…we need to…" Savannah's energy was spent, and the thought of a shower and a good night's sleep sounded too good to pass up. "OK, I'm too tired to argue."

"That's a first!" Jeremy retorted.

"Good night, Jeremy. Savannah and I are going to get better acquainted."

As Savannah and Rosita left Jeremy alone in the living room, he wondered if the situation could get any worse.

"Good evening Mr. President, I just wanted to let you know how disappointed I was to hear about the trip to China being canceled."

"The *what?*"

"The trip to China. In the spirit of growing our teamwork, you had asked Secretary of State Woolridge and I to go to China to—"

"Oh, shut up!" The President turned to walk away from his Vice President.

"Yes sir, you have a good evening as well."

Admiral Adair seldom allowed himself the indulgence of gloating. This evening would be the rare exception.

12

For the past 36 hours, buses had filled every artery heading into Washington D.C. The Blue, Red, Yellow, Green, Orange, and Silver Metro lines were packed with passengers, as were the platforms, stairs, and escalators heading down to them. Flights into Reagan, Dulles, and Baltimore's BWI were all overbooked. Taxi, Lyft, and Uber drivers struggled to keep up with demand, even overtaxing the scheduling apps. The fact that the event was held on a Saturday at least avoided the workday rush, but the transportation system was so crowded that some travelers had been trying to get into the city for almost 24 hours.

In daily and weekly calls to state and local Mustang teams, Minnie Carpenter urged people to plan ahead, travel early, expect delays, and not be surprised if some people didn't make it into the city.

The National Park Service's headquarters, located a few blocks away from the National Mall, would serve as the organizing point for federal support of the gathering. Over 600 Park Service employees were deployed around the Mall. They were accompanied by 250 members of the U.S. Park Police and 500 officers from the Metropolitan Police Department. Although it was a chaotic scene, there were astonishingly few reports of conflict or damage.

Now, at 10:00 a.m., the gathering extended the full length of the Mall's 1.9-miles from the Capitol Building to the Lincoln Memorial. Although the Mall's crowd sizes are notoriously difficult to estimate, National Park Service personnel hadn't seen this large an assembly in at least 20 years, perhaps longer. Some expected the final number to exceed one million. It was going to be a historic day in the nation's capital.

"What do you mean *we aren't covering it live*?" National News Service's News Director Simon Gonzales had been summoned to NNS President Aimee Abernathy's office for an urgent meeting. He was shocked to learn the meeting's subject.

"We just don't consider this event significant enough to warrant live coverage." Having been with NNS for 15 years, Aimee Abernathy had advanced rapidly through the ranks of production assistant, producer, executive producer, news director to her current role atop one of the nation's leading cable news organizations.

"But we already have six crews there."

"It is fine to have the crews there to capture footage in case something happens, but we're not going live."

"This doesn't make any sense. We have been meeting for the last week about this. You're the one who said to send out the crews for all-day live coverage. What changed?"

"As you know, we're always assessing our priorities; we've simply decided to dial this back a bit."

Gonzales shook his head in disbelief. "OK, you're the boss. I'll get the word out."

"Thank you, Simon. Don't worry; we'll cover the event. Keep everyone ready to go live if anything breaks."

For a week, crews had been working to set up and connect over 300 large screens around the Mall. The screens were part of a complex audio/video system that would be integral to keeping attendees engaged with what was happening on the main stage outside the Capitol Building. For the past hour, the screens had been playing clips from Elijah Mustang's 2016 campaign, his running mate Admiral Adair's ascension to Vice President, and grassroots Mustang meetings throughout the country. A small countdown clock, which was started at 60 minutes, filled the screen as the final seconds leading to the formal event's kickoff were ticking away.

3, 2, 1—then fireworks filled the sky. Videos welcomed a county music star to the stage to sing a stirring rendition of "The Star-Spangled Banner." An opening prayer was offered. The crowd remained standing for the Pledge of Allegiance.

Emceeing the day's events, comedian Dylan Cash had ardently supported Elijah Mustang early in his campaign, a decision that took a toll on Cash's career, but one he never regretted.

The eight-hour day from noon to 8:00 p.m. was segmented into 25-30-minute speeches and performances, separated by two-minute transition video bumpers. As Cash stepped to the microphone, the event was officially underway.

"Excuse me, has anyone lost a set of keys?" Cash raised the keys in the air. "They are from a Ford Taurus. Just raise your hands if these are yours." The laughter cascaded down the Mall as the sound passed from east to west.

"OK, that's one of the goofiest jokes I've ever told, and I got a million laughs. Wait 'til ya'll hear my good stuff."

"I want to thank you for meeting with me today. As we have already discussed, everything I'm going to share with you is off the record." President McCoy's press secretary had asked for representatives from six major network and cable news outlets to come to the White House for an off-the-record meeting, which was the White House's bargaining chip in exchange for the press agreement to downplay the Mustang event.

"The President is concerned about certain movements by the Chinese navy. They are becoming increasingly aggressive, and their motives are unclear."

"What kind of movements?" a reporter asked.

"I can't discuss that at this time, but they are very disconcerting."

"What is the President doing about the situation?"

The administration official had expected that question.

"The President had plans for a meeting with the Chinese to discuss this concern, but those plans were interrupted."

"What do you mean *interrupted*?"

"Remember, this is off the record. The President doesn't want to impugn the Vice President's integrity. He had organized a meeting with high-ranking officials in the Chinese administration, and the Vice President was to accompany Secretary of State Woolridge to represent U.S. interests. Given Adair's career in the Navy, his insight would have been invaluable in this meeting. However, Adair backed out of the trip at the last minute to participate in the campaign event that's underway on the Mall."

"He refused to go, even though the President asked?"

"That's all I have today."

The press secretary walked toward the door before turning back and reemphasizing, "Remember, off-the-record."

The day at the Mall had progressed as planned. Speakers included politicians who had aligned with the Mustang movement. There was a salute to war Veterans, a rock band performance, a preacher who discussed the foundational importance of the national motto 'In God We Trust,' interspersed with jokes from Dylan Cash and videos from Elijah's campaign.

The National News Service had included in its hourly news cycle a brief segment about the event, primarily highlighting Elijah's absence by describing it as "an event featuring an eclectic mix of speakers and topics that even its founder, Elijah Mustang, chose to skip."

At 4 p.m., the event was officially half over. That time slot had been set aside for Minnie Carpenter to discuss what the Mustang Movement represented. Although a seasoned professional, leader, and CEO, she had never spoken to an assembly approaching this event's numbers. As she stepped up to the podium, she felt a tinge of nerves.

"Good evening, fine people of Mustang-land. I hope you have had a good day. It is truly my honor to be here to represent you. My task is to tell the world about some of the Mustang platform we've been working hard to develop. I'm going to share what it means to be a Mustang."

Over the past three weeks, Minnie Carpenter had met with network and cable news executives to ensure the event was covered live. She shared with them just how far the Mustang movement had reached, ensuring them there would be national interest in the gathering. At the news outlets' suggestion, she even moved around a couple of speakers. This event was one of Minnie's proudest accomplishments. Unfortunately, only one call from President McCoy undid everything she had done and pushed the event off live TV.

"We Mustangs believe in is the U.S. Constitution, the cornerstone of our country. We believe it is the most perfect governing document ever written. We acknowledge there may be times and circumstances that warrant its update, but our founders laid out a means by which it can be amended. As Mustangs, we believe in the Constitution.

"We also believe that elected officials should serve only for a short season as they take time away from their normal lives and professions. We do *not* believe that public service via elected office should become a career. To that end, we ask that candidates aligning themselves with the Mustang movement commit to no more than one six-year term as U.S. senator; two two-year terms as U.S. representative; and never more than eight years in office at any local, state, or national level. We understand these term limits may put us at a short-term disadvantage by missing the benefits of incumbency, but we believe our nation will be stronger in the long term."

Minnie also covered topics including individual liberty; commitment to maintaining civility during the campaign; respect for healthy debate; promising to eschew corporate donations; embracing diversity—not just of race, gender, and ethnicity, but also diversity of thought; and strengthening local and state governments while deemphasizing Washington's power.

"As I close, I want to assure those of you watching us at home that this isn't a temporary movement that is going to go away. Hundreds of thousands of us gathering here today pledge our commitment that we're not done. We're not done taking back our country from special interests, career politicians, and big-money donors. Today is not a crescendo; today is just the beginning. *We're not done*!!

13

At the conclusion of the meeting with the press secretary, all six news representatives rushed back to their respective organizations in hopes of being the first to cover the shocking story of the Vice President's insubordination. By 6:00 p.m., the news began to break with headlines including:

Adair chooses politics over country.

Sources confirm Veep campaigning when asked to serve.

Chinese threat grows as Adair campaigns.

Adair ignores President McCoy's call to duty.

Networks prepared headline stories for the 6:30 p.m. time slot. Cable new outlets rushed the story to run even earlier. All networks lined up commentators to discuss Admiral Adair's appearance at the Mustang rally. Some even suggested the Vice President should resign.

The Vice President was scheduled to be on the dais at 7:30 p.m. as the evening's last speaker. The breaking news led outlets to reverse their earlier plans and to air it live.

Vice President Adair had been backstage for the past three hours preparing for his speech, meeting with Mustang leaders, and occasionally shaking hands and chatting with supporters close to the stage. At 7:00 p.m., an aide whispered in his ear about the rapidly evolving story of his China trip. Adair nodded his head in understanding. He had to quickly decide how to address this new information or whether to address it at all. It was definitely a curve ball he felt he should have seen coming. Unfortunately, he underestimated exactly how low the President would go.

"We're continuing to follow this breaking news from Washington. Sources have confirmed with the National News Service that President McCoy asked Vice President Jackson Adair to accompany Secretary of State Barry Woolridge for high-level meetings with the Chinese to address a growing concern with military exercises in the Pacific. However, Adair refused the President's request and instead is giving a campaign speech this evening to a group of supporters here in Washington. Political experts of all parties are in shock, none of whom can remember a time a sitting vice president had refused such an important presidential request. Rumors of the two men's strained relationship have been circulating for months, but this rebuff appears to be a new low. The move has some even calling for Adair's resignation. We're going to take you live to the National Mall, where Adair is about to address his supporters. Let's go there now.

As the penultimate speaker concluded and the last bumper video ran, Dylan Cash strode to the podium one last time.

"OK, folks, I know everyone is tired. You all had travel adventures just to get here. You've laughed, cried, and cheered for the last eight hours—and that's just for my crappy jokes; but now we're coming to the grand finale, the big ending, the *pièce de résistance*. Our next speaker personifies everything we stand for—integrity, duty, and honor. Ladies and gentlemen, I know you're ready for our final speaker. Let's give it up for the Vice President of the United States, Jackson Carter Adair!"

As Adair strode from the backstage toward the stage's entrance, an aide ran to his side with a printed copy of his speech he had left in the chair.

"No thanks, I don't need that. I'm going off script. Tell them to turn off the teleprompter."

Adair approached the microphone as cheers went on for minutes. Chants of "Adair! Adair!" rang through the Mall. An already enthusiastic crowd was finally ready for the speaker they had been waiting all day to hear. It was pure euphoria.

Meanwhile, Americans watching from home were treated to a vastly different perspective. As Adair waved to the crowd, television viewers saw a scrolling text with variations of earlier headlines announcing Adair's shunning the President's request for assistance.

"Thank you! Thank you! What an honor it is to appear before a group of Americans who refuse to conform to what this world says you must follow. They say you have to pick between two political parties who think they have all of the power. But *you* dare to say there is a different way! A way that you are forging one step at a time. You're marching through the jungle with machetes in hand clearing a path for those who will come behind you because *you're not done!*"

The motto drew boisterous cheers from the crowd.

"For 30 years, I served in the United States Navy, the greatest collection of brains, brawn, and balls ever assembled in one group. Hooyah!"

Adair received a "Hooyah" in return from thousands of fellow sailors and midshipmen.

"During those 30 years, I had more than my share of interfacing with politics; and I thought I understood everything I needed to know about the political animal. However, over recent months, I've come to understand that from the inside she is a vastly different kind of beast. Today I'm going to tell you what our American political system has become and how as Mustangs we're going to offer something new and fresh to an America thirsting for change.

"Number one, there is a vacuum of integrity among our elected officials. The truth has been subordinated beneath an insatiable quest for power. This subordination has become so commonplace that honesty is no longer considered a virtue, but instead a weakness. As Mustangs we must find our way back to that place where integrity matters. We're here today to appeal to all Americans to embrace the truth in everything you do."

Adair again turned to look into the camera.

"This lack of integrity is not limited to our elected officials but has extended to our sacred institutions, which we once trusted but which have blurred the lines so much that they are no longer distinguishable from our politicians. One such example is most likely scrolling across the bottom of your screen as I speak. I am making a plea to the American voters today to give the Mustang movement a chance. In return, we promise to respect you; your vote; and, most importantly, your intelligence. This unholy alliance between politicians and the media, the Fourth Estate, thinks you're too dumb to question reports like you're seeing today. They think you're going to take this report hook, line, and sinker. My promise to you is that we're always going to respect you and do everything within our power to earn your respect in return."

"Did you hear what he said? Do we keep the news ticker rolling?"

"I don't know! Let me call HQ."

As Adair predicted, every news organization reporting live on the event featured a breaking news feed chastising him for ignoring the President's request to go to China.

"HQ said to keep it going but to intersperse some other

news."

"What other news?"

"It doesn't matter; just find something else to mix in!"

Adair continued his assault on politicians, touting an absence of leadership, accountability, and transparency. He promised the Mustang movement would be a force for change. By the time he got to his last point, most networks had removed the news ticker altogether.

"Lastly, we have completely lost the meaning of public service. Public servants are supposed to be servants of you, the American citizens. Today I'm calling on the hundreds of thousands gathered here today on this 6th day of May 2017, may this be the day we return to a culture of public service. I'm challenging you to be servants who improve your communities, jobs, places of worship, and families. I know you've started that process, but I'm here to tell you that"—Adair paused for effect—"you're not..." The crowd responded, "DONE! WE'RE NOT DONE!! WE'RE NOT DONE!! WE'RE NOT DONE!!"

14

"Hey, Beau, hand me that hammer."

"Here you go, Mr. Mustang."

"Come on, Beau; I've told you to call me Elijah."

"I guess you know you're all over the news."

"I don't watch much news these days, Beau."

"There was like a million people in Washington yesterday. They called it a gathering of Mustangs. There were speeches, performances, and stuff. Dylan Cash was the emcee."

"Any relation to Johnny?"

"Who? Oh, Johnny Cash, no I don't think so. Dylan is a comedian, who has a TV show and has been in some movies. It was a big deal for him to be there."

"Beau, I'm really impressed with what you've done on the cabin. You've been here just a couple of weeks; and you've repaired the stairs, the front porch, the back porch, and the roof. You're an awfully hard worker."

"Thank you, sir. I want to earn my keep. I'm hoping we can be out of your way soon."

"You haven't been in my way, Beau. I've only been here a night or two since you and Meghan moved in. You've actually helped me by keeping an eye on the cabin. Since I've been gone so much, we haven't had much of a chance to talk. Where's home for you, Beau?"

"Meghan and I are both from Portsmouth, Ohio. It is a small town just across the Ohio River from Kentucky."

"Do you have family there?"

Beau lowered his head, obviously troubled by the question. "My mom's in the Southern Ohio Correctional Facility. Gonna be there another 5 to 10 years."

"I'm sorry, Beau, I wasn't trying to pry."

"It's OK. She's been in and out of jail my whole life. That's where my dad should be. He's an Outlaw; I mean he's a member of the Outlaw biker gang. Not exactly a great guy. That's why we ended up here in Tennessee. We just wanted to get a fresh start, away from our bad influences."

"Beau, what if I told you we weren't all that different. My mom OD'd when I was six. I never knew who my dad was. My grandparents stepped in and raised me. They gave me a wonderful childhood. They didn't have much, but they gave me all I had."

Beau looked askance at Elijah. "For real? You had no parents, and you're still this famous dude on TV? Huh."

Elijah shook his head and said mockingly. "Famous dude?"

"Well, you are."

Elijah continued, ignoring Beau's comments. "My grand-parents never let me accept my circumstances as a crutch or an excuse. I made lots of mistakes growing up, but they were all of my own creation. Beau, I honestly believe that one of the greatest challenges facing our next generation—your generation—is the absence of personal responsibility."

"Mr. Mustang—I mean, Elijah—Meghan and I are hoping to be out of your way in just a few weeks. I have a big job that I'm hoping to get that will get us back on our feet."

"Beau, I wasn't talking about you. You've really impressed me with your work ethic and your desire to provide for your family."

"Living in someone else's house isn't exactly providing for my family."

"Tell you what, Beau, before you pursue that big job, I may have my own big job for you."

"What kind of big job?"

"Let me make a few phone calls. I hope to tell you more tomorrow."

Hey, Luke, are things any better?

No

I'm sorry.

Princess Leia has actually moved into my house.

What?

She and my mom are becoming best friends.

That's awesome.

No, it's not. It sucks.

What's she doing there?

She says she's here to warn me—actually, she wants me to warn you.

Warn me? About what?

She says they are looking for you too. The storm troopers.

Oh, that's not good.

Nope

Luke, I gotta admit, I'm a little scared.

I understand.

Do you think you could come visit me in Tatooine?

I don't know, maybe.

"Jeremy! Are you coming down for breakfast?"

Gotta go, Han, we'll text more later.

As Jeremy started down the stairs, he was met with the smell of warm biscuits just out of the oven. Their primary aromatic competition was bacon frying in the skillet.

"Are you hungry, Jeremy?" Rosita queried.

"Did you make homemade biscuits?"

Before Rosita could respond, Savannah entered the kitchen, covered in flour. "Your mom is teaching me how to prepare made-from-scratch biscuits. She's awesome."

At the sight of Savannah, Jeremy dropped his head, pretending to be disappointed. "Are you still here?"

"Jeremy, be nice!" Rosita chastised.

Although Jeremy outwardly protested Savannah's staying at his house, he was secretly happy she was there. With his father's death, the mood in the house had been dark for the past three weeks. Savannah's presence had lifted Rosita's spirits and helped occupy Jeremy's mind.

"Jeremy, have you spoken with Leonard?" Savannah probed.

"Not really."

"What do you mean, 'not really'? Either you've spoken with him, or you haven't," Savannah snapped.

Jeremy sighed heavily while chewing a biscuit. "I haven't technically spoken with him, but we might have texted...

maybe."

"And he's OK?" Savannah asked nervously.

"Yes, he's fine."

"What did he say? Did you warn him? Does he know what happened to your dad?" Savannah fired off the questions in rapid succession.

"Which of those three questions do you want me to answer first?"

Before Savannah could respond, Rosita joined the melee. "Jeremy, if your friend Leonard is mixed up in this, you need to let him know."

"I did, Mom. To be honest, he asked me to come see him." As Jeremy spoke the last word, he knew he had said too much.

"Then we need to go to him!" Rosita exclaimed.

"Now hang on, Mom! What do you mean *we*? You're not going anywhere."

"Great. It will just be you and me," Savannah declared.

"No, I didn't say that!"

"Great, I'll go get packed," Savannah announced as she placed her plate in the sink.

"I'll help you," Rosita exclaimed as they both disappeared from the kitchen.

"Wait a minute! Pack for what? I didn't even say we were going anywhere." Unfortunately, the only audience for Jeremy's protestations were biscuits, gravy, and bacon; and none of them responded.

Hey, Han, are you still in Tatooine?

Yes, why?

Tatooine was Leonard's code name for Saratoga Springs, Utah, his hideaway for the past six months. Situated on the Western shore of Utah Lake, 30 miles south of Salt Lake City, Saratoga Springs was the location of the Intelligence Community Comprehensive National Cybersecurity Initiative Data Center, also known as the Utah Data Center (UDC). Led by the National Security Agency, the UDC is a data storage facility serving the intelligence divisions of many U.S. governmental agencies.

UDC's proximity was the impetus for locating Mouse Trap's Omnia servers in an industrial park two miles south on Highway 68. Dozens of times throughout his tenure with Mouse Trap, Leonard had visited the location of Topaz Systems, a shell company maintaining the Omnia servers. His trips were intended to ensure Omnia's servers continued operating uninterrupted. Leonard's last visit to Saratoga Springs was to inform the crew that the Middle Eastern Bank, which they were told the servers supported, was ceasing operations, necessitating the facility's shutdown.

While the crew dutifully executed Leonard's directions, shutting down the servers, and closing the facility, Leonard had difficulty walking away. Surrounded by hundreds of computers housing exabytes of data, Leonard was in his happy place. As he considered his post-Mouse Trap options, he decided to make the server farm his home, at least for a while. His new 20,000-square-foot residence was 19,000 square feet larger than his apartment in Bethesda, Maryland. Leonard was living large—literally.

Apparently, Princess Leia thinks we need to come and make sure you're safe.

Really? She asked about me?

She's worried something's going to happen to you like it did my dad.

So, you're really coming?

Yep. Princess Leia too.

How soon?

Looks like we're leaving now. See you in however fast we can drive 2,000 miles.

Well, OK then.

"Are you using all of those outlets?"

"Yes, my desktop, monitor, iPad, and iPhone are all plugged in."

"Do we have any more power strips?"

"I heard we're all out, but you can check in the kitchen.

That's the last place I saw one not being used."

Less than a month after initiating efforts to resurrect Mouse Trap, Ezekiel "Zeke" Gibson was finally gaining traction. The camp's activity center, which hosted an initial meeting of fewer than ten, was now bulging at the seams with over 75 Mouse Trap team members at the camp each day. Zeke bolstered his recruitment success by reaching into his personal bank account to provide payroll for returning staff.

Zeke had also funded refurbishment of three bunkhouses and six cabins, more than doubling the workspace. Teams were situated throughout the camp with every corner occupied. Zeke consistently heard from each associate that successfully restarting Mouse Trap was going to be next to impossible without using Omnia.

With the recognized importance of restarting Omnia, a half-dozen team members had converted one of the cabins into an Omnia war room, attempting to recreate the basic system architecture using sheets of large white drawing paper that was now plastered on all four walls. Easton Brummett was explaining the predicament to Zeke and Ovchenko.

"The first thing we need is a means to communicate to our hundreds—well, maybe thousands—of other team members to let them know we're restarting. As you know, Omnia was the only way we could communicate with one another. We didn't retain any contact information outside the system. Without that, we're working blind."

Victor insisted on tight Mouse Trap security, hiring a

former nuclear weapons chief to design the security protocol. A major element of that protocol was the requirement that all communication among team members was compartmentalized in Omnia's messaging app. All backup and redundancies were also conducted through Omnia. Contingency planning never envisioned a scenario in which Omnia wouldn't be available.

"We are presented with the same challenge in contacting our field assets. We can't reestablish our political connections without Omnia. We can't connect with our friends in the media, sports, entertainment, government, or corporate world without—"

"We get it, *without Omnia*," Zeke interrupted. "You folks keep plugging away. Get us in a position to restart, and Andrei and I will have Omnia up and running soon."

Ovchenko and Zeke left the war room, retreating out the door to a small cabin that had been converted to Zeke's personal office. Ovchenko was still shadowed by four of his most trusted Blackforce assets.

"We need to talk, Andrei. Can we do it without your friends?"

Ovchenko gave a slight nod, and his men stood down. He and Zeke disappeared behind the cabin door.

"Andrei, what is the latest on Omnia? I'm having to make payroll out of my pocket for 75 team members. I can't keep this up forever. We have to access our funding."

"Breakthrough is imminent," Ovchenko's offered in his signature succinct reply.

"What kind of breakthrough?"

"I have person working inside who will lead me to Omnia within week."

"Working on the inside? Who is it?"

Ovchenko spun around and opened the door to leave. He turned back to Zeke as he stepped through the threshold. "One week."

15

"As you know, McCoy is trying to gain traction with this idea of a new kind of tax, which he calls a *wealth tax*. You all know Constance Lyons. Her firm has collected some important data to share with you this morning. Constance, you have the floor."

The gathering was a strategic meeting of the highest-ranking Republicans from both the Senate and House of Representatives. The group caucused regularly to ensure they remained aligned in their efforts to thwart McCoy in particular and their Democrat counterparts in general.

Constance stood before her clients as she had done dozens of times before. "We've polled 2,500 likely voters, resulting in a margin of error of plus or minus four percent, so we are confident about the results. 53% of voters state that they are opposed to the wealth tax; 20% are strongly opposed for a total opposition of 73%. 89% of Republican respondents are opposed while 59% of Democrats are opposed;

therefore, even most Democrats aren't in favor of the tax. Only those Democrats who consider themselves 'very liberal' favor the tax by more than 50%. This is definitely a losing issue for McCoy."

A Republican senator offered a suggestion. "Although we now have a 51-49 majority in the Senate, the Democrats have the majority in the House. Since this is such a losing proposition for McCoy, what if we kept the idea alive and told McCoy we would support his Democrat colleagues' drafting a bill? We could privately keep him pushing for it while publicly speaking out against it."

"Why would you want to do that? Wouldn't that be a waste of everyone's time?" The speaker was Kyle Harmon, who had the distinction of being the first person elected to the U.S. Senate running as a Mustang. During Elijah's run for president, Harmon adopted much of the same platform, but more importantly, the same positive optimistic demeanor that was so appealing to voters. That campaign approach resonated with New Hampshire voters, sending shock waves through both Republican and Democrat political structures. Without Harmon's vote, the Senate would favor Republicans by the thinnest of margins at 50-49. Although Harmon had never formally aligned himself with the Republicans, months of courtship resulted in his attending this strategic gathering—leading some Republicans to count Harmon in their majority, doubling their lead from 1 to 2. "Don't you have more productive ways to be spending your time?" Harmon asked.

Received as rhetorical, Harmon's questions yielded no

replies.

"We have some sample data suggesting that giving Mc-Coy enough support to keep the wealth tax idea alive could bolster the overall Republican approval ratings by three to five percent; therefore, the idea has merit." Clicking through a series of charts and graphs, Constance reinforced her position.

"What about our donor base? What are their thoughts?" A Republican senator asked.

Constance clicked rapidly through a few slides. "Yes, we have that data. Our donors who gave over $100,000 were almost universally opposed to the tax. We estimate that if we could keep McCoy talking about the tax for at least six months, we could raise between $5 million and $10 million."

"Wait a minute. Why are we talking about fundraising? How is that relevant to a discussion about taxes?" As with his other questions, Harmon's response was ignored.

"$5 million to $10 million. That's not bad. How long do you think McCoy would keep pushing this tax?"

"It is his signature issue. I think we could string this along even beyond six months." Constance clicked to another slide with a line graph. "This graph shows that our analysis suggests we'd have a declining return on investment every month beyond the sixth month; nevertheless, there would be a return."

"Excuse me...*excuse me*. Can anyone hear me? More importantly, can you even hear yourself? Do you hear what you're saying?" Harmon challenged.

"This is an excellent analysis, as usual, Constance."

"Thank you. This next slide shows…"

Harmon finally shook his head and walked out of the room. No one even noticed the margin had just dropped from 51-49 to 50-49.

"But I don't wanna go!"

"I'm sorry; it's time."

"I'm not going!"

"We have to. Mom is gonna help you pack your things."

"No!!!"

"Honey, we have to."

"What's all of the commotion up here?"

"I don't wanna go, Papa E.!"

In the three weeks Beau's family had stayed with Elijah, four-year-old Destiny had given Elijah the affectionate moniker 'Papa E,' which made Elijah smile every time he heard Destiny's sweet voice utter it.

"You don't have to go anywhere, Destiny."

"Dad says we do."

"What's this all about, Beau?"

Beau Trenton shook his head, unable to look Elijah in the eye. "Elijah, I told you yesterday that we'd been here long enough. It's time we move on."

"Move on?" Elijah asked incredulously. "Where are you going to move on to?"

"We'll figure it out. We always do."

"So, did that big job you mentioned yesterday work out?"

"I'm expecting to hear something any day now."

"I see." Elijah nodded in understanding. "Destiny, your daddy and I are gonna walk outside a minute. Are you OK to hang out here with Clyde and play for a while?"

"Sure."

"Come on, Beau. Let's talk."

Elijah led Beau down the stairs of the cabin and out the back door. They walked to the edge of the patio, where Elijah gestured for Beau to take a seat in a sturdy Adirondack chair beside a fire pit.

"So, you're just gonna pack up the family and leave? Is that right, Beau?"

"It's time for us to go."

"But you don't have anywhere to go, do you?"

Beau didn't respond.

"Beau, I'm not gonna sugarcoat this. You're letting your stubborn, prideful masculinity take priority over providing for your family."

Beau stood, pacing rapidly. "But that's the point! I'm not providing for my family. You are!"

"What if I told you that earlier this year I had estimates prepared for all of the work you've done in the three weeks you've been here? Beau, you've done over $5,000 worth of work in that short time. You are smart, a hard worker, and really good at what you do."

"But you've provided the kids a place to stay, food, clothes, toys. That's probably worth more than $5,000."

"Beau, nobody's keeping score! I'm not, and you shouldn't either. Let's get one conversation behind us so that we can move on to the next. You're not going anywhere. Meghan and the kids aren't going anywhere. You're staying with me and Clyde. It is not a topic for debate. Now, for the more important discussion Beau, what's your long-term goal? What's your dream?"

"I'm not—"

"Beau, I'm serious. What's your big dream?"

After a heavy sigh of both relief and resignation, Beau allowed himself to follow Elijah down this new path. "I guess I'd like to own my own construction company, Beau Trenton construction. I'd like to build houses for families. That's my dream."

"That's an admirable dream, Beau."

"Yes sir. I understand it's not going to happen anytime soon."

"Beau, did you know that I run an organization known as Promise Ministries? Most of the nights I've been away from the cabin I've been tending to ministry business. For the past 25 years, we've been building homes in Central and South America. What would you say if I told you we had built over 1,000 houses?"

"Wow, that's awesome!"

"You know what's missing? Building homes right here in America. We've done a lot of work here, but we've never considered building homes. Your family's time here with me has made me realize this is a huge gap in our ministry. Walk with me, Beau."

Beau and Elijah walked into the edge of the woods.

"Beau, I have 40 acres here on top of this ridge. I'm

using a half acre for my cabin. I'd like to make better use of this property. I met with the Promise Ministries' leadership team last night, and they approved an expansion. We know there are many other families like yours right here in East Tennessee who just need a little boost. A big part of that boost is a place to stay. We'd like to offer you a job building the first Promise cabin here on this property. Your family can continue to stay with me while you're building it. I've already ordered the cabin kit. We're going to pay you a salary to oversee construction. What do you say?"

A tear began to roll down Beau's cheek as he worked to muster a response.

"Now dang it, Beau. Don't start that. I'll be a slobbering mess. I'm going to take that as a 'yes.' Let's go tell Destiny the good news that she doesn't have to move. Clyde will be so excited!"

As Elijah took a couple of steps back towards the cabin, Beau froze in place.

"Elijah, thank you."

"You're welcome, Beau. Now let's go. You have a lot of work to do."

"Let's call it a night, Jeremy. We've been on the road for 14 hours. We just crossed into Nebraska. Lincoln is halfway to Leonard."

"I think I can make it another hour or two," Jeremy protested.

"Come on, Jeremy. I'm tired. Let's stop."

"Not yet."

"Your mom's right. You *are* stubborn."

Jeremy turned up the radio three notches in hopes of drowning out his navigator.

"You're rude, too!" Savannah exclaimed. "Come on, Jeremy; I'm tired and hungry."

Obviously angry, Jeremy pushed the button to silence the radio. "You know, I was planning on making this trip by myself. I could have made it a lot faster without you! I'm trying to get to Leonard, and you want to stop. Just because you're a hot blonde doesn't mean you always get your way!"

As Jeremy huffed, a smile began to show on Savannah's face, angering Jeremy even more.

"What are you smiling about?!" Jeremy scolded.

"You said I was a hot blonde," Savannah cooed.

"Well...I...uh...didn't mean, a—"

"What *did* you mean, Jeremy?" Savannah capitalized on Jeremy's nervousness.

"That's just what Leonard calls you. Anyway, there's a Hampton Inn at the next exit. We're stopping for the night," Jeremy declared.

"OK. How many rooms are we getting?" Savannah teased.

"Two rooms!! We're getting two rooms!!" Jeremy screamed.

In a hushed tone just loud enough for Jeremy to hear, Savannah muttered, "Jeremy said I was a hot blonde."

"Oh, shut up!"

16

"We have to rethink everything. We were working on the false assumption that we were on a level playing field. We were obviously naïve in that assumption," a Mustang leader asserted.

"Let's not focus exclusively on the negatives. So much good came out of the day that we can build on."

Four days after *We're Not Done 2017*, the Mustang leadership team met at the Knoxville headquarters for an after-action review of the event. Two perspectives emerged from the discussion.

The positive perspective was that the event was an undeniable success. Close to a million U.S. citizens gathered peacefully in the nation's capital to signal to the world that a new movement was effervescing. The clear message was that Elijah Mustang's 2016 presidential run was just the beginning. Mustangs were on the rise.

The more critical perspective was that the image seared

into the minds of most Americans watching the event via TV was the media's reporting that Admiral Adair had shirked his patriotic duty to country and instead opted for political campaigning. Since the event, a few news stories had questioned the veracity of the initial reporting about Admiral Adair; however, first impressions were difficult to overcome.

"Going forward we must take our message directly to the American people—not through the media, Hollywood, or any other intermediary," another Mustang emphasized.

"I'm as frustrated as any of you, but we have to channel our frustration constructively. We can't let our emotions lead us to do something we'll regret." Minnie Carpenter was doing her best to keep the discussion focused, but that task was becoming a challenge. In addition to the 12 leadership team members, the gathering included representatives from each state delegation, a constituency that seemed most frustrated by the media's handling of the event.

A member of the Alabama delegation seemed to summarize the situation most eloquently. "Here's the deal. We had around 40,000 Alabamans on the Mall. We were all excited; and by the end of the day, we were ready to run through a brick wall to wrestle this country away from the dadgum politicians. Then we got home, and everyone was asking why the Vice President didn't go to China like the President asked. We didn't know what they were talking about. They said they thought we were going to be different and not be politicians like the Democrats and Republicans. The highest high became the lowest low. Kinda like lining up to kick a game-winning field goal, the kick coming up short, and the other team running it back for a touchdown with no time left on the clock. Heartbreaking!!"

"I understand everyone's frustration. I really do."

Admiral Adair had joined the meeting via video from his Naval Observatory home.

"I want to again apologize for being at the center of this storm. I can assure you that the President and I have had some intense conversations on this topic over the past four days. He, of course, denies any involvement in the false reporting. I agree with the sentiment that we need to take our message directly to the people. I'm not sure exactly what that will look like, but I think it is the strategy with the most merit."

"Has anyone heard anything from Elijah? I would love to hear his thoughts on this."

Minnie knew the 'Elijah question' would come. It always did. Unfortunately, she had no good answer. "As you know, we reached out to Elijah several times leading up to the event. In this season of his life, Elijah seems intent on staying out of the limelight. I think we have to honor his wishes."

"Minnie, this is Kyle from Kentucky. We've spent the last three days squirrelled away in a state park's meeting room trying to figure this out. I think we have a proposal that could change everything. Is it OK if we share it with the team?"

"Yes, Kyle, we'd love to hear it."

"Are you sure this is the right place?" Savannah squinted,

looking through the windshield of Jeremy's Cherokee. "It says Topaz Systems on the building. Is that what we're looking for?"

"It's the right address. Let me text him."

Han, this is Luke, we just got to Tatooine…I think.

"What did he say?" Savannah asked nervously.

"Nothing yet. That's weird. Leonard's usually one of those guys that texts right back. Let me try again."

Han, this is Luke, where are you? I think we're in Tatooine.

"Still nothing. I know this is the right place. There's a door on the left. Let's go see if it's open."

"You mean, *just go in?*" Savannah instinctively grabbed Jeremy's forearm. "Jeremy, what if this isn't it? We can't just barge in."

"Quit being a baby. Come on, let's go."

Jeremy exited the vehicle and Savannah followed, scurrying around the car to grab Jeremy's arm.

"What are you doing?" Jeremy growled.

"Jeremy, I don't think this is good idea. I have a bad feeling about this."

Jeremy shook his head, letting out a deep sigh. "We're gonna be fine. Come on, let's go."

He looked around the building still seeing no signs of life outside or through the deeply tinted windows. Walking to the door, he was surprised to find it unlocked.

"Great! Let's go in," Jeremy declared.

Savannah moved behind Jeremy, grabbing his belt from the back.

"Leonard?" Jeremy called out.

"Let's go down this hallway and see what we can find."

"Jeremy, you know this is exactly how slasher movies go. A young couple walking down a dark hallway."

"We're not a couple," Jeremy corrected.

"You know what I mean."

"Come on, let's keep going."

"Jeremy, did you hear something?!" Savannah whispered.

"I think I did. It was coming from this direction. Let's go."

"You want to walk TOWARD the weird noise?" Savannah cried. "You really *haven't* watched any slasher movies, have you?"

Jeremy continued cautiously down the dark hallway feeling his way along the wall. Savannah ducked closely behind.

"I think I feel a light switch." As Jeremy flipped the switch, light flooded the hallway.

Before Jeremy could react, he saw a figure immediately in front of him, arms raised with an object in hand crashing quickly toward Jeremy's head. Savannah's scream pierced the air.

"Leonard?!"

"Jeremy?" Leonard squinted, lowering his hands.

"Yes, it's me."

"What are you doing here now?"

"I told you we were coming."

"I know, but it's 6:15 in the morning. I was sleeping. I didn't know you'd come this early."

"I told you we were on our way. I tried to text you."

"I just told you that I was asleep!"

Savannah shook her head in amazement at the exchange. "How long are you guys gonna keep this up?"

Jeremy smiled, chuckling at the dustup. "I'm sorry, Leonard. I didn't know it was so early."

"It's OK. It's good to see you."

As Jeremy and Leonard shared a reunion embrace, Savannah noticed the 'weapon' in Leonard's hand.

"A keyboard? You were going to fight an intruder with a keyboard? *Really?*"

"Leonard, you probably remember Savannah."

"Hi." Leonard's succinct response was that of a stereotypically shy computer nerd, uncomfortably awkward around ladies, particularly hot blondes.

"Hi, Leonard. It's nice to see you again."

"Hi," Leonard repeated, having exhausted his 'talking with girls' vocabulary.

"So, how about you show us around the place, Leonard?" Jeremy interjected, rescuing his colleague from Savannah.

"Let's go this way first." Leonard led the two down a short hallway, then into a corner office.

"This was the office of the manager. He had a big space with a bathroom, couch, flat- screen TV on the wall, chair, and huge desk. For the last six months, this has been my home. There's even a shower down the hall."

"What's down this way, Leonard?" Jeremy wondered.

Ignoring Jeremy's question, Leonard walked past Savannah, stepping to the side as if she had a 'wet paint' sign attached to her. "Let's go back down the hall to the left next."

"The building is 20,000 square feet with 15,000 dedicated to servers, which are all in this room." Leonard opened a large door revealing cabinets of servers from wall to wall and floor to ceiling.

"Wow, this is much bigger than I was expecting—and colder," Savannah observed.

"I guess. I've just been here so many times it feels like home to me," Leonard responded, as if discussing an old friend.

As Leonard was talking, Jeremy's head turned slightly askew, as if a light bulb went off in his head. "Leonard, is this what I think it is?"

"Yes, Jeremy, let me introduce you to Omnia."

"Wow, this is impressive," Savannah muttered.

"I had no idea this was all here in Utah." Jeremy looked around the room in wonderment. His initial thoughts of the room's size were replaced with remembering how vast Omnia's capabilities were. That recollection made the room seem much too small.

"With computers, they could be anywhere," Leonard announced in a 'well duh' tone.

As Jeremy peered around the room, uneasiness overtook him as the second mental light bulb lit up. "I have a question, Leonard. We both agreed that we would shut down Omnia. If that's the case, why are all of the server lights flashing?"

"Well…I…uh…guess we need to talk about that, Jeremy."

"Mr. President, I think we need to seriously consider moving on from the wealth tax initiative. We don't seem to be getting any traction in Congress, and it is polling really badly in all demographics. We can advance many other initiatives more successfully."

It was a one-on-one meeting Chief of Staff Riley Indigo had been trying to arrange for the past three days. He was hoping to talk some sense into his boss to move beyond his signature issue that was going nowhere.

"I'm not ready to give up just yet, Riley. This is what I campaigned on and what garnered the support of millions of Americans."

"Yes sir, it's just—"

"I know what you're going to say, Riley. We didn't even garner 50% of the popular vote. I understand that, but I may have an ace in the hole."

At age 44, Indigo was a rising star in the Democrat Party. His magnetic personality coupled with his natural leadership skills helped him transition smoothly from a corporate senior vice president's role into his first foray into politics as McCoy's campaign manager. He joined the team with only a few months left in the campaign, reviving McCoy's stock just enough to ensure the three-way election would leave no candidate with the requisite 270 electoral votes. Once the decision was left to the House of Representatives, Indigo turned on his charm, convincing enough congressmen that they couldn't trust the outsider Elijah Mustang and that Mitch McCoy was the logical selection. Even McCoy didn't fully understand the role Indigo played in his presidential election and had no clue who was responsible for placing him on the campaign team.

"Sir, if I may ask, what kind of ace in the hole?"

"Well...I had an interesting visit yesterday from two members of the Senate, including the Majority Whip."

"The Republicans? Why didn't you ask me to join you? What did they want?" Indigo fired off the questions in quick succession.

"Believe it or not, they wanted to discuss the wealth tax. They commissioned an independent study that showed the wealth tax could actually raise the country's overall GDP by over 4%. They wouldn't commit to anything, but they are open to continuing the dialogue."

"I see." That was all Indigo could trust himself to utter as he rose from his chair to pace around the Oval Office. Thoughts raced through his mind including "You fool, you know they're just playing you." and "Are you really this stupid?"—answered quickly by "Yes, I know you're this stupid."

"Believe me, Riley, I have the same suspicions you may have about the Republican's motives; but I think we at least need to see where this leads."

"Yes sir, I understand. I'll have our staff review the study and work with the Majority's staff."

"Thank you, Riley. That's all for now."

Again, Indigo's thoughts moved rapidly through a series of unspoken responses. "*That's all for now*?' As if I'm your servant? You do understand the only reason you're behind the Resolute Desk is because of how easily you are manipulated, don't you? Of course, you don't. That's OK; you will soon enough."

Finally, Indigo had thought enough that he could muster an acceptable verbal response. "Yes sir, thank you. Have a good day."

17

"Leonard, I know I don't need to remind you that we both agreed Omnia should be destroyed." Jeremy gestured exaggeratedly toward the large bank of computers. "This doesn't look destroyed."

"I...uh...I can explain, Jeremy."

"I certainly hope so! This is extremely dangerous, Leonard!" Jeremy's voice rose much higher than he realized.

"Come on, Jeremy; back off a little and let Leonard talk." Savannah's softer side tried to come to Leonard's rescue.

"Jeremy, Omnia has been my life for the past 20 years. I couldn't bring myself to just destroy her."

"*Her*? Now Omnia is a *her*?"

"I didn't mean it in a weird way."

"Leonard, you know that Victor has used Omnia to collect information that destroys people!"

"I understand now that Victor used her—I mean it—to do some really bad things, but that's because Victor was really bad. Omnia is just a machine. It's an awesome, amazing machine; but it's still just a machine. In the right people's hands, it could be a force for good."

"I'm still waiting for a good reason why I hear humming and see blinking lights."

"I shut it down completely; I really did. It sat idle for three months. You gotta understand Jeremy, I was here all by myself. Omnia was just down the hallway, and I didn't think it would hurt if I restarted her just for me."

"Just for *you*? How do you know it's just for *you*? You know Ovchenko's been trying to restart it. How do you know he hasn't been logging in from wherever he is?"

"I made sure he can't. I'm the only one with login access, and the only way anyone else could ever log in is through your account."

Jeremy stared at Leonard in a confused daze. "What do you mean, *through my account*?"

I installed a firewall between you and every other user. You have to log in with your fingerprint; it is impossible for anyone else to gain access.

"And you're sure this firewall is working? Ovchenko has no way to get access?"

Just as Jeremy spoke, he heard a door open and foot-steps coming briskly in his direction.

"Someone's here!" Savannah whispered.

"Are you expecting someone, Leonard?"

"Thirty-two million seven hundred fifty-thousand dollars," the voice demanded.

Jeremy's mind couldn't process what his eyes were seeing. "Ovchenko? What's going on?"

"I warned you," Ovchenko reminded.

Jeremy lurched toward Ovchenko; but before he could take a step, two of Ovchenko's black-clad henchmen grabbed Jeremy's arms from behind, rendering him unable to move.

"Let me go!" Jeremy exclaimed. "What are you doing here? How did you find us?!"

"Had good help!" Ovchenko declared.

Anger rose in Jeremy as he spun to glare at Savannah. "What did you do?!"

"What? You think I helped him? It wasn't me?!" Savannah shrieked.

"Then who?"

"I'm sorry, Jeremy," Leonard responded despondently.

Ovchenko's henchmen placed black hoods over Savannah and Jeremy, securing them with ropes around their ankles and torso.

"Remember, you said you wouldn't hurt them," Leonard reminded.

"Ladies and gentlemen of the jury, you are serving on one of the most important trials in decades. It involves power, corruption, greed, and ultimately murder. You are going to hear testimony that will frighten, shock, and probably anger you. You are going to see a video that you may be unable to mentally purge for weeks or even months; this video evidence will show the cold-blooded murder of United States Senator and vice-presidential candidate Grant Wembley by this man, Victor Youngblood."

For 40 years, Victor worked meticulously to build his empire of wealth, power, and access to the world's elite until he became the most powerful man in the world. Mouse Trap controlled dozens of the world's largest corporations; hundreds of politicians from both political parties; and the most powerful voices in Hollywood, music, sports, and the media. The fact that Victor was sitting in a courtroom, feet shackled in chains, as a result of the trickery of his 23-year-old protégé, Jeremy Prince, and a computer nerd named Leonard left Victor's friends, enemies, and everyone in between stunned. It also left Victor the opportunity of a lifetime.

Savannah's hood was removed first, leaving her terrified peering into her captors' faces. She struggled to move, but the zip ties secured around both ankles and the legs of the chair kept her legs from moving. Ties around her wrists ran through a back spindle of the chair, rendering her unable to move her arms. The duct tape around her mouth ensured she would be unable to speak.

Ovchenko then removed Jeremy's hood, causing him to cycle through the sensations of confusion and fear.

"I...I'm sorry. You gotta understand, they have my mom. They said they would kill her if I told you they were here."

Jeremy attempted to lurch toward Ovchenko but was unable to move.

"They promised me they wouldn't hurt you. That was

part of the deal. This is all going to be OK in the end," Leonard muttered, appearing also to try to convince himself.

Ovchenko stepped in, shoving Leonard back several feet into a wall.

"Computer boy going with us. Computers will be moved to different location. You will be taken back to Virginia. Stay away from us, and you will be left alone. I see you again, you will die. Your family will die. Your friends will die. You understand?"

A tear began to roll down Savannah's cheek as fear consumed her soul.

Jeremy's response was anger. He tried to stand but was still unable to move. He grunted through the duct tape, and his glare shot daggers through Leonard.

"I'm sorry Jeremy. I promise this was the only way," Leonard whimpered.

"Get fingerprints," Ovchenko commanded to one of his men. The man grabbed Jeremy's arm and placed his hand on a pad. The pad displayed an outline of a hand, the fingertips blinked, then the screen turned green.

"This work?" Ovchenko asked Leonard.

"Yes, it worked. Omnia is unlocked."

"Remember, if I see you again, your friends will die. You have been warned."

Ovchenko motioned for two of his men to escort Leonard out of the room as he led the way out the door. Four other men paired off with Jeremy and Savannah. After a brief struggle, the henchmen removed Jeremy and Savannah from the chairs but again bound their hands and feet before carrying them out to a van. After a 15-minute drive to Cedar Valley Airport, they'd be on a private plane back to Abingdon, Virginia. In less than six hours, Jeremy would be safe and sound in him mom's living room. The only question that remained was how long he would stay there.

18

*T*wo months later...

"Excuse me! Excuse me, guys. Do you have a minute?"

"Nah, dude, we're headed down to 5 Guys for some burgers."

"Are you guys familiar with the Mustang movement?" Eric Mathis asked.

"Uhh...we're just trying to grab some lunch. We're really hungry."

"Can I give you a brochure? It explains everything we stand for, how we operate, our leadership structure."

"Seriously, we're not into politics. Just trying to grab some chow."

"But that's just it! We're not into politics either. We—"

The response caused the duo to finally break stride, turn back to Eric, and burst into laughter. "Not into politics? Dude, that's all y'all are. You know how the TV has nothing but political ads for the last few weeks before an election and everybody hates it and can't wait until the election is over? Man, that's y'all every single day!"

"But—"

"Gonna grab a burger. Later."

Eric Mathis plopped down on a nearby bench, dejected with his hands under his chin. It was the fourth consecutive encounter in which he had been rebuffed. The 18-year-old was the ultimate Mustang. Overjoyed that the first time he was old enough to vote he could vote for Elijah Mustang. He was at the Washington Mall's Mustang event and every other Mustang gathering he could find. Therefore, he was beyond discouraged that he wasn't successful in recruiting new members to the movement. This scene was being repeated throughout the country.

The unfair reporting on the *We're Not Done 2017* event so aggrieved the Mustang movement that they voted overwhelmingly to take their message directly to the voters. They were assertive in creating a presence among the people. Almost every local Mustang chapter leased a space from which to launch this initiative. Storefronts, free-standing buildings, and kiosks in shopping malls were transformed into Mustang outposts. This particular exchange happened in the Paducah Oaks Mall in Paducah, Kentucky. Similar altercations were becoming more common throughout the country as Mustangs worked to share their message with their neighbors. Much to the Mustangs' dismay, this effort was becoming increasingly irritating to fellow citizens.

"Do you see him?"

"No, but there's blood on this limb. He must be going this way."

"Are you sure? We've been following him for close to an hour. I don't even know where we are."

Will Trout paused to take in his surroundings. After a brief 360-degree survey, he had to agree with his brother, Seth; but he didn't want to admit it.

"We're just a couple of farms over from our place, Seth. Don't worry; I can get us back. Come on; let's keep going."

"Are you sure?"

Before Will could answer, the brothers were startled by an unfamiliar voice.

"Halt! Do not move!"

Before either could respond, they were surrounded by four black-clad men, each brandishing an AK-103.

"OK!! OK!! We're not moving!!" Seth screamed.

"On ground!!"

In abject terror, the brothers kneeled on the ground.

"I told you we were too far from home!!"

"No talking!"

Their hands were secured behind their backs with zip ties, and black hoods were draped over their heads. They were stood on their feet and marched away to a destination they were sure meant certain doom.

"What do you think?"

"I think it's going to be fine, Beau."

"I don't know. I'm nervous."

"Beau, you've passed every inspection so far. There's no reason to think this will be any different." One of Elijah's primary goals had been building Beau's confidence. It was a challenging task, but one Elijah embraced.

"I'm nervous," Beau repeated.

"Yeah, you mentioned that."

Beau Trenton totally immersed himself in Elijah's Promise Cabin project. A manufacturer supplied the cabin kit, while Beau found the perfect spot on the property for the cabin site, cleared the land, applied for the building permits, and laid the footers and slab.

After the cabin company erected the structure, Beau was responsible for building a stone fireplace as well as completing the plumbing, HVAC, electrical, insulation, cabinets, countertops, and flooring. He had finished a week earlier and spent the last few days on a final punch list. The verdict on his work was about to be read as the Roane County building inspector approached Elijah and Beau.

"Well, what do you think, Ted?" Elijah asked.

The inspector stood with hands in both jacket pockets, looking down at the ground, shaking his head disappointedly. "Well, Elijah, I have some news to pass along."

"I knew it. What is it, the electrical? I knew I should have used thicker gauge wire."

Elijah glared at his protégé. "Would you let him finish! OK, Ted, what's the story?"

"Well, you see…" The inspector then looked up smiling, extended a hand to Beau, and continued, "Congratulations, you passed."

"I passed? *Seriously?*"

"Beau, you've passed every other inspection with flying colors. Why did you think this would be any different?" the inspector responded.

"That's what I told him, Ted."

"Elijah, you've got a good one here. You need to hang on to him. I am looking forward to the next cabins."

The 'next cabins' were Cabins 2, 3, and 4. As Beau surveyed the property for the first cabin location, he identified several flat spots atop the ridge that would be perfect building sites. With progress moving along nicely on the first cabin, Elijah presented to his Promise Ministries Board a larger vision for the Promise Cabin project as he better understood the urgent need for housing in Roane County. The Board voted unanimously to move forward with three more cabins that would keep Beau busy for the next 18 months.

"Elijah, I have to run to another inspection. Great job, Beau. Keep up the good work."

"Yes sir, thank you."

As Ted left Elijah and Beau alone, the two shared a celebratory hug for the completion of the first Promise Cabin.

"Elijah, do you have any plans tomorrow night?"

"No, not really, Beau."

"Well, Meghan—actually Meghan and I—wanted to know if you would come over for dinner. You know…to celebrate."

"Beau, I would be honored to come to your house for dinner."

Four weeks into the project, Beau mustered the nerve to speak with Elijah about his plans to move himself and his family out of the cabin. Beau argued that the Promise Cabin project had put the family on stable enough footing that they could afford to rent their own place. They had found a small house four miles down the road from Elijah's that would be perfect for their young family. At first, Elijah had protested; but for every point he made, Beau had a counterpoint that Elijah found difficult to contest.

Beau's desire to establish a home for his family caused Elijah to remember an adage his grandfather often quoted— "No home is large enough for two families." Elijah knew this was true; but he was dismayed by the thought of Beau, Meghan, Destiny, and Trevor moving out. In a moment of introspection, Elijah realized that it wasn't Beau's family who was dependent on him; he was becoming dependent on them. He had to admit that Beau and his family may have been filling a void left by his own family.

Elijah's wife succumbed to breast cancer almost seven years earlier. Daughter Shelly and her husband were 600 miles away in Florida. Daughter Kathi and her husband were 350 miles away in South Carolina, an especially difficult distance as they were also parents to Elijah's first grandchild, who wasn't yet one year old. His most recent loss was his youngest daughter, Rachel. Her absence was a source of both pride and sorrow for Elijah as she accepted a position with Promise Ministries to serve in rural Brazil, 4,837 miles from home, an exact distance Elijah had committed to memory.

Although Elijah wanted the Trentons to stay with him, he knew it was time for them to make their own home.

"I know you old people like to eat early, so plan on coming around 5:30."

"Old people?!" Elijah protested.

"OK, what time do you normally eat dinner?" Beau kidded.

Elijah smirked, "See you at 5:30."

"Andrei, what have you done?!" Zeke Gibson exclaimed incredulously.

"They were intruders," Ovchenko responded flatly.

"No, Andrei, they weren't. They were just teenage boys hunting."

"Teenage boy intruders."

Zeke was now pacing, arms flailing. "They live just down the road, Andrei. They were hunting, and they shot a buck and wounded him. They came down our way trying to find him." Zeke was now fully animated. "They are 15- and 17-year-old boys! Your men zip-tied their hands and put black hoods over their heads. They must be terrified, and I'm sure their parents are looking for them and have probably already called the police."

Ovchenko sat stoically with no response.

"Andrei, things are different now. We don't have the connections we used to have. We have to tread more lightly.

If the police come, we don't have an explanation. Where are the boys now?"

"Intruders in cabin."

"I'm gonna go fix this; then you and I must have a serious conversation."

Ovchenko offered no response. For the past two months, tension had grown between Ovchenko and Zeke. Zeke understood the limited capabilities his depleted Mouse Trap remnant had and made his moves tactfully and methodically like a surgeon wielding a delicate instrument. Ovchenko, on the other hand, was a hammer; and to him everything was a nail. He only knew blunt force and wasn't afraid to exercise it. The clash of these two men was inevitable and would be coming to a head sooner than Zeke could have predicted.

As Zeke approached the cabin door, he knew his tactic with the boys was paramount. He had to dial back the tension created by Ovchenko's men; at the same time, he couldn't have the boys going back to wherever they came from spouting off their story to friends; family; classmates; and particularly, the police.

"Well, hello young men. I guess today has brought more adventure than you could ever have imagined."

"Yes sir," Seth Trout muttered nervously.

"I told you not to say anything!" Will Trout smacked his younger brother in the chest.

Zeke chuckled to try to ease the tension. "It's OK, gentlemen. I understand your nervousness. It's been a big day. Let's start with introductions. My name is Ezekiel, but you can call me Zeke."

Crossing his arms and looking suspiciously at Zeke, Will replied, "I'm Will; this is my little brother, Seth."

"Hi, Will and Seth. It is good to meet you. I promise you that we'll have you home in just a bit."

"*Home?*" Seth asked hopefully.

"I bet you're hungry." Zeke yelled to his chef, "Hey, Susan, you got those burgers yet?"

On cue, the cabin door opened; the chef entered with platters of bacon double cheeseburgers and a mountain of fries.

"You guys dig in," Zeke encouraged.

Seth was the first to grab a bite with the reluctant Will following.

Zeke knew the next part of the conversation would be best received on a full stomach.

"I know we have some explaining to do, gentlemen. I'm terribly sorry about how you were treated. It was a big misunderstanding. I'm going to let you in on something if I can trust you."

Both boys shook their head in agreement.

"I'm serious. I really need to know that I can trust you with what I tell you."

"Yes sir," Seth responded, while Zeke got an "OK" from Will.

"We have a big project going on here in the woods. I can't say who I'm with, and I can't say exactly what we're doing; but it could mean big things for this area."

"Big things?" Seth asked.

"*Big things,*" Zeke emphasized. "But we're at a stage in

the project where absolute secrecy is required. We can't let anyone know what we're doing. That's why you were detained. Our security team thought you were spies—whoops, I'm not supposed to use that word. They thought you were… well, they thought you weren't supposed to be here."

"*Spies?*" Seth asked, eyes wide open.

"Forget I said that. Look, I know this is going to be hard, but you can't tell anyone about today. You can't say you were detained, and you can't say you met us."

"Why not?" Seth asked disappointingly.

"If word gets out about the project, the agency—I mean people—in charge, will move it somewhere else, and this area will miss out on a huge opportunity."

"What kind of opportunity?" Will asked, now fully interested.

"I'm sorry, but I've already said more than I should. So, do we have a deal? Can I trust you guys to keep this a secret between us?"

Both boys nodded in agreement.

"Not a word, right guys?" Zeke sought a second confirmation.

"No sir."

"Great! We're going to get you home. Our security forces found that big buck you guys shot. It was an eight-pointer! You should be proud,"

"You found it?" Will asked excitedly.

"Yep. We have it loaded in the back of a truck. You guys are going to hop in the truck, and we'll get you home. The driver is a guy who was driving down the road and saw the two of you trying to carry this big buck home. That's our story. Got it?"

"Yes sir."

"OK, you boys have a great rest of the day and enjoy that venison."

Zeke left the cabin passing by Ovchenko, who had been listening outside the window.

"Andrei, we're going to have that serious conversation soon." Zeke didn't look back to see Ovchenko's foreboding grin.

"Ladies and gentlemen of the jury, have you reached a verdict?"

"We have, Your Honor."

"And the verdict is unanimous?"

"Yes, Your Honor."

"Very well. Will the foreperson read the verdict?"

"We the jury in the case of Victor Youngblood find the defendant guilty of first-degree murder."

The courtroom was in shock. The media rushed out furiously to file a news report. Victor showed no emotion.

In his cabin, Zeke Gibson reached into his jacket pocket, pulled out the envelope, removed the list, and crossed off item #4.

19

JULY 27, 2017

"**U**nconfirmed reports are originating from the Mc-Coy White House that a major announcement is forthcoming regarding President McCoy's long-awaited wealth tax. With us this morning is Alice Finkle, chair of the Federation for Fair Taxation. Ms. Finkle, what are your thoughts on the rumored wealth tax?"

"Thank you for having me. I believe this is a long-overdue announcement. Among first-world countries, America has the greatest gap between the top and bottom 10%. The wealth tax is a small step to try to correct that injustice."

"Also joining us this morning is Bart Henninger, vice-chair of the Republican Party. Mr. Henninger, what are your thoughts on this new tax?"

"It is the most imbecilic idea the Democrats have had in decades, and that's saying something because they've had a lot of terrible ideas. This tax would hit family farms and small businesses, cripple the economy, and ultimately make our country weaker and poorer."

"Lastly, we have Kinsey Davenport joining us as leader of the Mustang movement in the state of Delaware. Kinsey, what is the Mustangs' perspective on the tax?"

"We have many concerns about the tax, chief among them being that American voters haven't been given a chance to weigh in. It seems like we should ask those who will have to pay the tax what they think."

"We asked them what they thought during the election. That's why McCoy was elected."

"McCoy received less than 50% of the votes. The American people don't want this!"

"Those forgotten souls on the bottom of the economic ladder most certainly want this!"

Over the last six months, Mustangs have pursued commentary positions on news and talk shows with the intent of demonstrating how Mustangs were different from the traditional parties. However, many viewers went from hearing two people to hearing three arguing about a topic. Some people were reminded of the famous Mark Twain quote "Never argue with a fool, onlookers may not be able to tell the difference."

"There's no way this will ever pass in Congress!"

"We won't know unless we try!"

"Why don't we ask the voters what they think?"

"We already know what they think!"

<CLICK>

"Thank you for coming today. The President is eager to hear your reports about how you'd use additional funding from the wealth tax. I know your staffs have been working hard to compile the information."

Chief of Staff Riley Indigo was chairing the Cabinet meeting. Indigo encouraged President McCoy to listen and ask questions, a task McCoy begrudgingly accepted.

"Let's start with Transportation."

"Yes sir, the increase in the DOT budget would be approximately $8 billion. With this additional funding, we could repair over 200 of the highest priority bridges and over 1,000 miles of interstate roadway, upgrade 1,000 miles of rail lines, and invest in the FAA to improve customer experience at 100 of the nation's busiest airports."

"Great job! Transportation, you set a high bar." McCoy sounded like a child on Christmas morning.

"How about Defense?"

"Yes sir, as you know, you asked us to focus on domestic priorities. Much of our additional funding would go to the Army Corps of Engineers. We'd repair over 250 of the highest priority locks, dams, and levee systems. We'd also address our long under-funded environmental legacy at over 50 bases. Finally, we'd invest $10 billion in sustainability, ensuring that at least 50% of our facilities would be certified Gold in the Leadership in Energy and Environmental Design."

"Wonderful, that sounds—"

"That's it?! With billions more added to Defense, this

is all you came up with? I know for a fact that the secretary of the Navy asked for an upgrade to the Naval Sea Systems budget to retrofit three carriers that desperately need repair."

There was no response.

The silence following Admiral Adair's interjection was beyond awkward. In the three months since the Mustang event, tensions between the President and Vice President had gone from bad to worse. Adair attempted to forge a working relationship, but McCoy rebuffed every attempt. Finally, Adair accepted that the relationship would be like a married couple who'd agreed to live in the same house for the kids' benefit, but any pretense of reconciliation was gone. The two were at loggerheads.

"...or the Air Force's request for accelerated development of the B-21."

Not only did the Cabinet members not respond to Adair, but most wouldn't make eye contact. Due to the dispute between the President and Vice President, McCoy had established a strict rule that no one in his Cabinet was permitted to respond to any of Adair's comments. The Cabinet members considered this rule beyond juvenile, but none wanted to test their mercurial leader's temper.

"...or the Army's new Abram's tank."

Adair knew there would be no response. Nevertheless, he felt compelled to defend the military, which he'd spent his entire career serving.

Indigo decided to break the awkwardness and move on.

"Let's hear from Commerce."

For the next two hours, the Cabinet members went through their gift bags presenting McCoy exactly what he wanted to hear. McCoy left the meeting energized, knowing he'd soon be sharing the same list with 320 million Americans, whom he was sure would embrace his tax with newfound acceptance.

"Remove all clothing, raise both arms above your head, spread your feet apart three feet, and open your mouth."

Victor Youngblood complied.

"A guard with rubber gloves examined every orifice to ensure no contraband would be brought into the prison. Three armed guards stood watch."

After a two-month trial, Victor was found guilty of first-degree murder of U.S. Senator and vice-presidential hopeful Grant Wembley. During the investigation leading up to the trial, the government's primary evidence was one video of Wembley's murder and another of Victor confessing to the crime. Both videos were from Victor's own Mouse Trap surveillance system.

The murder video was filmed in the Killpecker Sand Dunes, a remote area of Wyoming. Shot from a surveillance drone, the footage showed two men dressed in black bashing large rocks against Wembley's head, sending him sprawling to the ground with Victor standing beside them providing direction. During the investigation, the two men in black were never identified.

The second video was shot from an undetermined office location with Victor uttering, "Yes, I killed a United States' senator; and nobody is going to do anything about it." The video included a conversation in which Victor confessed, "Yes, *Jeremy*, I killed a United States' senator." However, someone had edited out the word "Jeremy" and cropped the video so that only Victor was in view. The video editing wasn't the investigation's only oddity. Before Victor's arrest, Jeremy spent weeks compiling information tying Victor to Senator Wembley's murder and dozens of other murders. He handed the evidence over to the Sweetwater County, Wyoming's sheriff to help secure Victor's arrest. When the case was elevated to the federal court system, the evidence was passed along; however, it inexplicably disappeared before the trial.

As the trial approached, Jeremy expected to be the star witness. He had compiled damning evidence and was Victor's right-hand man for over a year. His work trapped Victor into confessing to the crime. Thus, he was certain he would be called to testify; but that call never came. Jeremy even called the prosecutor's office; however, his messages were never returned.

In the end, the two videos were enough to convince a jury to convict Victor. The unusual circumstances didn't end with the trial. The judge sentenced Victor to life imprisonment without the possibility of parole. The judge noted that the crime was so heinous that Victor would serve his sentence in the United States Penitentiary, Administrative Maximum Facility in Fremont County, Colorado. Known as ADX

Florence, it houses the most dangerous criminals requiring the most stringent controls. The prison's occupants include international terrorists, drug kingpins, domestic mass murders, gang leaders, spies, and now Victor Youngblood.

"Your new home is H-Unit. You will spend your entire time there without contact with other prisoners. You will spend 23 hours a day in your cell and one hour a day outside in a cage by yourself. Your meals will be provided to you through a slit in the door. You will have no friends. You will make no friends. Get dressed. We're going to take you to your new home."

After hearing confirmation of Victor's arrival at ADX Florence, Zeke Gibson reached into his jacket pocket, pulled out the envelope, removed the list, and crossed off item #5.

"Meghan, I believe that was the best apple cobbler I've ever had."

"Thank you, Elijah. I know you're lyin', but it's still nice to hear."

"No, really, it was delicious."

"It was the least we could do for everything you've done for us."

"Elijah, do you mind if I ask you a question?" Beau joined the conversation.

"Of course not, Beau, ask away."

"It's kind of a serious question."

"OK, I will do my best to answer."

"Why do you do this—help people like us?"

"We've been through this, Beau. I had extra room and work that needed to be done. You needed some room and were looking for work. It was the perfect fit."

"No, I don't mean just us. Why do you help people? You travel all over South America, Central America—and I don't know where else—just to help people. You were almost president of The United States. You are a big deal. You could do anything you wanted, but instead you spend all your time helping people."

"You just said I could do anything I wanted. This is what I want to do. I want to help people."

"But why? That's what I'm asking. Why do you want to help people?"

"That's a fair question, Beau." Elijah took a deep breath to collect his thoughts. "We've spent enough time together that you know I became a Christian at age 21 after a really bad truck wreck."

"Yes, I remember the story," Beau acknowledged.

"The first couple of years as a new Christian were really difficult. I was working hard to get Promise Transportation off the ground. I was a very hands-on practical guy in every area of my life except for my Christian life. My struggle was that I couldn't see or touch Jesus. I had a lot of doubt about who Jesus was or even if He existed. I would pray to Him; but more times than not, I didn't sense that anyone was listening."

"I am glad you said that because a lot of times I feel exactly the same way," Beau interjected.

"Then one day everything clicked. I was reading in the Gospel of Matthew about Jesus having a private meeting with His disciples. He tells a story about the people who will inherit the Kingdom of God. He says those people gave Him something to eat when He was hungry. When He was thirsty, they gave Him something to drink. When He was a stranger, they invited Him in. When He was naked, they clothed Him. When He was sick or in prison, they visited Him. Then people responded, 'Jesus, we don't remember seeing you hungry or thirsty or naked or in prison.' Jesus answered, 'When you do things for other people, especially those in need, you do it for Me.'

"See, Beau, I couldn't find Jesus because I was looking in the wrong places. If you open your eyes, Jesus is all around us. When I'm in the midst of serving others, I feel Him the most. That's why I've told you that I'm not doing *you* a favor by offering a little help to you and your family. You are offering me the opportunity to encounter Jesus."

Meghan looked at Beau with a knowing glance. "You're right; this must be what it's like."

A tear began to well in the corner of Beau's eyes. "I know."

A confused Elijah asked, "What *what's* like?"

Beau wiped the tears from his face and looked directly into Elijah's eyes. "You know that Meghan and I didn't have much of a family life growing up. We both said last night

that spending time with you must be what it's like to have a
real dad."

20

"**I**s everything a go with the press conference, Riley?"

"Yes sir, everything is on schedule. I don't suppose another attempt at convincing you not to do this would work, would it?"

The President chuckled at his chief of staff's comment. "No, Riley, you know I'm very resolute about this. I admit I'm struggling to make inroads with my own party, but I just wrapped up a meeting with the Republican leadership who reaffirmed their commitment to pursuing the wealth tax. I think this is truly a chance at a significant bipartisan achievement. I'm going to give it a try."

"Yes sir, I understand."

"On May 6, 2016, this movement was born in this very building. Friends, family, and supporters of Elijah Mustang assembled here to convince him to run for President. In the 15 months since that historic day, the movement's accomplishments have been many and varied. You've all had a role in our success. As you know, today we are gathering to take a cold hard assessment of where we are. Minnie Carpenter continued, "Thomas Jefferson once wrote, 'Honesty is the first chapter in the book of wisdom.'"

Twenty-five of the Mustang movement's leaders were handpicked for this assembly in the Knoxville Convention Center's Cumberland Room. The normal Mustang protocol of an open invitation to all state and local Mustang leaders was bypassed for this gathering. In the previous three months, the movement began to experience some fracturing as blocs adopted varying methods to vent their frustrations with the media and the two major political parties. Some vented less elegantly than others, revealing a sharp edge that the movement hadn't previously demonstrated. As a result, Minnie Carpenter organized this more intimate gathering to chart a course forward. She hoped she would find the right words to motivate her colleagues.

"Let's get honest. Within two months of that day in May 2016 when the movement was started, our approval rating grew from being unknown to 30%. By Election Day, we were viewed favorably by a staggering 70% of those polled. That rating stayed high for six months after the election. Then everything changed. Over the last three months, we've seen a sharp decline with less than half the population viewing us positively. We're at about the same level as Democrats and Republicans. After the campaign, we hired Brett Taylor to help us understand the movement's status. We've brought him back to help us with the sober assessment that must be done to understand where we've wandered off course. Brett, the floor is yours."

As Taylor took the podium, he could sense great unease in the room. As an adherent of the Mustang movement himself, Taylor understood how important this gathering was and how challenging his task was going to be. He breathed deeply and started his presentation. Slide one showed a boxer sprawled on the canvas.

"This picture was taken on February 11, 1990, in Tokyo, Japan. Mike Tyson was destined for another first-round knockout of the next unknown fighter to challenge him in the ring. Buster Douglas was a 42-1 underdog. Mike Tyson was the undisputed, undefeated heavyweight champion of the world with a record of 37-0. He had known nothing but success. Early in the fight when Buster Douglas began landing some punches, Tyson wasn't sure what to do. Douglas continued his onslaught until finally in the 10th round Tyson's legs began to wobble, his vision blurred, and he ultimately fell to the canvas as you see in this picture. He was in unchartered territory."

Taylor took a step toward the gathering for effect. "I'm here today to tell you that you're like Mike Tyson was in 1990. You've known nothing but success; but over the past few months, you've been punched in the face and your vision is blurred. The good news is that you're not a Mike Tyson yet. You're not in the 10th round yet. You haven't been defeated, but you are hurt and disoriented. What you do over the next six months will determine whether you can regain your footing and continue this fight *or* you end up like the Mike Tyson we see in this photo."

Taylor advanced the presentation beyond the Tyson photo to a series of charts. "We've collected a lot of data to help understand where we strayed off course. First, our outposts in the community have been received very negatively with 78% of those surveyed saying they disagree or strongly disagree that they have helped our cause. Second, the ambassadors we've had on TV talk shows have muddied the message. Most of those surveyed say there's no difference among Mustangs, Democrats, and Republicans. We've had similar negative responses to our radio and TV ads, emails, and direct mails. Essentially everything we've tried over the past three months has been an abject failure. We have to face the prospect that although we have tried to differentiate ourselves from the two major parties, the public views us as becoming more of the same."

One of the team members asked Taylor, "Is there any good news?"

"Well, I'm not sure whether it's good news or not, but somehow the movement has become untethered from its founder. Elijah still has a 71% favorable rating, which we can build on."

"Isn't that it?" another asked. "Elijah is the key. How can we convince him to rejoin us?"

It was a question no one was able to answer.

As the President ascended to the podium, the press corps stood at the ready. They had been given advance notice that the President was going to make a major tax announcement, but no other details were provided. It was the worst-kept secret in Washington that the subject was going to be the President's cornerstone initiative, the wealth tax.

"Thank you for coming to today's briefing. Our country finds itself in troubled financial times. Too many have too little while too few have too much. We have the greatest discrepancy of any first-world country between the wealth of the top 10% and that of the bottom 10%. This is due to our antiquated tax system, which focuses almost exclusively on income. Today, I'm announcing a new revenue model for our country that will level the playing field, help those that need it most, and provide much needed funding for many of our nation's neglected priorities.

"I'm announcing the American Wealth Reinvestment Act, which will provide a tax cut for 70% of the population while funding roads, bridges, dams, levees, airports, and many other national priorities. On the tax side, this act will only impact wealth over $5M with a small 5% tax. Therefore, while 100% of the population will realize this tax's benefits, only 2% will have to pay the tax.

"I understand some of you are likely skeptical about our ability to get this initiative through Congress, but I believe this can be a bi-partisan initiative. In fact, discussions with my colleagues across the aisle are well underway and trending in a positive direction.

"I will not be taking questions today, but my staff will be

sharing much more information soon. Thank you for coming today and for reporting on this historic initiative."

Within 30 minutes of McCoy's concluding remarks, 30 Republican senators and congressmen had gathered on the
steps of the Capitol. They had also attracted a large throng
of reporters. The Republican Senate leader stepped to a
bank of microphones to speak.

"As you just heard, our reckless President showed yet
again this evening how out of touch he is with the American
people and with leaders in Washington. After almost a year
in office, he has been unable to garner a single supporter
from his own party for this ridiculous wealth tax. Tonight,
he seemed to suggest that Republicans are somehow going
to get behind this recklessness. I am here representing the
hundreds of leaders in the GOP caucus, I can state unequiv-
ocally that not a single one of us will sponsor, vote for, or otherwise support anything resembling a tax on wealth. Zero
chance. It is a dead idea, like every other idea this President
has offered."

As the Republicans' press conference concluded, McCoy
turned off the TV, slouched in his chair, and sat stunned and
stewing for five minutes. Riley Indigo, the only other person
remaining in the Oval Office, was prepared for a volcanic

reaction as he sat silently waiting for the President to speak first.

McCoy rose from his chair and paced nervously around the office before removing his shoes and socks and kneeling on the rug in front of the Resolute Desk. He then placed his hands on the rug as Indigo observed his boss down on the carpet on all fours.

"Uh, sir, is everything OK?"

Ignoring Indigo's question, McCoy began to take deep breaths while performing the cat-cow yoga pose, intermittently arching his back, then lowering it, arching, then lowering. With each of the President's movements, Indigo grew increasingly uncomfortable. He glanced at the door to see if there was a clear path for him to slip out. There wasn't.

"Uh, sir…"

Finally, after one last deep breath, the President rose to his feet and sat on the couch, rejoining his chief of staff.

"I've been working on some relaxation techniques that my wife suggested. I think they really work."

"Sir, that was a wonderful suggestion."

"OK, back to the matter at hand, Riley. I think we just got played by the Republican scumbags."

"I'm afraid you're right, sir."

"Go ahead, it's just you and me. Go ahead and give me your 'I told you so.'"

"I don't see any value in that, sir."

"It's OK, Riley. You don't have to say it. You warned me not to trust them, but I didn't listen."

"My advice is to give this a few days to settle down; then

we can chart a course forward."

"Good advice, Riley. Let's call it a night."

"Yes sir."

"Can't believe I got played."

Riley Indigo knew it was neither the first nor the last time McCoy would be manipulated.

"Good night, sir."

21

"Turn on computer."

Leonard hung his head before replying to the inane comment for the 100th time in the past two months.

"Look. You see that little green light? I've told you over and over that the computer is on. It just takes time to recreate—"

"Computer working?" Ovchenko interrupted.

"Yes, it's working; but everything isn't reprogrammed yet. You can't just—"

"One week."

Leonard shook his head in disgust. "No, it's not going to be ready in one week. You've been saying 'one week' for the last six weeks, and I've been telling you it won't happen that fast unless I get some help."

The last three months had been hectic and harried for Leonard Applebaum. Immediately following his reluctant betrayal of Jeremy and Savannah, Leonard was given the task of overseeing Omnia's movement from Utah to an undisclosed location. For two weeks, Leonard meticulously inventoried and labeled the hundreds of Omnia's components, including servers, data storage devices, uninterruptible power supply devices, thousands of feet of cables, and dozens of racks. After the components were finally boxed and ready for transport, Leonard was blindfolded, led to a plane, and flown to Omnia's new home. Still blindfolded, he was led into a nondescript metal building before the blindfold was removed.

Leonard spent the next two weeks putting the pieces of the puzzle back together. After reconstructing Omnia's hardware, Leonard was again blindfolded and led to a plane before ultimately being brought to Mouse Trap's temporary headquarters in a camp in the middle of the North Carolina woods. Ovchenko assumed responsibility for restarting Omnia and wanted Leonard where he could follow his every action.

"You will start computer. No help."

"I've tried explaining this before, Omnia works by accessing the target databases, learning the administrative login, mimicking the admin login, and surreptitiously logging in without anyone knowing. We spent years creating those logins. Omnia has been powered down for weeks. We've lost all the admin logins, which must be recreated, including the ones for the CIA, the Treasury, banks, the IRS, the FBI, Transportation, and hundreds of others. It isn't something that's going to happen in a week, a month, or probably even a year."

As Leonard was still speaking, Ovchenko pounded on the table where Leonard was working, breaking two table legs, and sending the monitor and keyboard crashing to the floor. He grabbed Leonard by the back of the neck and pulled him until they were nose-to-nose.

"You are no working hard. We still know where family is. Get computer on soon or family will pay."

"No! We had a deal! I got Jeremy to Colorado, and you promised you'd leave my family alone!"

"Turn on computer!"

As he had done repeatedly, Ovchenko left Leonard's workspace unsatisfied and angry. His patience was clearly approaching its limit.

Leonard knew he had only one avenue out of this mess. It was finally time he tried it.

"Riley, I have an idea!"

"Sir, you startled me."

Riley Indigo had served as the President's chief of staff for close to a year. Whenever the President wished to see him, a staff member would summon Indigo to the Oval Office. That McCoy had come to Indigo's office for this discussion was a first.

"Riley, I want to take your thoughts back to the campaign trail. You joined our team in the last six months of the campaign, and you turned things around."

"Thank you, sir."

"This isn't a compliment. I'm going somewhere with this. What do you remember that worked best to correct our course?"

"Well, sir, it seemed to be when you addressed a crowd. You really have a gift for connecting with your audience."

"Yes, I do." McCoy immodestly observed.

"You were especially good with the greatest achievers. The bigger the movers and shakers in the crowd, the better you were. In fact, you were at your peak speaking with supporters in Washington, New York, and Hollywood."

"Yes, you're right. I do rise to the occasion."

"Maybe that's it, sir."

"Maybe *what's* it?"

"We put you back in front of today's biggest influencers." Riley cocked his head.

"That's a great idea! How about we go back to Hollywood?"

"It is definitely something we could pursue."

"I've got it. I'd like to have a private meeting with, let's say, 200 or 300 supporters in Hollywood. All the A-listers. We've put too much effort into the wealth tax to just walk away because we can't get support here in Washington. Tell them I'll be there in person. I'll give a speech and can provide them with talking points they can share with their fans and followers. We won't even ask for donations. How soon could you pull that plan together?"

"Well, I'm not sure, but—"

"I'd like to do it within a month, Riley. Can you do it?"

"Sir, I'll certainly do my best."

"Let's get this going as soon as we can." McCoy took a step out the door before turning back. "I knew I could count on you, Riley." Then McCoy was gone.

Indigo smiled, then made a call on his personal cell phone. "Yeah, things are progressing in a positive direction."

"Come on, guys. You have to pick up the pace! We're supposed to reopen in just a couple of weeks, and we don't even have electricity."

"I understand, Jeremy; but we are working as fast as we can. We've worked the past three Saturdays."

"I know you are working hard, but there's not enough of you. How about bringing in another crew to help accelerate the schedule."

"I'll look into it, Jeremy."

"Do more than look into it. Do it!"

"I'll see what I can do."

The last three years had been unimaginable for Jeremy Prince. He had experienced inconceivable power; wealth beyond his wildest dreams; abject terror in being part of the world's most dangerous organization; a murder investigation and arrest; and most recently, his father's death—all by the age of 24. His new reality was being leader of the family business after he and his mom made the difficult decision to rebuild and reopen Prince's Hardware.

"Is everything OK, Jeremy?"

"Yeah, everything's good, Mom. Just trying to keep

things moving."

Rosita sensed everything was more than *good* with Jeremy. She didn't remember seeing him happier. The new role as head of the family business was fitting him well, but Rosita knew that wasn't the real source of his happiness. She knew he was enjoying his first true long-term relationship. Rosita was even ready to call it *love.*

Jeremy had never had a problem attracting lady friends. Strikingly handsome with a natural athletic build, Jeremy had many female companions through the years although none for more than a few weeks. Rosita knew her son's new long-term relationship meant he had either fallen head-over-heels, was becoming a mature adult, or maybe both.

"Where's Savannah?"

"I'm here, Mom."

Although Savannah and Jeremy were neither married nor engaged, Rosita insisted that Savannah call her 'Mom.' After a month of protest, Savannah finally acquiesced.

"I went to the store and got three paint samples for you to consider for the interior."

"I really like the tan," Jeremy interjected.

"That was my favorite too," Savannah agreed.

"Tan it is," Rosita declared.

Savannah Lynch was born in Charleston, South Carolina. The middle child of five. She grew up in Thurston House, named after her great-great-great-great-great-grandfather Josiah Thurston, a wealthy shipping magnate, who immigrated to Charleston from Scotland. Thurston House was situated in The Battery, the historic district where most homes date their origin to the 17th century. The third-floor balcony of the 8,000-square-foot mansion provided a perfect perch looking toward iconic Fort Sumter. Although many surrounding homes were by then museums opened each year to thousands of tourists, Thurston House remained a private residence.

Savannah's father, William, was a partner in South Carolina's premier law firm and was among the wealthiest and most powerful South Carolinians. As a third-generation attorney and fourth-generation Yale graduate, William's heritage also set the trajectory for his and wife Abigail's children. Like her two older siblings, Savannah started in pre-law at Yale. However, after three semesters, she knew law would not be her career path. Although brilliant, Savannah's aptitude was not in unending hours poring over legal cases. An extravert, she was at ease with everyone and particularly skilled at convincing others to do what she wanted.

After more than a few heart-to-hearts with her parents, she convinced them to allow her to pursue a career in public relations and transfer from Yale University, which she felt was suffocating. After obtaining a bachelor's degree from Georgetown and a master's from Penn State, she disappointed her parents by not returning to South Carolina but instead taking a PR position with Youngblood and Associates in Washington, D.C. Arguing that D.C. was the most corrupt city in the country, her parents forbade her to move there. Savannah, by then 23, argued that she was an adult and could live and work where she pleased. The dispute was so bitter that her parents parted ways with their middle child, declaring her persona non grata. They felt vindicated when Savannah's employer, Victor Youngblood, was incarcerated for murder. For her parents, it was the ultimate 'We told you so.'

Savannah was determined to never look back. After the drama with Jeremy, Leonard, and Ovchenko in Utah, she decided to stay in Abingdon, renting an apartment a couple of miles from Jeremy and Rosita. It wasn't long until the sparks that began on their journey to Utah started to smolder. She found that their budding relationship brought her the greatest joy she had ever felt. She was finally at a place of peace that she was never able to find in her South Carolina mansion.

"You are coming to dinner tonight, right, Savannah?"

"Yeah, Mom, I'll be there."

As the three spoke, Jeremy felt a buzz in his pocket. Pulling out his phone, he was shocked to read the text from a sender he hadn't heard from in seven months.

Hey, Luke, this is Han. I'm in big trouble. I need your help.

22

"Too slow! Everything too slow!!"

Andrei Ovchenko barged into Zeke's cabin.

"Calm down, Andrei! What are you talking about?"

"Too slow!! Must move faster!" The diminutive Russian stood over Zeke, who was still seated at his desk.

Ovchenko tilted his head so that his eye patch was facing Zeke, a tactic causing most opponents to squirm.

Zeke rose from his chair as Ovchenko took a step closer, now poking Zeke in the chest.

"Andrei, if you'd like to have a conversation, that's fine; but you have to calm down."

"Too late for calm. Calm long enough. Computer boy Leonard too slow."

Zeke decided to try to turn the tables by assuming an offensive position. "Now, Andrei, I've been hearing reports from several of our team members that you've been overly aggressive with them. That's not how we—"

Ovchenko didn't let Zeke finish. "We've worked for months with no progress. Too slow."

"That's not true, Andre. We've made incredible progress. We have over 100 team members on site. We're rebuilding our network of assets. Leonard is working on Omnia. We've tapped into one of our Cayman accounts to fund our restart efforts."

"Too slow!"

"Andrei, it took Victor 40 years to build Mouse Trap. We're trying to rebuild it and have only been here four months."

As Zeke spoke, Andrei knocked on the inside of the cabin door. Four of Ovchenko's Blackforce members knew that was the signal to enter.

"I am now in charge. You can leave the camp or work for me," Ovchenko declared.

"This is outrageous! I'm not working for you."

The henchmen moved toward Zeke.

"*Two options*," Ovchenko repeated.

"Victor would never stand for this!"

"Victor not here."

"I most certainly WILL NOT work for you!"

Ovchenko nodded to his men, who grabbed the 78-year-old Zeke by the arms and forcibly led him out of the cabin.

"Take your hands off me!!" Ovchenko's men didn't comply.

As the Blackforce team led Zeke to an awaiting SUV, Ovchenko sat in the seat of power. Blackforce was now in charge, and things were about to get interesting in the

Pisgah Camp for Disadvantaged Children.

The Y-12 National Security Complex in Oak Ridge, Tennessee, is a nuclear weapons manufacturing facility responsible for uranium parts for every weapon in the U.S. arsenal. Constructed in the mid-1940s as part of the Manhattan Project, Y-12 has hosted scores of high-level visitors including admirals; generals; congressmen; senators; presidents; and on this day, the Vice President of the United States.

"Yes, sir, the project is moving along smoothly. The cranes you see being erected will be the largest free-standing tower cranes in North America. They are required to move construction materials and equipment safely and efficiently around the jobsite," the project manager explained.

The project is the Uranium Processing Facility, a multi-billion-dollar U.S. investment to modernize uranium production, much of which is still ongoing in the original World War II era facilities.

"The UPF is a national priority that must be completed on schedule. The nation is counting on you to deliver."

"Yes, Mr. Vice President, UPF is our highest priority project. So far, we've met all our major milestones on or ahead of schedule. We are all focused on UPF's success."

"That's what I wanted to hear. I understand you have higher priorities than babysitting a cake eater from Washington, so I really appreciate your taking the time to brief me today. I'll get out of your way, but I want you to know that we stand at the ready if there's anything we can do in Washington to keep this project on track."

"Thank you, sir, it is good to know we have your support."

The local dignitaries shook hands with Vice President Adair and exchanged their well-wishes. Adair, his small entourage, and the Secret Service detail loaded into three SUVs and headed west on Bear Creek Road, ostensibly for a return trip to the airport. The caravan passed through the guard portal without incident, then two miles down the road made an abrupt left turn onto a gravel road leading into a densely forested ridge. The gravel road, used by the Y-12 protective force to patrol the facility perimeter, provided the perfect cover for Vice President Adair's afternoon plans. The group reached the crest of the ridge where a clearing was cut in the woods. Awaiting the group were three Y-12 security vehicles and a non-descript black Ford F-150 four-door Supercrew pickup truck with darkly tinted windows.

"Mr. Vice President, you know I'm obligated to try to talk you out of this." Conner Fitzgerald had the honor of being head of the Vice President's Secret Service detail. Vice President Adair had personally planned this visit a week earlier. He knew he'd need the Secret Service's cooperation to fully execute his planned detour. Both Adair and Fitzgerald knew they'd need to keep those in the know to an absolute minimum.

"I understand, Conner. Your objection is noted."

"Alright then, Plan Bravo is a go. Remember, we have a two-hour window where we should be safe. Beyond that, we're going to get questions no one will want to answer,"

Fitzgerald cautioned.

"Roger that, Conner. Let's go."

Fitzgerald turned to the remaining assembly. "OK, you're all to sit tight here. We should be back in less than two hours. Remember, complete radio silence must be observed."

With those words, Conner Fitzgerald, two of his most trusted Secret Service agents, and the Vice President climbed into the F-150 and headed back down the hill toward the real reason for the Vice President's visit to East Tennessee.

"Hey, Babe, can you hand me the screwdriver?"

"Is the Craftsman OK?"

"Yeah, that's perfect."

"This is the last shelf, right?"

"Definitely. I'm wiped out."

Jeremy Prince was standing on the counter stretching to hang yet another display shelf bracket. He and Savannah had been working all day. Although it had been a productive day, both were tired and ready for dinner. As Jeremy reached to secure the last screw, his cell phone on the counter beeped.

"Looks like you got a text, Jeremy."

"It's OK. I'll get it later."

Savannah instinctively reached for the phone to read the text.

"Hey, Jeremy, I think you got someone else's text by mistake. This one is meant for someone named Luke. This is funny; it is from a guy named Han—you know, like Star

Wars, Han and Luke."

Jeremy sighed, hoping Savannah wouldn't pursue the subject any further. His hopes weren't realized as Savannah scrolled through the phone.

"Looks like you've received several texts from this Han guy. It sounds like he's in trouble. It says, 'Please help. Text me as soon as you can. I'm sorry I let you and Leia down.' This sounds serious, Jeremy. Who is this?"

Jeremy climbed down from the counter, put his screwdriver on the shelf, removed his hat, and prepared for a difficult conversation. He raised his head to look Savannah in the eye, took a deep breath, and responded, "It's Leonard."

"What?!? *Leonard?* How? Where is he? He sounds frantic!"

"I don't know where he is."

"Why haven't you responded to any of these texts?"

"You remember that he betrayed us, right?" Jeremy protested, now fully engaged in the conversation.

"Jeremy, they had his mom! He didn't have a choice. You would have done the same thing!"

Jeremy walked three steps away from Savannah, working to collect his thoughts, then turned back to continue his defense. "Remember we had a long discussion about this when we got back from Utah. We could take Ovchenko's offer, walk away, and get on with our lives; or we could spend who knows how long trying to chase them down with no guarantee we'd ever find them. We both agreed it was time to put that chapter behind us and try to start fresh. You remember that conversation, right?"

"Yes, Jeremy, I remember; but Leonard really sounds scared."

"How do we know it's not another trap? How do we know Ovchenko isn't using him to lure us back in?"

"What would Ovchenko need with us? He had us and let us go. We've been back in your hometown for three months. He doesn't need to lure us back in. If he wants us, he could easily find us. I think Leonard really is in trouble! At least text him back and see what's going on."

Jeremy stood silent for a few moments, considering Savannah's proposal before responding, "OK, but I've got a bad feeling about this."

Hey, Han, sorry to hear about your troubles. What can I do to help?

23

"The foundation is looking good, Beau. When do you think it will be finished?"

"I'm thinking it should be ready in a week or so. The cabin kit is coming in three weeks; I should have the foundation done well before then."

Elijah stepped back to survey the surroundings. "I think you chose a good site for Cabin #2. It is far enough away from the first one to have some privacy, and it has a nice view down into the valley."

As Elijah was speaking, the sound of a muffler in the distance was growing closer.

"Is that sound coming from the driveway?" Beau asked.

"I think so. I wasn't expecting any company."

Elijah and Beau walked toward Elijah's cabin just in time to see a Harley pull up next to the cabin and stop beside Beau's car. The rider slowly shut off the engine; lowered the kickstand; and removed his helmet, glasses, and facemask. The length of his beard was rivaled only by that of his hair.

Every inch of his body was covered in leather, tattoos, or both. At 6'3"and 240 pounds, he was as physically imposing as he was visually intimidating.

"Oh no," Beau said as he froze in his tracks 50 feet from the rider.

"What? Who is it?" Elijah asked anxiously.

The rider saw Beau, spread his arms wide, and exclaimed, "Daddy's home!"

Elijah, mouth agape, muttered, "That's your dad?"

Beau didn't answer but walked briskly toward the rider; Elijah followed closely behind.

"What are you doing here?" Beau shouted angrily.

"It's good to see you too, Son."

"It's not good to see you. How did you find me?"

"Call to Meghan's aunt. A couple of visits around town. Boss man here's a celebrity." The rider gestured toward Elijah. "It wasn't too hard."

"I got nothing to say to you," Beau declared.

"I hear I have a new grandson. I'd like to see him."

"Well, you're not going to see him. Just get back on your motorcycle and drive away. I don't want to see you. One of the reasons we moved to Tennessee was to get away from you."

"Awww, now don't break your daddy's heart," the rider mocked.

"I don't want to see you now, and I never want to see you again."

The rider shook his head in disgust at Beau, then turned to gesture toward Elijah. "You workin' for the help now?"

"The *what?*" a confused Beau asked.

"You know us Trentons are proud people. And now you're workin' for this Black boy?"

"*Boy?*" Elijah responded, equal parts amused and insulted. "I'm almost 60!"

"He's more of a man than you'll ever be," Beau shouted with his fists clenched.

Sensing the situation spiraling out of control, Elijah attempted to mediate. "I think it's best that you just get on your motorcycle and drive away."

Now angry, the rider snarled, "This is not your concern, boy. Go back and climb on the porch where you belong."

Elijah had worked for decades to develop a gentle spirit and controlled countenance. It took a lot to stir his anger. The rider had sufficiently stirred. "If you call me boy again, I'm gonna stuff that tailpipe up your—"

As Elijah spoke, the rider took a step in his direction, grabbed him by the throat, and shoved him to the ground. Beau grabbed the rider from behind as Elijah managed to stand to his feet. As the melee reached a crescendo, the sound of gravel beneath tires could be heard growing louder with each second until the black Ford F-150 pulled within a foot of the rider's bike. Two men in suits burst from the truck and approached the brawl.

"Everything OK here, folks?" As a seasoned Secret Service agent, Conner Fitzgerald first tried to quell the fracas with diplomacy. He knew the detail wasn't even supposed to be here. Getting into a fight with a civilian would be the last thing they'd want.

"Yeah, I think everything's good," Elijah interjected. "Our friend here was just leaving, right?"

The rider sized up the situation and slowly put on his facemask, glasses, and helmet. Turning to Beau for one final word, he said, "Look forward to seeing my grandson." He started the motorcycle, spun rocks on the onlookers, and tore down the driveway.

"I'm really sorry about that, Elijah," Beau cried.

"It's OK, Beau."

"I mean, those names he called you."

"Beau, as a black man growing up in Tennessee in the '60s, I assure you I've been called much worse."

"Looks like we showed up just in time. My name is Agent Fitzgerald. Mr. Mustang, it is a privilege to meet you."

"It is nice to meet you, Agent Fitzgerald."

"You're probably wondering why we're here. I have someone who would like to speak with you." Conner gestured toward the F-150 as the passenger emerged from the back seat, escorted by the third member of the Secret Service detail.

"Hello, Elijah, it's been a while."

Walking toward his old friend, Elijah offered a heartfelt embrace and exclaimed, "Jackson!"

Beau stood, gape-jawed, muttering mostly to himself, "That's the Vice President of the United States."

Jeremy raised his phone to show Savannah. "OK, are you

happy? I sent it; now let's wait to see if he—" <beep>.

"Look, he's responded already!" Savannah proclaimed.

Hey, Luke. I'm so sorry about Utah. I didn't have any choice. They had Mom. It was terrible. I am really sorry.

It's OK. I understand. That's all in the past. What kind of trouble are you in now?

I've been with Darth Vader since Utah. He has a guard with me all the time. He's trying to get me to start Omnia, but it is taking too long and he's threatening my family again.

"Is Darth Vader, Ovchenko?" Savannah asked.

"Yes."

Where are you?

I don't know. They blindfolded me and brought me here. Somewhere in the woods.

In the woods? Where?

I don't know. There are a lot of trees.

Gee, Han, in the woods with trees. That's really helpful.

Savannah, who was watching over Jeremy's shoulder, smacked him on the head.

It looks like some kind of old camp. They've rebuilt a lot of the buildings, but I can't tell where it is. They won't let me talk with anyone.

If you find out anything, let me know. I'm with Princess Leia and we'll do what we can to help.

"I'm Princess Leia? That's awesome!" Savannah gushed. Jeremy just shook his head.

OK. I will see if I can find out anything more. Thank you for texting back. I'm really scared.

I understand. Let me know what you find out.

"I feel so sorry for Leonard. We have to help him!" Savannah paced frantically.

"I will try, but I'm gonna need more than 'at a camp in the woods with trees.'"

"Zeke is gone. I am in charge. We have new rules."

Andrei Ovchenko called a meeting of the entire Mouse Trap remnant working at the camp. With the group up to 120, the space was becoming a hub of hectic activity. Mouse Trap's network of contacts was being reestablished. Financial resources were being recovered. Leonard Applebaum was working to restart Omnia. Only he and the guard assigned to watch his every move were absent from this gathering.

"Wait a minute, where's Zeke?" a team member asked.

"Zeke is gone," Ovchenko growled.

"Where is he? Zeke is the reason I came back to Mouse Trap."

"Not here," Ovchenko repeated.

"Yes, you established that; but where is he?"

Ovchenko ignored the question.

"First new rule. No more weekends away. You must work."

There was an immediate outcry among the team. Most team members arrived at camp late each Sunday evening, spent the week in the cabins and bunkhouses, and left for their homes on Thursday evening. Zeke knew a three-day weekend away from the camp would keep the team fresh and energized. Ovchenko didn't share that sentiment.

"Everything too slow. Must work harder."

"Count me out. I'm here because I want to be, not because I have to be."

"Me too."

"Same for me."

Ovchenko ignored the objections. "Second rule. No one leaves camp unless I say so. Cameras are on entire perimeter. We will monitor all activity."

During the week, it was not uncommon for team members to drive into nearby Asheville to get away from the camp for a few hours. Zeke had a back exit created so the team could leave without disturbing the camp's main entrance on Ox Creek Road, continuing the ruse that the 400-acre camp was unoccupied.

"That's ridiculous!"

"You know this isn't a prison, right?"

"Third rule. No cell phones in camp. Cell phones mean no work. Must work harder."

"Victor would never support this!"

"We're all adults here, you know!"

"To maintain security, many more on Blackforce team. You will listen to their commands."

On cue, five heavily armed Blackforce members emerged to stand beside Ovchenko, terrifying the assembly.

"There will be no questions."

"It is so good to see you, my friend," Elijah said admiringly.

"It has been too long," Adair agreed.

Although the two only met during the 2016 campaign, they bonded quickly, both being cut from the cloth of integrity, humility, and service. Conventional wisdom calls for a presidential running mate to be diverse from the presidential candidate so as to reach a broader voter constituency. However, nothing about the Mustang for President Campaign was conventional; therefore, selecting a running mate much like himself greatly comforted Elijah. The two men didn't realize how much they had missed one another until this unlikely reunion.

"You look great, Elijah. I see that civilian life is treating you well."

"Probably better than being stuck in Washington every

day."

"You know this is your fault, right? You asked me to make the sacrifice and run for office with the understanding we'd be doing this together. You got off the hook, and I have to serve under Mitch McCoy."

"The Lord works in mysterious ways, Admiral."

As both men chuckled, Beau cleared his throat, caught in the awkward fringes of the conversation.

"I'm sorry, Jackson; this is my friend, Beau. Beau, this is Jackson Adair."

"It is nice to meet you, Mr. Vice President." Beau extended a hand, not remembering the last time he was so nervous.

"Beau is a master carpenter helping to build cabins out here for the ministry. He's doing a wonderful job!"

Adair nodded his head in approval. "That is a fine-looking cabin for sure. Is the gentleman on the motorcycle also involved in the ministry?"

"Not exactly. We don't need to get into that, Jackson. I am curious what brings you to my little corner of the world."

Beau used that segue to leave the two men to their reunion.

"There is something I'd like to discuss with you."

"Why don't we go inside the cabin and get more comfortable." Elijah gestured toward the cabin door.

"Sounds good, but my hall pass expires in less than an hour; this visit will have to be brief."

The two men entered the cabin as the Secret Service detail positioned themselves around the perimeter. Elijah led Adair to a large wooden chair with a red plaid cushion.

Elijah settled into a chair directly opposite with a small rough-hewn coffee table separating the two men.

"Elijah, you know it's been close to a year since we've seen one another."

Elijah knew this conversation was inevitable; thus, he dove right in.

"I know I walked out on you. As soon as the election results were in and the decision was left to the House of Representatives, I knew our chances were zero. I already had more politics than I cared to experience so I withdrew to my ministry. In hindsight, I see that left you and the rest of the leadership team to clean up my mess."

"Elijah, I'm not here to discuss what anyone should or shouldn't have done. That's all water under the bridge. I'm here to talk about the movement you started. Elijah, do you know what's been happening the past nine months?"

"I'll admit that I've had tunnel vision since the election. My focus has been almost exclusively on ministry work. If it doesn't involve that, assume I don't know anything."

That was the answer Adair was hoping to hear so that he could be the first to let Elijah know that the movement was still alive.

"Elijah, let me give you a quick history lesson. You may not know that our movement includes one senator and four congressmen who were elected to office and are now serving. Since the election, six books have been written about you and the election. At last count, over 50 colleges have classes examining your campaign. You are still the topic of many news talk shows. There was even a country song named

'Heart of a Mustang' that reached #1 on the Billboard charts for five weeks."

Elijah nodded, taking in everything Adair had shared. "Jackson, you used the word *history*. This is all interesting, but it is in the past."

"Wait a second, Elijah; there's more. Do you remember we raised $90 million before the election? What if I told you we've raised $150 million *since* the election? And do you recall the community teams chartered to help spread the word about the campaign? We had around 250 at the time of the election. They haven't gone away. We now have over 300! This summer we had a gathering on the Mall in Washington. Over a million Mustangs—that's what citizens who support the movement call themselves—met to let the world know that we're not done. That's what you told us, that after the election is over the movement isn't over. '*We're not done.*' We've all taken that slogan to heart."

"That's all wonderful, Jackson; it really is, but I'm not sure what I can do to help you. Sounds like things are going well."

"That's exactly it, Elijah. Things *haven't* been going well over the past few months. Immediately after the election, the Mustang movement's approval rating was at 70% and stayed that high for months. Then we made some bad decisions, and it appears we've lost our way."

Elijah nodded in agreement. "Bad decisions like those terrible TV ads and the jerks you put on the news programs to debate with the Democrats and Republicans?"

Adair flashed a broad smile. "So, you *have* been paying

attention!"

Recognizing he'd given away too much, Elijah attempted to backpedal. "Well, I saw a commercial when I was eating dinner at Beau's."

"Elijah, enough beating around the bush. We need you. The movement needs you. *I* need you. Throughout the campaign, you kept telling us to be different than the other guys. We couldn't just blend in and become like the Republicans and Democrats. Unfortunately, that's exactly what we've become, just another political movement."

"Jackson, I hear your genuine concern; and I know you went to great lengths to come here and meet with me; but I'm done with politics. I'm doing exactly what I'm supposed to be doing, serving other people."

"Exactly, Elijah! I'm done with politics too! We all are! That's exactly the point! We need to do things differently. I'm just unsure how. That's where we need your help! I'm not asking for any kind of commitment. We have a meeting planned next month with our leadership team. Everyone is disheartened with the way things have been going. If you would just come and speak with them, I know it would mean so much to the team. They—we—all need a word of encouragement to help us find our way back."

With Elijah's pause and deep sigh, Adair knew he was making inroads.

"Can you at least give me some time to think about it?" Elijah offered cautiously.

"Absolutely, Elijah!"

"If I did come to speak, it would not be about politics,"

Elijah cautioned.

"Exactly."

"And I wouldn't be agreeing to anything long term."

"Definitely not."

"And there's a good chance everyone will leave really disappointed."

"Elijah, there's a void within the movement that only you can fill. You could read them the phone book, and everyone would be encouraged."

"Leave me your contact information, and I'll let you know something in a week or two."

"You have a deal, my friend."

Adair and Elijah exchanged parting words, and the Secret Service detail loaded their passenger into the truck for the return trip to Y-12.

As the truck drove away, Beau rejoined Elijah. "Wow, it's not every day the Vice President of the United States comes to your house for a personal visit. What did he want?"

Elijah watched as the truck disappeared down Sugar Grove Valley Road. "I'm afraid he is looking for something that I can't provide."

24

So, let me get this straight. You were abducted by a group of guys wearing all black, speaking with a foreign accent, and carrying automatic weapons."

"Yes, I swear that's what happened," Seth Trout shrieked.

"We're not supposed to be talking about this," big brother Will Trout muttered ominously.

"You shut up!" Agnes Trout, their mom, exclaimed.

"And you're saying this happened down at the old abandoned 4H camp?"

"Yep, but it ain't abandoned no more," Seth groaned.

The meeting was happening at the City Hall in Bull Gap, North Carolina, population 847. The City Hall was a repurposed double-wide trailer that served as home to the mayor, fire department, city clerk, and the entire police department consisting of a chief and a single deputy, who attended today's gathering. The chief was serving as primary inquisitor.

"Agnes, the boys were four hours late coming home from

hunting. Their story is that they were abducted by two foreigners, blindfolded, held hostage, but then released without harm. Oh, and they gave the boys an eight-point buck."

"I told you they wouldn't believe us," Will maintained.

"That's what Seth has been telling me for over a month. I even grounded them and told 'em if they tell the truth I'll let them go huntin' again. Seth keeps telling me this same story."

It was the deputy's turn to chime in. "Agnes, I drive by that camp every day, and I haven't seen any signs of life. That old gate is still up."

"If ya'll want a bunch of foreigners runnin' around Bull Gap, don't blame me if something bad happens," Agnes declared.

"How 'bout this, Agnes; I'll have the deputy poke around a little, and we'll let you know if he finds anything."

"What do you boys think?" Agnes asked.

"You gotta go up into the woods where the camp is. You can't just look at the gate from the road," Seth cautioned.

"Sounds like we got a deal. I'll send the deputy, and we'll let you know what we find out."

"This is a real bad idea," Will pronounced.

"That's not possible. The inmate is in the SHU. He isn't allowed face-to-face visits. We don't break protocol. Yes, I understand there are unique situations but...yes sir, but...this is highly unusual...yes, sir, I understand." The warden slammed down the phone, cracking the receiver's housing.

At the United States Penitentiary, Administrative Maximum Facility in Fremont County, Colorado, visitation protocol was that Special Housing Unit inmates were only allowed visits via video conferences. However, the call from a highly placed individual to the warden not only allowed a face-to-face meeting but ensured the meeting would occur in a private room normally set aside for attorney-client sessions. The warden was still fuming.

The two men first locked eyes, then smiled, then engaged in a long embrace before taking seats across from one another at the table.

"It is good to see you, old friend. You look healthy as a horse. You seem to be enduring your incarceration remarkably well," Zeke observed.

"Not bad for an old man of 76," Victor agreed.

"Wow, are you that old? How do you even remember your age?"

"I take your age and subtract two."

The two men shared a hearty laugh. It was a laugh Victor Youngblood hadn't enjoyed in close to a year. Although he prided himself on a laser-like ability to stay task-focused, not allowing himself to become emotionally attached to his team members, Zeke was the lone exception.

Ezekiel "Zeke" Gibson joined Youngblood and Associates in 1969. It was a new company in a new field known as public relations. Zeke was 30 and drawn to the company's charismatic leader, 28-year-old Victor Youngblood. Victor was building a company on the misdeeds of Washington's movers and shakers, who needed to find ways to wriggle themselves out of sticky situations. Fortunately for Victor, Washington was a target-rich environment for sticky situations. He provided cover for numerous forms of scandal including financial; relational; and, of course, sexual. In 1973, Victor was called upon by a secretive group known as The Council, who found themselves embroiled in a mushrooming problem that would later be known as Watergate. Before investigators could link The Council to Watergate, Victor extricated them from the situation without a hint of involvement.

Indebted to Victor, The Council brought him into their inner circle. They had found a resource who proved to be invaluable. In The Council, Victor found power, wealth, and connections waiting to be fully exploited. In understanding The Council's potential, Victor saw the need to start his own clandestine organization, he would call Mouse Trap. Launching this new enterprise, Victor designated his friend Zeke as Mouse Trap employee # 0001. For the next 43 years, Victor grew Mouse Trap into the largest and most powerful organization in the world. Zeke Gibson had a front-row seat throughout the entire journey, serving as chief operations officer for over 30 years.

"How are things progressing?" Although he was happy to see a friendly face, Victor was ready to get down to business.

"The Washington initiative is going well and should bear fruit soon."

"How about the restart?"

"We've hit a bit of a snag at the camp."

"What kind of a snag?"

"Ovchenko. He…uh…kicked me out of the camp and put himself in charge."

The normally stoic Victor Youngblood broke into a smile followed closely by a seemingly unstoppable hearty laugh.

"He kicked you out?" The question caused Victor to laugh even harder.

"It wasn't that funny," Zeke snarled. "His men treated these 78-year-old bones like I was still 30."

"And he put himself in charge?" Victor asked, trying to keep a straight face.

"Yes, but—"

Victor again burst into gleeful laughter, stumbling over to the wall, trying to regain his composure.

Finally having enough of his boss's chastisement, Zeke felt the need to fight back. "You know, if you hadn't grown so close to Jeremy Prince and let him trick you into this predicament, none of this would be necessary."

"Touché, old friend, touché. Don't worry; everything is going according to plan. Are you preparing for #6?"

"I am," Zeke confirmed.

"Good."

"It's good to see you again, Victor. I am looking forward us being back together."

"Soon enough, my friend, soon enough."

As Zeke and Victor exited the room, three guards were waiting outside the door to escort Victor back to his cell. He also had a special visitor awaiting in the warden.

"I don't know who you think you are or what connections

you have, but rest assured that behind these walls, I make the rules. Do you understand?"

Victor just smiled as he brushed by the warden on the way back to his cell.

"Director, I understand you wanted to see me."

"Yes, Thomas, thank you for coming. Please take a seat."

Four years into a 10-year term, FBI Director Gavin Thompson reveled in his job. He loved being a Washington power broker and fancied himself one of the town's elite. With a career pinballing between the private sector and various government roles, Thompson was working to be accepted by the career FBI's rank and file but was having limited success.

"How's your family, Thomas?"

"Doing well, Director. Thank you for asking." Hanover knew Thompson really didn't care about his family but used the greeting as a segue into the real topic.

"You're probably curious about this meeting, Thomas."

"A bit, yes sir."

"Well, Thomas, I have an assignment for you. I want you to convene a special task force. You will lead this endeavor and report directly to me."

As chief of the Criminal Enterprise Branch, Thomas Hanover had a significant role within the Bureau with responsibility for 300 employees, including agents, analysts, and administrative staff. Although he served in a critical position, he was still several layers below the director in the Bureau's mammoth bureaucracy. As a 35-year Bureau veteran, he preferred to stay out of the bureaucratic limelight. Unfortunately, he was being pulled into its tractor beams.

"OK, sir." Hanover knew he couldn't share his true feelings on the matter; thus, he kept his response succinct.

"Thomas, do you recall about a year or so ago we discussed a substantial amount of information you received regarding Victor Youngblood and his enterprise?"

"I do remember, sir."

"I'd like your task force to dig into that information and report back to me with what you find."

Hanover scratched his head, looked askance, and addressed Thompson. "Sir, isn't this the same information I discussed with you a few weeks after we received it?"

"Yes, it is, Thomas."

"And the same information that you told me to stand down on?"

"Yes, Thomas."

"Not being disrespectful, sir, but this is also the same information that I brought to you during Youngblood's trial and that I said could ensure his conviction."

"Thomas, are you aware that Youngblood was found guilty and sentenced to life in prison at ADX in Colorado?"

"Yes sir, I am aware of that."

"OK, Thomas, I want you to form a task force large enough to be effective but small enough to keep the information contained. Again, you will report to me. I'll work out the details with your chain of command. You are to discuss your task force with no one but me. Your team is to discuss it with no one but you."

"Yes sir, I understand."

"I'll give you a couple weeks to gather information, but I'd like an update as soon as possible."

"Yes sir, we'll get working on it."

"I knew I could count on you, Thomas. You are one of the best."

As Hanover left the office, he knew he should feel a sense of pride that Director Thompson had entrusted him with this great responsibility; however, he couldn't seem to shake a distinct feeling of anxiety. It was a feeling that would soon prove to be well-founded.

The venue was familiar. During the 2016 presidential campaign, then Campaign Manager Riley Indigo had commissioned three gatherings at the Palazzo di Amore in Beverly Hills. The 53,000-square-foot mansion featured 23 bathrooms, 12 bedrooms, a bowling alley, a 3,000-bottle wine cellar, a theater, and a ballroom that could accommodate 250 guests. It was the perfect venue for the McCoy For President's three events, each garnering more than $10 million in campaign contributions. These events attracted A-list celebrities, all-star athletes, tech CEOs, and many of the world's billionaires.

During each gathering, candidate Mitch McCoy regaled the crowd with his policy positions, with each gathering

ending in a standing ovation. It was this recollection of being adored that led President McCoy to suggest this first
post-election gathering. The President had arrived at the
venue 30 minutes earlier, entering through a side door to
prepare himself for what he was sure would be a memorable
evening. As he straightened his tie in a mirror inside the
5,000-square-foot master suite, he could feel the energy in
the mansion begin to effervesce. He pulled back the curtain
inside the suite to look down on the crowd milling about in
the ballroom. Although he was the President of the United States, he had a few butterflies encountering such star
power. This fixation on star power made the scene he was
witnessing even more curious.

"Umm...Riley, something is not exactly right."

"What's that, sir?"

"Are we early?"

"No sir, guests were to arrive an hour ago."

"Did they leave?"

"Of course not, sir. Why?"

McCoy pulled the curtains even more tightly, just leaving
a crack from which he could peer through the window.

"I'm not recognizing very many faces. In fact, I'm not
recognizing ANY faces."

"Just a moment, sir; let me check with Chelsea."

Chelsea Solomon, Riley Indigo's executive assistant, had
shouldered most of the responsibility for organizing the
event and was in the ballroom mingling with the crowd.

"Hey, Chelsea, can you come up to the President's suite?"

"This is very bizarre, Riley," the President declared,

unable to stop looking out the window.

"Yes sir. Here's Chelsea now. She should be able to shed some light on the situation."

Chelsea passed through the President's Secret Service detail and entered the suite.

The President was the first to speak. "Who are those people!?"

Indigo provided more substance to the President's abrupt question. "Chelsea, thank you for coming. The President has been observing the ballroom and was looking for a few more familiar faces."

Before Chelsea could respond, the President again interjected, "MORE familiar faces? I don't see ANY familiar faces!"

Chelsea cleared her throat, knowing she was about to deliver disappointing news. "Yes sir, about that. You've been busy, and we haven't had a chance to speak in the last week or so."

"Yes, *go on!*" the President urged.

"Well...we've had a few...OK, several cancellations in the last few days. It just seems to be a busy time of year. However, we still have some impressive guests."

McCoy again walked to the window. "Impressive? OK, tell me who that guy is in the red tie with the wine glass."

Chelsea joined the president. "Oh, he was one of the writers for 'The Golden Girls.'"

"Golden Girls?" McCoy scrunched his face in disapproval. "And that lady in the pink dress?"

"She won the Bronze Medal in archery in the 2000

Olympics."

McCoy huffed and shook his head in disapproval. "Bronze in archery?"

"And that guy in the red blazer. He looks familiar."

"Oh yes, that's Big Bob Boatright, who invented Big Bob's Bacon Burger. These are not hamburgers with bacon *on* them; they are burgers that are actually made from 100% bacon. You've probably seen his infomercials on TV."

McCoy swung around to Indigo, his face red with anger. "Golden Girls? Bronze Medal? Infomercials? I hope you don't think I'm going to lower myself to speak to this freak show! I'm heading back to D.C. Riley; you stay and speak with them! And plan on having a heart-to-heart with me about this event when we both get back to D.C.!!"

"Yes sir, I understand."

The President rushed out the door with the Secret Service in tow. Chelsea followed, returning to the esteemed guests.

Now alone, Riley Indigo smiled, knowing things were going exactly according to plan.

25

In the heart of Kingston, Tennessee, lies the American Eagle Diner, which has served as a central landmark in the life of Elijah Mustang for 25 years. It is five miles south of his Sugar Grove Valley cabin and 10 miles north of his primary home on Watts Bar Lake. The diner was central to Elijah's forays into politics.

When Elijah was convinced to run for Congress in 1994, he came to feel the pulse of the citizenry in the early mornings at the American Eagle Diner. During these morning sessions, he befriended an eclectic group of gentlemen who call themselves the Liars, Thieves, and Jokers Club, or LTJ for short. After successful runs for Congress in 1994 and 1996, Elijah stepped away from politics but continued his breakfast meetings with his friends.

His friendship with the LTJ members served him again in 2016 when he stepped into the presidential campaign, seeking their insight into various current events. As Elijah's popularity grew, so too did the American Eagle Diner's and with it the popularity of the LTJ Club. During the height of the presidential campaign, all major network and cable news outlets reported form the diner, noting it was Elijah's unofficial campaign headquarters. The LTJ Club members could be found signing autographs for travelers who took the short detour from nearby Interstate 40.

As with any enterprising business, the diner's owner capitalized on the situation by adding interstate billboards, signs on the front of the building noting 'Home of Elijah Mustang,' and even a life-size cutout of Elijah for patrons to pose for pictures. Although business had become less frenetic, the diner was still a busy place and a popular stop for both tourists and locals.

"Did ya'll see where that drug dealer in Florida was arrested and they found him hiding over $1,000?"

"Heck, Ted, $1,000 ain't much. Drug dealers usually have a lot more than that."

"Naw, y'all don't understand; it is *where* he was hiding it."

"Where was he hiding it?"

"Take a guess."

"In his hat?"

"Nope."

"In his socks?"

"Nope."

"Dadgum, Ted, just tell us."

"Y'all are not gonna believe this. He had a $1,000 stuffed up his hind end!"

"If I was that police officer, I'd just let him keep it."

As the LTJ Club hooted at Ted Beckett's story, they began hearing a commotion coming from the direction of the front door. Whispers led to murmurs, then shouts, and finally a standing ovation.

"What in the world's going on? We haven't had this kind of hullabaloo since—"

"Elijah was here," Percy Glanville interrupted.

As Percy spoke, a familiar face emerged from the crowd and approached the table.

"You fellas mind if I join you this morning?"

"Elijah Mustang! It is good to see you!"

Handshakes and hugs were exchanged around the table. It was Elijah's first visit to his old stomping ground since the election nine months earlier. For the intrinsically humble Elijah, the adoring reaction he received upon his arrival was one of the reasons he had avoided returning.

"What in the world have you been up to, Elijah?"

"Mostly ministry work. I've been traveling a lot. I'm working on a cabin project down in Sugar Grove Valley. I've been keeping myself busy."

"We've missed you. It's good to have you back."

"I've missed you fellas, but I haven't missed all this fuss," Elijah whispered.

On cue, he was approached by a young fan. "Mr. Mustang, could I please have your autograph?"

As Elijah obliged, a half-dozen other patrons lined up for autographs and photos. When the crowd subsided, he reengaged with his friends.

"Like I said, I don't miss this fuss."

"What brings you in today?"

Elijah interlocked his fingers, put both hands on his chin, and sighed. "Well, I was considering coming out of my semi-exile, but I think I may just go back and hide in the cabin."

As Elijah was speaking, Ted Beckett's attention was drawn to the diner TV. "Hey, Tracy, could you turn up the TV?"

We have breaking news from Tennessee. Photos have emerged of Vice President Adair visiting with failed presidential hopeful Elijah Mustang. These photos show Adair visiting Mustang at what appears to be a cabin deep in the woods. Mustang has rarely been seen in public since the 2016 election. It is unclear what Adair's purpose was for the visit. We have an eyewitness who captured these pictures.

"I was at Mustang's cabin when this big SUV drove up the driveway. Two big dudes in suits got out of the vehicle and threatened me until I left. When I got to the end of the driveway, I stopped and took these pictures. This is where Mustang is hiding out. It is just off I-40, exit 352, down a road called Sugar Grove Valley."

Elijah shook his head in disgust. "Hey, Tracy, would you mind turning that off."

"What was that you were saying about hiding in the cabin, Elijah?"

After another successful day in the challenging Prince's Hardware rebuild project, Jeremy and Savannah retreated to her Abingdon apartment. Jeremy was sitting on one end of the couch; Savannah stretched out with her head on Jeremy's lap. Exhausted from a long day at work, they hadn't even mustered enough energy to turn on the TV.

"Do you ever think about the future?" Jeremy delved.

"Of course, everyone thinks about the future."

"What do you see when you think about your future?"

"You know, Jeremy, the girl is supposed to be the one asking 'where do you see us in six months, or a year, or a—'"

"No, I'm not asking like *that*, I'm asking—"

Savannah sprang up, spun around, and looked Jeremy in the eye with a wry grin on her face. "What exactly are you asking?"

The Savannah experience had proven to be unlike anything Jeremy had ever encountered. He was usually the one who made the girl feel awkward and giddy with his boyish good looks, deep green eyes, and devil-may-care grin; but Savannah had turned the tables. The more time he spent with her, the more nervous she made him. That night was no exception.

"Well...I'm...uh...asking about what you think about the...uh...future—"

"Yes, we've covered that." Savannah moved in closer, her lips now inches away from Jeremy's. "What about the future?"

<Beep>

As Jeremy stammered to manage a response, his cell phone provided a merciful respite.

"It's Leonard." Jeremy held the phone up to show Savannah.

"What did he say?!" Savannah exclaimed.

"He just wants to know if we're here."

"Text him back!"

"Yeah, I know how texting works," Jeremy smirked.

Yes, I'm here with Leia.

"You know it's *Princess* Leia, right?" Savannah smiled as Jeremy rolled his eyes.

Things are really bad here. Vader has taken over. I'm not supposed to have a phone.

Do you have any more information about where you are?

I saw a sign on the door that said Pisgah. I don't really know what that means.

Do you have any more information to let us know where you are?

"Hey, is that a cell phone?! That's not allowed in here!"

Han are you there?

"I'm worried about him, Jeremy. It's been 15 minutes since he replied."

"I'm worried too. Let's do some research on Pisgah and see what we find out."

"OK, Riley, let's talk about what happened Saturday night."

"Yes sir, I assume you mean with the event in Hollywood."

"I mean with the freak show in Hollywood!" President McCoy barked. "I'm the President of the United States, the most powerful man in the world. I traveled all the way across the country, and the people there didn't even have the respect to show up!" The President was now pacing around the Oval Office, arms flailing.

"Yes sir. I did make a few phone calls."

McCoy spun around to face his chief of staff. "*And?* What did you find out?"

"I'm working under the premise that you've hired me to always tell you the truth, even if it might not be what you want to hear."

"Hell, Riley, just spit it out," McCoy demanded.

It was now Riley's turn to pace around the office. "I agree the event was an embarrassment, so I talked with over 20 of Hollywood's most prominent individuals. Of course, some wouldn't give me an honest answer, at least in the beginning. However, the more people I spoke with, the more the story began to unfold." Riley's back was turned to the President.

"Riley, am I going to have to call the Secret Service in here to beat it out of you?"

Riley turned to face the President, speaking apologetically. "It sounds like there's some sort of intricate network of influencers in Hollywood who determine which events the 'A-listers' should attend. This network was highly active and in our court during the campaign. Wherever we showed up, the 'A-listers' got the word to show up as well. Of course, wherever the 'A-listers' go, the crowd will also go."

"And these influencers, you're telling me that for some reason they're not in our court now that we're in office?"

"Not exactly. It's not that they're against us; it's more that the network is down. I spoke with agents and a few stars. Some said they didn't even know we were coming to Hollywood. Others said they knew but weren't sure whether to come or not, so they erred on the side of caution and stayed home."

"This sounds too incredible to be true. Do you believe them, Riley?"

"I believe that the President of the United States attended a private gathering in Hollywood and no one of significance came to the party. This network outage—for lack of a better term—appears to be the only plausible explanation."

McCoy shook his head in disbelief. "OK, Riley, if I follow you down this rabbit hole, what's the explanation for the network outage, as you call it?"

Riley again walked away from the President, sighed deeply, and appeared to struggle to organize his thoughts. "Mr. President, you said this was too incredible to be true, but you haven't heard the most bizarre part of the story. Apparently, the network is down because its organizer is in prison."

"*In prison*? Who is it?"

"Mr. President, it appears the man behind the curtain, the mastermind of this 'A-lister' network, could be Victor Youngblood."

McCoy burst into mock laughter. "Riley, this is nonsense. Youngblood was my Republican opponent's running mate! Why would he help to organize *our* campaign events? Oh, I forgot; he's also a murderer! Surely you don't believe this!"

"I'm not sure what I believe, sir. I'll say I've heard a consistent story from enough different people that I'm not ready to eliminate Youngblood as a possibility."

McCoy shook his head. "My chief of staff has lost his mind. I'm not even a year into my term, and you've gone absolutely mad!"

"I've done some other research, sir. Director Thompson from the FBI has a piece of the puzzle as well. He's meeting privately with you and me tomorrow to share some salient information. I understand your skepticism, but I'm asking you to keep an open mind until you hear what he has to say."

"OK, Riley, but I'm going to give you a short leash on this. I don't want us wasting our time on wild conspiracy theories."

"Yes sir, I understand."

As the exchange concluded, another step was taken in a well-laid scheme that started over a year earlier. There were still more steps to be taken, but the lure was finally in the water just waiting for the big fish to take the bait.

26

Grady Shumpert had been the deputy in Bull Gap, North Carolina, for five years. Each day on his way into town, he drove by the entrance to the abandoned 4H camp. The wild story the Trout boys told was the cause of this morning's stop.

As Grady exited the patrol car, he walked to the gate to look up the gravel driveway, overgrown with waist-high weeds. As the driveway disappeared into the woods, Grady saw no signs of life. Walking 50 yards up and down the road, he saw nothing of significance. Taking out his radio, he reported back to the chief.

"Yeah, Chief, I'm down at the old 4H camp where the Trout boys made up that story. I don't see anything out of the ordinary."

"Did you go up to the camp?"

"No, I just looked up from the road, but I didn't see anything."

"The boys said they were at the camp and that people were there."

"Chief, surely you don't believe that story."

"Just go check. That way I can tell Agnes we followed up."

"OK, I'll check. I'll be right back."

As Grady turned off the radio, he cursed his chief for the waste-of-time snipe hunt on which he was about to embark.

Grady again walked toward the gate and stopped to crane his neck to look up the driveway. He pondered lying to his boss that he'd walked up the driveway; then, on the off chance this was a test, he climbed the gate and headed toward the camp.

"Intruder! We have an intruder! Go get Ovchenko!"

The only excitement the central commend video monitor normally captured was the occasional deer and an even rarer black bear. A police officer approaching the camp was unchartered territory.

As Ovchenko frantically entered the central command center, he watched the series of monitors as Grady slowly ascended the hill in the direction of the compound. Situated in the back third of the 400-acre camp, the collection of buildings was a five-minute walk from the gate.

"Everyone, inside the building!" Ovchenko barked. His Blackforce team scurried around the camp to ensure everyone was hidden. Ovchenko knew that he needed to keep the intruder out of the buildings and that he'd need an emissary without an accent. "You!" Ovchenko pointed to the security monitor. "You are American?"

"Yes, I'm from Alabama, I—"

"You go see police. You make up story and keep him out of buildings."

"What kind of story?"

"You make up! Now go!" Ovchenko pushed this man out of the cabin and into the great unknown.

As Grady made it to the top of the driveway, he began to see signs of life. While tall grass had overcome the driveway at the bottom of the hill, fresh gravel and tire tracks were evident throughout the area he was entering. His first glimpse of the camp structures also revealed that the camp was certainly no longer abandoned. New construction was obvious as old structures were being repaired and a handful of new structures dotted the landscape. As he reached for his radio, he was startled by an unexpected voice.

"Can I help you, Officer?"

"Oh…uh…hello. I didn't expect to see anyone here. I thought this place was abandoned."

"It is mostly abandoned, but we're working on that."

"*We?*" Grady questioned.

"I'm with a non-profit. We bought this place a while back, and we're trying to do some work to make it a camp for kids with special needs. We've made some progress; but as you can see, we still have a lot of work to do."

"Oh, a camp for kids with special needs. That's wonderful."

"Is there something I can help you with, Officer?"

"Well…this is going to sound crazy; but a couple of boys said that they came up here and—I'm sort of embarrassed to even say this—said they were abducted by guys dressed in black with big guns."

Ovchenko's man laughed heartily. "That must be those two boys hunting!" He continued laughing.

"Yes, do you know them?"

"Not really, but they came up, said they were late getting home, and asked us for a ride home. I'm guessing the big guys with guns story was their excuse for being late."

"That was my theory too," Grady affirmed. "You've really done a lot of work here."

"Thank you. We've still got a lot to go."

"Is there a reason you're not using the main gate?"

"We just found the back entrance was better for us to get supplies up to the site."

"Seems like that would be a longer drive and curvier."

"Maybe, we'll give the main entrance a try next time. Is there anything else I can do for you, Officer?"

Grady looked around the camp. "You really have done a lot of work here. You mind if I look around a little?"

"I certainly don't mind, but I was getting ready to pack up for the day."

"I'll be quick."

As Grady approached the large activity center, Ovchenko

whispered into the radio network to his men, "If police come in, shoot him."

Grady took one step up to the door, reached for the doorknob, then turned back to his host.

"You know, I really need to get back to town. I'm sorry to bother you. Best of luck in your work with the kids. That's very admirable."

"Thank you, Officer. Please let me know if there's anything we can do for you."

As Grady descended the hill, he radioed back to his boss, "Yeah, Chief, I just left the old camp. We gotta talk."

"So, I, uh, wanted to finish the conversation we started the other day," Jeremy babbled.

"Oh, great, me too!" Savannah chirped.

"We were talking about—"

"Pisgah."

"Huh?"

"I Googled *Pisgah* and *woods*, and the first several hits involved the Pisgah National Forest in North Carolina."

"Oh."

"Leonard said he was in the woods and saw something that said Pisgah on it. That *has* to be it. He's in the Pisgah National Forest!"

"What has to be what?" Rosita quizzed, walking into the living room.

Savannah rose from the couch to greet Rosita. "Oh,

Mom, you remember us telling you about our friend Leonard. He sounds like he's in trouble, but all he could tell us was that he's in the woods and saw a sign with the word *Pisgah*." Savannah showed Rosita the tablet she was using for the search. "I think he's here in North Carolina in the Pisgah National Forest."

"If your friend is in trouble, you should go check on him!" Rosita implored.

Jeremy, who had been doing his own search on his phone while Rosita and Savannah talked, chimed in, "The Pisgah National Forest is 800 square miles. We can't just take off looking for him in an area that large!"

"Have you heard from him lately?" Savannah wondered.

"Not since last night."

"Jeremy, we have to go to North Carolina," Savannah pleaded.

"Let's just give him a little longer. We really need more information."

"I'm worried about him. He sounded very frantic."

"Come on, Savannah; I'll go with you." Rosita grabbed Savannah's arm.

"Mom! It's 100 miles from here. You don't just get in the car and drive," Jeremy yelped.

"We're going soon, with or without you," Savannah insisted.

Jeremy sighed. "I'll go; we just have to have a plan."

"OK, but we're making plans tomorrow. Got it?"

"We'll talk again tomorrow," Jeremy conceded.

"As long as we talk on the way to North Carolina,"

Savannah quipped.

Jeremy left the room without retort. The conversation went absolutely nothing like Jeremy had planned.

"Gavin, I want to thank you for coming to meet with us to-day, we—"

Before Riley could finish the introductions, McCoy interrupted, eager to get on with the meeting.

"Riley tells me you have some information about Victor Youngblood."

In the Oval Office were President Mitch McCoy, Chief of Staff Riley Indigo, and FBI Director Gavin Thompson.

"Well, sir, I'd say we have some preliminary information."

"*And?*" McCoy scowled.

"We're still putting the pieces together, but it appears that Youngblood was the head of a very far-reaching organization involved in…well, lots of things."

"Lots of things?" McCoy fumed. "You're the director of the freaking FBI; I expect a more thorough report than *lots of things.*"

"Well, sir, as you know, he was convicted of murder and is serving life in prison. It appears that there were more… many more…murders involving his organization."

McCoy, disinterested in murder, continued pushing for the information for which he had beckoned Thompson to his office. "How about the campaign? Was he involved in the campaign?"

A confused Thompson responded, "Well, yes sir, he was your Republican opponent's running mate."

Now enraged, McCoy slammed the desk. "I mean, was he involved in *my* campaign?!"

"As I said, sir, this is all preliminary. I have a task force that is being organized that will begin determining the depth and breadth of Youngblood's enterprise."

"How soon? How soon do you expect results?"

"Sir, it may be a while. We have a mountain of information to review, we—"

"*Soon.* Come back to me soon with a report and sooner than that if you have any important information."

"Sooner than soon, sir?" Thompson wondered.

"Just go!" the President roared.

"Yes, sir. I'll get back with you as soon as possible."

Riley walked Thompson to the door, shaking hands on the way out, the two quickly exchanging a knowing glance.

"I don't like this, Riley. I don't like this at all."

"Agreed, sir. We definitely have to keep our eye on the ball."

27

"Where are money people?" Ovchenko snarled. "The financial team is supposed to be in Cabin 3, but there's only one left."

"One left? Where are others?"

"They just left and didn't come back."

"New Rule #2 was no leaving the camp!" Ovchenko screamed.

"Yes sir, I don't think many on the team are observing new Rule #2."

"You are security. Your job to keep them here."

With a ramp-up in security, Ovchenko deployed to the camp a group of seasoned Blackforce members, most of whom had come from Mother Russia with their leader. Augmenting the group was a domestic contingent whose previous function had been building security at Mouse Trap's headquarters in Bethesda, Maryland. The unfortunate soul currently engaged with Andrei Ovchenko was in the latter group and unfamiliar with typical Blackforce tactics.

"Keep them here? What am I supposed to do? Hold them at gunpoint?" the guard chuckled.

"Your job to keep them here," Ovchenko repeated.

"But...uh...I don't know what you want me to do."

"How many here?"

The guard picked up a tablet from the table and reviewed the day's log. As he scanned the results, he realized he had the misfortune of giving Ovchenko the bad news.

"Our numbers are down a little."

"How many?"

"Uh...well..."

Ovchenko growled, took two steps to close the gap, and pointed a stubby finger. "How many?"

"Well...there's a total of 35, 20 of whom are in the security force."

"Only 15 workers left?"

"I'm afraid so."

With Zeke's absence and the oppression of Ovchenko's tightening grip, team members began to slip away one by one. Although the remnant had peaked at 145, over 100 had left and never came back in the seven days since Ovchenko announced the new rules.

"Where have they gone?" The normally stoic Ovchenko began to stalk about the security cabin like a hungry lion.

"I don't know; I assume they've all gone home."

"This home!" Ovchenko raged.

As a Soviet general through the 1980's and head of Blackforce for 25 years, Ovchenko was unaccustomed to his underlings' not following orders. When he laid down the new camp rules, he never thought that they might not be followed. He was in unchartered waters.

"Have to think."

With those parting words, Ovchenko stormed out of the cabin into what would be for the first time in decades an uncertain future.

"Look, he's here!" For the second time in less than a week, Elijah Mustang walked into the American Eagle Diner, again attracting a crowd of admirers. After shaking hands, posing for photos, and signing autographs for 20 minutes, Elijah finally made his way to a table in the back corner of the diner.

"I see things haven't changed much in the year you were in exile."

"Sadly not," Elijah confessed.

"How's Beau doing?"

"Beau is doing great. He has really been a blessing to me."

Elijah attempted to meet with Stephen Roberts, his friend and pastor, at least once a month, with the recent meetings held in the privacy of the pastor's office. This was the first meeting in public in over a year.

"I think the last time we met in the Eagle you were contemplating a run for president. That turned out to be an interesting journey," Pastor Roberts observed.

"*Interesting* is one word for it," Elijah snickered.

"Elijah, are you at peace with your decision to run for president? Do you have any regrets?"

Elijah looked around the restaurant, aware that many eyes were still watching him. "I do have regrets; but as I have contemplated and prayed about them, I sense they are mostly grounded in selfishness."

Pastor Roberts cocked his head in confusion. "*Selfishness?* How so?"

"My regrets are around all the attention and notoriety I've received. I'm extremely uncomfortable with that, but that discomfort is selfishly all about me. I also know that many people are encouraged about the movement we started, and some are still working to keep it alive."

"How about you, Elijah? Are you working to keep it alive?"

"I haven't been, but that's part of why I asked you to lunch. A few days ago, I had a visitor."

"The Vice President?" Pastor Roberts interrupted.

Elijah sighed. "I keep forgetting everyone knows about that. Yes, the Vice President. He's asked me to get involved again. I really don't want to; but again, my reluctance may be for selfish reasons."

"What has he asked you to do?"

"Nothing specific, just to show up, reengage, and try to encourage the movement."

"And? What are you going to do?"

"As I pray, I keep hearing Philippians 2:3-4."

"Do nothing out of selfish ambition or vain conceit. Rather, in humility value others above yourselves, not looking to your own interests but each of you to the interests of the others," Pastor Roberts quoted from memory.

"Yep. That's the one. The only challenge, I think they are looking for a different message than the one I think I'm supposed to give them."

"You said they didn't ask for anything specific. They just asked for you."

"Yeah, that's what they said."

"Then that's what you should give them."

"Yeah, that's what I'm afraid of."

"It looks like there are three main routes to get from Abingdon to the Pisgah National Forest. We can take Highway 421 over to 11 East down to I-26; *or* we can take I-81 to get to 11 East; *or* we can just take the interstate all the way, which is longer, but faster."

Jeremy didn't answer or even look up from his phone.

"Are you even listening to me?" Savannah growled.

"Yes, I'm listening. I still don't know where we'd be going. Like I told you before, the forest is 800 square miles, including dozens of towns and probably hundreds of miles of trails. I just don't want to go running through the woods without a plan."

Savannah joined Jeremy on the couch, grasping his hands. "Jeremy, I agree; but we can't just leave Leonard there. He needs us."

"I've texted him several times but with no response. We

really need more information about where he is."

"I know you're right; I just feel helpless not being able to do anything," Savannah admitted.

As Savannah spoke, the doorbell rang. "I'll get it," Rosita called out from the kitchen.

"Let's go back through what we know. He's in the woods in a cabin, probably near the Pisgah National Forest," Savannah persisted.

"Jeremy, there's someone here to see you," Rosita announced, entering the living room.

Jeremy looked up, surprised to see two men in suits.

"Hello, Jeremy. My name is Thomas Hanover. I'm with the FBI. Do you have a moment that we could speak in private?"

"Calm down, Grady, and tell me exactly what you saw." The Bull Gap Chief of Police was sitting behind his desk, trying to calm his amped-up deputy.

"There's definitely something going on at that camp."

"You said the guy told you it was a camp for kids with special needs."

"Yeah, that's what he said; but that's definitely not the case."

"Why don't you think so?"

"As soon as I took a few steps up the driveway, I noticed surveillance cameras hanging in the trees. There were dozens of them all the way to the camp."

"In this day and age, having a surveillance system isn't unusual," the chief reasoned.

"And when I got to the top of the hill with the cabins and buildings, I noticed on the backside of the hill there were over a dozen vehicles parked, mostly black SUVs."

"I'm still waiting for the nefarious part of the story."

"And there was just one guy there like he was sent out to get me to leave."

"You said he admitted the Trout boys were there."

"Yes, he said they had gotten lost hunting and he took them home."

"Doesn't that sound like a more believable story than a bunch of foreign guys wearing black with automatic weapons capturing them?"

"Chief, I'm telling you something is going on. I was going to go into one of the cabins; but I sensed that dozens of eyes were watching me, and something told me not to open the door."

"Grady, I'm canceling your Netflix subscription. You've been watching too many of those crazy shows."

"Chief, something ain't right at that camp. I think we need to call the State Police and the FBI and find out what's really going on," Grady implored.

"You're right, Grady. I'll call them right now." The chief picked up the phone, pretending to dial. "Uh…yeah…FBI, this is the Bull Gap, North Carolina police department. We need y'all to send a couple of dozen agents down here. My deputy has a bad feeling that a bunch of eyes are watching him and there may be a criminal enterprise at work here in our tiny hamlet. OK, great, we'll see y'all soon." The chief put down the phone and looked up to his deputy. "OK, Grady, they are sending down a bunch of guys as soon as possible. Stand by."

"Chief, I'm serious."

"And I'm serious. This is all your imagination, Grady."

"I'm gonna keep an eye on that camp."

"Grady, you stay away from that camp. The last thing we need is a harassment complaint."

"Stay away? You gotta be kidding me!"

"Grady, for the last time, stay away from that camp!"

Grady stormed out of the chief's office. Frustrated, he paced in the parking lot, contemplating his next move, a move that would soon come from an unexpected source.

"Jeremy, thank you for meeting with me today."

"What exactly does the FBI think I can help with?"

Jeremy and Hanover had retreated to the home office. Jeremy was sitting behind the desk; Hanover was in the guest chair on the other side of the desk.

"I'm here about some information the FBI received. On October 23, 2016, you emailed the FBI. Do you recall that email?"

"I do." Jeremy was perplexed and slightly agitated.

Hanover opened a portfolio, removed a sheet of paper, put on his glasses, and read, "Director Thompson, my name is Jeremy Prince. For the past 18 months, I've worked for

Victor Youngblood in an organization known as Mouse Trap. During this time, I've learned that Youngblood is responsible for many crimes, including theft, extortion, bribery, and several hundred murders. All the evidence you need was just placed on an FBI server J://evidence/victoryoungblood. If you need any assistance putting the pieces together, do not hesitate to contact me." Placing the sheet back in his portfolio, Hanover announced, "I'm here to discuss this email."

As Hanover was reading, the anger in Jeremy began to surge to the point he rose from his chair and paced around the room.

"You want to discuss this email *now*? *Now*? I sent that last October. I put my life and my friend's life in grave danger to collect this information, and you sat on it for almost a year!" Jeremy's frustration had not yet reached a crescendo. "You have no idea what I've been through this past year, and you did nothing. Because of your inaction and your incompetence, this organization is rebuilding. They are responsible for my father's death; and now, all this time later, you show up at my house and want to discuss this email?! You better have a damn good story!"

Hanover wasn't sure what to expect from this meeting with Jeremy. As he contemplated the possible reactions, infuriation was not among them. Remembering that his primary objective was to elicit Jeremy's help, he opted for apologetic diplomacy as a first salvo.

"Jeremy, I'm terribly sorry it has taken us so long to follow up. I wish I had a better explanation than government bureaucracy, but I'm afraid I don't."

"Government bureaucracy?! I called the Bureau three times during Youngblood's trial offering to help you with the information and even to testify. No one ever called me back." Jeremy was still pacing the floor of the small office.

"You do understand that Victor Youngblood was found guilty of murder and will spend the rest of his life behind bars?" Hanover had remained seated in hopes of lowering the tension.

"Yes, I'm aware of that; but this is much bigger than Victor. He was the leader, but there were hundreds...more like thousands of others involved."

"That's why I'm here today, Jeremy. We do want to pursue the information you sent, and we want to bring to justice everyone who broke the law. I realize we have some work to do to regain your trust, but we really would like your help."

Jeremy pondered Hanover's response and walked back to stand behind his desk. "What do you want from me?"

"Jeremy, you uploaded over two terabytes of information. A secondary question is how you accessed a secure FBI server, but the primary help we need from you is sorting through this mountain of information."

"You're actually serious about going after Mouse Trap?"

"I'm not exactly sure what Mouse Trap is; but if that's Youngblood's organization, yes, we're serious about going after them. The director has commissioned a task force specifically for this purpose."

"Hang on, did you say the director, as in FBI Director Gavin Thompson?"

"Yes. Why?"

Jeremy plopped down in his chair and, for the first time in the conversation, flashed a wry smile. "How far are you willing to take this investigation?" Jeremy asked provocatively.

"We'll take it wherever it leads."

Jeremy scooted to the front of his chair and placed his elbows on the desk. "You have no idea what you're getting into."

"Why don't you help me understand that." Hanover finally sensed a crack in Jeremy's resistance.

"If I did agree to help, what would you want from me?"

"I want you to come to D.C. with me. I want you to be a special consultant to the task force. I have a plane waiting at the Highlands Airport just three miles away. We'll be on the ground in D.C. in less than an hour."

Jeremy pondered the proposal for a few moments before declaring, "I need some time with my family, but I'm in."

The two men shook hands. Jeremy asked the agents to wait outside while he spoke with Savannah and Rosita. The discussion quickly became animated.

"But what about Leonard?" Savannah implored.

"Babe, there's nothing for us to do about Leonard. We have no idea how to find him. Maybe looking through the information about Mouse Trap will give us a clue."

"I'm nervous about this Jeremy!" Rosita exclaimed.

"I'll be fine, Mom. I've handled much worse than the FBI."

"When will you be back?" Savannah reluctantly asked.

"I'm sure it will just be a day or so. I'm going to help

them understand the information they have, and then I'll be back. I promise."

As the trio exchanged hugs, Jeremy stuffed an extra set of clothes in a backpack and was out the door.

28

"Do you think the rumor is true?" Eric Mathis bubbled.

"You mean the rumor about Elijah?"

"Of course, that's what I mean."

"We've had Elijah rumors before, so I'll believe it when I see it."

Eric Mathis and his father Rick were among 75 people gathered at downtown Paducah, Kentucky's Mustang meeting hall to participate, via live video conference, in a meeting the Mustangs' leadership had called. Like many other local meetings around the country, the Paducah meeting's attendance was a testament to waning enthusiasm within the movement. Only six months before, crowds of over 200 were commonplace.

Since Mustangs met every month via video, specially called meetings were a rarity. Some important news was obviously forthcoming. As Rick noted, these gatherings almost always included rumors that Elijah was reengaging with the movement. The rumor had extra credence for this meeting due to Elijah's recent reappearance with Vice President Adair.

"I believe he's really going to be here this time," Eric responded.

"I hope you're right, Son. We need him."

"Jeremy, have you moved from the computer since last night?" Thomas Hanover wondered.

"Yes, I grabbed a few hours of sleep on the couch in the atrium."

"You know, I didn't expect you to review everything all at once."

"For the past year, I have worked hard to put all of this out of my mind. Reviewing all these files reminds me of the breadth and depth of everything Victor did."

The night before, Hanover and Jeremy landed at Reagan National Airport at 7 p.m. They hopped into an awaiting car and drove four miles up I-395 North to the J. Edgar Hoover Building, headquarters of the FBI. They took the elevator to the sixth floor where Hanover showed Jeremy the small office he would be using to search through the Youngblood information. Hanover expected Jeremy to head to the nearby Hotel Harrington for a good night's rest before starting his FBI assignment the next morning. Instead, Jeremy volunteered to immediately begin poring over the data.

"I'm having my first meeting with the task team tomorrow. I expect you to join us."

"I'm here for you, Boss."

After Hanover left, Jeremy returned to a Mouse Trap properties' database he had been seeking since his arrival. In the search window, he typed the words *North Carolina Pisgah*. There were three hits. The Pisgah Inn, his first hit, was in a suburban area on the outskirts of Asheville. That wasn't it. His second hit, The Pisgah Tire and Auto Center in Black Mountain, North Carolina, again was not what he was seeking. The third hit was the Pisgah Camp for Disadvantaged Children in Bull Gap, North Carolina. Bingo!

Minnie Carpenter looked toward her producer who started the countdown, 3, 2, 1...

"Good evening, Mustangs. Welcome to this specially called meeting. We're joined today by Mustang groups from all 50 states with over 250 local groups participating. We have some special guests joining us from Washington—all three of our Mustang congressmen—Martinez, Gabriel, and Sharp—and our Mustang senator, Kyle Harmon. We also are honored to have the Vice President of the United States, Jackson Adair joining us via video. Vice President Adair, I will yield the floor to you."

As the producer switched the signal source to the Washington D.C. feed, Adair spoke.

"Thank you, Minnie. It is always an honor to be among

my fellow countrymen who take time out of their busy lives to invest in this movement, but more importantly to invest in their country. After retiring from a 30-year career in the Navy, I experienced an unfamiliar sense of melancholy. During my time in uniform, we enjoyed victories in the Persian Gulf. We were privileged to help deliver new carriers, battleships, and cruisers. Most importantly, I had the honor of leading the finest men and women this country has ever known. When I retired, I was faced with the possibility that the best of my life was behind me. How could anything possibly compare to the United States Navy? But then a new challenge was presented to me. It came from a most unlikely source, the CEO of a trucking company in Knoxville, Tennessee. When Elijah Mustang asked me to join his campaign leadership team just over a year ago, I could have not predicted where this road would lead. The road has had its share of twists, turns, and unexpected detours; but the journey has been worth every moment I invested. I am thankful Elijah afforded me this opportunity. Speaking of Elijah, I know we have all missed him; so, it is my great honor to introduce the founder of our movement, speaking to us live from our headquarters in Knoxville, Tennessee. Ladies and gentlemen, Elijah Mustang."

Elijah wasn't sure what kind of reception he would experience. He would understand if the team were angry with him. He walked away from the movement just as it was beginning to gain traction. He hoped at least some would remember his positive contributions, even if they were over a year ago. He was unprepared for what was about to happen.

The applause was immediate and sustained. Elijah gestured three times toward the camera to signal an end to the praise, but the crowd didn't oblige until minutes later when Minnie finally hushed the team.

Elijah swallowed hard, licked his lips, and began.

"Wow. That was a welcome I neither expected nor deserved but thank you. Minnie, I really appreciate you having me here today. Vice President Adair, I could never earn those kind words; but please know that I cherish each one.

"I had prepared a few remarks and shared them with the Vice President. They included an apology for being away so long and an explanation of where I've been. However, the Vice President encouraged me to move beyond the past and focus my time on the future, so I will honor his request. I do want to start by letting you know that I've been watching the good work you've been doing, and I'm amazed at what you've accomplished as a grassroots organization with little outside support. You've been able to keep this engine turning. Well done!

"So, let's talk about what Vice President Adair invited me to speak about—where this movement goes from here. It seems to me that we have three paths from which to choose. Path number one is to return to our normal lives, give up this idea of a new movement, and be satisfied that we gave it a good run. Based on what I see here today, I don't think you are considering that path. I'm going to ask you to turn on your mics and let me know if I am correct. Is this movement done?"

Elijah heard prolonged chants of "We're not done!

We're not done!" He raised his hands to take back the floor.

"OK, I got it. We're not going down the first path. The second path is to keep the movement going but doing just like the other guys. What I'm understanding from Vice President Adair is that you've tried that path for the past several months with disappointing results. You've tried to engage the public on political matters, but they don't seem interested in politics. You've purchased ads on traditional and social media with limited success. You've engaged with the mainstream parties debating current events on news and talk shows, only to get pulled into their world of conflict and partisan rancor. I don't believe this second path leads to success.

"That leaves us with the third path, which is to remain actively engaged in trying to make our country a more perfect union but doing so in a way that's never been done before. I'm going to offer you my vision of this path and do my best to share it with honesty, candor, and love.

"We all started in this movement as a means to improve our country. We saw its flaws and imperfections and knew there had to be a better way. We loved our communities and were troubled by the direction many were heading. In our country, we saw arguing, bickering, and fighting over every imaginable issue. Within many of our communities, we saw poverty, hunger, too many kids raised in single-parent homes, addiction, and destroyed families; and we refused to stand by and let these problems continue. As a result, we started a political movement in hopes of making things better." Elijah paused and breathed deeply.

"I think we had it all wrong—or at least, we had it all backwards. Our concerns about our country and our communities led us to try to gain a voice in Washington. What if we changed our priorities and focused first on serving in our communities? I've made no secret that I'm a follower of Jesus Christ. The 23rd chapter of the Gospel of Matthew describes a time when Jesus was speaking to a large crowd. He criticized the church leaders for tying heavy loads on the people's shoulders, while the leaders were unwilling to lift a finger to move them. He said the leaders loved the place of honor at banquets and loved to be greeted with respect in the marketplaces. Jesus offered an alternative path. He said that the greatest among you will be your servant, that those who exalt themselves will be humbled, and that those who humble themselves will be exalted.

"Therefore, my vision for the third path is that the Mustang movement become one of service in the communities you call home. Show your neighbors that you are willing to make a positive difference right where you live. Fix the broken playground. Clean up the litter-strewn park. Paint the community center. Repair the dilapidated ball field. Volunteer at your local Boys and Girls Clubs to help kids with their homework. The list is endless. Be known as servants in your community. Imagine the good that millions of you can do right where you live. Maybe that will lead to some sort of political end—maybe not, but I guarantee it will lead to improvements in your communities and a sense of fulfilment within your souls.

Elijah again paused to let his words sink in.

"I realize you were probably expecting a different message from me, a message of how we can take back our country and ascend to the highest offices in Washington. Before we can do that, we have to take back Mayfield, and Chattanooga, and Boulder, and Bangor, and thousands of other communities where you are meeting this very evening. These communities need us more, serving right there at home, than they do in Washington. So, I challenge you to at least give this course of action a try. Before you leave this evening, I challenge you to make a list of how you could make your hometowns better places to live. I guarantee you will be glad you did.

"One thing we've accomplished over the last 15 months is to capture the American people's attention. They've been watching, and now they're waiting to see what this movement is all about. Let's take these next few months and show them that we care about them and their communities. Let's show them what we're made of. Let's show them *we're not done*!"

"Wait a minute! Where's everyone going? We haven't done our list!" Eric Mathis cried.

"We can do that later," a dejected attendee replied.

"But Elijah challenged us to do it before we left," Eric implored.

"We waited a year to hear from Elijah, and this was his message?" another attendee lamented to no one in particular.

"Come back! Come back, everyone! We need to make our list!"

"Hey, kid, most of us already volunteer. I'm a deacon at my church. Bob's on the United Way board. Scott does Boy Scouts. Volunteering in the community isn't a groundbreaking idea."

"But this is different. This is everyone banding together as a force for good."

No one was listening, so Eric took a step on a chair and stood on a table.

"Listen everybody! I'm gonna go over to the corner and start a list for anyone who wants to join me. Come on, let's show them what we're made of!"

Eric, his father, and five others joined the group as the rest of the disappointed crowd headed for the door. And the Mustang movement ambled along its steep uphill climb.

29

Jeremy arrived at the FBI office early after a night where he found little sleep. Questions had bombarded his mind as he was being reintroduced to the motherlode of information from Mouse Trap. He was eager to have one of those questions answered.

Searching the database for 'Blackforce,' he was surprised to find a comprehensive list of all Blackforce operators, including Andrei Ovchenko. He recalled that Victor kept everything about Blackforce separate from Mouse Trap; but on a lark, he queried the search engine. This FBI assignment was going to take longer than Jeremy thought; but if this first nugget were any indication, it would be worthy of his time. He knew he needed to make one call to clear his schedule for the next few days.

"Hey, Babe, how are things at home?"

"Oh, Jeremy, it is great to hear your voice! Are you OK?"

"Yeah, I'm good. How's Mom?"

"She's OK. She misses you. Are you coming home today?"

"I don't think it will be today. You know how I've been texting you about how much information Leonard and I uploaded to the FBI database? The FBI has formed a task force to sort through that information. They asked me to stay here a couple of days to help them understand what they have."

"A couple of days? I don't like the sound of that."

"Seriously, it won't be long. I do have some good news though."

"We could use some good news."

"I think I may know where Leonard is. I searched through a massive database of properties owned by Mouse Trap's organizations. One is the Pisgah Camp for Disadvantaged Children in Bull Gap, North Carolina. That has to be it."

"Awesome. So, you have to come home so we can go get Leonard."

"I will. I promise that's the first thing I'll do in—"

"I know, a couple of days. Jeremy, that can wait. The FBI has waited over a year. We have to take care of Leonard now!"

"I promise we will really soon. I'm sorry, but I have to go. The task force kickoff meeting is starting."

"Jeremy, I'm worried about Leonard."

"Me too. We'll get him soon. I gotta run. I will talk to you later tonight or tomorrow."

"Jeremy, I miss you and I love—" Jeremy was gone.

"Any idea why we are here?" Billy Murdoch asked.

"I'm guessing you were given the same reason I was. Special task force. Report to the northeast classified conference room for more details," Elizabeth Sanders replied.

As Elizabeth spoke, she was startled as the conference room door burst open, and she heard, "18 points, 6 assists, and 5 rebounds! Not a bad night wouldn't you say?"

"Oh great, the superstar is on the task force," Elizabeth rolled her eyes as she spoke.

At age 38, Ben Gossett was trying hard to hold on to his youth. His receding hairline and expanding waistline revealed that he was losing the battle. Captain of his high school basketball team, president of his fraternity in college, and a high-potential employee for most of his FBI career, Ben had always been an achiever. Although known to be a bit eccentric, Ben was recognized as one of the most brilliant minds in the Bureau. He was three questions short of a perfect score on his SAT and graduated from Vanderbilt with bachelor's and master's degrees in accounting with only one B in five years. His exuberant personality didn't fit the accountant stereotype because Ben loved to be the center of attention, a love that was on full display.

"This is a task force, which sounds about right 'cause *force* is a good word to describe me. Watch this." Ben stepped to the right, then quickly to the left, then back to the right, swinging his arms with each movement. "Know what that is?"

"Is it a dance? Are you a dancer?" Billy asked jokingly.

"*Cats,* you're auditioning for *Cats*?" Elizabeth interjected. "Ooh, you'd be a good Mr. Mistoffelees."

"No! Not *Cats* or a dance. It's my killer crossover."

"What's a crossover?" Elizabeth probed.

Energized by the question, Ben continued, "It's my crossover dribble. I dribble to the right." Ben air dribbled, pretending he had a basketball. "Then I quickly dribble to the left, leaving the defender in the dust. I used it last night in the league."

"The league? You are talking about the FBI rec league, right?" Elizabeth asked.

"That's right!" Ben eagerly replied.

"You're in the C league, right?" Billy queried.

"Yep, C league, baby! C is for champions," Ben exclaimed, still pantomiming his dribble.

"Umm, no, C isn't for champions; it's like the bottom league," Billy continued.

Ben ignored the comment. "Did I mention that I got 18 points, 6 assists, and 5 rebounds?"

"I heard Wally over in Public Affairs mentioning that he plays in the C league. Do you know Wally? He's 71. You're playing against guys that are in their 70's. Yeah, very impressive," Elizabeth mocked.

"Most of the points came on my crossover. Did you know they've started calling me the ankle-breaker because of my crossover?"

"Nobody calls you the ankle-breaker," Billy retorted.

"If anyone's ankle breaks, it's because you are playing against senior citizens with osteoporosis," Elizabeth quipped.

As Billy was speaking, the team's fourth member, Lucy Cross, entered the room.

Noticing the new addition, Ben tried again to impress. "Hey, Lucy, watch this."

"That's nice, Ben. Have you started taking a modern dance class?"

Elizabeth and Billy burst into laughter.

"No! It's not a dance move; it's my killer crossover. They call me the ankle-breaker!"

"No, they don't," Billy insisted.

"OK, Ankle-breaker, take a seat. It's time to get started." Thomas Hanover, the group's leader, entered the room, taking control of the conversation. "As you know, you've been asked to join a task force. You've all been selected for your respective areas of expertise. Billy Murdoch, you're here to cover banking and finance. Lucy Cross, identity theft. Elizabeth Sanders, real estate. Ankle-breaker, with whom I have the pleasure of working every day, you are here for your accounting prowess. Get settled in because this team may be in place for a while."

Ben, who showed his ability to quickly be serious, asked, "Thomas, this sounds a little unusual. What's the case?"

Thomas Hanover was a Bureau veteran serving for over 35 years. He had worked in a dozen field offices before settling in to headquarters five years earlier. Life at the J. Edgar Hoover Building suited Hanover better than most. He understood the bureaucracy well enough to pay its penance so that he could focus most of his time on the Bureau's primary mission, investigation.

As Thomas pressed a handheld clicker, the conference room screen awoke with the words *Task Force Terracotta*.

"Welcome to Task Force Terracotta. You're all high performers, so I'm going to go through this information quickly. I know you'll ask questions along the way."

Thomas clicked the remote, and the image of a middle-aged man filled the screen. "This is Ronald Shumate, whose residence is just outside Atlanta in Alpharetta, Georgia." Thomas clicked again. "This is Mr. Shumate's house." A two-story red brick home appeared on the screen. "Mr. Shumate owns a real estate business. He does well. Last year he made $1.2 million, and his total net worth is almost $7 million."

"Let me guess, drugs?" Elizabeth asked.

"Nope, not drugs," Thomas replied as he clicked again. "These are his birth certificate, Social Security information, driver's license, passport—all the usual ID information."

"Securities fraud?" Billy asked.

"Tax evasion?" Lucy decided to join the guessing game.

Thomas returned to the screen with Shumate's face. "No, neither securities nor taxes are the issue. In fact, Mr. Shumate has done absolutely nothing wrong."

"Because Mr. Shumate has done absolutely nothing," Ben interjected.

"What do you mean he's done nothing?" Billy looked askance at Ben.

"Mr. Shumate doesn't exist. Am I right, Thomas?" Ben deduced.

"Why would that be your theory, Ben?" an interested Thomas responded.

"First, you have Lucy on this team, meaning there's an

identity issue. At a minimum, he's not who he says he is. Second, if he's a real estate guy worth $7 million in the Atlanta area, he's not living in that two-story house in Alpharetta. At most, that house goes for $750,000. He's gonna live in Buckhead, Druid Hills, or Dunwoody. Third, you put the Social Security number, passport, and birth certificate on the screen; so, there's obviously an issue with those. Lastly, there's something weird about that picture. It looks almost too real like it's a virtual photo, not a real one."

Elizabeth got up to walk closer to the screen. "I see what you mean. This image *isn't* real."

Thomas responded with a nod to Ben. "Excellent job, Ben, you nailed it. There is no Ronald Shumate; at least this guy isn't Ronald Shumate. Let's back up for a second. Everyone remembers a guy named Victor Youngblood, right?"

"Of course, he was the Republican nominee for vice president," Elizabeth blurted.

"He was the nominee only after he murdered the prior vice-presidential nominee," Billy interjected.

"Exactly," Thomas then displayed on the screen a photo of Victor. "After Youngblood's arrest, the Bureau received an unusual email from someone who said he worked for Youngblood. He claimed there was a clandestine organization known as Mouse Trap, which was responsible for thousands of deaths and the illicit accumulation of billions of dollars of wealth. With the email, he also provided a list of tens of thousands of names that were purported to be false identities."

"Hang on, did you say *thousands* of deaths?" Lucy

inquired.

"Yes, thousands of deaths," Hanover responded.

"You said the FBI received this information after Young-blood's arrest. That was like a year ago. Has this investigation been active with another team? Surely we haven't been sitting on it all this time."

"We were asked to hold the investigation for a while; but with this team, we're now starting in earnest." Hanover hoped the terse reply would satisfy this new team, but he correctly suspected it would not. "Asked to hold it? Who asked you to hold it?"

"Our leadership asked...actually directed...us to hold it. I know you probably have questions about that, but I'm going to ask you to set that aside for the time being so we can focus on the work we've been asked to do. Is everyone clear on that?"

All nodded, albeit reluctantly.

"Back to the list of false identities, we wanted to see if there was any credence to this claim; consequently, we randomly selected one name to further investigate," Thomas explained.

"Ronald Shumate," Ben muttered.

Thomas continued. "At first, everything seemed legit, but we double-checked the birth certificate against the records from 1982 when Mr. Shumate was supposedly born at Emory University Hospital in Atlanta. The original records from 1982 were actually on microfiche at Emory. His birth records weren't there."

"But there was a legitimate birth certificate and social

security number for him?" Lucy asked.

"*Completely* legitimate," Thomas responded.

"This is a big deal," Lucy cautioned, sensing this was not a normal case of identity theft. "Someone had to have access to internal government records to create Mr. Shumate's identity. That's the only way this could happen."

Allowing Lucy to ponder, Thomas continued. "We also searched the real estate records for the agency he purportedly owned. We found that almost every sale he made was to someone on the list we got in the email."

"So, he was only buying and selling real estate from other Youngblood people?" Billy probed.

"Exactly," Hanover confirmed as he continued his presentation. "Lastly, we sent agents to the house in Alpharetta. It had furniture, and the power was still on. They asked neighbors about the house, and the story was that the owner travels a lot, shows up every few months, and hadn't been there in a while. We checked his financial records, and there had had been no activity over the past six months. There's definitely something strange going on."

"And how many Ronald Shumates are there?" Elizabeth prodded.

"Over 40,000, if you believe the email we received." Thomas responded.

"Holy crap! And there's only four of us!" Billy exclaimed.

"Well, there are actually five." Hanover opened the door to signal Jeremy's entrance. "Team, I mentioned that this information came in an email from someone who worked for Youngblood. Meet that someone, Jeremy Prince. Don't let his youth fool you; Jeremy quickly caught Youngblood's attention and soared through the ranks of leadership until he was named head of the Mouse Trap organization. Jeremy was also responsible for orchestrating the plot resulting in Youngblood's arrest. We're lucky to have him on our team to help sort through this mountain of information."

Jeremy looked perplexed at Hanover. "On the team? No, I'm just here for a couple of days to get you started."

Hanover ignored Jeremy's protest and continued with the introductions. After each team member had shaken Jeremy's hand, all returned to their seats with Jeremy sitting among them. As he sat, he mumbled, "But...I'm not actually on the team."

"So, this task force—Terracotta—I'm guessing it is named for the Terracotta Army in China, a bunch of empty vessels designed to look like real people," Ben deduced.

"It is indeed. Your job is to take this investigation to the next level. See if we just happened to pick the one guy that's bogus. I'm guessing we're not that lucky. Dig into as many identities as you can to see if this is as big as it seems. Everything you need is on the shared drive. Ladies and gentlemen, this will be your home for a while."

"Did he sound OK?" Rosita asked nervously.

"He did. To be honest, he sounded energized."

"Did he say when he was coming home?"

"He said in a couple of days, but I sense it will be longer."

"What about your friend Leonard?"

"That's the good news. Jeremy thinks he knows where Leonard is."

"Really? Where?"

"At a camp for disadvantaged kids; at least that's what they say it is. It is in a little town called…," Savannah looked at her notes, "Bull Gap."

"What are you going to do?" Rosita prodded.

"What do you mean?"

"What are you going to do about Leonard?"

"Well, I guess I'm going to wait on Jeremy to get back. I don't really have a choice."

Rosita stood with her hands on her hips. "What do you mean you don't have a choice? You're a strong professional woman perfectly capable of driving to Bull Snort, North Carolina."

Savannah chuckled. "It's Bull Gap."

"You know what I'm thinking?"

"What are you thinking, Mom?"

"I'm thinking we have a road trip ahead of us."

"Now hang on. What do you mean *we*?"

Rosita headed to the kitchen. "I'll get the keys. You drive; I'll navigate."

"Wait, Mom, it's ten o'clock."

Rosita was already in the garage.

"OK, we'll go; but let's wait until tomorrow morning. We can't do anything this late anyway."

Rosita put her hands on her hips. "Are you sure this isn't a tactic to get the old lady off the subject? If it is, it won't work."

"I promise mom, we'll go in the morning. Let's just get a good night's sleep so we'll be fully rested for tomorrow."

Rosita sighed. "OK, but we're going early, right?"

"Right."

30

"So, this is Bull Gap?" Rosita asked.

"This is it. It appears there's not much to it," Savannah confirmed.

"Where is this camp supposed to be?"

"I'm not sure, but it can't be too far away. Let's ask some folks and see if they know where it is."

Upon arriving in the metropolis of Bull Gap, North Carolina, the ladies stopped at the Bull Gap Café to get some lunch and possibly help with a few unanswered questions.

"Are you ladies ready to order?"

"Yes, I'll have the soup and salad," Savannah answered.

"How about you, ma'am?"

Rosita took one last look at the menu. "I'll have the double cheeseburger, large fries, and a large coke. Oh, and I'll have the banana pudding for dessert."

"Are you hungry, Mom?" Savannah chuckled.

"We have a big day ahead of us."

Rosita's comment prompted Savannah to ask the waitress for directions. "Oh, yes ma'am, we're looking for a camp and hoping you can help us. It's called the Pisgah Camp for Disadvantaged Children. Are you familiar with it?"

"No, honey, I don't know anything about a camp. I'm sorry."

"No problem. We'll ask around town. Surely someone knows where it is."

Savannah was overheard at a table behind them.

"Excuse me, ma'am, my name is Grady Shumpert. I'm the deputy here in Bull Gap."

"Nice to meet you, Deputy. I'm Savannah, and this is Rosita."

"Pleased to make your acquaintance. I don't mean to eavesdrop, but did I hear you ask the waitress about the Pisgah Camp for Disadvantaged Children?" Grady whispered.

"Yes, we did! Do you know where it is?" Rosita exclaimed.

"Do you mind if I join you for a minute?"

"Of course, Deputy. Pull up a chair."

Grady sat at the table, removed his hat, and glanced around the room to ensure no one was watching. He whispered, "Can I ask why you're interested in the camp?"

Savannah and Rosita looked at one another, wondering if they should get the police involved. Savannah opted for a subtle opening.

"We have a friend that we're looking for, and we heard he may be there."

Grady nodded slowly. "And this friend, he works at the camp?"

"We think he might."

"Do you know anything about the camp?" Grady quizzed.

Suspecting Grady was hiding something, Savannah asked her own question. "Do *you* know anything about the camp?"

Caught off guard, Grady sat back in his chair, collecting his thoughts. "It might not be safe for you to go there."

Savannah cocked her head. "Not safe? Why not?"

"It might not be a camp for kids. It might be something else."

"What kind of *something else*?" It was Rosita's turn to ask a question.

Unsure how to proceed, Grady huffed, "Well...I...I'm not really supposed to talk about it."

Seeing the deputy as their most promising lead, Savannah decided to come clean, at least somewhat clean.

"OK, here's what we know. Our friend's name is Leonard. He's a really good guy, but he got mixed up with some really bad people. Some of those people are at that camp, and we think they may be holding Leonard against his will."

"I knew it!" Grady exclaimed, then quickly realized he was speaking too loudly and returned to a whisper. "OK, I'm gonna be honest with you ladies; but you can't tell anyone, OK?"

Both Rosita and Savannah nodded in agreement, anxious to hear what Grady was going to reveal.

"I was at the camp earlier this week, and I knew something wasn't right. One thing I know for sure, it ain't a camp for kids. I told the chief, but he doesn't believe me." Grady lowered his head in embarrassment. "He told me not to go back to the camp."

"I believe you," Savannah said, placing her hand on Grady's arm, causing him to look up.

"You do?"

"I do. I can confirm it is definitely not a camp for kids. There are some bad guys at that camp...I mean really BAD," Savannah spilled.

"And your friend Leonard is with them?"

"He's with them, but not willingly. I am sorry to ask this after what the chief said, but would you help us find him? Would you show us to the camp?"

Grady's heart raced. "I don't know. I'm really not supposed to."

"Would you at least show us where it is, and we'll go ourselves."

"No! You can't go up there by yourselves," Grady protested.

"We have to find our friend. We *really* think he's in trouble," Savannah pleaded.

Grady scratched his chin, thinking through his options. "OK, but here's the deal." Grady looked at Rosita. "Ma'am, I'm sorry; but the camp is way up a long, steep road that we can't drive up. I'll go, but I'll only take her." Grady gestured toward Savannah.

"What do you mean? I can walk up a hill!" Rosita objected.

"Look, I really shouldn't go, and I really shouldn't take either of you; but I'll take..." Grady tried to remember Savannah's name.

"Savannah."

"I'll take Savannah. That's my final offer. Ma'am, we'll need someone to drop us off. They have cameras everywhere, so we'll need you to be our driver. Do you think you can do that?"

"I don't want to be the driver. I want to go!" Rosita objected.

"Mom, remember, this is about Leonard. I think the deputy is right. He and I will go, and you will be our central command. You'll drop us off, then head back into town to wait for our call to pick us up."

"*Central command*," Rosita blurted. "Don't give it a fancy name; it's just a place for the old lady to wait while the kids go on their adventure."

"Sounds like we have a deal," Savannah announced.

Grady pounced on Rosita's acquiescence. "Great, now here's the plan…"

"Who's going to the game tonight?" Eric Mathis asked as he joined his friends at the McCracken County High School cafeteria.

"We're playing Carlisle County, right?"

"Yeah. They are a tiny school, but somehow they always have a good basketball team."

"Hey, Blake, come on over and join us." Eric noticed his friend Blake St. Pierre, who normally joined his group, sitting at a table by himself.

Blake didn't acknowledge Eric's call. Managing high-functioning autism is difficult in any situation but is magnified under the lens of a 21st century high school. Eric was among the few students at McCracken County High to establish a friendship with Blake, a friendship that usually involved sitting together for lunch.

"Hey, Blake, come on over!" Eric repeated. Again, Blake ignored the request, prompting Eric to go to his friend's table.

"Hey, Blake, is everything OK?" Eric said softly.

Eric rocked in his chair and shook his head slightly back and forth.

"What is it, Blake? What's wrong?"

Blake's rocking increased.

"It's OK, Blake. You don't have to tell me."

Blake pulled out his cell phone, opened Instagram, navigated to a video, and handed the phone to Eric.

Eric took the phone and hit play. As he watched, he became furious but was careful not to show his emotions to Blake. He viewed the entire 60-second video and handed the phone back to Blake.

"I understand why you're upset, Blake. I'm really sorry. I know how hard you've worked on this." Thinking for a moment, Eric continued, "Blake, I know this is something you wanted to do yourself, but would it be OK if I got some guys to come over and help?"

Blake's rocking slowed, and he nodded gently.

"Sounds great. We'll be there tomorrow."

"Mrs. Prince keep your phone handy. We'll call as soon as we're ready to be picked up," Grady whispered as the car approached the drop-off point.

Still unhappy with her assignment, Rosita just grunted.

"That means she agrees," Savannah interpreted.

Knowing the patrol car would be detected by the surveillance cameras surrounding the property, Grady had Rosita drive her 2016 Cadillac SRX. Now two hours past sunset, the car's graphite color blended into the trees, concealing its presence.

"OK, now slow down. Stop at the deer crossing sign just ahead. It's about 100 yards from the gate. We'll walk the rest of the way."

Rosita eased the SUV to a stop as Savannah and Grady unbuckled their seatbelts.

"Mom, we'll call soon. Don't worry; we'll be fine."

"I know you will. I would be fine too."

Grady and Savannah eased out of the vehicle as Rosita resumed full speed and disappeared around the curve.

"OK. The camp is at the top of this hill. There's a driveway down the road, but the cameras will be fixed on it; so, let's try to make our way through the woods," Grady whispered.

Grady and Savannah slowly worked their way up the hill, slipping on the leaves slickened by a recent summer rain. As they zigzagged among the trees, Grady glimpsed what he thought he saw on his last trip to the camp.

"Look over to the left. It has to be what, 25 vehicles? I knew I saw them before, but the guy who greeted me told me he was the only one here. Let's keep working up the hill."

Over the next knoll, the pair found exactly what they were seeking.

"Look, there are lights on in every building," Savannah declared.

"And people are walking around in each one," Grady confirmed.

"Let's work our way closer to see if we can find Leonard," Savannah coaxed.

Grady grabbed Savannah's arm and gestured upwards into the trees. "Surveillance cameras. We're going to have to be really careful the rest of the way."

Savannah nodded.

"Look!" Savannah whispered. "That small cabin on the left. That…that figure in the window sitting at a computer. That could be Leonard."

"How can you know that?"

"I don't know for sure, but it looks like his silhouette. And look, there's a guard near the door. And look at the roof. It looks like a lot of cables are going into the cabin, more than in any of the other structures; like it's the computer cabin. That *has* to be Leonard."

"I don't know…" before Grady could finish his sentence, Savannah was hurrying toward the cabin. "Savannah, wait. Where are you going?"

Grady followed trying to keep pace.

The cabin was a small 20-by 40-foot structure. It had windows on the north, east, and west sides. With the guard milling about outside the west window, Savannah tiptoed to the east window to get a closer look. As she slowly rose to peer into the cabin, her suspicions were confirmed. Leonard!

Grady finally caught up to his cohort and grabbed her by her arm, pulling her back to the ground.

"What are you doing? This is crazy!" he implored.

"I was right. It is Leonard!"

Savannah shook loose of Grady's grip and again rose to look into the window, this time tapping gently. The sound caught Leonard off guard and caused him to jump. Finding his bearings, he realized the sound was coming from the window. Rather than going toward the window, he instinctively backed away.

Seeing the window could be opened by pulling at the bottom, Savannah eased it ajar and whispered, "Leonard, it's me, Savannah."

Perplexed, Leonard scrunched his face and refocused his eyes. "Savannah?"

"Yes, it's me."

Leonard looked around to ensure no one was watching and eased over to the window.

"Savannah, what are you doing here?"

"Jeremy got your texts. We're here to get you out."

Nodding his head in fear, Leonard stuttered, "Yyyyyou shouldn't have come! It's not safe, not safe at all."

"I know; that's why we're here."

"Who's *we*? Is Jeremy here too?" Leonard asked.

"No, but I'm with a deputy. He'll help us get out of here."

"You shouldn't have come," Leonard groaned.

"Why not, what—"

Before Savannah could finish her sentence, bright lights flooded the entire camp, and the pair were surrounded by six heavily armed guards and a short one-eyed Russian general.

"On the ground, *now*!!" the guards commanded.

"You shouldn't have come," Leonard again stammered.

"Hello, Savannah," Ovchenko howled in his trademark accent. "Computer boy is right. You shouldn't have come."

31

"Hello."

"Hey, Mom. I've been trying to reach Savannah, but my calls go straight to voicemail. It's like she's turned it off. She never turns her phone off. Is she there with you?"

"With me?" Rosita repeated.

"Yeah, is she there with you?"

"Uh…no, she's…uh…she ran an errand. She should be back any minute now."

"What kind of errand?"

"Oh…uh…just an errand here in Abingdon, where both Savannah and I currently are."

"Is everything OK, Mom? You sound sort of strange."

"Yes, everything is great here in Abingdon."

"OK, Mom. Would you ask Savannah to call me when she gets back from her errand there in, you know…Abingdon?"

"Sure thing. Will do. You have a great day."

"Um…OK, you too, Mom."

"That was weird," Jeremy thought as he ended the call.

"Whew, that was close," Rosita blurted.

"I know it's been a long day. Most of you have already worked over 12 hours today. We can postpone this status meeting until tomorrow morning. You may be fresher then."

The members of Task Force Terracotta responded in unison that they wanted to proceed with the meeting that evening. Thomas Hanover, the leader, was correct; the team had worked for over 12 hours. However, they all were as energized as when they started.

"OK, I got it; you want to meet," Hanover responded, hands in the air in surrender. "Jeremy, are you up for a long evening?" Jeremy had spent the day in his workspace reacquainting himself with the exabytes of Mouse Trap data he hadn't seen in almost a year. Even he had forgotten the breadth and depth of what Victor Youngblood had accomplished. Or perhaps he had intentionally filed it away in a place where he hoped his mind would never need to go again. However, his research confirmed he really had no choice. "I'm ready, Thomas."

Hanover cocked his head and took a seat at the head of the table. "OK then, let's get started. Throughout the day, I've been getting messages from you saying that this could be much bigger than any of us imagined. I'm curious to hear what you've discovered in the first day on this team. Lucy let's start with you. What have you been able to learn about some of these questionable identities?"

The identity theft expert rose from her chair, took a position in front of the screen, and clicked the remote to begin her PowerPoint presentation. "You gave us a list of thousands of individuals. I thought I would start with a random sample of 100 just to have a population I could digest. First, I confirmed all 100 have legit Social Security numbers, driver licenses, and birth certificates. All were registered to vote. I thought maybe this was a political party thing; but there were 54 Democrats and 46 Republicans. Out of the 100, three were in Miami, four in Los Angeles, two in Dallas, and three in Minneapolis. So, I had field agents from those sites go to the home address of each. Much like the first name you gave us, all 11 were in nice homes, all with the power still on. In all cases, no one came to the door."

Lucy paused before advancing to the next slide. "This is absolutely brilliant. I have no idea how they pulled this off. They all have social media accounts; and get this, they all have over 1,000 friends."

"Over 1,000 friends?" Ben Gossett pondered. "It's like they want to hide in a crowd."

"I'm not following, Ben," Thomas noted.

"If you're on social media and you are among a group of 25 or 50 friends, you will eventually stand out. If you're not real, people will begin to question who you are. They will probably ask mutual friends. But if you are in a group of 1,000, you're going to get lost in the group."

Lucy continued, "And here are a few pictures. Like the one we saw of Mr. Shumate in Georgia, they look a little too real. I need to spend more time investigating, but there's definitely something not right here. And I only looked at 100 out of 40,000." Lucy shook her head. "This is unbelievable."

"Great work, Lucy. Who's next?"

"Hang on a second, Thomas." Jeremy raised a hand. "I get it that you have to check the boxes that you've researched everything. But can we move things along? I can confirm that Mouse Trap owned over 40,000 identities. You don't really have to spend much time knocking on the doors of empty houses. This is so much bigger than identity theft. You don't understand what—or who—you're dealing with here."

"I appreciate that, Jeremy. I assure you that we're going to move this along as quickly as we can, but we do have a process we must follow." Thomas's answer did not assuage Jeremy's desire to move along more rapidly, but it did inspire him to take a seat. "OK, who's up?" Thomas asked.

"I'll go next," Billy Murdoch offered as he took the remote from Lucy. He clicked to his intro slide that read, 'Billy Murdoch: Banking and Finance.' "We thought it would make sense to start with the 100 identities Lucy mentioned. Let's start simple. The 100 identities had over 400 U.S. bank accounts, brokerage accounts, and other investment accounts with a total value of just over $500 million."

"What? $500 million?" Thomas asked incredulously.

"And notice I said U.S. accounts. I see evidence that most also have foreign accounts. It will take more time to dig into those. They invested in a wide range of instruments; but I noticed a disproportionate amount invested in commodities, such as gold, silver, and oil. Take a look at this graph, which plots ten years of investments. Notice anything strange?"

"It looks like this person always bought when the market was low and always sold when it was high," Ben interjected, "almost like they knew when the price was going to fluctuate."

"Yeah, exactly like that," Billy confirmed. "Some of you may have already done the mental math: 100 people—or rather, identities—had a worth of $500 million. That's $5 million per identity. If we are talking about 40,000 identities at $5 million per, that's—"

"Two-hundred billion dollars," Ben declared.

Thomas Hanover's mouth dropped as he looked at Jeremy.

Jeremy just shook his head. "And you're barely scratching the surface of everything Mouse Trap is about."

"OK, Elizabeth, let's see if you can top that. What did you discover about Mouse Trap's real estate?"

"Again, working with the 100-identity sample size, this is a map of the U.S. showing the properties these individuals owned. As you can see, they own or co-own properties in over 30 states. They own 220 homes, over 100 commercial buildings, and 20,000 acres of land. That's an average of 200 acres per identity. At 40,000 identities, that is 8 million acres, or land roughly the size of the state of Maryland."

Working to comprehend everything he was hearing, Hanover called for the final report of the already late evening from Ben Gossett, his accounting genius, who stood before the group.

"So, an obvious question is 'how.' *How could a single clandestine organization, no matter how brilliant, acquire all this wealth?* The answer is simple—accounting. I know, everyone thinks accounting is boring; but it is truly the most fascinating occupation on the planet, and you're getting a glimpse why. I've quickly examined all 100 of our sample population, and every single one appears to be perfectly legitimate. They pay taxes, always on time. A few have even been audited, but all passed without a single finding. They all invest in legitimate holdings. There's not a single blemish that would draw any investigator's attention. I can't extrapolate the 40,000-identity deal like everyone else; but I will tell you that this Mouse Trap thing—whatever it is—employs a boatload of accountants somewhere, somehow. It is a thing of beauty."

"I'm stunned. I don't even know where to begin or what to ask," Thomas confessed.

"I'll tell you what to ask," Jeremy interjected. "Ask *why*. Why would an organization amass this kind of wealth and power? It has to be more than just the act of acquiring it. There has to be a larger motive behind it. Any guesses?"

The lack of a response revealed a relationship gap between the 25-year-old visitor and the seasoned FBI agents. They were not yet interested in playing Jeremy's guessing game, a reality Thomas recognized.

"Wow, I had no idea it was 10 o'clock. This has been an impressive day of work. Great job. Jeremy has given us a provocative question for our homework. Let's call it a night and start fresh again tomorrow."

32

"Look, there it is; Meadow Street, turn here."

"What's the house number?"

"It's 413. That looks like the house in the video. Wasn't the kid's name St. Pierre? That's the name on the mailbox."

"Yep, that's it. Pull over here."

"Did you see the video?"

"Of course, I saw the video. The last I checked about five million people had seen it."

"It's so awful what they did to that kid."

"I can't believe that would happen right here in Paducah, Kentucky."

"That's why it is important that we find out more of the story. Let's set up the camera here on the sidewalk. Shoot in the direction of the house, and I'll report from right in front."

"Let's go see if anyone's home first."

"Hey, it looks like there are several kids out back."

"Umm...Tony, you're gonna want to come see this."

"Oh wow. I'll get the camera. I think this is going to be a different story than we thought."

"That's an understatement!"

"Deputy Shumpert, what's your 10-20?"

"I repeat, Deputy Shumpert, what's your 10-20?"

"Dang-it Grady, where are you?"

Bull Gap Chief of Police Warren Bodkin knew his only deputy very well; and he knew that with all of Grady's warts and imperfections, at least he could be counted on to respond to a radio call. The fact that Grady had not responded concerned Chief Bodkin, who decided to try the heartbeat of the community, the Bull Gap Café.

"Good morning, Gayle. You got a fresh pot going?"

"You know I do, Chief. You want a large?"

"That would be much appreciated, Gayle."

Chief Bodkin took a couple of steps around the café, looking out the front window, then turned back to the waitress.

"Say, Gayle, you haven't seen Grady lately, have you?"

"He was in for lunch yesterday, but I haven't seen him since."

"Did you happen to hear him say where he was going?"

"I don't think so. Is something wrong?" Gayle responded, pouring a fresh cup of coffee.

"No, no, nothing's wrong. Just doing my rounds."

"You know, come to think of it, I did see him talking with two ladies yesterday at lunch, ladies I hadn't seen before. One was fairly young, and the other was a little older."

Chief Bodkin's interest was piqued. "Two ladies? Do you remember anything about them, or did you overhear any of the conversation?"

"Warren, I thought you said nothing was wrong."

"Nothing is wrong, I just—just answer the question, Gayle."

"I didn't hear any of the conversation; but I did notice they were talking in a low voice, almost a whisper. And I think they left together."

"Did you happen to notice what they were driving?"

"No, I'm sorry; I didn't."

"Thanks for the information, Gayle. The coffee was good as always. Just let me know if you see Grady or those ladies, OK?"

"Will do. Glad to hear nothing is wrong."

Chief Bodkin ignored Gayle's parting words as he hurried to his police cruiser on the lookout for his deputy and two ladies. He was officially concerned.

33

"Excuse me, sir, I'm sorry to bother you; but I wanted to show you some contraband we received in the mail." The officer handed a box to the warden.

"A cell phone? I don't understand; we get cell phones in the mail every week. Just throw it in the trash like you always do."

"Yes sir, but I just want to make sure. Did you see which inmate it was addressed to?"

Flipping the box over to see the addressee was Victor Youngblood, the warden quickly cycled through shock, confusion, frustration, and anger. He knew he couldn't let his subordinate see him lose his cool, so he took a deep breath before excusing the officer. "Thank you. That'll be all."

The confused officer was unsure how to proceed. "Umm...do you want me to take the phone?"

"No, leave it here. I'll handle it. Please close the door on your way out."

At the sound of the closing door, the warden immediately dialed his cell phone. "Melinda, I just got a package for Youngblood. This is getting ridiculous. We allowed him to have visitors off-hours. He gets special meals. He uses the prison phone when he wants. Now he is getting his own cell phone?"

"Warden, we've talked about this before. You know this goes way above me."

"It doesn't make sense. If they are going to make all of these accommodations, why not just transfer him to a facility where he can have these privileges normally?"

"Because that's not what we've been asked to do."

"Where is this coming from, Melinda?"

"You're asking questions I can't answer."

"You *can't* answer, or you *won't* answer?" The warden's voice was rising.

"It doesn't matter. We have to do what we've been told to do."

"Oh, now we're being *told*; a moment ago, you said we were being asked."

"If you do it willingly, you're being asked. If you object, then yes, you're being told. It's up to you which it is."

"This is unbelievable. Someday this mess is all going to blow up, and we're going to be held accountable. I can't believe I'm a party to it."

"Any more questions, Warden?"

"Yes, a thousand more questions, but I understand what I've been told to do."

"You know I told you and boyfriend to walk away. I told you, 'No follow.' You no listen, and you brought police. This bad."

The scene was intense. Savannah and Deputy Grady Shumpert were secured to chairs, their hands and feet zip-tied to the spindles. They had endured hours of interrogation. A terrified Leonard was in the back of the room wracked with guilt for his role in Savannah's capture.

"I'm sorry. I'm just *so* sorry," Leonard mumbled.

Led by Andrei Ovchenko and supported by three armed guards ready to engage at a moment's notice, the interrogation had begun at 11 the night before and had recently passed the eight-hour mark. The questions were simple: "Who sent you?" "Why are you here?" "Who knows you're here?"

Satisfactory answers to the questions had yet to be extracted.

"You know the police are going to be looking for me. You know you can't keep me here," Grady protested.

"Don't worry; you won't be here—or anywhere—much longer," Ovchenko threatened.

Ready to continue the questioning, Ovchenko heard a commotion from outside the cabin.

"Stop!! Stop!!"

The cabin door opened, and to Ovchenko's astonishment in walked Zeke Gibson, who had been evicted from the camp by Ovchenko less than two weeks earlier. As Zeke entered, one of the guards instinctively pointed a gun directly at him. Zeke grabbed the barrel of the gun and pushed it away.

"Don't you ever point that gun at me again!" It was a side of 78-year-old Zeke Gibson that most had not seen.

Zeke was engaged in a cell phone conversation that was consuming his focus. "Yes, I made it here to the cabin with Ovchenko. As you know, Leonard is here; but you're not going to believe this—Savannah is here too, but she's tied to a chair. Ovchenko has captured one of the local police officers, who is also tied to a chair. Yes, this is an unexpected problem."

"I told you to leave camp. I told you—" Ovchenko tried to regain the upper hand, but Zeke was not interested.

"That's enough, Andrei. Stop talking."

Ovchenko's face turned as red as the Soviet flag. "You don't tell me to—"

"Yes, I'll let you speak with him."

Zeke handed the phone to Ovchenko. "It's for you."

Taking a step away from Zeke, Ovchenko raised both hands in objection and asked, "Who?"

"It's Victor. He wants to speak with you."

Ovchenko's mouth flew open as he tried to comprehend Zeke's words. "Victor? Victor in prison."

"Victor is on the phone," Zeke responded. "I recommend you take the call."

Ovchenko carefully took Zeke's phone as if he were grabbing a thorny bush. "Victor?"

The room's occupants observed the interaction with great interest. Ovchenko's men stood cautiously. Savannah and the deputy wondered how the call might alter their fate. Zeke offered only a knowing smile.

"Yes, Victor, I understand." Without making eye contact, Ovchenko handed the phone back to Zeke, barked an order in Russian to his men, and then proceeded swiftly out the door without a word. His men followed closely behind.

The brusque exit left Zeke, Leonard, Savannah, and the deputy alone in the cabin. Zeke began making amends.

"Leonard, you cut the zip ties on the officer while I release Savannah." As he cut the zip ties around Savannah's ankles, he began the process of mending fences.

"I can't begin to tell you how sorry I am about how you've been treated. That includes you too, Leonard. None of this should have happened. It wasn't supposed to be this way."

As she was freed, Savannah massaged her wrists and ankles to try to comfort the raw skin that had suffered from hours of zip ties.

"I...I'm not sure what just happened here. Is that really Victor on the phone? Where did Ovchenko go? What are you doing here?" Savannah babbled.

In his most diplomatic and grandfatherly tone, Zeke answered, "I'd like to address each of your questions. Please let me explain."

"And I guarantee you the police will be here any moment; so, I hope you have a good explanation," the deputy interjected in his most assertive tone.

"Yes, Officer, I understand," Zeke confirmed.

In mid-conversation with Zeke, Victor sensed he was not

alone. He had been allowed to leave his cell and conduct the call in privacy from the corner of an exercise yard. His privacy was interrupted as he turned to see the warden accompanied by two guards within 10 feet. He held the phone to his side and engaged the trio.

"Is there something I can do for you?" Victor asked.

The question caused the already on-edge warden to take a step in Victor's direction. "You understand I am still the warden of this facility?"

"I do."

"And you asked if there is something *you* can do for *me*?"

Victor didn't respond.

"You…an inmate, a murderer…having a cell phone conversation as if you are the boss."

"You, sir, are most definitely the boss," Victor retorted.

"If it were up to me, you wouldn't have that cell phone," the warden snapped.

"We've already established that you are the boss." Victor extended an arm to offer the phone to the warden. "If you would like to take the cell phone, it is yours."

The warden snarled, knowing that confiscating the phone would raise the ire of his boss and whoever up the food chain was calling the shots. He took a step away from Victor. "Just know that I'm watching every move you make."

Victor looked at his surroundings, raised both hands, and quipped, "I assumed as much."

The warden lowered his head and walked away with the two guards in tow.

"I'm sorry, Zeke. I'm back."

$\mathcal{Q}$

"Victor, I've got Savannah, Leonard, and Officer... I'm sorry; I didn't catch your name."

"It's *Deputy* Grady Shumpert."

"I've got Savannah, Leonard and..." Reading Grady's badge, Zeke continued, "Deputy Grady Shumpert of the Bull Gap, North Carolina Police Department. I'm going to put you on speaker."

It was an opportunity for Victor to demonstrate his charm and personality, which had helped him create the world's largest white-collar criminal organization and amass the greatest wealth ever known.

"Savannah, I'm so sorry to hear about the ordeal you've been through. Please understand that this was never supposed to happen. You are a treasured team member who has my utmost respect."

"*Former* team member," Savannah attempted to correct.

"And Leonard, I can honestly say I've never worked with a more brilliant mind than yours. I don't think any individual has contributed more to our success than you have. I'm sorry that Andrei has treated you so poorly. I will do everything I can to make it up to you."

"Thhhhank you, Victor." Leonard couldn't help but feel pride, even if the compliment came from a boss who ordered his murder less than a year earlier.

"And Deputy Shumpert, you have been caught in our messy misunderstanding. Of course, you'll be released to return to your department. I'm sorry about the inconvenience."

"I'm going to step away from the call, but Zeke will fill you in on the details of where we go from here. I think you'll be excited about what he has to say."

"Where I want to go from here is home," Savannah retorted.

"I look forward to our next opportunity to interact. Good day." Victor was gone.

"Zeke, I don't know what Victor is planning; by the way, isn't he in prison?" Savannah growled.

"If you'll give me a moment, I will explain all that I can." Zeke continued, "Things are going to move quickly from here. First, Andrei and his team are leaving the camp. They have been instructed to return to their base of operations in Pittsburgh and await further instructions. A team of 25 accompanied me here with the assignment to close down the camp. They will remove any evidence that we have been here. That task should be completed in just a few hours."

"Mustering his most authoritative tone, Deputy Shumpert announced, "I'm afraid I can't let you tamper with the evidence. This entire camp is a crime scene that must be secured."

"Deputy, as Victor said, I am sincerely sorry that you have been entangled in our mess. We're going to return you safely to town, and we promise never to return."

"This isn't a negotiation. I represent the law in Bull Gap, I—"

"I assure you, Deputy, this is going to turn out just fine." Zeke knocked on the inside of the door, prompting three members of the Mouse Trap's Greenforce security team to enter. "These gentlemen will see that you get safely back to town."

"I'm not leaving without Savannah," Deputy Shumpert demanded.

"I'm sorry; that's not possible. Savannah and I have further business that doesn't involve the Bull Gap Police Department. Again, I assure you, you will be treated humanely."

"No, I'm not leaving—" As Deputy Shumpert protested, three Greenforce members carried him out the door.

Savannah stepped in to intervene, but one of the members of Greenforce stopped her.

Zeke mustered all of his 78 years to speak in an assuring, grandfatherly tone. "Savannah, he'll be fine. I just want a few minutes of your time. We have some business to discuss."

Savannah knew her only option was to listen.

34

"**A**nswer! Answer! Answer!" Rosita pleaded. For the last six hours, she had been calling Savannah's cell phone; but each time the call went directly to voicemail. Over those six hours, she progressed from interest to concern to something just short of all-out panic. She was in a strange town where she knew no one. Her normal response would be to call Jeremy, but she knew she couldn't involve him—at least not yet. To make matters worse, she hadn't eaten in over 12 hours. At least this last hurdle could be cleared with breakfast at the Bull Gap Café, where she had just parked her Cadillac SRX.

As she walked in, the smell of hot coffee brewing and bacon frying temporarily distracted her from her worries.

"Good morning, ma'am. Can I pour you some coffee?"

"Yes please, cream, no sugar."

"Are you ready to order, or do you need a minute to look over the menu?"

"I think I'm ready. I'll have the Hungry Bear Platter with

extra bacon and a large whole milk."

"Yes ma'am, we'll have that ready for you in a jiff." The waitress took a step away from the table but then turned back to Rosita. "Excuse me, ma'am, weren't you in here yesterday with your daughter?"

"Not exactly. She's my son's girlfriend."

"Oh, that's nice for you to spend time with her. I hope you are enjoying Bull Gap. It is a beautiful place."

Rosita felt a lump swell in her stomach. She realized a moment too late that her hunger had clouded her judgment and that she may have put their plan in jeopardy. She knew she at least had to try to recover. "Yes, we're very much enjoying Bull Gap. We've been hiking and taking in the beautiful scenery. My son's girlfriend is over at the hotel getting cleaned up. This old lady was hungry, and she told me to come on over. She should be joining me shortly."

"That's great. We'll have your food out to you shortly."

Rosita tried to remain calm, but her heart rate was quickening.

The waitress passed the order along to the chef and then sent a quick text, ensuring her phone was below the counter where no one could see.

One of the ladies that met with the deputy is in the café RIGHT NOW and she just lied to me about the other one – something is definitely not right.

"Savannah, Leonard, please take a seat. I need to explain to you what's been happening here. When Victor was arrested, we knew we had to evacuate all our resources from the Mouse Trap headquarters in Bethesda. Of course, Jeremy helped us with that objective as he emailed all employees informing them that Mouse Trap was shutting down."

"Wait a minute." Savannah raised a hand to interrupt Zeke. "You don't expect me to believe Victor *wanted* Mouse Trap to be shut down."

"Before his unfortunate arrest, of course he didn't. But, after Jeremy's deception, Victor resorted to an alternative plan, which involved pausing Mouse Trap for a necessary time. During that pause, Victor knew Mouse Trap couldn't be allowed to completely atrophy; consequently, I was tasked with keeping a remnant going until it was time to restart."

"But something happened that you weren't expecting," Savannah interjected.

Zeke nodded. "Ovchenko. He is a loose cannon. Victor is the only person who has ever been able to control him. But it's OK; we've made great progress here, especially with Leonard's work on Omnia. We're ready for the next step."

"So, what's the next step?" Savannah asked.

"A full restart of Mouse Trap. Everything and everyone back to Bethesda to our headquarters." Zeke turned to Leonard. "We've even moved Omnia's hardware into a building in Bethesda, right next to Mouse Trap headquarters. That's where you were taken after Utah. You were reassembling Omnia in Bethesda. You won't have to take any more trips to Utah. Omnia will be right beside you."

"But how are you moving back in? Won't the government...the FBI be watching?" Savannah queried.

"All that has been addressed. We wouldn't be moving back in if there were still a threat," Zeke asserted.

"And who's in charge? Victor's in jail, and most of the remaining leaders have scattered across the globe."

"All that is being addressed as well. In fact, that's why the two of you are still here. You are among Victor's most trusted executives. We'd like for you to rejoin us."

Savannah's response was an involuntary chuckle coupled with a shake of the head. "You gotta big kidding me," she blurted. "Rejoin Mouse Trap? Do you really think we're that dumb?"

"Hear me out," Zeke insisted. "Victor has a plan to restore Mouse Trap to an even grander level. You'll have a front seat for the ride. Of course, you'll be well-compensated financially; but more than anything, you'll have a key role in making all this happen."

"I still don't understand how you think Victor is going to do anything. He's in prison for the rest of his life," Savannah insisted.

"You will understand. You just have to be patient."

"I *don't* have to be patient." Finally tired of Zeke's sales pitch, Savannah stood to take control of the conversation. "I will never return to Mouse Trap *or* Victor *or* you! I'm done with Mouse Trap, and I'm done with this conversation. Come on Leonard, let's get out of here."

As Savannah took two steps towards the door and grabbed the doorknob, she noticed Leonard wasn't moving.

"Come on, Leonard. I have a car in town."

Leonard closed his eyes, then looked up at Zeke. "We're really going to get Omnia up and running back at the office?"

"It's already installed in Bethesda. It's just waiting for you to finish restarting it," Zeke said temptingly.

"Leonard, come on; we gotta go," Savannah urged.

"And I could go back to my old office and my old job?" Leonard asked.

"Not exactly. We have a new office for you, double the size of your old one. Victor plans to increase Omnia's capabilities, and he's counting on you to lead that effort."

"Leonard, you can't seriously be considering this," Savannah scolded.

"Omnia is all I've ever known. I started working on her—um, it—when I was 17. I don't know how to do anything else."

"She's waiting for you, Leonard. She's been lonely."

"Oh, stop it. *She's* a machine. She's an *it*," Savannah protested.

"What do you say, Leonard? Are you in? Can we count on you?" Zeke tempted.

Leonard walked to the door where Savannah was standing. "You gotta understand. I've spent my whole life here. It's like my home; and sometimes you just have to go home. Please understand." As Leonard embraced Savannah, he whispered into her ear, "Trust me; I have a plan."

Savannah mustered the strength to suppress her surprise and continued her incredulous tone. "I honestly don't believe this, Leonard. After everything they put you through, you're really going back?"

"You've chosen wisely Leonard." Zeke beamed. "I know you'll be happy back with us. Savannah, I'm deeply sorry you won't be joining us; but you've made your decision clear. I have a driver who will return you to town."

Savannah headed out the door without responding to Zeke. She looked back at Leonard and thought, "I hope you know what you're doing."

As Savannah was loaded into a car for the trip back to Bull's Gap, Zeke worked out the final details to close the camp, signifying full operational transfer back at Bethesda. He reached into his jacket pocket, pulled out the envelope, removed the list, and crossed off item #6.

"Hungry Bear Platter with extra bacon."

"Oh, it looks delicious."

"Do you need anything else?"

"No, thank you."

As Rosita began slicing the country ham, the café door opened. In her peripheral vision, she saw a figure approaching her table.

"Excuse me, ma'am." The Bull Gap police chief was now standing over Rosita, making her uneasy.

"Yes, Officer, what can I do for you?"

"Do you mind if I join you for a moment?"

"Umm…sure…have a seat." Rosita could feel the sweat

beading up on her brow.

"Thank you." The chief sat down, removed his hat, and extended a hand. "I'm Warren Bodkin. I'm the chief of police here in Bull Gap."

"Hello, my name is Rosita." She decided to withhold her last name until she knew what the chief wanted.

"I'm sorry to interrupt your breakfast, but I just had a quick question. You're here visiting Bull Gap, right?"

"That's correct."

"Were you here in the café yesterday as well?"

Rosita knew this line of question was going in a direction she didn't like. She decided to be as succinct and factual as possible, while trying to seem calm.

"Yes, I was."

"I don't blame you; this café is a hidden treasure here in little Bull Gap. Were you here with someone else yesterday?"

"Yes, I was with my son's girlfriend."

"Oh, I see. Where are you ladies visiting us from?"

"We're from Virginia."

"Virginia's a beautiful state. Where is she now, your son's girlfriend?"

"She's in the room getting ready. She'll be joining me shortly."

As Rosita spoke, the café door again swung open; and Savannah approached the table.

"Hi, Mom. Who's your friend?"

Rosita did her best to hide her equally strong feelings of excitement and surprise to see Savanah's smiling face. "This is the Bull Gap chief of police. He's joined me for breakfast."

"Hi, I'm Savannah. I'm dating Rosita's son. Rosita and I are having a short bonding trip in your beautiful community. We absolutely love it here."

When Zeke's men drove Savannah back to town, her cell phone was returned. She found several text messages and voicemails from Rosita, the last stating she would be at the café.

"Yes, we are blessed to live in such a beautiful part of the country." The chief scratched his head trying to determine where to go next with the discussion. "Umm, I've been trying to get in touch with my deputy. I was wondering if the two of you may have seen him."

Savannah nodded her head. "Yes, one of your officers did join us here yesterday—much like you have today. He gave us ideas on things to do in the area."

"He didn't leave with you?" the chief pressed.

"Leave with us?" Savannah demurred.

Sensing he was getting the runaround, the chief decided to ramp things up a bit. "Yes, leave *with you*. When you left the café yesterday, did the deputy leave at the same time you did?"

Before Savannah could respond, the café door opened and in walked Deputy Shumpert. He strolled in the direction of a table on the other side of the café before being hailed by the chief.

"Grady?"

The deputy spun around to see his boss. "Oh, good morning, Chief." He walked over to the table where the trio were sitting.

The chief stood and bellowed, "Grady, where have you been?"

"What do you mean, Chief?"

"I mean, you have been gone for almost an entire day. Where have you been?" the chief huffed.

As he was transported out of the camp, Grady spent some 'quality time' with three members of Zeke's Greenforce. He was given two options. Option one was to report everything he had seen and bring more law enforcement officers to the camp. Grady was cautioned that option would lead to scorn and ridicule because within an hour the camp would be completely emptied of signs that Mouse Trap had ever been there. Option two was to come up with a story that he had been on patrol and that he and the chief had missed one another.

"I've just been on patrol," Grady advised. "Why? Is something wrong?"

"Grady, I've been trying to get in touch with you on the radio, on your cell phone; I've been by your house, and I couldn't find you anywhere."

"Gosh, sorry Chief, I guess we've just been on different schedules."

The suspicious chief wasn't quite ready to back off. "And you haven't been anywhere with the ladies?"

The look of confusion brought Savannah to the rescue. "You may not remember, but yesterday you gave Rosita and me ideas for sights to see in the area."

"Oh yes, I remember. I hope you've had a good time visiting our town."

"It has certainly been an adventure!" Savannah exclaimed.

The chief chewed on his cheek and then finally conceded, "I'm sorry to bother you ladies. You have a good day. Let's go to the office, Grady. You need a refresher on radio and cell phone response protocol."

"Yes sir."

Grady followed behind the chief. Before leaving the café, he quickly turned back to Savannah, touched the brim of his hat, and smiled.

"You have some explaining to do," Rosita blurted.

"All in due time, Mom."

"Papa Eli, will you read a book to me?"

Before Elijah could respond, Meghan interjected, "No, Destiny, it's too late; we're about to go home."

"It's never too late to read a book," Elijah protested, "and besides, you haven't been over in almost a month. I had to beg Beau to have you come over. The least you can do is let me read her a book."

"Please, Mom!!" Destiny pleaded.

"It's almost nine o'clock. It's already past your bedtime," Meghan insisted.

"Looks like Beau is settled in for a while," Elijah observed as Beau was captivated by the screen on his cell phone.

Looking up, Beau offered excitedly, "You gotta see this. Where's the remote on your TV?"

"It's on the table. Why?"

"I gotta stream this story on your TV," Beau proclaimed as he sprang to grab the remote.

"You gotta do what?" a confused Elijah responded.

"I found a story linked on Twitter, and I want to screencast my phone to your TV to show you."

"Just when I think I understand the new technology, I find out how dumb I really am," Elijah admitted to no one in particular.

"OK, I got it; now watch," Beau instructed.

"Good evening, this is NewsChannel 8's Cam Marigold reporting live from Paducah, Kentucky. Yesterday, this video was uploaded to various social media outlets and went viral with over five million views in less than 24 hours. The video shows four teenagers destroying and defacing an elaborate treehouse. In the disturbing video, the teens are laughing and joking as they lay waste to the structure. In the most alarming part of the video, the treehouse's builder, a special needs, screams in protest as the vandals demolish his masterpiece. His objections lead to more laughter from the teens as they shove him to the ground and walk away from the scene.

"Since the video has gone viral, NewsChannel 8 has discovered the treehouse's builder is Blake St. Pierre, who worked on the treehouse for three months. It was going to be a birthday present to his younger brother, who turns 10 next week. We're excited to report there's a happy ending to

this troubling story. Here is a video of St. Pierre's treehouse just a day after the destruction. You heard that correctly; this video was filmed AFTER the destruction. Eric Mathis, a senior at McCracken County High School, organized the rebuilding effort; and the response was overwhelming. We asked Eric how he got involved.

"First of all, Blake is my friend. We eat lunch together every day at school. I saw the video of the destroyed treehouse and we just wanted to do what we could to try and make things right. I texted some friends, who texted more friends; and the next thing we knew, 50 people showed up this morning to help Blake rebuild the treehouse. A local lumberyard even donated materials. It was important to us to rebuild it exactly like Blake had it. Fortunately, with so many people helping, we were able to do that in a few hours."

Beau paused the video. This is the part I wanted you to see. Now listen to this:

"What is our motivation? As I said, Blake is my friend, so I wanted to help him; but there's more to it than that. You remember Elijah Mustang, right? Yeah, of course you do. The dude was so close to being president. What people liked about him was that he wasn't a politician. Instead of dividing people, he tried to bring them closer. The Mustang movement— that's what it's called—is still alive. It isn't a political movement; it's a movement to serve in our communities to

*make them better. Many of us here are part of that move-
ment, and helping Blake is just a small part of that. Projects
like this are happening all over America. Mustangs are making a difference one treehouse at a time. If you haven't heard
about them in your community, just wait; you will. Mustang
projects are going to be everywhere.*

Beau turned off the TV.

"See, I told you you'd want to see that!"

"Someone actually listened?" Elijah asked rhetorically as
he gazed out the window. "They *actually* listened."

"You know we have to call Jeremy," Savannah fretted. "When
I turned on my phone, I had a dozen missed calls and even
more texts. He knows it's not like me to not call or text right
back."

Savannah and Rosita were on I-26 traveling back to
Abingdon. Approaching the Cherokee National Forest, they
were 30 minutes into their journey home. Although they
had much to discuss, both were exhausted; and the initial
leg of the trip had proven to be a quiet ride with the silence
interrupted by Savannah's provocative question.

"I know," Rosita gulped. "What are we going to say?"

"I see three options. Option one, tell him the truth, the
whole story of exactly what happened. Option two, be vague
and hope Jeremy doesn't ask too many questions. Option
three, outright lie."

An awkward pause filled the SUV.

"Option one is probably the right way to go, isn't it?" Savannah queried.

"Option two wouldn't be bad. Just sort of beat around the bush," Rosita volunteered.

"I'm thinking Jeremy's too smart for option two."

More silence.

"Option three it is!" Savannah blurted. "Here's our story. We were working down at the store, and time got away from us. The battery ran down on my phone, which is why I didn't call back. I just turned it on while driving back home from the store and saw his messages. Sound OK?"

"Sounds OK to me," Rosita concurred.

"OK, let's call."

Savannah called Jeremy's cell using the Cadillac's hands-free app.

"Where have you been?" Jeremy answered.

"Jeremy, I'm so sorry. Mom and I have been working down at the store, and time got away from us. The battery on my phone went dead, and I'm just seeing your calls and texts. I'm so sorry to take so long to call back." Savannah prayed she sounded convincing enough.

"So, everything's OK?" Jeremy quizzed.

"Oh yes, everything's great! We've just been working down at the store and just like Savannah said, time got away from us," Rosita repeated the story as she pantomimed a silent chuckle to Savannah.

"Where are you guys? Are you driving somewhere?"

"Yes, we're just driving home from the store," Savannah volunteered.

"Yep, just right here in Abingdon, driving home," Rosita echoed.

"Mom, are you OK? You sound weird."

"I'm wonderful. Life here in Abingdon is the bee's knees."

"OK, I have no idea what that means. Savannah, did you take Mom to a bar or something?"

"No, we've both been working too much. Your mom's just really tired."

"Something's not right," Jeremy prodded.

"You're correct; something's not right. You're not here with us." Savannah worked to change the subject. "When are you coming home? You were supposed to be gone only a couple of days. You're already past that."

"I know. *I know.*" Jeremy was now on the defensive. "We have a few more meetings; then I'll be home. I don't know exactly when, but it will be soon. In fact, we have a meeting starting shortly. I'll call back as soon as I can."

"OK. We miss you," Savannah proclaimed. "Please hurry home."

"Will do. Love you both."

"Love you too, honey."

As the call was disconnected, Rosita and Savannah looked pensively at one another.

"Do you think he bought it?"

"I think so. At least I hope so," Savannah responded.

As Jeremy hung up the phone, he said softly to himself, "I still think something's not right."

35

"I want to thank everyone for participating in this call on such short notice. We have teams from all 50 states dialed in, and we have a good turnout here at our headquarters in Knoxville."

Minnie Carpenter was addressing a special meeting/teleconference of the Mustangs. "I'm happy to say we also have Elijah here with us."

Elijah waived to the camera.

"I hope everyone has seen the news report from Kentucky, where one of our own, Eric Mathis, enlisted the help of others to rebuild a treehouse for a young man who had his work destroyed by heartless bullies. As a prelude to the rest of this meeting, I'd like to show the full video."

The news report of the tree house's destruction and reconstruction, along with the interview with Eric Mathis, was played on the screen. Afterwards, applause could be heard in every location where the Mustangs were gathered.

"What a moving video!" Minnie boasted. "And I'm excited to say we're joined by Eric Mathis accompanying his fellow Mustangs from Paducah, Kentucky." Again, applause followed Minnie's introduction. "I'm going to send the video feed to Paducah, and Eric has agreed to share a few words with us. Eric, take it away."

"Well...uh...*wow*, I've never spoken before this many people. I'm kinda nervous. You know, I'm just 18. Anyway, I've been a big fan of Mr. Mustang ever since he announced he was running for president. I was so bummed he didn't win, but I didn't give up. I knew he had started something big...something that couldn't end. When he encouraged us a few days ago to make a difference in our communities, I knew we had to try. When I found out Blake's treehouse had been destroyed, I knew we had to do something. I mostly did it for my friend Blake, but I'm glad I got to give a shout out to the Mustangs. Anyway...that's all I have to say."

Blake's parting words brought even more applause.

The video feed returned to headquarters, where Minnie retook the mic. "You said a lot, but more importantly you *did* a lot. I'm so thankful for you, Eric, and so glad you're on our team. I'm curious if there are other stories like Eric's that didn't make the news but that made a difference. Please use the raised hand feature on your video screen if you would like to share a story."

The Mustang video system had the capability for people in remote locations to click a button on their screens to signal to headquarters they would like to speak. At headquarters, 12 raised hands could be seen. Within two seconds of Minnie's request, all 12 spaces were taken; dozens more were clicked but not seen.

"Wow, that's amazing. All 12 slots are taken. OK, let's hear the stories."

For the next hour, Mustangs shared stories of serving in their communities, cleaning up parks, providing firewood to needy families, building wheelchair ramps, providing meals to nursing homes, helping kids with homework after school, and many more. Realizing these stories could go on for hours, Minnie intervened.

"Wow! That's the word that keeps coming to mind, simply *WOW*! I know you could share many more stories with us, but Elijah wanted to say a few words."

Elijah's introduction brought cheers. He could be seen on the screen clapping toward the screen to gesture his return applause.

Then Elijah began speaking. "Thank you, thank you, *thank you*! Not just for how you are serving your communities, but for encouraging me. I can't begin to express how these stories have moved my heart. You are amazing people. I want to highlight something important that Eric shared as he was telling us about the treehouse project. He said, 'Mostly, I did it for Blake.' He didn't rebuild that treehouse to be on TV or to promote this movement. He did it because his friend was hurting, and he felt he could make a difference. That attitude has to be the heart of our movement. We don't serve our communities in hopes of getting individual or Mustang glory. We serve our communities because we love them. Please don't forget that. If you serve enough—and from the stories, it sounds like you do—others will see the difference we're making; and maybe, they'll want to get on board too. This is not a political movement; it is a service movement. And you've inspired me to continue serving! Thank you!

"OK, let's hear what everyone has been working on. Billy let's start with you. What's going on with banking and finance?" As leader of Task Force Terracotta, Thomas Hanover took his usual seat at the head of the table.

Billy began, "I researched another 100 accounts—"

"Do we have to go through this same thing again?" Motivated by a desire to return to Abingdon and a general interest in advancing the investigation, Jeremy interrupted Billy's report.

All eyes turned to Jeremy as Hanover tried to keep the meeting afloat. "This is our protocol, Jeremy. I know you're new to this, but this is our process. We gather data, analyze the data, and report our results. We—"

"Yeah, I get it. I'm not FBI. I'm just a young guy in my 20s, but I can give you the quick version of what you're about to hear. You discovered hundreds of millions more dollars tied to Mouse Trap. They own thousands of acres of lands and hundreds of buildings. You confirmed that another 1,000 identities are legit but really fake. Can we fast forward through this part?"

Indulging his young visitor, Hanover asked, "Jeremy, what do you think we should be discussing?"

"Do you remember the question I asked in our meeting? Why would Youngblood be amassing this much wealth and property? What is his motivation? Has anyone thought about that?"

Lucy Cross was the first to answer. "Probably power."

"Yes! That's definitely a huge part of it." Jeremy was excited that someone was responding. "This is so much deeper than just accumulating stuff. You know why Victor is in prison, right?"

"Murder," Ben responded.

"Exactly. Do you think that murder is the only one he's responsible for?" Jeremy coaxed.

"Jeremy, I told you before—murder isn't in our purview. We're supposed to investigate banking, finance, accounting, identity theft, and real estate," Hanover cautioned.

"Yeah, I know; but the murders and the white-collar stuff are inseparable. Let me show you something else."

Jeremy took the keyboard connected to the large screen and logged in to his account. He searched his common drive and found a folder he had been amassing from mining Mouse Trap data.

"I've combined all of the identities, companies, and organizations owned by Mouse Trap; and I searched the political contributions. In total, the Mouse Trap entities donated...are you ready for this...*$375 million* to Lionel Ireland's campaign."

"So, Youngblood was obviously a big Republican," Billy Murdoch interjected.

"Which makes sense because he's in jail for killing the

Republican vice-presidential candidate that he was conveniently selected to replace. This is all starting to make sense!" Elizabeth Sanders cried.

Jeremy smiled and raised a hand. "Starting to make sense, huh? Then I'm about to blow your mind. Guess how much Mouse Trap donated to President McCoy's campaign?"

"*What?* Why would he donate to the opponent's campaign?" Lucy Cross asked.

"I'm glad you are all starting to ask the *why* questions. They are important, but they have to wait. Back to McCoy, Youngblood's organization donated over $400M to Mitch McCoy's campaign."

"Wait a minute. He donated hundreds of millions of dollars to *both* campaigns? That doesn't make any sense," Hanover interjected.

"How much did he donate to Mustang?" Ben blurted.

"Zero. He donated exactly zero to Mustang," Jeremy marveled.

"This is wild!" Lucy exclaimed.

"McCoy's campaign spent right at $1 billion. That means Youngblood was responsible for 40% of our sitting president's campaign financing," Billy gasped.

"Let me summarize what you just said," Jeremy offered. "The greatest criminal in the history of the world—a thief, gangster, and murderer—is responsible for our current President's election."

"Do you think McCoy knows this?" Billy asked.

"That is a great question, one we must answer," Hanover proclaimed.

"Are you sure we want to go down that road?" Lucy cautioned.

"We don't have any choice. We're already standing right in the middle of it," Hanover responded.

"Standing in the middle of a road isn't usually a good thing," Billy noted.

"I just gotta figure out where we go from here," Hanover cautioned. "Our next move is critical."

On his way out of the J. Edgar Hoover Building's conference room, Jeremy reached into the cabinet that held the meeting participants' personal cell phones. These devices are forbidden in the Sensitive Compartmented Information Facility, or SCIF, which is set aside for Top Secret subjects. As Jeremy ran his finger across the glass to unlock his screen, he saw that he had one new text message.

Hey Luke, this is Han, are you there?

Jeremy hadn't heard from Leonard in over a week. With his heart racing, he noticed the text was sent almost two hours earlier.

Hey Han, I'm here! Are you OK?

I'm good now. I got my phone back from Darth Vader. You won't believe it, he was kicked out of the camp by Darth

Sidious! It's been crazy here.

Jeremy and Leonard had created code names for each person they might encounter. Jeremy quickly realized Leonard's memory of the code names was more reliable than his.

Han you're going to have to help me remember who Darth Sidious is.

You know we can't use real names.

I know just give me a hint.

OK, you remember who Darth Vader is, right?

Jeremy knew all too well who carried that pseudonym: Andrei Ovchenko, the man responsible for thousands of deaths, including his father's.

Of course, I know Vader.

Well Sidious was Vader's boss.

Jeremy thought, "Wait a minute; that means he is talking about Victor Youngblood. But how is that possible? Victor's in prison."

You mean VY?

Yes, but delete that text he is Darth Sidious.

How was Sidious in the camp? Isn't he in prison?

Yes, he's still in prison but it is a really long story I'm sure Leia will tell you the details.

Jeremy was still trying to process that Victor Youngblood was back in the picture, but then Leonard was texting about Savannah.

You saw Leia?

Of course, she was in the camp with a policeman.

In the camp…meaning in North Carolina?

Yeah, it's been crazy, but everything is good now.

Is she still in the camp with you now?

No and I'm not even in the camp anymore you won't believe where I am.

Jeremy shook his head in disbelief and then spoke to his phone as a surrogate for expressing what he really wanted to say to Leonard. "Savannah is for some reason in a camp in North Carolina with Ovchenko, and you want me to play guessing games. Come on, Leonard!"

Is Leia safe?

Yeah, I'm sure she's fine Luke you won't believe where I am.

You're sure she's fine? Don't you know if she's fine?

Yeah, she's fine OK you won't guess so I'll just tell you, I'm back at the Death Star.

"The Death Star?" Jeremy thought, "Surely Leonard doesn't mean he's back at Mouse Trap's headquarters in Bethesda. How is that even possible? It's been abandoned for almost a year."

You mean back where we used to work?

Yep I know it's crazy.

Why would you go back there?

I have a plan.

What kind of a plan?

A plan to find out what's going on.

Han you gotta be careful.

I will I gotta go but I'll text you back when I can - you have to trust me I know what I'm doing.

OK Han please be careful.

I will Luke I'll be in touch soon.

As Jeremy looked up from his phone, he was working hard to process everything Leonard had shared with him. Savannah was in the forefront of his mind. Thinking back on the last few days, he recalled a strange phone conversation with his mom. Surely, she wasn't involved. He returned to his phone and called Savannah.

"Jeremy! It's great to hear from you!" Savannah exclaimed.

"Hey, Babe; it is great to hear your voice. I just wanted to check in and see how you were doing."

"I'm doing good, but I'm missing a certain guy."

"That's good. I'm missing a certain gal. How's Mom doing?"

"She's good. She's already in bed for the night. Do you want me to wake her?"

"No, don't do that. I was curious. *So*, everything's been quiet the past few days?"

Savannah's heart began to race because it wasn't like Jeremy to be this inquisitive. Something was up. She despised lying to him, but she knew she couldn't tell him about going to the camp—at least she wasn't ready to just yet.

"Well, you know the store's staying busy, but it's a good kind of busy."

"So, nothing out of the ordinary? Just staying busy there in Abingdon at the store?"

"Enough about me, how about you? Is your FBI assignment almost over? Are you coming home soon?"

"As a matter of fact, I am. I'm coming home tomorrow morning."

"Jeremy, that's awesome! I have missed you so much!"

"I've missed you too. I can't wait to get back home. We have so much to talk about...to catch up on."

"We certainly do. I love you, Jeremy."

"Love you, too, Babe. See you tomorrow."

Yep...Savannah knew that *Jeremy knew*. She wasn't sure how, but she would have to tell Jeremy the truth—the whole truth—sooner than she had planned.

36

"Do we have another truck coming? This one's almost full."

"Yeah, Percy's on the way with his truck, and he's bringing his 14-foot trailer."

"That's good; but at this rate, we'll fill it up in an hour."

"Speaking of this rate, how about we take a break."

"Best idea I've heard all day."

Kingston, Tennessee, is located on the shores of Watts Bar Lake, whose water level is regulated by the Tennessee Valley Authority's Watts Bar Dam 40 miles downstream. From late spring to early fall, the lake's level is maintained at 741 feet above sea level. In late October, it is dropped to 736 feet in order to mitigate flooding during the wetter season. This five-foot drop exposes a sandy shoreline that accumulates brush, logs, fishing paraphernalia, trash, and other debris during the summer. As a service to the city of Kingston, Elijah had recruited the Liars, Thieves and Jokers

Club for shoreline cleanup duty.

"I want to thank you gentlemen for coming out today. As you can tell from our full truck, this cleanup was sorely needed," Elijah praised.

"I have one complaint about Ted," Bubba Driscoll quipped.

"What's that, Bubba?" Ted challenged.

"I'm finding your toxic masculinity very discomforting."

"My *what*?"

"Your toxic masculinity. Don't act like you don't know what you're doing."

"Heck, Bubba, I ain't actin'; I really don't know what I'm doin'."

"It's your 24-inch chainsaw, Ted. Do you really need a chainsaw that big, or are you simply trying to reinforce traditional dominant male gender roles?"

Ted Beckett stared at Bubba Driscoll in abject confusion, then looked down at his chainsaw, then back at Bubba, then up at the rest of the crowd, now fully engrossed in the conversation.

"Bubba, I ain't got a clue what you're talking about!"

"I'm talkin' about your dadgum toxic masculinity."

"Come on, guys; we gotta get back to work. Percy just arrived with the trailer," Elijah announced.

Still confused, Ted walked back to the shoreline with Elijah. "I never did understand what Bubba was sayin' about my chainsaw. Toxic somethin' or other."

Putting his arm around Ted, Elijah said, "Ted, your chainsaw is perfect. Thanks for coming out today."

Overhearing the conversation, Bubba walked past Elijah and Ted and mumbled, "Toxic, toxic, toxic, nothing but toxic masculinity."

"Hey, Elijah. Any luck in getting Clyde to do some work? He's just sittin' on the shoreline watching."

"Nah, Clyde's more of a watch dog than a work dog," Elijah chuckled.

"Ain't that the truth," Bubba quipped, nodding his head.

"Who's that coming?" Ted wondered.

The guys looked up and saw three full-size sedans pulling into the Kingston United Methodist Church's parking lot. Exiting their vehicles, a group of men were walking toward the cleanup crew.

"Elijah Mustang, it is so good to see you!" the man said, extending a hand in greeting.

"Good morning, Senator Chambers. It is good to see you too." Elijah removed a glove and shook hands with Senator Rodney Chambers, Republican from Tennessee, who had just been elected to his third term representing the Volunteer State.

"We were wondering if you could use some help," Chambers inquired.

"Sure, we can always use more help," Elijah responded.

"That's great; we'll get—"

Before Senator Chambers could finish, Clyde released an uncharacteristic bark and moved toward him.

"Clyde, calm down, buddy. It's OK. He's a friend."

Clyde continued growling and advancing. Just before Clyde reached the Senator, Elijah grabbed him by the collar.

"I'm really sorry, Senator. Don't know what's gotten into him."

"No problem, Elijah."

"I'll put him in the truck," Elijah offered, leading Clyde by the collar.

"Here are your clothes." An aide handed Chambers a pair of jeans, a flannel shirt, gloves, and a pair of work boots—all brand new with tags.

He got dressed and joined the LTJ Club along the shore-line. Moments later, an aide announced, "OK, everyone look over here." She began taking pictures.

"Elijah, you mind if we get a picture together?" the senator asked.

"Sure, OK." Elijah smiled for the camera, realizing what was happening.

After five more minutes of photos, the aide called out to Senator Chambers, "OK, I think we got everything."

"Elijah, I can't thank you enough for what you people are doing to help out our communities. I'm a big supporter of the Mustang movement. Outstanding work, just outstanding."

Chambers climbed back on the shoreline, walked to the car, and drove away with taillights winking at the LTJ Club.

Clyde once again growled from the cab of Elijah's truck.

"Always said dogs were a good judge of character," Bubba Driscoll mused.

Rosita Prince was as tough as they come; she had to be. Born into poverty in rural Oaxaca, Mexico, Rosita's parents were migrant workers who came to the United States to pick strawberries each year from February through June. Rosita started accompanying her parents at age ten, working 14-hour days in the sweltering heat. She waited years and studied diligently to finally become a U.S. citizen. In her early 20s, she met Walter, the love of her life, and moved to Abingdon, Virginia, where long hours in the strawberry fields were replaced by long hours at the hardware store. Growing a small business requires a lot of blood and sweat, as Walter and Rosita Prince would often attest. Rosita's most recent trial was the loss of her beloved Walter. The greatest solace in recent months was in having Jeremy back home. He offered a small glimpse of the husband she missed so terribly. With Savannah as the daughter she never had, Rosita felt a joy she had never experienced. Although she tried to deeply bury her grief, life without Walter still brought her an unshakeable sting. Four months since the tragic passing of Walter, his blue eyes and kind heart remained foremost in her mind as she went to bed every night and woke every morning. This morning was no different. As she worked to raise her 64-year-old body from bed, she squinted at the clock, knowing she had to be misreading it. 10:30? Surely not. Usually up by 5:30 every morning, Rosita's only explanation was that the power must have gone out at 10:30 the night before. She put on her slippers and stumbled out the bedroom door and down the hallway toward the top of the stairs. The bright morning sun only contributed to her confusion. As if her senses needed one more challenge, the smell of bacon wafted up to meet her on her way down the steps.

"Well, good morning, Mom. Or should I say good *afternoon*?" Savannah teased.

"Is it really…" Rosita struggled to manage the words.

"10:30? Yep, it sure is." Savannah giggled. "I was getting worried about you."

"Why didn't you wake me up?"

"Mom, we've been through a lot the last few days. You didn't sleep at all when we were in North Carolina, and you've barely slept since we got back. Your body needed the rest."

Rosita sighed heavily. "I guess you're right. I can't remember the last time I slept this late."

"But I have some good news—well, sorta good news," Savannah confided.

"What kind of good news?"

"Jeremy is coming home this morning. In fact, he should be here soon."

"That's great news!! *Wait a minute.* Why did you say *sorta* good news? Is something wrong?" Rosita prodded.

"No, not really *wrong*," Savannah hedged.

"What then?" Rosita pleaded.

"Well, I'm not 100% sure, but I think he knows about our little adventure. I'm not sure *how* he knows, but I think he knows."

"Oh," Rosita gulped. "What do we do?"

Savannah paced around the room and then turned back to Rosita. "I've already decided; I'm not going to lie to him.

I'm not going to volunteer anything; but whatever he asks, I'm going to answer honestly."

Rosita nodded her head in agreement. "That's a good plan. Let's stick with that."

"Mom, having him gone these few days made me understand how much I miss him and need him."

"And *love* him?" Rosita asked.

Savannah sighed, "Yeah, that too."

A broad smile consumed Rosita round face as she looked out the front window. "Looks like you don't have to wait any longer."

Savannah whirled around to see Jeremy walking up the driveway. She ran to the door to meet him.

"You are never allowed to leave me again!" Savannah threatened as she wrapped her arms around Jeremy.

"I tried that the first week after he went to college. It didn't work," Rosita deadpanned.

"I missed you too," Jeremy bubbled. "It is good to be back home."

"Have you had breakfast? I've got bacon and pancakes going," Savannah offered.

"No, I haven't. Just a cup of coffee at a gas station." Jeremy noticed his mom uncharacteristically disheveled. "Mom, are those your pajamas?"

Rosita blushed as Savannah chuckled.

"Can you believe your mom slept past 10 o'clock?"

Jeremy stood gape-jawed, staring at his mom. "Are you sick?"

Rosita waved both arms in protest. "No, I'm not sick. Just

catching up on my sleep. We've been busy while you were gone."

Seeing a segue to the primary topic of interest, Jeremy pursued, "Busy? Busy doing *what?*"

Rosita and Savannah looked at each other, unsure what to say. As Rosita bit her tongue, Savannah managed a subtle shake of the head in her direction. Deciding to break the awkward silence, Savannah spoke first, "You know, busy do-ing—"

Before Savannah could finish her sentence, Rosita blurt-ed out, "We've been to North Carolina to check on your friend Leonard. Savannah went to a camp in the mountains with a deputy, but they were captured. They found Leonard. He's fine, and everyone is going back to somewhere to work for someone named Victor."

Savannah looked at Rosita disapprovingly. "*Mom!*"

"You said we were going to be honest with him. I was just being honest," Rosita protested.

"Honest?" Jeremy observed. "That's a refreshing change."

"Look, Jeremy, it's a really long story; and we're going to tell you everything," Savannah assured. "But it's going to take some time. Let's eat some breakfast; I know you both are hungry. Then we'll have plenty of time to talk."

Jeremy hesitated. "You are going to tell me everything, right?"

"*Everything,*" Savannah repeated.

"Great, now let's eat!" Rosita cackled. "I'm starving."

"Thank you for agreeing to meet with me, Director Thompson."

"Certainly, Thomas. We have worked together for many years, and I've never heard you this insistent to meet. I'm happy to accommodate you."

"I'm glad you understand; I wouldn't insist on meeting if it wasn't an urgent matter of national security." Thomas Hanover was uncharacteristically nervous.

"And if I didn't understand the urgency, your request to meet in the SCIF certainly drives that point home."

Hanover knew that if a meeting ever fit the definition of *sensitive,* this one did, especially since it involved the FBI Director.

"As you know, our Task Force Terracotta has been commissioned."

"I do. I'm the one who commissioned it."

"Yes sir. I realize we are just getting started, but we've already uncovered some significant information."

"You haven't been underway for even a week, have you?" Director Thompson asked.

"No, sir, just four days."

"Hmm. Please continue."

"We've found that Victor Youngblood's organization, known as Mouse Trap, is much more far-reaching than we imagined. Although we're just in the early stages of investigating, I think we're looking at the largest and most powerful criminal organization that has ever existed."

"And you've come to this conclusion in four days?" Thompson asked skeptically.

"It's not a conclusion yet, just a strong suspicion. But that isn't why I asked to meet."

"Then, by all means, continue."

"We are finding that Youngblood's organization was very engaged politically. They accumulated huge sums of money and then funneled it into the campaigns of politicians."

"While certainly illegal, it shouldn't be surprising that criminal organizations donate money to politicians."

"No sir, that isn't a surprise; but the amount and the particular politicians are."

"*And?*" Thompson's patience was wearing thin as he waited for Hanover to fully unpack his message.

"Youngblood donated several hundred-million dollars to politicians in the 2016 election cycle."

Thompson began chuckling. "Thomas, you can't possibly mean several *hundred-million*. With the campaign finance laws in place, it would all be disclosed."

"I will spare you the transactional details, but Youngblood had an intricate plan to pull off this scheme. I hesitate to say this about a criminal organization, but it was brilliant."

Hanover could see the wheels in Thompson's head spinning, so he decided it was time to drop the real bombshell.

"And sir, we have been able to trace donations totaling $400 million to President McCoy."

Thompson's face was ashen, his heart raced, and sweat began accumulating on his upper lip. He worked to generate a cogent response. "And again, I will ask, you've been able to gather this information in only four days?"

"Yes sir. We have a resource on the team who has been invaluable. We have been able to secure Jeremy Prince. You may recall that Prince was the individual that sent us the information about Youngblood and his organization. In his early 20s, he rose to be Youngblood's right-hand man, even ascending to the head of Mouse Trap while Youngblood ran for vice president."

Thompson got up from his chair and walked over to the corner of the SCIF. He kept his back to Hanover until he could compose himself. It was taking an awkward amount of time, prompting Hanover to finally speak.

"Director, is everything OK?"

Thompson breathed deeply, then turned back to Hanover. "Yes, Thomas, I'm just trying to take all this in. You've certainly given me a lot to think about."

"Yes sir, I know this is a lot; I hope you now understand why I wanted to meet with you."

"I most certainly do. Is there anything else, Thomas? I have other meetings that I postponed."

Taken aback by Director Thompson's abrupt desire to end the meeting, Hanover mustered a similarly abrupt response. "No sir. I understand your schedule is tight, and I sincerely appreciate your meeting with me. I'll report back as we get more information."

Hanover closed his portfolio and stood to leave.

"Yes, Thomas, please do." Thompson managed a parting handshake as Hanover left the room.

Thompson returned to his office, closed the door, and

made a call on his cell phone.

"We have a problem. This is unfolding faster than we expected. Jeremy Prince is involved. Yes sir, I understand."

"Seriously? Leonard is going back to work for Mouse Trap?" Jeremy asked astonished.

For an hour, Savannah and Rosita had been explaining to Jeremy every detail of their trip to North Carolina. This conversation was illuminating for Jeremy and redemptive for Savannah and Rosita. They hadn't realized the heavy burden keeping their trip a secret had become.

"Not just Mouse Trap, he's going back to work for Victor," Savannah explained.

"How is that even possible? Victor is in a maximum-security prison with a life sentence."

"I can't explain it. All I can tell you is that Victor was on the phone. I heard his voice myself. I don't know how, but Victor is back in charge of Mouse Trap." Savannah shook her head in disbelief as she spoke.

"That's crazy. I want to contact Leonard; but I'm concerned that would put him...and maybe us, in danger," Jeremy mused.

"Here's the weird thing—the last words Leonard whispered to me as we were leaving the camp were 'I've got a plan,'" Savannah revealed.

Jeremy cocked his head. "*A plan*? What kind of a plan?"

Savannah raised both hands in the air. "He didn't say. I

told him I was leaving and tried to convince him to go with me. He said he was staying; and then as he hugged me to leave, he just whispered, 'I have a plan.'"

"Whoa now, back up a second. Leonard hugged you?" Jeremy squinted.

"That's the part of this story you find hard to accept?" Savannah smirked.

"You have to understand that Leonard isn't a hugger… or a talker…or a participator in any form of interaction with other human beings. Are you sure this was Leonard and not some Mouse Trap AI creation?" Jeremy teased.

"Stop joking around, Jeremy; this is really serious. We have to figure out what we are going to do," Savannah insisted.

"Right now, I don't plan to *do* anything. I recall the last time we all three agreed not to do anything." Jeremy looked at his mom, who crossed her arms in protest. "You two decided to strike out on your own and try to be heroes. I need you to promise to never do anything like that again. Agreed?"

Rosita turned and walked away, uttering only an exaggerated "humph."

"I think that means she agrees," Savannah chuckled.

"How about you? Do you agree?" Jeremy queried.

With the two left by themselves, Jeremy saw this as the perfect time to drive home his point.

Jeremy sighed. "I don't want to make this a big dramatic moment of conflict, but I think this is an important discussion for us. These last few months with you here in Abingdon have been some of the best in my life. I love…I mean,

I hope we're always together. I just want us to agree to be totally honest with each other, even if it is a difficult conversation. Are you on board with that?"

Savannah smiled scooted next to Jeremy on the couch; and breathed, "Yeah, I'm on board with that." Then she tilted her head ever-so-slightly and offered a long, deep kiss. "And I love you too. I'm glad you're home, you handsome boy."

37

Thomas Hanover was in the middle of a staff meeting as he felt his phone buzz in his pocket. Peeking to see who was calling, he knew this was one he wanted to take. He excused himself from the staff meeting and answered the phone in the hallway outside. "Jeremy?"

"Yeah, it's me."

"I was a few hours away from sending agents to find you."

After the unexpected text exchange with Leonard, Jeremy left Washington D.C. without talking with Hanover or any other member of Task Force Terracotta. He knew he was needed in Abingdon and didn't have time to explain to the FBI where he was going. He also knew he owed this call to Hanover, both to explain his absence and to convey the new information Savannah had shared.

"I needed to return to Abingdon for some personal business. I'm sorry I didn't have a chance to discuss it with you in advance."

"Everything OK at home?"

"Yeah, it's OK. How's the investigation going?"

"I can't say much on this line, but I had an interesting meeting with the Director. I shared what we've found so far, and the reaction was interesting." Hanover was conflicted as he recognized he was talking with a private citizen on a non-secure line, but he also knew the contributions Jeremy had made to the investigation and felt an obligation to keep him in the loop.

"An interesting reaction? How so?"

"The Director seemed caught off guard."

"You mean surprised? Telling the FBI Director, the sitting president received hundreds of millions of dollars of illegal campaign contributions was probably a shock to him." Jeremy speculated.

"That's just it. It wasn't like he was surprised to find out about the contributions; it was almost like he was surprised to find out that *I* knew about them."

Aware that Director Thompson had been a Victor Youngblood Mouse Trap asset for many years, Jeremy was waiting for just the right time to reveal this nugget of information to Hanover. He wasn't trying to keep information from the FBI. In fact, Thompson's link to Mouse Trap was included in the exabytes of information he had already provided the FBI, if they just knew where to look. Instead, Jeremy was trying to share the breadth and depth of Mouse Trap's activities in digestible bites. If he spilled the entire Mouse Trap saga to Hanover, Jeremy would likely come across as a conspiracy nut who would be ignored. He understood that he must reveal the Mouse Trap puzzle one piece at a time. However, this particular piece wasn't ready to be revealed.

"You think he knew?" Jeremy quizzed.

"I'm not sure. It was just a really strange meeting."

"I have some information I need to share with you, Thomas." Jeremy felt that Victor's renewed involvement with Mouse Trap warranted being shared with the FBI, even if he didn't have all the facts.

"What kind of information?" Hanover asked.

"This is going to sound unbelievable, but I want you to know this is coming from a 100% reliable source," Jeremy divulged.

"You have my attention, Jeremy."

"What's the last thing you heard about Victor Young-blood?"

"That he's spending 23 hours a day in a 7-by-12 box at ADX Florence. He's scheduled to be there until he assumes room temperature," Hanover announced.

"What if I told you that Youngblood is active with Mouse Trap again?"

"That's not possible at Florence. It's not some local jail where the inmates run the show. It's the real deal. I've been there many times to interrogate prisoners."

"I understand." Jeremy paused for effect. "But what if this time is different? What if Youngblood is somehow able to communicate with his Mouse Trap team from Florence?"

"Jeremy, I'm not making myself clear; that's not possible at Florence."

"Have I told you anything about Youngblood that has

proven to be false?" Jeremy probed.

"No, everything has proven to be true; but it has all been past activities, he—"

"Thomas, I'll take that as a *no*. Mouse Trap is reorganizing, and Victor is leading it. I don't know how, but he's in charge. If you want proof—at least proof that Mouse Trap is reorganizing, go to the Youngblood and Associates building in Bethesda, where you will find a flurry of activity."

"And you know this *how*?"

"Do two things: go check Bethesda and go check Florence. Victor's back, Thomas, and that should scare the hell out of everyone."

"Mr. President, thank you for meeting with us on short notice." Chief of Staff Riley Indigo entered the Oval Office with FBI Director Gavin Thompson following closely behind.

"You said this was about Youngblood, right?" The President sneered.

"Yes sir, we—," Indigo began.

"It has been over a week. I told you I wanted a report from you as soon as possible." Stalking around the Oval Office, President McCoy was waving his arms.

"I'm sorry, sir; but it is an extremely complicated case. It has taken us a while to gather credible information," Thompson interjected.

"I don't want to hear your excuses. Come on, spill it. What have you found out?"

Thompson and Indigo stared at one another for a moment before Indigo nodded for Thompson to proceed.

McCoy's patience was wearing thin. "Would someone start talking and now!"

Thompson opened a portfolio and began speaking. "Mr. President, you may recall the last time we met there was concern that Victor Youngblood's organization may have been actively involved in the 2016 presidential campaign."

"Yes, of course I recall," McCoy snapped. "The real question is whether he was involved in *my* campaign."

Thompson paused for effect. "Yes sir, we have reason to believe he was *very* involved in your campaign." Thompson pulled a sheet from his portfolio. "So far, we have traced over $100 million in donations to the McCoy for President campaign to entities controlled by Youngblood—entities such as businesses, individuals, PACs, and labor unions."

McCoy stood, mouth open working to utter a response. "Did you say *over $100 million?*"

The $100 million was, of course, a fabricated number. The real number was four times that amount, but this conversation was not about accounting precision but about eliciting the desired response. Both Thompson and Indigo knew $100 million would do the trick.

"Yes sir, I'm afraid that's accurate—over $100 million."

Stumbling over to the sofa and sitting down, McCoy struggled to form a cogent sentence. "How is that...what could they...are you sure?"

Thompson nodded solemnly. "That's why it has taken us a few days to get back with you. We wanted to triple check everything."

"I obviously knew nothing about this. There's no way I could have known. You both know that, right?"

Before either could relieve McCoy with an answer, Indigo raised the heat several more degrees.

"There's more, sir," Indigo cautioned.

"More? How could there be *more?*!" McCoy howled.

"I received a call this morning from a reporter at the *Times*. He told me they were working on a story about the McCoy campaign receiving large illegal contributions. He wanted to know if we had a comment or if anyone was available for an interview."

"I hope you said, 'Hell no!'" McCoy was back on his feet.

"Of course, I told him we didn't comment on wild fishing expeditions."

Turning back to Thompson, McCoy pointed his finger. "This is your fault. There has to be a leak in your organization. How else could they know?"

"I first heard about the reporter's question this morning. We'll obviously investigate to determine if we are the source," Thompson assured.

"Riley, you are going to earn your salary. I want a damage-control plan in place as soon as possible. Thompson, I expect a daily briefing on this investigation, including updates on the leaker's identity."

"Yes sir, we'll get working on this immediately," Riley assured. "You can trust us, sir."

"Then go; *go now* and get started!" McCoy demanded.

As Thompson and Indigo left the Oval Office, McCoy

slammed the door behind them.

"The President seemed very upset," Thompson observed.

"He most certainly did." Indigo turned to Thompson and offered the slightest hint of a smile.

"Can I please speak with Warden Polivick?"

"May I ask who's calling?"

"Thomas Hanover with the FBI."

"Just a moment, Mr. Hanover."

Henry Polivick, Florence ADX's warden, and Thomas Hanover, chief of the FBI's Criminal Enterprise Branch, were members of the Federal Government's Senior Executive Service, or SES, the highest level of civil servants who are not political appointees. Both men were also members of the Justice Department; therefore, their paths had crossed on several occasions including senior departmental retreats, seminars, and training. Although not close friends, the two had become professional acquaintances.

"Thomas, to what do I owe the pleasure?" Polivick quipped.

"Henry, great to hear from you. How's the family?"

"Kids are growing like weeds. How are things in D.C.?"

"As slow and bloated as ever. When's the last time you were here?"

"Not since our exhilarating diversity training in July."

"You mean the training that you almost failed?" Hanover

quipped.

"Passing grade was an 80. I made it over the line comfortably with an 82."

Both men chuckled.

"I'm sure you didn't call to talk about diversity training."

"No, Henry, I have a question about one of your inmates."

"Which one?"

"A high profile one, Victor Youngblood."

Polivick was silent.

"Henry, you still there?"

"Yes, I'm here Thomas." Polivick's tone had had quickly gone from jovial and friendly to somber and quiet.

"So, my question is, is there anything unusual about Youngblood?" Hanover tested.

Again, no response.

"Henry?"

"Thomas, this may not be a great topic for the phone."

Growing concerned that Jeremy might be on to something, Hanover searched for a way to advance the conversation. "I understand. You want me to call you back on the STE?" Hanover asked, referring to the Secure Terminal Equipment line set aside for sensitive calls.

"You been to Colorado lately, Thomas? It is beautiful this time of year."

"I haven't, Henry. Should I arrange a trip?"

"Only if you want an answer to your question."

"See you tomorrow, Henry."

"Looking forward to it, Thomas."

38

Hey Luke this is Han are you there?

Jeremy was just getting his first cup of coffee for the day when he heard the "bleep" on his phone. He was excited to hear from his friend but still concerned about Leonard's precarious situation.

Yeah I'm here.

Things are crazy here at the death star, you won't believe how much is going on.

Are you safe, Han?

Yeah, I'm fine, people are everywhere and my office is huge!

Han you gotta be careful.

As Leonard was typing a response, he felt a hand on his shoulder, causing him to jump and squeal simultaneously.

"I'm sorry, Leonard; I didn't mean to startle you." Zeke Gibson, the acting head of Mouse Trap, was standing at Leonard's desk. His heart pounding, Leonard wondered how long Zeke been standing there and if he had seen his texts.

"Oh…uh…no problem," Leonard muttered. As he looked up from his desk, still trying to compose himself, he continued, "I was just texting tech support, and I—"

"Leonard, I'd like for you to meet Cassidy Ramirez, your new assistant administrator. She's been assigned to help you get Omnia back up to full speed a little faster."

In the throes of the disquieting visit, Leonard hadn't noticed the only thing that would make him more nervous than Zeke's catching him off guard—a beautiful female. As he looked at his new guest, his mouth involuntarily fell open.

"Mmmmmy *what?*" Cassidy Ramirez stood at the entrance to Leonard's office. She was 5' 3", only because she was wearing three-inch heels. Her black leather pants were the perfect match for her leopard print sweater. Deep-red curly hair cascaded halfway down her shoulder. As she stepped toward Leonard, he wasn't certain what was more unsettling, her captivating smile or her bright green eyes.

"It's nice to meet you, Leonard. I have heard so much about you. I really look forward to working for you."

Leonard looked at Cassidy, then to Zeke, and back again

to Cassidy. He attempted to speak, but his voice was stubbornly uncooperative. The awkward silence was interrupted by a "bleep" on this phone.

Han you there?

"Sounds like you got a text," Cassidy announced.

"Probably tech support getting back with you," Zeke observed.

Leonard remained frozen, hoping somehow this was all a dream or more likely a nightmare.

"Leonard, I know you are making great progress in rebuilding Omnia, but we felt that you could use some help. Cassidy has computer science degrees from MIT and Northwestern. She'll be a great addition to your team."

"Zeke gave me a quick tour of Omnia. Pretty impressive," Cassidy interjected.

Leonard's phone bleeped again.

Han everything OK?

Again, Leonard ignored it.

"Well, Leonard, I've got things to do," Zeke chirped. "I'll leave you two to get acquainted."

"Wwwait…wwwhat…you're leaving, and she's ssstaying?"

"Don't worry, Leonard. I let Cassidy know it takes a while for you to warm up. You guys will be fine. Be gentle with him, Cassidy."

Cassidy chuckled. "Gentle's not exactly my style."

"Keep up the good work, Leonard," Zeke uttered while closing the door on his way out.

Cassidy walked around Leonard's desk and stood directly behind him looking at his screen. "What are you working on?"

"Ummm...computer...working on computer."

"I can see that silly." Cassidy put her hands on Leonard's shoulders and leaned in cheek-to-cheek with Leonard to look at his dual 42-inch monitors. "What part of Omnia are you rebuilding now?"

Cassidy's invasion of his personal space caused Leonard's throat to tighten and his heart rate to find another gear. However, his greatest concern was bladder control, which was rapidly approaching involuntary status.

Han, just let me know you're OK.

"Who's Han?" Cassidy quizzed.

"Nnnnobody." Leonard flipped over his cell phone as he sighed heavily.

"We're going to make a great team, Leonard. Can't wait to get started."

"Ugh!" Leonard muttered to himself.

The alarm sounded at 4:00 a.m. Thomas Hanover showered, shaved, kissed his sleeping wife, and by 4:45 a.m. was out the door of his home in McClean, Virginia. With light traffic on the Dulles Access Road and his FBI credentials allowing him to breeze through TSA checkpoints, he was sitting at his gate by 5:30, a full hour before his flight. United Flight 1108 had an uneventful landing in Denver 10 minutes before the scheduled arrival time of 8:33 a.m. Mountain Time. The rental car was waiting as scheduled, and the two-hour drive to ADX Florence positioned him 15 minutes early for his 11 a.m. meeting with Warden Polivick.

"Thomas, I see you're punctual as always." The warden extended a hand to his guest.

"It is good to see you, Henry. Thank you for agreeing to meet with me."

The two acquaintances exchanged updates on kids, complaints about Justice Department bureaucracy, and how they both were dreading the upcoming training on zero-based budgeting. Then they got down to the real reason for Hanover's visit.

"When we spoke on the phone, I sensed that something's up with Youngblood." Hanover steered the conversation.

The warden shook his head, trying to find the right words. "I've been warden at Florence for six years and in the federal system for 22. I've never seen anything close to this."

"Close to what?" Hanover wondered.

"You gotta really be careful, Thomas."

"What do you mean?"

"Youngblood has friends in extremely high places."

"You mean *had* friends in high places, right? At ADX Florence you don't have friends."

"It's supposed to be that way," the warden mumbled.

"Henry, what exactly are you trying to tell me?"

The warden ignored the question. "What did you enter as the purpose for your travel?"

"Henry, I don't understand what you mean?"

The warden stood up from his desk and walked to the window. "On your travel request, what did you enter as the purpose?"

"I said I was going to interview Youngblood. I'm leading a task force that is investigating his organization. It makes sense that I would—"

"Then he knows you're coming," the warden deadpanned.

"What? How? He's cut off from the outside world."

"Thomas…," the warden sighed, "…he has a cell phone."

"What?" Hanover asked incredulously.

"I can't get into any more. I shouldn't have told you, but you should know that he has a cell phone."

"How?"

"Don't ask me *how* or *why* or *anything more* because I can't tell you," the warden snapped.

"I'm sorry, Henry, I didn't mean to—"

"It's OK. This situation has just become untenable. I know you didn't come to speak with me. I'll take you to meet with Youngblood; but, Thomas, please be careful."

Unsure how to respond, Hanover just nodded in agreement.

"Jeremy, did you order the plumbing supplies yesterday? Jeremy? *Jeremy!*"

"Oh, I'm sorry, Mom. What did you say?"

"Did you order the plumbing supplies?"

"I think so, but I'm not sure. Let me look." Jeremy searched the hardware store's order history on his computer. "Oh, it looks like I didn't. I'll do it this afternoon."

"Jeremy, are you OK?" Rosita queried. "You seem distracted."

"Yeah, Mom, I'm fine."

"Savannah said you were worried about Leonard."

"I'm sure everything is fine with Leonard. I'll get the plumbing supplies ordered right away."

"You know you can't do that," Rosita protested.

"Do *what*, Mom?"

"Just dismiss your mom like that."

Jeremy sighed and lowered his head. "I'm sorry, Mom. I was texting Leonard last night, and he just sort of dropped offline. Seriously, I'm sure it's nothing."

"Savannah doesn't think it's nothing," Rosita blurted.

As Jeremy was working on a response, Savannah entered the office.

"Hey, Mom, can you come out to the store for a second? There's a guy with a question about the chainsaws that we can't answer."

"OK, I'll be right there."

As Rosita walked by Jeremy and out the office door, Jeremy mouthed to Savannah, "Thank you." Savannah responded with a subtle wink.

JOHN FORD CLAYTON

39

Thomas Hanover was led to a small interview booth. On both sides of his seat were solid cinder block walls painted a dull white. Directly in front of him was two-inch-thick glass with a round stainless-steel louvered port through which inmates and their visitors could communicate.

After a short wait, the door opposite Hanover opened. A guard entered the room followed closely by a man wearing leg irons, handcuffs, and stomach chains. A second guard followed. The guards positioned the prisoner on a small stainless-steel stool, ensuring he was well-balanced. As he raised his head, Hanover was struck by the sight of Victor Youngblood in chains. For weeks, Hanover had studied this genius criminal mastermind and had subconsciously built Youngblood into a larger-than-life figure, who was now at the mercy of two prison guards in rural Colorado.

As Hanover studied his subject, he was impressed at how well-groomed Victor was. With deep-blue eyes and salt-and-pepper hair, Victor seemed to be someone more at home in the halls of Congress than at ADX Florence, except for the chains and orange jumpsuit. He wrestled to move beyond this juxtaposition. Besides, he had come for business, not psychoanalysis.

As the two briefly sized each other up, Hanover was the first to break the silence.

"Mr. Youngblood, my name is Thomas Hanover. I'm with the FBI in Washington. I have some questions for you."

"OK," Victor succinctly responded.

"Mr. Youngblood, you were the head of an organization known as Mouse Trap. Is that correct?"

"*Mouse Trap?* I'm not familiar with that name. I led a team of professionals focusing on public relations, marketing, consulting, and project management at Youngblood and Associates."

Hanover looked up from his pad and nodded as if to say, "OK, so that's how it's going to be." He laid his pad on the table and paused in an awkward silence before resuming. "So, your story is that you don't know anything about Mouse Trap?"

"Mr. Hanover, it's not my *story*. I truly don't know anything about a mouse trap."

Again, Hanover nodded and then opened his tablet. "Mr. Youngblood, I recognize you have been able to operate right under the noses of the federal government for decades, but I want to share with you what we know."

Victor didn't respond or change his expression.

"We know that you have operated Mouse Trap since at least the '80's. We know that you have amassed an extreme amount of wealth, totaling in the hundreds of billions. We know that you have vast holdings in real estate and equity in thousands of companies. We know that you have many highly placed individuals whom you consider assets, individuals such as athletes, movie stars, and politicians. We also know that your organization is responsible for hundreds of murders beyond the one that landed you in this prison for the rest of your life."

Again, Victor didn't respond.

"You may be interested to know how we have obtained this information. You were kind enough to keep it all organized in your computer system known as Omnia, whose complete contents are now in FBI custody. It's all there— every bribe, theft, and murder—fully documented. We have an FBI task force whose sole responsibility is to sort through every sordid detail of what your organization has done."

"I wasn't aware the FBI had such a vivid imagination." It was the first response Hanover had elicited from Victor.

Ignoring Victor's remark, Hanover continued, "And we even have some breaking news. We've found that Mouse Trap—*your* organization—is rebuilding. Everyone is moving back into your Bethesda headquarters. You must really be proud."

Victor returned to silence.

"Is any of this information resonating with you, Mr. Youngblood?" Hanover paused, waiting for a response that did not come. "Since we already know everything I've shared with you, you may be wondering why I am here. We know even your best-kept secret. Not only is Mouse Trap reorganizing, but you, Mr. Youngblood, are directing those efforts from right here at Florence."

"Mr. Hanover, you are aware that 23 of the 24 hours in each day I'm confined to a 7-by-12-foot cell. The remaining hour is spent outside my cell in chains like these. The FBI has lost its mind if it is chasing the ghost of Victor Youngblood. I've been sentenced to live the rest of my days in this godforsaken hell hole."

"See, you think we don't know what you're doing. That you're getting away with this right out in the open. You think you have friends in high places who are going to look the other way. The reason I'm here, the reason I traveled 2,000 miles to meet with you face-to-face is to let you know that it's over. Your days of running a criminal organization from federal prison are over. The rebuilding of Mouse Trap is over. Your days of making a mockery of the U.S. justice system are over. Mr. Youngblood, I hope you've enjoyed your moment of freedom here at Florence because everything is about to change."

With the last statement, Hanover nodded to the guards to lead Victor back to his cell; Hanover stood to leave, but before the guards could move, Victor asked, "That's it?"

Taken aback by the response, Hanover turned back to Youngblood and looked askance at him and responded, "What did you say?"

"You flew all the way from Washington D.C. to Colorado and all you did was tell a man who's already sentenced to life in prison, in the most secure prison in the country, that you're going to get him? Mr. Hanover, the taxpayers of this country expect more from their civil servants."

Hanover began to snarl at being called on the carpet by a convicted murderer. "Mr. Youngblood, you're—"

"I'm what?" Victor taunted.

Hanover leapt to his feet and slammed the stainless-steel table. "You're a killer, Mr. Youngblood, a cold-blooded killer. Guards, take this man back to his cell!"

As the guards reached for his arms, Victor softly muttered, "Wait."

The guards obliged, returning to their posts on either side of Victor.

"Guards return this man to his cell," Hanover repeated even more loudly.

The guards stood still as Victor offered Hanover a faint smile.

Hanover sat back down in his chair, stunned at the guards' deference to Victor.

Just as Hanover was about to respond, Victor softly uttered, "OK, I'm ready, Javier."

Each guard grabbed an arm and helped Victor to his feet.

"You have a safe trip back to Washington, Mr. Hanover."

"Please remove these chains, Javier."

As always, the guard complied.

Reaching into his pants leg, Victor pulled out his cell phone and tapped out a short text. Looking at the guards, he said, "Thank you. OK, let's go."

"You know way back in ancient history—I think it was like two weeks ago—you and I were having a conversation." Savannah plopped down on Jeremy's lap; her long legs stretched out over the arm of the loveseat. Reaching out her arm, she draped it around Jeremy's neck. "*An important conversation.*"

"An *important* conversation, huh?" Jeremy teased.

Touching the tip of Jeremy's nose, Savannah continued, "In fact, you were the one that initiated the conversation."

"Oh, I remember exactly the conversation we were having," Jeremy declared.

"You do?!"

"Yep. We were trying to decide if we should make the trek over to Blacksburg to watch Virginia Tech's first football game of the season. After all we've been through, I think we deserve the splurge. Let's do it!"

Drooping her shoulders, Savannah hung her head. "It wasn't about a stupid football game."

"It *wasn't?*"

"No! It was about the future, specifically about *our* future."

"Our future? Wow, that sounds serious," Jeremy cautioned.

"I hope it is serious."

Jeremy acquiesced, breathing deeply before he spoke.

"Are you happy here in Abingdon? I know it's not the big city of Washington, and we're not in the middle of the Mouse Trap excitement; but is it at least OK?"

Savannah scooched up to see Jeremy eye-to-eye. "It's not just OK, Jeremy; it is the happiest I have ever been in my life. I was raised with everything I could ever want except for someone who genuinely loved me just for me. I feel like I have that now."

"You do, Babe, I—"

Before Jeremy could get out the most important words of the conversation, his cell phone rang.

"Really?" Savannah blurted.

"It could be Leonard." Jeremy reached into his pocket to check his phone. He saw the number, sighed, and showed it to Savannah."

Incoming call – Thomas Hanover, FBI

"Go ahead, I know you need to take that." Savannah grimaced, hopping off Jeremy's lap.

"I can let it go to voicemail."

"No, take it," Savannah reluctantly insisted.

Jeremy nodded.

"This is Jeremy."

"Jeremy, this is Thomas Hanover. We've had a significant development in the Youngblood case. I can't get into the details over the phone, but I'm in Colorado driving to the airport. I have been to ADX Florence to interview Youngblood. I sense things are worse than we thought. I believe you are correct that Mouse Trap is being reconstructed and that Youngblood is at the center of it."

"Wait, you talked to Victor?" Jeremy marveled.

"Yes, he has an immense presence, even in chains and a prison jumpsuit. And we've had agents out to Bethesda. There's definitely something big going on."

"If Victor is involved, *big* isn't the right word."

"I know you have things to tend to at home, but I need you back in D.C. tomorrow. I'm briefing the team on what I discovered."

Jeremy winced and looked at Savannah, who was hearing Jeremy's end of the conversation.

"Are you still there, Jeremy?"

"Yeah, I'm here."

"We're meeting at 8 a.m. in the northeast conference room."

Jeremy looked at Savannah again. He thought about the future. He thought about how happy she was. He thought about how happy *he* was. He knew there was only one proper response.

"Thomas, I'm not going to make it tomorrow. I think I'm done with Task Force Terracotta."

Savannah looked to Jeremy and smiled.

"Jeremy, this is serious. After meeting with Youngblood, I have grave concerns about where this is going. I understand you've lived this firsthand, but I'm just fully realizing what Youngblood is capable of. I really need your expertise on the team."

"I'm sorry, Thomas; but I'm not going to make it."

"Look, if this is about compensation, I can arrange to make you a paid consultant. I can—"

"No, it's not about money, Thomas; it is about priorities. I finally understand what mine are."

"OK, Jeremy, I get it. I'm not going to be able to talk you into tomorrow's meeting, but we're going to talk again about coming back to the task force. We need you. Your country needs you."

"You guys have a great meeting, Thomas."

"I will talk with you soon, Jeremy."

Jeremy put down the phone and looked at Savannah.

"Now…about the future."

Quality Manufacturing occupied a 50,000-square-foot building in Northwest Pittsburgh, on the banks of the Ohio River. Built in the 1950s, the facility manufactured parts for the automotive industry until the late 1980s, when U.S. automobile manufacturers were increasingly going oversees to fulfill their supply chains. After closing in 1988, the building remained vacant until it was purchased in 1993 by Council Holding Corporation, a Mouse Trap business entity.

After a half-dozen similar sites were toured in early 1994, Andrei Ovchenko selected the Pittsburgh site for the headquarters of a new Mouse Trap asset that would be known as Blackforce. In the 27 years since, Ovchenko called the industrial site his home.

Inside the building, suites were built for each Blackforce

member to have their own space with a bedroom, bathroom, and small living room. A Central Command Center was created along with a training area, recreational area, dining hall, and kitchen.

Victor conceived Blackforce as an arm of Mouse Trap that would be responsible for the dirtiest of dirty jobs. The Soviet Union's demise provided the perfect opportunity to pluck General Andrei Ovchenko from the KGB's payroll. It proved to be a perfect marriage as the lethality of Ovchenko was rivaled only by his secrecy.

The previous year was hard on Ovchenko and his team of 60 as Mouse Trap's pause in operations left them stir-crazy and longing for a mission. The short trip to a camp in North Carolina at least provided a change of scenery but fell short of fulfilling Blackforce's desire to be back in the field. The text message Ovchenko received earlier that evening changed everything.

As Ovchenko stood in front his men, the normally stoic leader could not hide his enthusiasm. "Comrades, we have mission in Washington D.C. More missions to come soon. Blackforce is operational"

In Bethesda, Maryland, Zeke felt the buzz of a text message that read "Blackforce operational." He reached into his jacket pocket, pulled out the envelope, removed the list, and crossed off item #7.

40

"**G**ood morning, Mom. You look beautiful today. I hope you slept well."

As she did most days, Rosita Prince arrived at the hardware store at 7:30 a.m., an hour and a half before opening, usually an hour before Jeremy and Savannah arrived, making this morning's greeting unexpected.

Rosita scratched her head in confusion. "Wow, Savannah, you're here early and in a *really* good mood."

"I guess I am," Savannah agreed.

"What happened last night? Did you and Jeremy have wild—"

"Don't finish that sentence, Mom." Jeremy interrupted entering the office.

"You're here too? Did I miss daylight savings time or something?" Rosita blurted.

"No, we just thought we'd get the day started a little early."

Rosita stood with her hands on her hips. "You sound chipper too. What's up with you two?"

"It's just…we got some things squared away last night, and we're both really happy."

"*Things?* What kind of things?" Rosita then took a deep breath and swirled around to Jeremy. "Did you finally pop the question?"

Jeremy sighed and looked at Savannah. "I told you coming in early was a bad idea."

Savannah chuckled. "No, mom, but we are putting down roots here in Abingdon. The FBI called Jeremy last night and tried to get him to return to Washington, but he told them no. He's staying here with me—with us, I mean."

"You had it right the first time." Walking to Jeremy, Rosita put her arms around his waist and embraced him. "But I'm fine to reap the rewards of love if it means seeing my son and of course you, Savannah, more often."

"I think that's what it means, Mom," Savannah agreed.

"OK, enough love time, we all have to get to work," Jeremy declared, leaving the office.

Rosita turned to Savannah. "Now, let's get back to that part about me looking beautiful today."

"Large coffee, cream, no sugar, and a plain bagel."

Thomas Hanover was a creature of habit. He started every morning promptly at 6:00 as the first customer of the day at the Chesapeake Bagel Bakery, just a few blocks from his home in McClean, Virginia. Even on mornings like this, when his 1 a.m. arrival back from Colorado meant he would have only a few hours of sleep, he always arrived at the bakery at 6:00 a.m. and always had a large coffee, cream, no sugar, and a plain bagel.

"Have a good day, Mr. Hanover."

Perhaps his sleep deprivation caused the usually perceptive FBI professional to somehow miss the black SUV that pulled onto Old Dominion Drive behind his Ford Edge.

"We were supposed to meet at nine, right?" Billy Murdoch asked, looking at his watch.

"That's what my email said. I'm assuming we all got the same email since we're all here," Lucy Cross confirmed.

"When was the last time Thomas Hanover was late for a meeting?" Ben Gossett asked rhetorically.

"Not just late, but almost an hour late" Elizabeth Sanders lamented.

"His email said he was in Colorado yesterday visiting Youngblood in prison. Maybe he's still on Mountain Time."

"I'll try his cell phone." Ben Gossett volunteered.

"So, he really met with Youngblood?" Billy Murdoch questioned.

"Can't wait to hear what he found out."

"It went straight to voicemail," Ben announced.

"Should we call his home?"

"No, let's wait a little longer. He probably got stuck in

traffic."

It had been four days since Task Force Terracotta had met, but they had been an eventful four days. In addition to going to Colorado, Thomas Hanover had investigated Mouse Trap's headquarters in Bethesda and had met with FBI Director Thompson to share the team's initial findings. Jeremy Prince had left the team to return home to Abingdon. The four core team members continued diving into the case in their areas of expertise.

Continuing to unravel Mouse Trap's financial empire, Billy Murdoch had identified over $20 billion in assets that could be tied to Victor Youngblood. He knew he was just scratching the surface. Lucy Croft's count of faux identities was over 10,000. She conceded there were many more but moved beyond the investigation's counting phase to understand how these identities could be legitimate in all government systems, including the IRS's. Elizabeth Sanders found Mouse Trap's real estate holdings in all 50 states and over 30 foreign countries. Ben Gossett alternated between being impressed and terrified as he worked to unravel the accounting mechanisms Mouse Trap used to make everything the team had found appear to be completely legal. They all agreed they had never worked on a case remotely close to Task Force Terracotta.

"Hey, guys, did IT move our folder? I'm not finding anything on the J drive," Elizabeth Sanders quizzed.

"Everything was there last night, but I haven't logged on this morning," Lucy Cross replied.

"Yeah, I just checked too; and I can't find anything

either," Billy Murdoch declared.

"I'll call IT and see what's going on." Elizabeth dialed the speaker phone in the middle of the conference room table.

"You have reached the Federal Bureau of Investigation Information Technology Department. Please listen closely as our menu has changed."

Ben Gossett shook his head. "They know this is an internal helpline, right?"

"If you already have a ticket, please enter it now. If you are calling regarding help with your cell phone, press one. For help with a password, press two…"

"Crud, just press zero!" Ben exclaimed.

Elizabeth obliged.

"Thank you for calling the FBI helpdesk. This is Todd. Do you have a ticket number?"

"No, Todd, if we had a ticket number, we would have entered it when the recording *asked* if we had a ticket number," Ben smirked.

"Shhh." Elizabeth waved her arms at Ben. "No, we don't have a ticket number."

"OK, can I have your badge number and the number on your PC barcode?"

"Yes, it is—" Elizabeth started.

"Hey, Todd, can we bypass all the usual stuff. We just have a quick question," Ben muttered.

"I'm sorry; I can't proceed without—"

"Great!" Ben interrupted. "Todd, we just need to know if there's a shared drive named J drive on the Criminal

Enterprise Branch server. It used to have a folder on it named Terracotta. We just need to know where that folder was moved to. It was there last night and gone this morning."

"I really need your badge—"

"This is your chance, Todd; this is your chance to break free," Ben chirped. "Put down that IT script and show us what Todd is capable of doing."

"I can't."

"With that attitude, you can't. Todd, I think Dr. Seuss said it best, 'You have brains in your head. You have feet in your shoes. You can steer yourself any direction you choose.'"

"You know, we would have our answer by now if we had just given him our badge number," Elizabeth scolded.

The team heard a deep huff on the phone followed by a brief pause. "Did you say the *J* drive?"

"Yep, the *J* drive."

"I'm not finding a folder named Terracotta."

"Yeah, that's the point; we're not finding it either," Ben moaned. "We need to know where it is."

"Just a second." The team could hear the sound of a keyboard clicking in the background. "There's no folder named Terracotta anywhere on the server."

"That doesn't make sense; it was there last night."

"I looked at the backup file from the last two nights, and there's nothing named Terracotta. Anything else I can help you with?"

"You didn't help us with that," Ben quipped.

"No, nothing else. Thank you for checking," Elizabeth closed.

"Thank you for calling FBI IT. After the call, there will be a short survey—" Ben hit the speakerphone button to end the call.

"Anyone else have a bad feeling about this?" Billy Murdoch asked.

"And Thomas is late for a meeting. Something definitely feels wrong," Lucy confirmed.

"What should we do?" Elizabeth asked.

Before anyone could answer, the conference room's phone rang.

"Hey, maybe Todd found the folder," Ben proclaimed. He pushed the button to answer. "Did you find it, Todd?"

"Yes, this is Director Thompson. Is this the Task Force Terracotta room?"

Ben's face turned white as the other three shot him angry stares.

"Oh, yes sir, it is. I'm sorry; we were just on the phone with IT, and we thought they were calling back."

Ignoring the apology, Thompson continued in a clearly concerned tone. "Is the full team there?"

"Almost. Thomas Hanover hasn't arrived yet, but he should be here any minute."

"That's what I need to speak with the team about. Stay put. I will be there shortly."

"You're coming here to meet with us personally, sir?" Billy asked.

"Yes, please stay put. I'll be right there."

"Yes sir, we'll be here."

Thompson hung up the phone. The team sat in stunned

silence for a moment. Of the four team members, three had never met the Director of the FBI. Ben Gossett had only met him on the basketball court. For the FBI Director to personally meet with a staff-level team was abnormal and only served to further raise the team's suspicions.

"Surely this morning can't get any more bizarre." Ben Gossett, and the rest of Task Force Terracotta, was about to learn just how wrong he was.

"Javier, I need to go to the yard for a moment."

The guard opened Victor's cell door and led him down a hallway and out a side door to a small exercise yard.

He walked a few steps away from the guard and dialed his cell phone. "Yes, Andrei. How did this morning go? Excellent. I too am glad that Blackforce is operational again. I will be in touch soon."

Victor put the cell phone back in his pocket and walked back to the guard.

"OK, Javier, I'm ready to go back."

"I want to thank you for agreeing to meet with me on such short notice," Thompson began. "I'm afraid I must share some very troubling news."

The team sat in rapt attention.

"Earlier this morning, the Capitol Police responded to a

report of a body found in Columbia Heights. Based on the identification found on the body, they called the Bureau. It is with deep regret that I must share with you that the body has been confirmed to be that of Thomas Hanover."

The team gasped in unison; no one knew what to say.

"I understand this is a shock to each of you."

"Columbia Heights? That's a rough part of town. I assume there must have been a carjacking." Ben Gossett was the first to speak.

Thompson hung his head, unsure how to continue. "We're still working through the details." Then he nodded as if convincing himself to share more. "You were his team, so I feel obligated to share some pertinent information with you. I hope you understand this is Bureau sensitive and cannot be shared outside of this room."

All nodded in agreement, unsure where this conversation was going.

"We've recently come find that Thomas had been struggling with addiction. Apparently, it had been going on for some time, maybe a few years."

Ben laughed incredulously. "Thomas? No way, you gotta be wrong."

"He did an admirable job hiding it; but like so many in this country, he was addicted to opioids. He was found in an alley behind a known drug house. He had OD'd. The call was made by a known prostitute, who admitted spending the early morning hours with Thomas."

"Director, this is all wrong. Prostitutes? Drug house? Opioid addiction? This is not Thomas Hanover," Ben insisted.

"I understand it is going to take everyone awhile to process this news. It is a shock to me as well. Agents are visiting with Thomas' family now. They are going to be discreet with some of the details, but we know this is going to hit them the hardest," Thompson agreed.

Before other team members could speak, Thompson rose from his chair. "I'm so sorry to have to share this news with you. Remember, this information can't leave this room. I hope you understand that I need to return to my office since this is an active case involving a senior Bureau leader."

All nodded in understanding as Thompson shook each team member's hand before leaving the room.

"There's something bad, bad wrong here," Ben Gossett spoke ominously to the team.

"I...I don't even know what to say," Lucy stammered.

"We would have known if our boss was on opioids, right?" Billy offered.

"I worked in narcotics for four years. I would like to think I would have known," Lucy affirmed.

Working to put the pieces together in his mind, Ben hoped they would make more sense if expressed out loud.

"Let me summarize this situation. Thomas Hanover leads...well, led...an FBI investigation into one of the largest criminal organizations in the world. As we began unravelling their activities, Thomas visited the leader in prison and got important information that he had planned to share with us this morning. But before he could make it into the office, this clean-cut, drive-the-speed-limit, career FBI guy was found dead behind a drug house in Columbia Heights. That sound fishy to anyone else?"

"Don't forget, all of our evidence files against this criminal organization have mysteriously vanished. Yeah, I'd say *fishy* is a fair word to use," Billy concurred.

Before anyone else could speak, the door to the conference room opened and an aide announced, "Director Thompson called an all-hands meeting in the conference room starting in three minutes."

No one wanted to move.

"We're on our way," Ben responded.

All four looked at one another, but no one spoke a word. Finally, Ben turned to leave the room followed by the other three.

"I just had a really bad feeling." Lucy gulped. "What if we're next?"

41

"Javier, the captain would like to speak with you in the office."

Startled, the guard stood at attention. "Is there a problem, sir?"

"That'll be all, Javier."

The frightened guard managed a muted "yes sir" and walked away, briefly looking over his shoulder in the direction of the cell.

The warden had come to the maximum-security wing with three guards accompanying him.

"Open it," the warden commanded. A guard complied. Two guards entered the cell before the warden; stood the prisoner on his feet; and nodded all clear for the warden, who stepped into the now-crowded cell.

With equal parts anger and disgust, the warden said, "Thomas Hanover was my friend."

"Hanover? Was that the gentleman who visited me

yesterday?" Victor wondered.

The warden ignored Victor's mock question.

"You think you're getting away with this; but if it takes my dying breath to bring you to ultimate justice, I will see that it is done."

Victor didn't respond.

"Check his pants."

The guards frisked Victor and found the cell phone, holding it up for the warden to see.

The warden took a step toward the guard and grabbed it from his hand. He then shoved it in Victor's face.

"This is it. This is the end of your liberty, the end of you running your enterprise right under the nose of the federal government. I suspect this is going to tie you to much more than Thomas Hanover."

Again, Victor remained stoic.

Motioning for the guards to return Victor to his bed, the warden turned to leave and then turned back to Victor lamenting, "Thomas Hanover was a good man. He had a wife, four kids, and two grandchildren."

As the warden watched the cell door close, he saw a wry haunting smile that would be etched into his mind for the rest of his life, however long that might be.

"Welcome to Prince's Hardware. Chip said you asked to see me." As a duo turned around to face Jeremy, his mouth dropped open as his mind worked hard to process the out-of-context signals it was receiving.

"We need to talk."

"Ben? Lucy? What are you doing here?" As Jeremy's mind raced to catch up, he noticed the pair's disheveled appearance. "You two look awful."

"Have you heard about Thomas Hanover?" Ben asked ominously.

Jeremy nodded, thinking he understood the purpose of the unexpected visit. "Oh, I see. Thomas sent you. Look, I'm going to tell you the same thing I told him; I'm done with moonlighting for the FBI. I have a life here in Abingdon. I'm happy with the life we're making here. I'm not coming back."

"So, obviously you haven't heard," Lucy stammered.

Jeremy cocked his head and looked confused. "Haven't heard *what?*"

Ben and Lucy realized they hadn't decided who would explain to Jeremy the unraveling situation, and neither could find the words to speak.

In the awkward silence, Jeremy took a step away from the duo. "You guys are acting weird. Just tell me what's going on."

Ben managed to start the conversation. "Thomas is… dead."

Jeremy now became the one struggling to find the words. "He's…*what?*"

"He's dead. He was found yesterday morning," Lucy announced.

"Found? Where?" Jeremy mumbled.

Ben explained, "In an area of D.C. called Columbia Heights. It is a rough part of town."

"So, was he carjacked or something?"

"That's what makes a terrible situation even worse. We were told that he drove there himself and OD'd and that his death was called in by a prostitute."

Jeremy involuntarily chuckled. "OD'd? A prostitute? You guys are joking, right? We're talking about Thomas Hanover. That dude is as straight as the equator."

"I wish we were joking. Thomas wasn't just the team lead; he's been my mentor for over 10 years." Ben shook his head in disbelief.

Jeremy raised both hands in protest. "Here's why this doesn't make sense. I just spoke with Thomas night before last. He was on his way home from meeting with—" Before Jeremy could utter his next words, his mouth dropped open while blood quickly drained from his face.

"Victor Youngblood?" Lucy finished his sentence.

Taking a couple of steps away from Ben and Lucy, Jeremy turned his back to them. "I told him to be careful," Jeremy mumbled to himself. He then turned quickly back to his visitors. "*I told him to be careful!* I really did!"

"No one was more careful than Thomas," Ben confirmed.

"Now you guys have to be careful." Realizing he was part of 'you guys,' Jeremy corrected himself, "*We* have to be careful!"

"That's another reason we are here." Lucy took a step toward Jeremy, speaking in a hushed tone. "We don't know what to do. Do we go up the chain with this story? Do we keep the team going ourselves? Do we—"

"You lay low," Jeremy warned. "Don't do anything unless you are asked to do it. If they tell you to keep the task force going, you keep it going. If they tell you to stand down, you stand down. If you didn't understand what Victor is capable of, I am sure you do now."

"But we can't just sit back and let this happen. We owe it to Thomas to see this through," Ben objected.

"You are already in danger. *We* are already in danger. You gotta lay low. You gotta go back to D.C. Go back to your offices, act normal, and do what you're told," Jeremy cautioned.

"But—"

"Lay *low!*"

"I think I almost have Michigan fully connected. I need to run a few more tests; but I've been able to connect to the Treasury, Education, Agriculture and to the state police. I was in and out, and I confirmed Omnia was undetected." Cassidy Ramirez was assigned to assist Leonard with getting Omnia fully back online. One of Omnia's many capabilities was to find a back door into any computer system connected to the Internet. Leonard developed a program that would examine a computer system, determine who had the highest access rights, and replicate and retain that individual's login protocol. Upon logout, the program would remove any digital footprint indicating that the login ever happened.

Before Mouse Trap was disbanded and Omnia was shut down, the system had access to every department in the federal government, the governments of all 50 states, most major corporations, and every prominent private system in existence. After Omnia was shut down for almost a year, the logins had to be replicated.

"With Michigan, that's 31 states reconnected," Cassidy Ramirez continued.

Never looking up from his computer, Leonard began mumbling, "I didn't ask for any help. I didn't need any help. Why would they give me a big new office only to put someone in here with me? I'd rather be in my smaller old office and by myself."

"I'm sorry you feel that way," Cassidy exclaimed.

"I...wwwwasn't talking to you," Leonard stuttered.

Cassidy got up from her desk and walked over to Leonard's. "Leonard, I really am here to help." She leaned in to look over his shoulder at the computer screen. "What are you working on?"

Leonard shook his head nervously. "Just computer stuff."

"Is that the comms app?" Cassidy asked, pointing to Leonard's monitor.

Leonard quickly hit the Windows L keys to lock his screen.

"Don't you have something to do?" Leonard grimaced.

Cassidy nodded and acquiesced, walking back to her workstation. "I really am just here to help."

Cassidy was speaking the truth; however, she left out one

detail in her proclamation: exactly *whom* she was helping.

Washington Post – September 4, 2017

FBI MANAGER FOUND DEAD IN COLUMBIA HEIGHTS

D.C. police said the body of 59-year-old Thomas Hanover of McClean, Virginia, was found in the courtyard of an apartment complex in the 1100 block of Columbia Road NW in Columbia Heights.

At about 6:27 a.m., police responded to a report of a body being found. D.C. Fire and Emergency Medical Services personnel who arrived at the apartment complex determined Hanover was dead at the scene.

Hanover was the chief of the FBI's Criminal Enterprise Branch. The Bureau has not commented regarding whether Hanover was in the area investigating on the Bureau's behalf.

Sources have told the Post that Hanover was struggling with substance abuse and may have been in the area to purchase narcotics when the deal went bad. When asked about that report, the Bureau again declined to comment.

As Chief of the Criminal Enterprise Branch, Hanover led over 300 FBI employees responsible for investigations involving financial, organized, public, and drug-related crimes.

$\mathcal{Q}$

"Am I supposed to know Thomas Hanover?" President Mc-Coy asked, placing the newspaper on the Resolute Desk.

"Not personally, sir, but you should know that he was leading Task Force Terracotta, the Bureau team spearheading the Youngblood investigation," Riley Indigo reported ominously.

"Youngblood? Holy crap, Riley, you can't be serious." The President bowed his head and ran his fingers through his mousse-doused hair.

"I'm afraid there's more, sir."

McCoy stood and began pacing around the Oval Office like a cheetah prowling in a cage. "I told you...I told you I wanted a daily report on this, and it's been three or four days since I've heard anything about Youngblood." McCoy had now worked himself into an even greater lather. "Holy Mother of God."

"As I said, sir, there's more."

"Spit it out, Riley!" the President demanded.

"The day before Hanover's body was found, he visited Youngblood in prison. Reports are the exchange was quite tense."

"Prison? But Youngblood's in that maximum-security facility in where ... Utah?"

"Colorado, sir, ADX Florence. Youngblood is serving a life sentence."

"You're not suggesting Youngblood had anything to do with this agent's death, are you? The paper said there was no foul play suspected."

"Actually, the paper said the Bureau stated foul play was not suspected," Riley corrected.

"Quit playing games with me, Riley. Was there foul play or not?" McCoy barked.

"We're not sure, sir; but the signs are not good."

McCoy was still pacing frantically as his wheels continued spinning. "What about me? There's no way anyone could tie any of this to me, right?"

"Mr. President, do you recall our last discussion of a *Times* reporter asking about potential illegal donations to your campaign?"

"Of course, I remember that. *That's* what you and Director Thompson were supposed to be briefing me about daily!"

"That reporter has begun connecting some dots. He says he can trace the donations to Youngblood-affiliated entities."

McCoy ranted, "This is out of control, Riley; this is *completely* out of freaking control. Get Thompson in here now! I want the whole story."

"I understand, sir; but Director Thompson is in the Brussels meeting with his counterpart in Europol. He won't be back in the States until tomorrow evening."

"Damnit, Riley, I want to see both of you the minute he arrives; I don't care how late it is. Tell him not to stop to take a piss before he comes over to meet with me."

"Yes sir. We will see you tomorrow evening."

42

"All you're taking is a backpack? Are you sure you have enough clothes packed? You know we're going to be gone for ten days, right?"

"Yeah, Dad, I have enough clothes. They have washing machines in New Zealand, you know."

Henry Polivick started a tradition three kids and seven years ago. Upon graduating high school, each kid selected the destination of their choice for a one-on-one trip with their father. Henry's career in the Federal Bureau of Prisons often called for long days, business travel, and late-night phone calls. It was a career that brought Henry pride, but also regret that he wasn't always the father he wished he could be. Therefore, he was motivated to make these trips memorable.

This particular trip caused Henry a moment of reflection. Grant was his fourth and final child. Rebecca chose Maui. Shawn had requested a 10-day golfing trip in Scotland.

Valarie, an animal lover, had opted for a safari in Kenya. Each trip had brought lifelong memories and served as a first step into adulthood.

"Are you ready, Grant?"

"Ready, Dad."

While packing the car, Henry failed to notice the black SUV driving slowly down his street.

"OK, let's get going."

"Dad, are you expecting anyone?"

Grant was the first to see the SUV stop in front of the house, blocking the driveway.

Henry turned to see the vehicle. "No, I'm not."

A man in a dark suit got out of the back of the SUV and approached the duo.

"Mr. Polivick?"

"Yes?"

"I'm agent Cliff Vickery with the FBI. There's been an incident at Florence that we need to discuss with you."

"An incident? What kind of incident?" Henry grumbled.

"It's not something we can discuss here."

"Well, it's going to have to wait. I'm going to be on a plane in three hours, and I will be out of the country for the next ten days."

"I'm sorry, sir; we need to speak with you now." The agent gestured toward an open SUV door.

Becoming angry, Henry resolutely responded, "I'm not going with you or speaking with you until I return from my trip." Henry looked at Grant. "Go ahead and hop in the car, Son. I'll be right with you."

"Sir, I'm afraid—"

Henry took a step toward the agent. "Get back in your SUV and get out of my driveway!I have a plane to catch!"

The agent took out his cell phone and dialed a number. "Yes, he is refusing to come. I understand."

The agent handed the phone to Henry.

"Who is it?"

"It's the Director." The agent was referring to the Director of the Bureau of Prisons, Henry's bosses', bosses', boss.

"Yes, this is Henry Polivick." Henry walked away from the agent. "Sir, I understand; but I have had this trip planned for over a year. It has been on my leave schedule. I'm sorry, sir; I'm not going to cancel this trip. OK, sir, then I resign. Yes, I'm serious; I resign. I'm sorry too, but that's my choice. Yes, that's my final answer."

Henry handed the phone back to the agent, who put the phone to his ear. "Yes, sir, I understand."

The agent walked back to the SUV, reached into the front seat, and sifted through three envelopes before selecting one with a small letter "c" in the lower corner. He then walked back toward Henry and presented him the envelope.

"Have a good day, sir."

The agent got back into the car and drove away.

Curious, Henry opened the envelope.

I'm told you have a wife and four kids. I was feeling unusually generous, otherwise this could have ended differently. Enjoy your retirement.

VY

Henry folded the letter into fourths, walked to his garage, placed the envelope and letter in a trash can, then walked back and got into the driver's seat.

"OK, Grant, let's head to the airport. We have a plane to catch."

"Hey, Mom, do you know if..." Jeremy stopped in the doorway to the office, noticing his mom holding a photo of his late father.

"I'm sorry, Mom, I didn't mean to barge in."

"It's OK, Jeremy. It's just...well...sometimes I miss Walter more than others. This is one of those times."

"I understand, Mom. I miss him too. He was a great dad. He always made time for me."

"He loved being your dad more than anything."

Jeremy's conscience quickly went into debate mode. While this conversation was the perfect segue for the subject Jeremy wished to discuss with his mom, he feared it could also be construed as manipulating her raw emotions. He opted to tread lightly.

"He was my baseball coach, Scout leader, homework specialist, and ski instructor."

A smile grew on Rosita's face as she continued to stare at the photo. "He was all of those things and more. And he knew how to have fun."

Another segue, another step toward Jeremy's subject.

"I loved our trips to Smith Mountain Lake, especially when they weren't planned way in advance. I remember Dad would pick me up from school on Fridays and the three of us would go straight from school to the lake. What great memories!"

"Yes, they were, Jeremy."

"Say, Mom, did Dad ever sell the houseboat?"

It was the question Jeremy had come to ask in the first place. He just felt slimy for asking it in the midst of his mom's reminiscing.

"You know, I hadn't thought about that boat since Walter passed. Yes, we still have it. We didn't go to the lake very often after you went to college, but Walter could never part with it. As you said, it brought back so many great memories."

The conversation seemed to snap Rosita out of her melancholy and brought a smile to her face.

"I know you didn't come into the office to talk about Walter and boats. What did you want to ask?"

Little did she know, that's *exactly* what Jeremy came to discuss; but he quickly changed the subject.

"I just wanted to make sure we had ordered a shipment of ladders. We only have a few left."

"Yes, Jeremy, I ordered them last week."

"Sounds great, Mom."

Mission accomplished.

FBI Director Gavin Thompson entered the Oval Office, eyes bloodshot and back sore after two long days of meetings bracketed by eight-hour transatlantic flights, the most recent ending just minutes earlier.

"Where have you been?!" McCoy demanded.

Thompson looked at Riley Indigo as if to say, "I thought you told him where I was."

In response, Riley just shrugged and said, "I was in Brussels, sir, meeting with my EU counterpart."

Ignoring the response, McCoy launched, "This situation is completely out of control. We need to figure out how to get it back in the box, and I mean *tonight*!"

Anger and outrage—exactly the reactions Riley was hoping to elicit. He was ready to pour even more fuel on the already raging fire.

"Which situation, sir?" Thompson asked, knowing exactly the situation to which the President was referring.

"*Which* situation?" the President screamed, then turned to Riley. "I thought you briefed him!"

"Gavin, this is the matter involving the Youngblood donations possibly now complicated by Agent Hanover's death," Riley calmly explained.

"Oh, yes, of course." Thompson then turned back to the President. "I'm sorry, sir. We have so many pressing matters to discuss. In Brussels, Europol is concerned about a growing threat from—."

"I don't care about Brussels, Europol, or any threat," the President interrupted. "I want to know everything we have on your agent's death and if it can be traced to Youngblood."

"And if it can be traced to *you?*" a tired Director Thompson asked. Out of the corner of his eye, he noticed Riley mouthing, "Not yet."

"Exactly!" McCoy instinctively proclaimed, not recognizing his response's egocentric nature.

"Mr. President, I hope you'll understand if Gavin is not fully briefed on this subject. He's been in Europe for the last three days." Looking at his watch, Riley added, "It's approaching midnight."

"It's OK, Riley. On the plane, I read the report on Thomas' death; so, I do have a contemporary status."

"Well, spit it out! What does the report say?" McCoy demanded.

"Hanover was a stellar agent and an impeccable leader. He was also a devoted family man. His reputation is in direct contrast to the circumstances surrounding his death. As you know, his body was found in a rough part of the District by individuals you wouldn't expect him to associate with."

"Yes, yes! Riley has told me all about what a stellar professional Hanover was. Was Youngblood involved *or not?*" McCoy was now pleading.

"We did find surveillance video showing a black SUV following Hanover's vehicle the morning of his death. We got a partial plate and traced it to a business entity owned by Victor Youngblood. We also interviewed three people from the neighborhood where he was found. Two of them say they saw a man we confirmed had known affiliations with Youngblood. Although not enough yet to prosecute, the circumstantial evidence seems to overwhelmingly suggest

Youngblood's involvement."

"Oh, this is bad. This is really bad, Riley!"

Riley was impressed by his FBI colleague's performance, given that every scintilla of information he shared was completely fabricated. Now it was Riley's chance to turn the crank even tighter.

"I'm afraid I have more information, sir. Over the last couple of days, the media inquiries into your involvement with Youngblood have been increasing. The editor of the *New York Times* asked for an interview with you; they are publishing a story about Youngblood in the next day or two and want to give you an opportunity to comment."

"The *Times*? What kind of story? They were on our side throughout the campaign. Why are they turning on me now?" McCoy quivered.

"They wouldn't share any details, sir. I told them we didn't comment on speculation and innuendo."

"This is bad, Riley," McCoy repeated.

"Yes sir, we are approaching the worst-case scenario."

McCoy plopped down in his chair, hands on his cheeks, unconsciously making a fish face.

Riley was energized as this exchange was going exactly as he had intended although he knew he had to maintain a stoic demeanor.

"I have an idea, sir. Give me a day or so to assemble an inner circle who will serve as a crisis response team to covertly develop both a strategy and messaging. I believe this situation can be managed if we have the right people involved."

"Fine." McCoy waved a hand. "And whatever you do,

Riley, keep this out of the paper!"

"Yes sir. We will have a plan in place shortly."

With that last statement, McCoy and Thompson let themselves out of the Oval Office.

As the door shut, both men nodded in knowing agreement.

43

J eremy left Abingdon at 6 a.m. He knew he couldn't
share this adventure with Rosita or Savannah, so his
cover story was a meeting with the main owner of a fami-
ly-owned hardware store in Roanoke to discuss a potential
partnering arrangement to help the smaller stores compete
with the national home improvement giants. To avoid having to live with an outright lie, Jeremy met with Bell Hardware in Roanoke, where he and the owner commiserated
about the growing difficulty small-town stores were having
in staying afloat. Jeremy and the owner agreed they should
continue exploring ways to help one another.

With his conscience at least partially assuaged, Jeremy left Roanoke continuing southeast, navigating a series
of state and local highways before ultimately turning onto
Crystal Shores Drive. The Marina at Crystal Shores was largely unchanged from his last visit, which his best recollection
told him was approximately four years earlier.

Situated on Smith Mountain Lake, the Marina was created in the 1960s when Appalachian Power constructed a dam on the Roanoke River. Although the primary purpose was to provide affordable hydroelectric power to the region, Smith Mountain Lake quickly became one of Virginia's top recreational refuges. The 40-mile-long lake covers 22,000 acres, with its numerous fingers and coves creating 500 miles of shoreline. Over 20,000 residents call the area home. It held a special place in Jeremy's memory with summers filled with family, friends, food, and fishing.

The Prince's home at the lake was The Hammer, a 60-foot three-level houseboat. The lower level included four separate bedrooms, each boasting a queen bed. The middle level consisted of two more bedrooms, a large living room, a dining room, a full kitchen, two baths, and a shower. The upper level included a captain's flybridge and a large lounge area.

Jeremy knew his dad was a frugal, no-frills man. He always drove a pickup truck with at least 100,000 miles. His wardrobe was from the "50% off lowest ticketed price" rack. He took a bologna and American cheese sandwich for lunch every day. His one out-of-character splurge was The Hammer. Purchased in the late '90s when the store had three consecutive record-profit years, the houseboat was a wonderful family getaway. Two-and-a-half hours from Abingdon, it was far enough away to feel as if they were going on a trip, but close enough to enjoy over a weekend.

As Jeremy inserted the key into the boat's rear door, he felt an unexpected knot in his stomach. He wasn't sure if this discomfort's source was the memories of his dad, the uncertainty of what he might find inside the boat that had been undisturbed for over two years, or the precarious scheme on which he was about to embark.

He swallowed hard, then turned the knob. As he stepped inside, he detected a tinge of a musty smell. He flipped on a light and found the main level in good condition. Walking downstairs, he found the four bedrooms also intact. Up on the top deck, he walked toward the captain's chair and paused for a moment remembering that his father was happiest in this chair when Jeremy would sit on his lap and steer the boat. He told himself he didn't have time for reminiscing; there was work to be done.

Jeremy started by checking the boat's electrical system. Except for a couple of burned-out light bulbs, everything was in good working order. Then he checked the satellite system to ensure the coaxial cabling was working. Again, he was thrilled to find the TV was also in good working order. He went back to his truck for the equipment Leonard had instructed him to buy. Four trips later, the living room floor was filled with boxes. He then took out Leonard's detailed instructions.

Step one was to remove the existing satellite dish and replace it with the new device. Reading the box labeled *KVH TracPhone V11-IP Mini VSAT System*, he shook his head wondering how something so small could cost $60,000. It was the largest single purchase in this endeavor, which all-in exceeded $100,000. Jeremy tapped into his Cayman Island Mouse Trap bank account, which he had sworn he would never use. He reasoned that if there was ever a valid situation to deploy his ill-gotten gains, this undertaking was it.

Next, he followed Leonard's instruction and replaced the outdated coaxial wiring with high- speed ethernet cabling, which had added another $5,000 to the project cost. He then connected the ethernet cable to the Integrated CommBox Modem, or ICM. Lastly, he connected the ICM to a new Corsair One Pro i180 PC.

Checking Leonard's checklist, Jeremy was about to complete everything he had hoped to accomplish on this trip to the boat. Checking his phone, he saw that it was after 3 p.m. He had told Savannah and Rosita he would be home close to the 6 p.m. closing time. With a two-and-a-half-hour drive ahead of him, he didn't have much time left to waste.

Next, Jeremy powered on the PC. After the bootup routine, he followed Leonard's instruction to go to the browser Firefox. Leonard had typed in all caps, *DO NOT USE GOOGLE CHROME, SAFARI, MICROSOFT EXPLORER, OR EDGE. USE FIREFOX ONLY!* Jeremy then navigated a series of websites to test his connection. The first seven websites returned exactly what Leonard had predicted. Success! Jeremy then navigated to a secure video conferencing website, selected the conference and participant numbers, and found the intended person looking back at him on the screen.

"Can you hear me OK?" Jeremy asked.

"Loud and clear," Ben Gossett confirmed.

"Can you see me?" Jeremy peered more closely into the webcam. "Nice Hokies shirt. What kind of basketball team is

Virginia Tech going to have this year?"

Jeremy then went through a series of tests giving the participants control of the conference, shared a document on the screen, and connected Lucy Cross as a third party. All worked perfectly.

"I guess this means our little plan is a step closer to reality," Ben observed.

"Indeed, it does," Jeremy replied. "I'm running out of time and signing off."

"Roger that."

Lastly, Jeremy typed a long Internet address that Leonard had provided. He triple-checked before hitting *Enter* as the address was 24 digits and included a variety of letters—both upper and lower case, numbers, and special characters. After confirming his keystrokes, Jeremy squinted and pressed the Enter key. At speeds beyond human conceivability, the signal traveled from the PC, through the ethernet cable, to the modem, up to the VSAT system mounted on top of the boat, and finally to a satellite in geosynchronous orbit 22,236 miles into space. In less than a second, WELCOME TO OMNIA MESSENGER appeared on the screen.

Jeremy searched the address list and found his intended recipient.

Are you sure this is better than texting?

Yeah, I'm sure. It is totally secure. We have a dedicated satellite, and I have set permissions for this room to be only you and me. You can even call me Leonard, but it's also OK to keep calling me Han if you want.

Sounds good, Leonard.

You saw the part that it's OK to keep calling me Han, right?

Yep. So…anyway, I made it to the boat. Your instructions worked perfectly. All sites connected, and I was able to make a video conference call.

Did you try tying in a third party on the video?

Yes, it worked great. Everything is a go!

I need to head back home so that Savannah and mom don't get worried. Are you still safe?

Yeah, I'm good. They've given me an assistant who is a pain in the butt; however, everything is good overall. You still OK with this plan?

Not really, but it is the best we have. Let's move to the next step.

I'm in, Jeremy.

Me too, Leonard…I mean, Han.

When Mouse Trap was disbanded after Victor's arrest, the organization's unfathomable assets had to be quickly dispositioned such that they would be disassociated from Victor but efficiently retrievable when the appropriate time came. That retrieval had been in full swing for over four months with over 75% of the assets back in Mouse Trap's control. Among the leadership's most treasured assets was the Bombardier Challenger 650 jet. The luxury plane accommodated 12 passengers and had a range of 4,000 miles with speeds of Mach 0.85, or over 650 miles per hour.

With the plane now back in the Mouse Trap family, Zeke Gibson volunteered to be the first to take it on its rechristened maiden flight. Originating at College Park Maryland, a short drive from Mouse Trap headquarters in Bethesda, the plane arrived at Fremont County Airport, five miles north of Florence ADX.

"Good afternoon, old friend. It is good to see your face."

Victor walked toward the center of the prison yard to embrace his friend. Since Warden Polivick's 'retirement,' Victor was again in possession of his cell phone and was at liberty to go where he wanted, ensuring no guard followed him in the yard.

"You are looking well, Victor," Zeke observed, grasping his friend's arms, "especially for a man of advanced age subjected to solitary confinement in America's most secure prison."

Victor cocked his head. "Advanced age? You know, I'm

younger than you, right?"

"Yeah, you've reminded me of that every day over the past 40 years."

"It's still as true today as it was when we met."

Victor took a step away from his friend, signaling he was ready to move on to the business at hand.

"We're nearing the end of this phase of the mission. You're probably sensing in me a mix of satisfaction for a plan coming to fruition and excitement to reunite with our team."

Zeke hadn't seen his boss this happy in years. Over the last 11 months Victor had endured jail, a well-publicized trial, a conviction, and a life sentence in a maximum-security federal prison. Finally, this nightmare was only days away from being over.

"Everything is going according to plan back at headquarters. Omnia is back online, our team is almost at full strength, and our assets are being restored. All we need is our leader back at the helm."

"Riley has everything ready?" Victor questioned.

"Everything is ready. The call will be in two days."

"Good. I assumed you came in the Bombardier?"

"I did. I wanted to make sure it was still working properly before my boss rides in it."

Victor smiled. "What a professional. I've always known you to be willing to make sacrifices for the cause."

"And besides, I'm a 78-year-old man, emphasis on *old*. I can't be flying around the country commercial."

"Ah, now the truth comes out," Victor teased.

"OK, let's go over these final plans one more time. We've made it to the one-yard line; now we just have to punch it in for the touchdown."

"How about pizza for dinner!" Jeremy walked into the hardware store office at 6:30, 30 minutes after closing, with a large pepperoni pizza in hand.

"Oh, that's way better than the Captain Crunch I was planning on eating," Savannah responded as she hugged Jeremy.

"How was Roanoke?" Rosita asked, looking up from her desk.

"It was great. I met with Jerry Bell from Bell's Hardware. Like us, they are a single store trying to compete with the giants. Like us, they have struggles with cash flow, inventory, and credit lines. We both agreed it was just the beginning of the conversation, we plan to meet regularly to find ways to help each other survive. I think this relationship can really be good for the store."

"That's great! I'm glad you met with him," Rosita affirmed.

"Yeah, me too, Mom. But enough shop talk. I'm hungry; let's eat."

44

"Any idea why we're here?" Cassidy Ramirez wondered.

Leonard exhaled an exasperated sigh. "You got the same email I got. *Come to the auditorium for an important meeting.* That's all it said."

"I just thought maybe you had heard something from Zeke or one of the managers."

Leonard shook his head without making eye contact with Cassidy. "You've been with me literally every minute since you've been working here. If I had heard something, you would have heard it too."

As Mouse Trap grew, Victor needed to continually upgrade the Bethesda headquarters to accommodate a larger staff. One such upgrade was an 800-seat auditorium, completed in 2012. Victor was an inspirational leader, and he knew the importance of all-hands gatherings to keep the team motivated and focused. Before his incarceration, Victor held monthly team meetings as well as occasional specially called meetings in the auditorium.

Since Mouse Trap's reconstitution, this was the first time Zeke Gibson had called the entire team together and the first time the auditorium had been used. He knew today's announcement was a perfect fit for such a gathering.

Although he was never the captivating showman Victor was, Zeke's age and experience commanded the entire team's respect. He ascended the stage to respectful applause, which he quieted quickly with an acknowledging gesture. As he began to speak, Zeke had the team's full attention as all yearned to know why they had been assembled.

"What a gathering. Look around this room. Almost every seat is filled. Just a year ago, Mouse Trap had been disbanded. We all were forced to go our separate ways. We all assumed that was the end. That the organization that Victor so methodically built had come to an inauspicious end. But we should have known better. We should have known that Victor Youngblood would not go away that easily. But we'll discuss Victor in a few moments. For now, let's recap the incredible work you have done.

"We started this rebuilding effort five months ago in a small cabin in the mountains of North Carolina. We had six people show up for that first meeting. As of this morning, 87% of our staff is back at work; 77% of our field assets are reengaged; and 94% of Omnia's capabilities are back online."

Although he understood his true role in returning to Mouse Trap was the exact opposite of seeing the organization operational again, Leonard couldn't fully suppress a satisfied grin at the work he had done to restart Omnia—especially the Trojan horses that he would deploy at just the right time.

"Although in the past 40 years, Mouse Trap has had accomplishments beyond comprehension, I honestly believe our best days are still ahead of us. Let me explain why. The rest of the meeting will be Level 1 Classified."

With those words, the assembly in unison powered down cell phones, tablets, and laptops. One maxim in any Mouse Trap endeavor was absolute secrecy. It was understood that all discussions at or about Mouse Trap didn't leave the walls of Mouse Trap. The consequences of breaching this policy were as well understood as they were lethal. Taking that secrecy to the next level, Level 1 Classified meant the topic couldn't be discussed *within* Mouse Trap's walls and that all electronic devices were to be turned off before hearing a Level 1 Classified discussion.

After allowing sufficient time for devices to be powered down, Zeke continued.

"I know that you all followed with great interest the legal proceedings surrounding our leader and founder, Victor Youngblood. And I know that you are aware he was sentenced to life in prison without the possibility of parole in the nation's highest security prison, ADX Florence. I have good news for you. I returned yesterday from visiting Victor, and I can tell you he's in good health and great spirits. He sends each of you his best regards."

The news brought enthusiastic applause from the assembly.

"Now, I have even better news. Within a short period of time, likely a matter of days, Victor will be cleared of all charges; be released from prison; and will return to us, right here at Mouse Trap, where he will once again take his rightful place at the helm of the greatest and most powerful organization the world has never known. Victor is coming home!!"

After a loud collective gasp, the assembly leapt from their seats, screaming, and cheering with some wiping tears from their eyes. The celebration continued for another 15 minutes as Zeke walked into the audience and shook hands with as many team members as he could.

The meeting went even better than Zeke had dreamed. He knew the team respected Victor, but the response to Zeke's announcement was beyond respect; it demonstrated true adoration, exactly what Victor expected.

"Everything good, Mr. Youngblood?" The guard asked, noticing Victor smiling broadly and wiping a tear from his face.

Victor had watched the entire proceedings on his cell phone via live video streaming that Zeke arranged. He was overwhelmed by his team's response, and his heart raced with the thought of soon rejoining them.

"Everything is great, Javier. Thank you for asking."

"Have a nice evening, Mr. Youngblood."

"You too, Javier."

Can you chat?

As Jeremy was helping a customer in the paint section, he heard the distinctive ring tone he had assigned to Omnia Messenger. He hailed another store employee to assist the customer as he walked quickly back to the solitude of his office.

Yeah, I'm here.

Just got out of a crazy meeting. You're not going to believe this. Victor's coming back.

What do you mean? Back to where?

Back here, to Mouse Trap.

That's not possible, Leonard. He's serving a life sentence in a federal prison for murder. He's not coming back to Mouse Trap.

Jeremy, he's coming back. I don't know how, but Zeke just made a Level 1 Classified announcement to the full team. He said he's coming back.

Just as Leonard hit the enter key to send his message, he was startled by a voice coming from just over his shoulder.

"What are you doing? That was a Level 1 Classified meeting. We're not supposed to be talking with anyone about that," Cassidy insisted.

Lurching from his seat, Leonard quickly turned his head to face Cassidy.

"Dddddon't ever sneak up on me like that!" Leonard stuttered.

"I wasn't sneaking," Cassidy protested.

Trying to end the conversation, Leonard responded offensively, "I have a Level 1 Clearance, and you don't. What are you doing looking at my screen?"

"What was that you were typing in? It didn't look like Omnia Messenger."

"I repeat—What are you doing looking at my screen?"

"I came to ask you a question and I just—"

"Have you reconnected Omnia to the State of Michigan Education Department?"

"No."

"Have you reconnected to the Strategic Petroleum Reserve?"

"No."

"Then get back to work; and if you make progress, maybe I won't report you to security for unauthorized access to Level 1 Classified communications."

Cassidy bit her lip, walked back to her desk, and muttered under her breath, "*Fine.*"

Hey, Leonard, you still there?

Yeah, sorry, had a brief interruption. Anyway, that's the news. Victor is coming back to Mouse Trap.

I don't see how, but I'll see what I can find out. Take care, Leonard.

You too, Jeremy.

As Cassidy Ramirez returned to her desk, she reached for her cell phone and typed a short text.

Leonard just messaged Jeremy about Victor's return. I confronted him, and he denied it; but I saw his screen. Thought you would want to know.

"Is everyone clear about what is going to happen tomorrow?" Chief of Staff Riley Indigo looked each one in the eye.

All attendees nodded in the affirmative; attendees who included some of the most powerful men in the world including the Secretaries of State, Justice, Defense, and Commerce; the Attorney General, and Director of the FBI.

"You are going to all be right here in my office tomorrow morning by 8 a.m."

Again, all agreed.

"Do you have the newspapers?" the Secretary of State asked.

Riley nodded. "You all understand that this is what we've been planning for." Riley wanted to ensure each man in the room was fully committed. After tomorrow, there would be no turning back.

"Ready, Riley. We are all ready."

45

Mitch McCoy was a creature of habit, starting each day at 6:30 a.m. He had brought to his bedroom breakfast consisting of avocado toast, quinoa, yogurt, and a glass of kombucha. He did yoga at 7:00 a.m., showered at 7:30 a.m., and was sitting at his Oval Office desk by precisely 8:00 a.m. His desk was to include fresh Copies of the *New York Times*, *Washington Post*, and *Wall Street Journal* stacked precisely in that order each morning.

As McCoy sat behind the Resolute Desk, he breathed a deep sigh. Although his presidency hadn't had the smoothest first year, it was still an overwhelming feeling knowing he was the most powerful man in the world—or so he thought.

His first glance at the *New York Times* caused his heart to skip a beat. The *Page One* headline read,

Convicted Murderer Victor Youngblood Revealed to be McCoy's Top Donor

What?! How could this be?! McCoy quickly scanned the article that opened,

President Mitch McCoy raised $1 billion during his 2016 presidential campaign. An investigation into McCoy's donors revealed that close to $400 million was contributed by individuals and businesses with direct ties to convicted murderer Victor Youngblood.

Quickly turning to the *Washington Post* and *Wall Street Journal*, McCoy found similar headlines and articles on the cover of both. He flipped back to the *New York Times* and saw three different *Page One* articles with varying twists on the emerging scandal. One even questioned whether McCoy's election should be overturned. McCoy slouched in his chair, his heart racing, his mind searching for what to do next.

"Riley!" he screamed. "Riley!" There was no response. McCoy leapt from his chair; threw open the Oval Office door; and stumbled down the hallway to the southwest corner of the West Wing, bursting into Riley Indigo's office.

"Riley!" McCoy screamed, entering the office. Although his eyesight was blurred by terror and confusion, McCoy could see the faces of Chief of Staff Riley Indigo; the FBI Director; the Attorney General; and Secretaries of State, Justice, Defense, and Commerce staring back at him.

"Mr. President are you OK?" a concerned Riley asked.

"No! I'm not OK, Riley! I'm not OK at all!!"

Turning to the others gathered in the office, Riley

requested, "Would you gentlemen give me a minute with the President?"

The group obliged, leaving Riley and McCoy alone.

"What's wrong, sir?"

McCoy slapped the newspapers down on Riley's desk. "That's what's wrong!"

Riley scanned the newspapers. "Oh, I see. This is a problem," Riley agreed.

"*A problem!?* This is more than a problem, Riley. This could impact my presidency!"

"I see is it a—"

"I thought you were working to get this under control!" McCoy interrupted.

"It's a complicated situation."

"You're damn right it's complicated. I barely even know Victor Youngblood!"

"What do you think we should do about this, sir?"

An astonished McCoy glared at his Chief of Staff. "What do *I* think we should do about this? What do *I* think? Riley this is *your* job to do something about. In fact, it was *your* job to make sure it never got to this point, and you're doing a piss poor job of that!"

"I see," Riley responded calmly. "I think I have an idea."

"What kind of idea?" McCoy demanded.

"I think I know just who to call."

"Who? Are you calling the *Times?* Demanding a retraction?"

"Please, sit down, Mr. President." Riley gestured to an open seat at the head of his conference table.

"You're right; this situation calls for a clear head and calm thought." McCoy took a seat.

Riley joined him at the conference table, grabbed the remote control from the table, and powered on the 50-inch screen hanging on the wall at the end of the conference table.

"Who are we calling?" McCoy growled.

Riley searched his phone for the contact, not looking up at McCoy. "Just need to find the number."

"What number? For who?"

"Here it is." Riley started dialing.

"Who are you calling?" McCoy was now frantic.

"Good morning, Riley." The distinguished gentleman on the screen nodded.

"Good morning. How are things in Colorado?" Riley asked.

"Colorado? Who is that?" McCoy stood and moved closer to the screen. "*Who* is that, Riley?"

"It's early here. Remember, we're on Mountain Time; it's just after 6 a.m."

"Sorry to get you out of bed so early, but you look like you had time to comb your hair," Riley joked.

"Who is that?" McCoy exploded.

"Mr. President, say hello to Victor Youngblood," Riley instructed.

McCoy's mouth flew open, his face pale. He struggled to be coherent. "But…Youngblood's in prison…how can…why is he…what's going—"

"Good morning, Mitch." Victor intentionally called

McCoy by his first name rather than addressing him as Mr. President.

"What...how—"

"You're gonna want to sit back down," Riley warned.

"Mitch, I hear you've gotten yourself into quite a situation. Finding your name in the newspaper for all the wrong reasons and associated with quite an unsavory character, at least that's what they've started calling me—*unsavory*."

"Is this some sort of joke, Riley? Who is this?"

"I assure you this is no Joke, Mitch. And Riley's correct; you will want to take a seat. We're just getting started."

"Getting started, with what? This is unacceptable, Riley. I demand to know what's going on."

"Let's start with the good news," Victor interjected. "Those newspaper articles you read this morning about the sinful things you've been doing. Those aren't real. Show him, Riley."

"These are the real morning papers," Riley said as he slid three newspapers in front of McCoy.

McCoy quickly flipped through the stack with stories about growing unemployment, rising sea levels, and the European Union's struggles.

"Wait, you're telling me that these are the real newspapers? The ones about me and—"

"Me?" Victor teased.

"Those weren't real?" McCoy grabbed the faux papers and looked again. "But these look authentic."

"Good. That's how they're supposed to look," Victor agreed.

"So, these stories were never published?" McCoy queried.

"No, at least not yet" Victor taunted.

"What do you mean, *not yet*?"

"Don't worry, Mitch; we'll get to that."

"But how did these papers get into the Oval Office?" McCoy challenged.

Riley raised a hand.

"Riley?" the confused McCoy blurted.

"Mitch, do you recall how you came to meet Riley Indigo?" Victor coaxed.

McCoy began retracing the steps in his mind. "Our campaign was struggling, particularly with funding. One of our leading donors thought Riley could help us. I brought him onboard as deputy campaign manager, and the coffers seemed to open up. After that, our campaign manager stepped down, and Riley was a natural fit. My trust in him led me to offering him the job as Chief of Staff."

"Good memory, Mitch. The news stories you saw this morning—although not published—are 100% true. I did funnel $400 million to your campaign. I am responsible for you being elected president."

"But, Riley, how could you…" McCoy was still working to make sense of this revelatory information.

"Mitch, Riley has been my trusted associate for over 20 years. His loyalty remains with me."

"Is that true, Riley?"

"Yes, it is," Riley corroborated.

"I am obviously going to expect your resignation

immediately."

"You're not understanding the situation, Mitch. Bring the others in, Riley."

Riley opened the door to his office, and in streamed the gentlemen who had recently been excused.

"What is this?" McCoy demanded.

"These gentlemen all work for me, Mitch. They are all my associates or assets. I placed them in your campaign, and Riley ensured they were in your administration."

"This is outrageous. This is a coup!" McCoy screamed.

"It is way more than a coup, Mitch. I need you to sit down and listen."

"I'm done here. I'm leaving this room. You're all fired, and you'll all be held accountable for these treasonous acts."

McCoy pushed through the group and made his way for the door. As he grabbed the knob, it would not turn. Trying again, he yelled back at Riley, "Open this door, *now!*"

"You need to sit down, Mitch!" Victor calmly directed.

"I'm not sitting down! I'm not going to be a party to this," McCoy stammered.

Riley walked toward his boss and gently cupped his arm. "You need to listen to Victor. You really don't have any more options."

McCoy banged on Riley's door. "Help, help! Secret Service, help!"

"No one's coming, sir. You really need to sit down."

McCoy yanked his arm away from Riley. "Don't insult me by calling me *sir.*"

Reluctantly, McCoy returned to the conference table,

though refusing to sit.

"OK, Mitch, here's the situation," Victor began. "As I stated, everything in those newspapers is true and if published would bring your presidency to an end. But that doesn't have to happen. Seated to your right is Attorney General Breland Fleming. Based on recently discovered information, Breland's team at the Justice Department has reopened my case."

Fleming placed a large folder in front of McCoy.

"What they have found is quite alarming. They have irrefutable evidence that completely exonerates me. It will show that I was not involved in the Senator's death and that I have been the victim of one this country's greatest legal travesties. I am an innocent man wrongly accused, convicted, and sentenced to this hellhole, Florence ADX."

McCoy noted that Victor was speaking from the prison's executive conference room and was dressed in a $2,000 suit. "Yeah, a real hell hole," McCoy thought.

"Here's what you're going to do. You are going to call a press conference. You are going to summarize what your Justice Department has discovered, and you are going to immediately pardon me rather than going through the mechanics of my legal team filing an appeal and waiting for the legal proceedings of a retrial that could take years."

McCoy scoffed, "Oh, *I am*? I'm going to pardon you, just like that?"

"You are," Victor assured.

"And if I don't, I supposed you're going to try to get some hack newspaper to write these stories about me?"

"The stories are already written, Mitch. And if you call the *New York Times*, *Washington Post*, and *Wall Street Journal* hack newspapers, then yes, that's what I'm going to do," Victor assured.

McCoy looked around the room. "And you're all in on this? My most trusted advisors. My Cabinet."

"We're all in, Mr. President," Riley affirmed.

McCoy picked up the faux papers and again read the damning stories about him. After a couple of minutes, McCoy tossed the papers onto the conference table; looked up at Victor; and demanded, "Call."

"What's that?" Riley asked.

"*Call*," McCoy repeated.

Victor smiled wryly. "Mitch thinks we're bluffing, and he's calling our bluff."

"Mr. President, I assure you this isn't a bluff. You need to listen to Victor," Riley interjected.

"*Call*," McCoy demanded for a third time.

"Very well. Mitch, I want you to understand that my associates and assets are not limited to those in this room. Your administration is really *my* administration. You'll come to understand that soon enough. Riley, open the door, and let the President go. Remember, Mitch, this is the path you have chosen."

McCoy walked toward the door, looked back at Riley who pushed a button under the desk to unlock the door.

"Good day, gentlemen," McCoy uttered as he left the conference room.

"Just as we expected," Victor proclaimed. "Riley, let's

take the next step."

"Yes sir. I understand."

46

"Any idea why we're here?" Lucy Cross asked, pacing nervously.

"No, but I have a feeling it isn't going to be good news." Ben Gossett was worried.

"The meeting notice did say 9 a.m., didn't it?" Elizabeth Sanders asked.

"That's what mine says," Billy Murdoch confirmed, checking his cell phone's calendar.

"That was 20 minutes ago. How long are we supposed to wait?" Ben questioned.

"For the FBI Director, I don't think there's a limit; we wait until he arrives," Lucy declared.

As Lucy spoke, the door to the J. Edgar Hoover Building's Executive Conference Room opened; and all four turned to see who was entering.

"I'm terribly sorry. The Director is running a few minutes late, but he should be here any minute. Please, everyone take a seat."

All four members of Task Force Terracotta had been afraid to sit in the leather and mahogany chairs. This was their first time in the room normally set aside for visits from the President, Cabinet members, congressmen, and foreign dignitaries. The group sensed the room selection held meaning; they just weren't sure what that was. They would soon find out.

"Please accept my apologies for running late," Director Gavin Thompson announced as he entered.

The quartet simultaneously rose from their chairs.

Ben interjected, "Oh, it's no problem, Director; we—"

"I'm not sure if you've had the opportunity to meet Attorney General Breland Fleming," Thompson declared, making quick introductions.

"We've also brought along a couple of our in-house legal team members to help with some details. Let's all have a seat."

This unexpected meeting with the FBI Director, who also brought along the Attorney General and FBI lawyers, was definitely going to be unlike any other meeting the team had previously experienced.

"I want to thank you for meeting with us," Thompson started. "I also want to thank you for your service to the country in Task Force Terracotta. I know it has been less than a week since we lost your leader, Agent Hanover. I want to start by asking everyone how you're doing in dealing with his loss."

The team members were confused about this meeting's

purpose, but they knew for sure it wasn't to ascertain their feelings about losing Thomas Hanover.

"We're all doing OK, Director Thompson. It was very sudden, so we're working through it a day at a time, but I think I can speak for the team when I say we're charging ahead and ready to go to work." Ben offered.

The other three members nodded in agreement.

"That's good to hear, but I would expect nothing less from professional agents of your caliber." Opening a portfolio, Thompson signaled a transition in the conversation.

"We'd like to discuss Task Force Terracotta with you. We know this task force has only been in place for a few weeks, but you have assembled a considerable amount of information. Agent Hanover briefed me about it shortly before his death. I need to inform you that we have another Agency investigation ongoing that also involves Victor Youngblood. That investigation has been in place for several months and has involved dozens of agents. It is concluding very soon, allowing us the luxury of redeploying Task Force Terracotta's assets to other Agency priorities."

"Wait, you're disbanding the task force?" a confused Lucy Cross asked.

"This team's objectives have been met by other Agency initiatives," Thompson responded.

"Uh...can we know what conclusions this other team has been able to make?" Ben Gossett wondered.

"I'm glad you asked that, Ken," Attorney General Fleming responded.

"Its...uh...Ben, sir."

Ignoring the correction, Fleming continued, "With more time and Agency resources than your small team was able to wield, we're very comfortable with the direction the Justice Department is going regarding Mr. Youngblood."

"So, we can't know what that direction is?" Ben asked with growing interest.

"That won't be your concern, Ken."

"It's Ben."

"In fact, due to the direction of the investigation, we must inform you of your legal obligations regarding nondisclosure of your Task Force Terracotta efforts."

Fleming nodded to the Justice Department attorneys, who handed letters to each member of the task force.

"These letters were written to protect you from inadvertent disclosure of Top-Secret information. They explain that penalties for violating your non-disclosure requirements aren't limited to your employment but can involve criminal penalties with up to 20 years in prison," Fleming declared.

"Wait a minute," Ben interjected. "We all know we aren't supposed to talk about Agency business outside the Agency. What's different about this case?"

"We're just trying to ensure you understand the nondisclosure directive. Nothing is different, Ben. We're just trying to protect you," Thompson assured.

Ben rose from his chair and took a step away in thought, then turned back. "*Nothing* is different? We're in the Executive Conference Room, meeting with the FBI Director and the Attorney General of The United States of America, and we're given personalized letters. Oh, *something's* different,

Thompson rose from his chair, walked over to Ben and put a hand on either shoulder, looked him in the eye, and smiled. "Like I said, Ben, we're just trying to protect you."

"Well, we have another meeting to get to," Fleming announced. "It was great to meet everyone, and I wish you all the best in your careers with the Bureau."

With that statement, the FBI Director, Attorney General, and the attorneys were out the door, leaving the task force alone.

After an awkward silence, Billy Murdoch was the first to speak. "Holy sh—"

"Exactly," Ben Gossett interrupted. "Anyone else get goosebumps when they said they were trying to protect us?"

The other three nodded in agreement.

"We're screwed," Billy Murdoch succinctly concluded.

"Mr. Vice President, I want to thank you for agreeing to meet with us. I am such an admirer of yours, particularly your decades of service in the United States Navy."

The speaker was Bart Henninger, vice chairman of the Republican Party. Henninger was joined by Senator Maggie Beaufort, Republican from Louisiana, and Senator Rodney Chambers, Republican from Tennessee.

"Thank you for those kind words. Please have a seat."

The trio all found seats and engaged in brief small talk until Vice President Adair steered the conversation back to business.

"What can I do for you today?"

It was Senator Chambers' turn to speak. "As a native Tennessean, I was so proud of the run that my fellow Volunteer, Elijah Mustang, made for president. Choosing you as his running mate even further solidified his good judgment. Although I am a Republican, I'm not afraid to say I was a vocal supporter of you and Elijah and you gentlemen got my vote."

"Thank you, Senator," Adair responded.

"And I admire that you've held to your guns after being elected Vice President and haven't aligned yourself with one of the two major parties. I'm sure there has been pressure to do so."

"Please excuse me, Senator, is there something specific I can do for you today?" Adair asked professionally, but pointedly.

The Senator chuckled. "Yes, I understand; the Navy didn't teach you to dawdle. What we'd like to ask is, if you'd indulge the three of us as guests in your next meeting of the Mustangs."

Adair cocked his head. "Why would you want to come to one of our meetings? I can tell you firsthand, they are not very exciting."

"We are such admirers of this service-centered approach you have adopted. We were so moved by the young men rebuilding that boy's treehouse and the national philanthropic movement it has inspired. Frankly, we'd like to get out of Washington D.C. and see how you do what you do."

"These are really more business meetings where we work out some of the boring administrative details. They don't really lend themselves to guests."

"Mr. Vice President, we would be so honored just to sit on the back row and watch—if that's not too much of an imposition." Chambers was the consummate politician, and Adair knew it.

"Of course, we would be honored to have you as our guests. We have a meeting coming up in a couple of weeks. I'll be in touch with your office when the details are finalized."

"Mr. Vice President, you are too gracious. We can't thank you enough."

"Happy to have you. Was there anything else I can do for you today?"

"No, we've taken enough of your time."

As the group exchanged handshakes and the Republican trio headed out the door, they had an unexpected encounter in the hallway.

"Mr. President, what a pleasure it is to see you," Senator Chambers babbled.

"What are you doing here?" McCoy jeered.

"We were paying your Vice President a visit, but we were just on the way out."

"Good," McCoy grunted.

McCoy was headed down the hallway toward Riley's office on the left; however, that encounter caused him to pause and glance to his right. He saw the Vice President's door open and Adair seated at his desk and decided to walk to his doorway.

"What was that all about?" McCoy pressed, his hand still on the doorway.

Adair barely looked up from his desk. "Just a short meeting."

"A meeting about what?"

"Did you need something?"

Adair had little respect for the President with tensions increasing over the preceding months.

"Are you part of his little rebellion?" McCoy gestured across the hallway to Riley Indigo's office.

"What are you talking about? Whose rebellion?"

McCoy decided to venture deeper into Adair's office to ascertain if his Vice President was being fully forthcoming.

"Riley and Youngblood's."

"Youngblood? Victor Youngblood?"

"Exactly. So, you *are* with them."

"Victor Youngblood and Riley Indigo, your chief of staff?"

"Stop avoiding the question."

"Remind me again. What exactly *is* the question?"

Taking another step into the Vice President's office, Mc-Coy was only six feet away from Adair.

"Are you working with Riley and Youngblood in this ridiculous coup stunt they are trying to pull?"

"Mr. President, I don't have the slightest idea what you're talking about," Adair insisted.

McCoy crossed his arms, peered at Adair for ten seconds, grunted, then wheeled around and left, heading back down the hallway to the Oval Office.

Adair watched in stunned silence before muttering to himself, "That was…odd."

It was an introduction to a subject Adair would come to understand sooner and more deeply that he could ever imagine.

"Are you sure this connection is secure?" Ben Gossett asked.

"I'm on a burner phone. You said you are too, right?"

"That's right."

"Then it must be secure. What's got you so scared?" Jeremy had walked behind the hardware store and was sitting on the loading dock off a now-empty alley.

"You're not going to believe this," Ben whispered. "The team was called to a meeting today with the Director of the FBI. But not *just* the Director of the FBI, but also the Attorney General of the United States. And they were joined by two sour-looking FBI lawyers. *And* we met in the Executive Conference Room, which is usually set aside for meetings with the President. It was crazy."

"I'm guessing they weren't there to give you a promotion," Jeremy surmised.

"Good guess. We were all handed personalized non-disclosure directives not to discuss the Youngblood case with anyone; and we were warned that if we did there would be criminal penalties."

Jeremy breathed deeply. "I have a feeling criminal

penalties would be the least of your worries."

"I think Thomas Hanover would agree with you."

"Did they say anything else about the case?"

"Yes…are you sure no one is listening?" Ben shuddered.

For good measure, Jeremy looked down the alley both ways and back into the store. "I assure you; I am alone."

"They said there was another agency team investigating Youngblood and that they had enough information from that other team that they could disband Task Force Terracotta. What do you think that means?"

Jeremy's heart raced as his mind began to piece together all the information he had recently come to understand.

"Jeremy? Are you still there?" Ben asked frantically.

"Yeah, Ben, I'm still here."

"What do you think that means, that they had another team investigating?"

"They are going to set him free." Jeremy shivered.

"What? No, there's no way. They know what Youngblood did. We have tons of evidence. The other team would have it too."

"No, Ben, this is all starting to make sense; it is *awful, terrible* sense, but it all fits."

"What all *fits?*"

"You've shared information with me, Ben. Now I feel obligated to share some with you. I have a friend on the inside of Mouse Trap. He told me they had a meeting a couple of days ago with everyone in Mouse Trap and had a big announcement that Victor would soon be returning."

"How? That still doesn't make sense. How is that

possible?"

"Think about who you just met with—the FBI Director and the Attorney General. Why would they—don't take this the wrong way—but why would they meet with a field-level team just to tell you they are disbanding. That's routine stuff, right?"

"Normally, yes."

"So, this is obviously something that is not at all routine. This other team they talked about— the only explanation is that they haven't been working to connect Victor to more crimes. They've been working to clear him."

Then it was Ben's turn to be silent.

"*Ben?*"

"I'm here. I'm just…this is just…unbelievable; but like you said, it makes sense. In fact, it's the only explanation for why we would be meeting with the upper echelon."

"If this is all true, the big question is what we are going to do about it."

"We have to do something, Jeremy. We both know what Victor is capable of doing. Of course, now he somehow has the FBI Director and Attorney General working for him."

"He always did," Jeremy muttered.

"What do you mean?"

"You would not begin to believe who in this country, and really around the world, works for Victor Youngblood. I agree that we need to try to do something to stop Victor, but I need to think about where to start."

"I think I have an idea. I think I know someone I can talk with about this." Ben suggested.

"Who is it?"

"You won't believe it."

47

I t started like every other day: arise, avocado toast, quinoa, yogurt, kombucha, yoga, shower, Oval Office, newspapers. McCoy flipped through each of the three newspapers, quickly scanning all the pages. What started as a wry smile grew into hearty laughter as McCoy rose quickly from his chair, opened the door to the Oval Office, strutted down the hallway, and burst into Riley Indigo's office. He was pleased to see Riley meeting with the Attorney General and Secretary of State, two of the key members of the coup.

"I knew it. It was all a bluff!" McCoy waved the newspapers in the air.

"What's that, sir?" Riley asked.

"Cut the *sir* crap. I knew that little show with Youngblood was designed to get me to cave. Well, I want to make myself clear; I'm not caving today, tomorrow, next week, or next year. I'm staying in this office; Youngblood's staying in prison; and as soon as I can figure out how, all of you will be joining him."

"I'm sorry; I'm not following, sir," Riley stressed.

"You threatened me, saying terrible news would be written about me if I didn't pardon Youngblood. Well, here we are 48 hours later, and you got nothing! Absolutely zilch! You Boy Scouts didn't know who you were dealing with."

Riley just looked at McCoy, nodded in agreement, and uttered, "Yes, sir, we definitely underestimated your steely resolve. Well done, sir."

"Hey, Jeremy, I was just checking my calendar. Do you know what's coming up in three days?" Rosita asked.

"Let's see, today's Sunday; three days would be Wednesday," Jeremy replied, not looking up from his magazine.

"Yes, it is Wednesday; but what's the date?"

"OK, today's the 10th; 10 plus 3 would be 13, so three days from now would be the 13th. Am I right?"

Rosita huffed, "Yes, it's September 13th; but do you know anything special about September 13th?"

Jeremy glanced over at Savannah, who grinned while shaking her head.

"Oh yeah, that's the day we get the big shipment of asphalt shingles down at the store. How could I have forgotten?" Jeremy confirmed.

"Jeremy! September 13th is Savannah's birthday!"

Jeremy looked at Savannah in mock shock. "Oh, your birthday is the 13th, really?"

"That's what they tell me," Savannah confirmed.

"And you know on birthdays people who love each other buy gifts, sometimes really nice gifts. Are you buying Savannah a gift, Jeremy?" Rosita wondered.

"Yeah, Jeremy, are you buying me a gift?" Savannah smiled, glad to help Rosita make Jeremy uncomfortable.

"Here's the thing. I'm not really much of a gift guy. I just feel like getting to work here with me is a gift you both get every day."

"No, *no, no*, Jeremy!" Rosita protested. "You gotta do better than that. I was thinking about something shiny, that costs a lot of money, fits on one's finger, has a diamond, and rhymes with engagement ring?"

"Mom!" Jeremy and Savannah responded in unison.

"Mom, that is a very private topic we don't need any motherly help with!" Jeremy exclaimed.

"Then I'll leave you two in private," Rosita responded, leaving the room.

"So, what do you think?" Savannah teased.

"About what?"

"About what your mom said?"

"I think I need to go to the store and get some Diet Coke. You need anything?"

"She needs a ring!" Rosita said, sticking her head back into the room.

"Sir, it is truly an honor to have you visit the Academy." David

Ferguson, Commandant of the United States Naval Academy, had just finished a VIP tour and was concluding the day with a meet-and-greet in his office.

"It has been too long since I've been back here. The last time was over a year ago when I made the announcement that I was running for vice president." Looking around the commandant's office, Admiral Adair admired the collection of battleship and carrier models. "You build these yourself?"

"A little something to pass the time when I'm at home. It keeps the blood pressure down."

"With all these tiny parts, it would have the opposite effect on me."

The small entourage accompanying the men laughed at the Vice President's joke.

The Commandant looked around the room and addressed the crowd. "I want to thank you all for your part in making this day a success. I know our midshipmen were encouraged by hearing our Vice President speak."

"It was my honor."

"Thank you for your service today. The Vice President and I would like to have a moment in private."

Immediately the Commandant's assistants left the office. Adair nodded to his small staff and Secret Service detail who also left, leaving the two men alone in the Commandant's office.

"So, he's here somewhere?" Adair asked.

"He's here."

"Is this cloak-and-dagger routine really necessary?"

"Wait until you hear what he has to say."

Ferguson walked over and knocked on a door in the corner of his office. When he did the door opened, and the real subject of the Vice President's visit emerged.

"The bathroom? You made him wait all this time in the bathroom?" Adair asked incredulously.

"Oh, it's OK, sir. I didn't mind. I really appreciate your taking time to meet with me. My name is Ben Gossett. I'm with the FBI."

Adair extended a hand, and Gossett took a seat.

At the beginning of his career with the FBI, Ben Gossett was given a two year assignment at United States Naval Academy to investigate accusations of fraudulent contractor billing. While at the Academy, Ben's Navy liaison was Lieutenant Commander David Ferguson, who later became the Academy's Commandant. Fortunately, Ben had maintained close relations with Ferguson through the years. When Ben contacted Ferguson about the recent events he'd experienced, Ferguson arranged today's "tour" on short notice to give Ben an opportunity to share his story with the Vice President.

"Commandant Ferguson tells me you've had an interesting last few weeks."

"Yes sir. That's an understatement. I think this is a story you'll want to hear."

Ben described to Adair the formation of Task Force Terracotta and the unbelievable discoveries they had made about Victor Youngblood in just the first few days. He explained that their leader, Thomas Hanover, had died in very suspicious circumstances the morning after meeting

Youngblood in prison. He detailed the frightening meeting the team had with the Attorney General and the FBI director. He also explained Jeremy's role in the early days helping the team begin to unravel Youngblood's vast empire. Lastly, he shared Jeremy's warning that Victor would be out of jail soon.

"I know this all sounds so…conspiratorial, but I assure you everything I'm telling you is true."

Adair sat quietly and listened without interruption to the entire story. When he saw that Ben was done, he nodded his head and rose from his chair, clearly pondering all he had heard. Then he turned back to Ben and Ferguson.

"This helps me understand an encounter I had with the President yesterday. He was clearly disturbed—more so than usual—and was mumbling a question, asking if I was part of the coup involving his chief of staff and—get this—Victor Youngblood."

"Jackson, are you sure you heard that right?" In the heat of the discussion, Ferguson let his guard down and called his friend by his first name rather than Vice President.

"I'm certain. I hadn't heard Youngblood's name since his trial, so that really wedged in my mind."

"This is huge; this is really huge," Ben mumbled.

Adair walked back and looked both men in the eye.

"This is absolutely critical—this conversation cannot be shared with another person. Do you understand? Not your spouse, your kids, your parents, your dog, no one."

"Yes sir," both responded.

"This is very troublesome. I've got to find out what's

going on."

The Vice President left the Commandant's office, without shaking hands or uttering a word of goodbye. It was clear, he was on a mission.

48

A rise, avocado toast, quinoa, yogurt, kombucha, yoga, shower, Oval Office, newspapers.

Mitch McCoy immediately saw the headline of the *New York Times:*

McCoy Wealth Tax Would Devastate Economy

The *Washington Post* and *Wall Street Journal* had similar headlines. As McCoy quickly scanned the articles, he saw all three referenced a study by a team of blue-ribbon economists from the American Economic Growth Institute. From a purely economic standpoint, the study concluded that a wealth tax would have a terribly regressive impact on the American economy. It predicted 10 to 20 million jobs lost, a transfer of over a trillion dollars of investments out of the U.S. into countries without a wealth tax, and a net reduction in tax revenue of over $400 billion annually.

Involving 200 world-class economists, it was touted as the broadest study ever done on a wealth tax. The same newspapers included editorials eulogizing McCoy's presidency as they claimed the study dealt a deadly blow to the cornerstone policy upon which McCoy had built his entire presidential campaign. They questioned his judgment in investing so much political and personal capital in what they concluded was a losing proposition.

A mixture of anger and frustration clouded McCoy's thoughts, preventing him from immediately connecting the stories to Riley Indigo and Victor Youngblood. When the mental haze cleared and McCoy began connecting the dots, his ire had a target, and it was just a few yards down the hallway.

Springing from his chair, McCoy attempted to burst through the Oval Office door; however, in his haste, he failed to turn the knob, resulting in his face slamming into the door. After regaining his bearings, he continued down the hallway and exploded into Riley's office.

"You really had to go for the wealth tax, you—" McCoy stopped two steps into the office as he was startled by the face staring at him on Riley's large screen.

"Good morning, Mitch. You seem troubled. Is something bothering you this morning?" Victor Youngblood asked.

"You!" McCoy blurted.

"Good morning, Mr. President," Riley responded, still seated behind his desk.

"And *you*!" McCoy pointed to Riley. "I thought you were

coming after me, not my platform."

"We wanted to give you more time to think about my offer. We have generously withheld the most damming stories in hopes that you'll come to your senses," Victor proclaimed. "But please understand, inaction on your part will lead to further escalation on ours."

McCoy turned to Riley, pleading, "But, I thought you believed in the wealth tax. You have defended it to the press hundreds of times."

Riley didn't respond.

"I will repeat my demand. You will call a press conference, announcing that your Justice Department discovered evidence exonerating me and that you are going to immediately pardon me. Do that today, and this all ends."

"And if I don't?" McCoy dared.

"We escalate. The next articles are already written," Victor confirmed.

"Let me guess; they will be about the unpaid parking tickets from when I was in Congress," McCoy goaded.

"I need an answer Mitch," Victor demanded.

"You need an answer?" McCoy repeated. "Here's what I've figured out. You can't turn those fake articles into real stories because they portray you as a criminal. When you implicate me, you are only hurting yourself." McCoy took a step towards the door, then turned back to the screen, and shook the newspaper at Victor. "My answer is the same as before: *No deal!*"

McCoy rushed out the door, slamming it behind him. It made a loud noise heard throughout the West Wing.

"Next level?" Riley inquired.

"Next level," Victor confirmed.

Among those hearing the commotion was Vice President Adair whose office was across the hall from Riley's. Recognizing an opening to test the veracity of Ben Gossett's story, he walked down the hall and knocked on the Oval Office door.

"Go away," McCoy wailed.

"I'd like to speak with you," Adair responded.

"What do you want?"

"Please open the door."

After an awkward silence, McCoy cracked the door open and peeked through the opening. "What do you want?"

"Can I come in?"

McCoy huffed, then walked away from the door. "Fine."

McCoy went back to his chair and plopped down. He buried his face in his hands nervously running his fingers through his hair.

"Is something bothering you?"

"*You* are right now."

Ignoring the insult, Adair continued, "A couple of days ago, you asked me about Riley and Victor Youngblood. Is there something we need to talk about?"

McCoy's head shot up. "What do *you* know about Riley and Youngblood?"

"I only know that you asked me about them. Why were

you asking? Is something wrong?"

McCoy snarled, "Everything's wrong. *Absolutely everything*!"

"Can you be more specific?"

McCoy took a few steps around the Oval Office and then spun back to Adair. "You still say you are not part of this." McCoy picked up the newspapers and waved them in the air.

Adair nodded his head and responded, "I don't even know what *this* is."

"*This!*" Adair opened the paper to the wealth tax headlines.

An underwhelmed Adair replied, "The wealth tax? This is all about the wealth tax?"

McCoy yelled, "No, it's not *about* the wealth tax; it's about Riley and other members of my Cabinet, and Youngblood, and my campaign, and my presidency, and…" McCoy took a step toward Adair, as always looking up to his Vice President, who was almost a foot taller; and continued, "… and you know nothing about any of this?"

"Mr. President, I know less about whatever this is than I did before I came in here."

"Hmmm," McCoy mumbled, plopping down on the sofa in front of the Resolute Desk.

Adair sat in the chair opposite McCoy. "Let's start with Victor Youngblood. You've said he's somehow involved in whatever has you troubled, but he's serving a life sentence for murder in a federal penitentiary. How is he involved?"

A scattered McCoy responded. "You just *think* he's serving a life sentence, but that's not really what's happening."

"*What?* How?"

Before McCoy could respond, the Oval Office door opened, and Riley Indigo entered with a folder. "Mr. President, I have some materials for you to…" Then Riley noticed Adair sitting with McCoy. "Oh, I'm terribly sorry, Mr. Vice President. Am I interrupting something?"

Adair stood and advised, "The President was just discussing—"

"We were just wrapping up," McCoy interrupted. "Jackson, I want to thank you for stopping by today. Although we don't always agree, I appreciate your input and candor."

"Thank you, Mr. President. You gentlemen have a good day."

49

"Hey, Dad, I just wanted to confirm that everyone will be at Sagaponack tonight. … Great, I have a few meetings first thing this morning; then we'll be on our way. … Yes, we'll take Air Force One into MacArthur, then Marine One directly to the property. See you this evening."

Woodrow Mitchell McCoy was born February 15, 1978. The middle child of Gloria and Eugene McCoy, Mitch was not as smart as his younger sister, Ophelia, and not as athletic as his older brother, Jerome. However, Mitch had the political skills of his father, a four-term congressman and three-term Democrat senator representing the state of Connecticut. Eugene's 26 years in Congress were the best of his life and had left him a rich man. At a salary ranging between $150,000 and $174,000, the math didn't compute for his current net worth in excess of $60 million; but it was a reality that Washington accepted and very few questioned.

Gloria and Eugene enjoyed a primary residence in

Greenwich, Connecticut, in the Belle Haven neighborhood. Their neighbors included CEOs; owners of professional sports teams; and, of course, other politicians. The 9,000-square-foot home included a private boathouse on Long Island Sound.

Their vacation getaway was on an 80-acre estate in Sagaponack, a village in the town of Southampton, New York, on Long Island. Sagaponack was situated on the Atlantic 150 miles by water from their primary home in Greenwich. The McCoys would typically take their 125-foot Westport yacht, making the journey to Sagaponack in approximately six hours depending on the weather.

Sagaponack was the destination of choice for family gatherings as the compound included a 7,500-square-foot primary residence and three 3,000-square-foot 'cottages' situated around the main house, all connected by covered walkways.

This late summer gathering would be the first time the entire family had been together since Mitch's inauguration; thus, there was an air of excitement, especially for Mitch, who saw his father as his hero. In his eyes, no one stood taller than Eugene McCoy. With the Victor Youngblood and Riley Indigo adventures ongoing at the White House, Mitch needed nothing more than quality time with his father. He would seek his advice on how to address the declining economy, how to deal with the Russians, and eventually what to do about the Victor Youngblood conundrum.

Thanks to Mouse Trap's extensive research capabilities, Mitch's worship of his father was no secret to Victor, as Mitch would soon discover. This vacation would be long remembered in the annals of the McCoy family history—but for all the wrong reasons.

"Where's Savannah?"

"She's wiped out and already headed up to bed."

"I thought she seemed tired this evening."

"Thanks for letting Savannah stay at the house tonight, Mom."

"Oh, Jeremy, her birthday is tomorrow; of course, I want her to stay."

"I know how you feel about us...well, I know you think a man and woman should be married to—"

"That's not something you're going to have to worry about much longer, right, Jeremy?" Rosita interrupted.

"Mom!" Jeremy protested although his huge grin tempered his response.

"I know, I know. It's not something you want to talk about with your mom. But you know, it's not just that you'll be getting a wife; I'll be getting the daughter I never had."

Jeremy sighed. "Yeah, Mom, I think you've mentioned that like a thousand times."

"Consider this a thousand and one."

"Javier, I'm very sorry that you have to work a double shift today." Victor was sitting beside Javier in a chair outside his cell.

"It's OK, Mr. Youngblood. I get off tomorrow morning at 8 and will get to spend the day with my kids."

"How are Julio and Rachel doing?" Victor asked, calling Javier's kids by their first names.

"They are doing well, Mr. Youngblood. Both are getting straight A's in school. I'm really proud of them."

"You should be proud, Javier. You are a great father."

"Thank you, Mr. Youngblood."

"Javier, you've treated me with great kindness while I've been here; so, I got something for you."

"What? You got something for *me*?"

"Javier, I'm not going to be here much longer, and I just wanted to show you my gratitude."

"Thank you, sir. I don't know what to say."

When Javier opened the small package, his mouth flew open. "Uh…Mr. Youngblood…is this—"

"I asked some of the other guards, and they said you were a bit of a watch connoisseur."

"I am, but this isn't just a watch; this is a Rolex. And not just any Rolex, but the GMT Master II. It's incredible."

"I'm glad you like it, Javier. You deserve it."

"But I can't—"

"Yes, you can, Javier."

"Thank you, Mr. Youngblood. I tell my wife all the time that I've never met anyone like you, and this just proves my point. You know there's no way I could ever repay you for this."

"It's a gift. I don't expect you to repay me."

"Thank you, Mr. Youngblood. Thank you very much."

"You're welcome, Javier."

50

Mitch McCoy didn't care that it was vacation in Saga-ponack, New York; he maintained his morning regi-men: arise, avocado toast, quinoa, yogurt, kombucha, yoga. He was in the middle of a full locust pose when he heard it.

"Mitch!"

He couldn't remember the last time he'd heard his mom scream like that. He sprung to his feet; rushed past the Secret Service agent stationed outside his cottage; and burst into the primary residence where he saw his mom apparent-ly tending to Eugene.

"What is it, Mom? Why did you scream?" Mitch asked.

"The newspaper. Look at the newspaper." Gloria shud-dered.

"The *newspaper*?" Mitch thought. "Oh no, Youngblood actually did it. He must have published the story about Mitch's campaign having been funded by a convicted mur-derer."

As the thoughts rushed through his mind, his wife and son entered the room, followed closely by his brother and sister, their families in tow. For maximum embarrassment, Youngblood had orchestrated this while Mitch was with his family.

"What's wrong, Mom?" Jerome asked.

"The newspaper. Look at the newspaper."

Lost in thought, Jeremy hadn't even stopped to read it. He knew it would be devastating.

His brother picked up the paper, quickly read a few paragraphs, and then looked at his father. "What is this? This can't be right," Jerome insisted.

"I can explain," Mitch started.

"Dad, this isn't true is it?"

"*Dad?*" Mitch wondered, "Why is the focus on Dad?"

His father's legs buckled as he fell to the ground.

As everyone else ran to check on the elder McCoy, Mitch picked up the newspaper that his brother had dropped. The headline took his breath away:

President McCoy's Father a Human Trafficker

As Mitch found a seat on a nearby ottoman, his knees buckled. He began to read,

Eugene McCoy—a four-term congressman, three-term senator, and the father of current President Mitch McCoy—has been identified as one of the leaders of a ten-year human

trafficking ring. The scheme brought impoverished Central American refugees to the United States for what they thought was a chance at freedom and the prospect of a new life but that turned out to be modern-day slave trade. The elder McCoy's role was to supply the refugees with immigrant visas and then to purge the visas from the immigration system once the refugees were in the U.S. The Times has learned that over 1,000 individuals have been lost to human traffickers directly due to McCoy's actions. While FBI officials declined to comment, sources have told the Times that an investigation is in the late stages and that numerous indictments will soon be returned.

"Dad, are you OK?" Ophelia asked.

"Call 911!" Gloria screamed.

"Don't call 911. I'm fine. The last thing we need is even MORE attention," Eugene lamented while sitting on the floor, his back against a couch.

Jerome turned to Mitch. "What did you know about this?"

"I...I...knew nothing, I swear."

"This is *your* FBI! You had to know!" Jerome demanded.

"I didn't know anything!" Mitch repeated.

"Is this true, Dad? Is *any* of this true?" Ophelia had scanned the article and was now holding the paper in the air.

"You know the media and how they twist things," Gloria insisted as Eugene offered no defense.

Then Mitch thought, "What if this was another one of Riley and Youngblood's fake papers? Surely that was it. Surely the *Times* wouldn't run such a damning hit piece without any advance notice. This had to be designed to shake Mitch and get him to cave to Youngblood's demands."

"I gotta go check something out," Mitch muttered as he walked out the door.

"Where are you going?" Gloria asked.

"I'll be right back."

"Strawberry cake?" Savannah beamed.

"It's your favorite, right?"

"Yeah, but how did you know? I've never told you that."

"Your sister might have told me."

"Wait, you talked to my sister?"

Ignoring the question, Jeremy lit the candles.

"It's going to take a lot of wind to blow out 25 candles."

"Oh, please!" Rosita smirked.

Savannah blew out the candles, Jeremy and Rosita sang happy birthday, and Rosita cut each person a huge slice of cake.

Waiting impatiently, Rosita couldn't stand it any longer.

"Great cake, Jeremy. What did you get Savannah for her birthday?"

Savannah chuckled as Jeremy slowly shot his mom an angry stare.

"*What?*" Rosita protested.

"Yeah, Jeremy, what did you get me?" Savannah teased.

"Mom, you want to give us some privacy?"

"Fine!" Rosita took her cake and went into the kitchen, trying to stay within earshot.

Jeremy left the room and returned with a stack of presents in his arms.

"OK, these have numbers on them. You have to open them in order from one to six."

"Six presents? Wow!"

"OK, open number one," Jeremy instructed.

"Seems sort of heavy. I'm guessing it's a casserole," Savannah chattered.

"Yep, you nailed it. I made you a casserole, baked it, put it in a box, and wrapped it. How did you know?"

Savannah ignored Jeremy's sarcasm and opened the package.

"A book?" She looked at Jeremy, then read more closely. "A textbook from a speech class. It has a sticker from Virginia Tech?" she wondered. Then the light bulb went on. "Oh, I see." Savannah laughed with Jeremy joining her.

"What is it?" Rosita yelled from the kitchen.

"You see, the first time I met Jeremy I was on assignment from Victor Youngblood. I was supposed to convince Jeremy he already knew me, so I acted like we were old friends from speech class at Virginia Tech. He bought it hook, line, and sinker."

"I did not. I had you figured out as a faker from the minute you walked in the door," Jeremy protested.

"Yeah, *right.*"

Not as amused as Jeremy and Savannah, Rosita shouted, "OK, that's great. Now what's number two?"

"Mom! You're supposed to be gone!"

Ignoring Rosita, Savannah opened the next package.

"A menu from the American Eagle Diner in Kingston, Tennessee. Ha! That's where we happened to coincidentally meet for the first time," Savannah confirmed.

"Yeah, *coincidentally.*" Jeremy chirped.

"So, this is like a walk down memory lane thing?" Savannah asked.

"Something like that," Jeremy concurred. "OK, number three."

Savannah opened the next package and observed, "A Richfield College t-shirt." Savannah held up the garment from the small Tennessee college where Jeremy started a faux protest that went viral when social justice warriors around the country came to join in solidarity, followed closely by dozens of members of the media. It was also where Jeremy caught Victor Youngblood's eye as someone who could pull off such an elaborate scheme. That's why Victor sent Savannah to size him up as a possible candidate for his organization.

"OK, we're halfway home," Jeremy announced.

Present number four was a Mouse Trap board game, the inspiration for the name of Victor Youngblood's nefarious enterprise. Victor loved the metaphor of the Mouse Trap game in which a lever is pulled, setting a wide-ranging series of events into motion, and ultimately trapping a mouse. Victor's Mouse Trap organization worked the same way with his broad network of assets and associates he could deploy to solve any problem, and the solution could not be traced back to him.

"I know we don't have great memories of working at Mouse Trap; but it is part of our story, warts and all," Jeremy declared.

"I love it."

Present number five was in a large envelope with a red bow attached. Savannah carefully opened it, pulled out a parchment-like document, and began to read.

"It's a Prince's Hardware stock certificate?" Savannah asked.

"It is," Jeremy verified.

"Umm, OK," a puzzled Savannah mumbled.

"You've worked so hard with Mom and me on the hardware store that I want you to not just be a helper but to have an ownership share. There's only one problem. You see, Dad was a great businessman who took pride in building the hardware store into a successful family enterprise. Several years ago, he incorporated the business. He wrote into the articles of incorporation a strict requirement that all stock owners must be members of the family."

Savannah smiled broadly. "I think I see where you're going with this."

Jeremy grabbed the sixth present, a small square box, then dropped to one knee. "Since I really want you to have ownership in the family business and there's only one way to make that happen, Savannah Lynch, would you please be my wife?"

"Yes!" Rosita blurted.

Savannah chuckled. "I think that's my line." She then

turned back to Jeremy and gushed, "Jeremy Prince, it would be the joy of my life to own a stake in Prince's Hardware store; and if that means we gotta get married, then I'm all in."

"*Yes!*" Rosita screamed.

"I love you, Jeremy!"

"I love you, Savannah."

"I love you both!" shouted Rosita.

"Let's go!" McCoy shouted to one of his Secret Service agents who had the misfortune of being on duty for McCoy's vacation.

"Excuse me, sir?" the confused agent responded.

McCoy tossed a set of keys to the agent. "Get in the driver's seat and drive," McCoy shouted as he entered the Lexus and slammed the door shut.

The agent opened the driver's-side door and peered at the visibly upset President.

"Is everything OK, sir?"

"No, everything is *not* OK. Get in the car and drive."

"Is there something we can do for you, sir?"

Now even more agitated, McCoy screamed, "You can get into the damn car and drive!!"

Seeking to calm the situation, the agent obliged by getting into the driver's seat and starting the engine.

"Where are we going, sir?"

"Find the nearest grocery story or convenience store or

whatever store that has a newspaper stand with the *Times*."

"Oh, sir, four copies of the *Times* were delivered to the house earlier this morning."

McCoy's frustration continued to rise. "I know that. I want another copy. Now, drive me to get a newspaper if you'd like to stay employed."

"Yes sir, as you know we have protocols we have to—"

McCoy realized he needed to moderate his approach if he was going to have any success. "Look, it's early in the morning. We're at Sagaponack. Aside from a smattering of reporter fools trying to catch a story, no one is out. This is my brother's car; no one will expect me to be in it. Just drive me down the road to Pierre's Market. It's less than a mile. We'll be back in five minutes. It can be our little secret."

"Sir, I can't just—"

"Imagine what a story you can tell your grandkids about that summer in 2017 when you and the President of the United States took a secret road trip."

The agent sighed, realized arguing with the President was a losing proposition. Against his better judgment, he started the engine.

"Where exactly are we going, sir?"

"It's just a short drive down Sagg Main. It should be on the left."

The agent's heart raced as he drove by the few members of the press corps who were working the morning shift. The President ducked down in the seat, and shockingly no one saw him or suspected he was in the non-descript Lexus.

"There's Pierre's Market. I just need to get a copy of the

Times." McCoy began to open the door.

"At least let me get the paper, Mr. President," the agent protested.

"Oh, all right," McCoy conceded.

The Secret Service agent exited the car, paid for the paper, and quickly returned to the car where he had left the President of the United States alone and unprotected.

"Here it is, sir. Now, we have to get back immediately."

Ignoring the agent's comment, McCoy grabbed the paper out of his hand. His heart sunk as he saw the same headline as in the newspaper delivered to the family compound. It was unclear which was racing more, his heart or his mind.

"Stop!" McCoy screamed, and the agent slammed on the brakes. McCoy got out of the car and walked to the end of a nearby driveway and took the neighbor's paper, opening it while standing out in the open.

The agent quickly exited the vehicle and ran to the President.

"Sir, I have to insist that you get back in the car and let me get you back to the house."

McCoy didn't respond but stared off into the distance. Then he got back into the car expressionless, not saying a word.

The agent made the return trip to the compound; but this time, the press spotted McCoy as he was too dazed to duck down into the seat.

As the car pulled back into the driveway and up to the main entrance, the Secret Service detail was just preparing to fan out around the small village in search of the

Commander in Chief.

The agent was peppered with questions that he tried to answer.

Stone-faced, McCoy walked into the house to find everyone aflutter.

"Where's Dad?" McCoy asked.

"He left. He and mom both" his sister, Ophelia, answered.

"Left? To go where?"

"Back home. He and Mom called the captain, and they are headed for the boat. They are going back to Greenwich."

"What did he say about the newspaper story?" McCoy asked.

"Not a word," his brother, Jerome, responded.

McCoy found the lead agent and said, "Get everything ready, we are headed back to Washington."

"You no-good downright scumbag of a human being. I didn't know such low-life slugs actually existed. You—"

Click. The screen went black.

"What happened?" the President asked.

"Looks like he hung up on you."

"Well, get him back on. I wasn't done!"

Flying back to the White House after the morning debacle that was the newspaper article about his father, President McCoy demanded that Riley Indigo conduct a video conference with Victor Youngblood. Although Riley was led to believe that McCoy was ready to concede to Victor's demands, the beginning of the call suggested otherwise.

"Mr. President, I don't think Victor is interested in you berating him."

"Just get him back on."

"I'm not going to do that. It's been a long day, and I'm going to be with my family." Riley began to gather his belongs.

"Wait, Riley. OK, I'll stop the name-calling. Just get him back on."

Rather than dialing the video conference, Riley used Victor's cell for a private conversation.

"He says he wants to talk to you. He says he'll calm down. … I'll ask." Riley held the phone to his chest and looked at McCoy. "And you're ready to grant his release and pardon?"

McCoy rolled his eyes. "Yes, we can talk about that."

Riley cocked his head. "Are we *talking* about that, or are we *doing* that?"

McCoy's anger rose again as he paced around Riley's office.

After a few moments, Riley returned to the call. "He's not ready. We'll go to the next step and try again in a couple of days."

"No! Wait! Don't hang up! I'm ready. Just get him on the video," McCoy insisted.

Riley looked skeptical but spoke once more to Victor. "I'm connecting you. Stand by."

After a moment, the large screen in Riley's office powered up with Victor Youngblood staring back.

"I just want to know *why* my dad? What did he ever do to you?" Riley pleaded, almost in tears.

"*You* did this to your dad, Mitch. You did this by dragging your feet," Victor responded.

"But my dad is retired. He is out of the limelight. He isn't bothering anyone. My dad is a good man."

Riley decided it was his turn to respond. "Your dad is not a good man. Every word in that story is true. Your dad profited from the suffering of other human beings."

Victor piled on. "And besides, good men don't accomplish great things. Good men coach Little League baseball and go to church and pay their utility bills on time. Great men don't allow themselves to be distracted by such drivel. Great men use good men as instruments to change the world. That's what we're doing here today, Mitch. We are changing the world."

McCoy got a sick feeling in the pit of his stomach. "Changing the world?"

"That's right, Mitch. This is a historic day, and only the three of us will ever understand that. You're going to be able to look back on this day as the one when your presidency changed forever."

"Just sign these, sir." Riley handed McCoy the papers endorsing the Justice Department's efforts to overturn Victor's conviction and granting him a full pardon.

McCoy knew this was the biggest mistake of his career and that he'd regret this decision for as long as he lived. After a deep breath with a stunted exhale, he grasped the pen and signed the papers anyway.

"Great decision, Mitch. I'll be seeing you soon," Victor declared.

"Seeing me? How?" a confused McCoy asked.

As the screen went black, McCoy couldn't conceive what madness the next few days would bring to the Mitch McCoy presidency.

51

SEPTEMBER 18, 2017

"What time is it?" Savannah mumbled.

"I'm sorry; I tried not to wake you," Jeremy apologized.

"What time?"

"It's early."

"What time?!"

"A little after five."

Since Savannah moved to Abingdon to be with Jeremy and work at the hardware store, Rosita insisted that the pair live separately, a stance she finally relaxed after the engagement. Night number six of living in the Prince household was starting earlier than Savannah had expected.

"Are you dressed already?" Savannah squinted rubbing her eyes.

"Yes, I am."

"Where are you going?"

"Don't you remember? I'm going to Roanoke this

morning to meet with Jerry Bell. He owns the small hardware store like ours. We're helping one another take on the big guys."

"But why so early?"

"We're going to meet before his store opens. That way, I should be home by lunch."

"Umm…OK. Drive safely." Savannah stretched to give Jeremy a goodbye kiss and rolled back over in bed.

"That was close," Jeremy thought. Then he was off to his real destination, The Hammer.

Arise, avocado toast, quinoa, yogurt, kombucha, yoga, shower, Oval Office, newspapers.

For the past five days, President Mitch McCoy had opened the morning newspapers as if lifting a rock in the desert hoping a rattlesnake didn't coil out. To McCoy's pleasant surprise, for the past five days there had been nothing but mundane, harmless articles. Maybe the media were feeling generous. Ha! If that were the case, they wouldn't have published the hit piece on his father. Maybe they had dug up all the dirt they could on McCoy and his family. The last several weeks had been brutal. Dug up all the dirt? No way. The media could always find new dirt, even if they had to fabricate it.

Was it possible his concession to Victor Youngblood was paying dividends? Was it coincidental that the negative stories stopped at exactly the same time he finally agreed to

Victor's demands? Surely not.

With a deep breath, McCoy decided it was time to lift today's rock. He unrolled the paper, squinted, and finally took a peek. Was he seeing things? This had to be his imagination playing tricks on him. To his amazement, the headline said,

Why 2018 May be McCoy's Year

Mitch quickly scanned the article, which outlined several reasons why the Mitch McCoy presidency could thrive in 2018. The economy was poised for a rebound. His staff was finally in place to advance his signature initiatives. Key allies in Europe and Asia viewed him favorably.

As he finished reading, Mitch experienced something that he'd almost forgotten how to do - smile. The thought led to a chuckle and then a full-on laugh.

Riley! He had to go see Riley.

Walking into Riley Indigo's office, McCoy waved the paper above his head.

"Have you read the morning news?" McCoy bubbled.

"Congratulations, sir. It's about time you had some good press."

McCoy uncharacteristically sat down in Riley's visitor chair. "We need to find ways to make this happen."

"Make what happen?" Riley quizzed.

"The things that will make my presidency thrive in 2018."

"Don't worry; you did that last week."

"You mean—"

"Yes, your agreement with Victor. Oh, sir, 2018 is going

to be a highly productive year for all of us. And don't worry; you'll get plenty of credit."

McCoy cocked his head. "I'm not following you, Riley."

"That's OK, sir; it will all play out in due time."

The smile finally drained from McCoy's face. "You're speaking in code, Riley."

Riley grabbed the paper from McCoy's hand. "This article. You do understand this article is a product of your agreement with Victor. In fact, it was written by one of Victor's assets."

"But...I—"

"Like I said earlier, you'll get plenty of credit. 2018 really is going to be a great year for, among other things, the McCoy presidency," Riley promised.

The thought brought a reserved smile back to the President's face.

"Mr. President, are you ready for the big day tomorrow?"

"*Big day*? What's happening tomorrow?"

"Victor will be here. Tomorrow's the day you announce the new evidence that has been discovered and you officially declare his release."

"Victor will be here at the White House?"

"Oh, here's your speech." Riley then handed the President a stapled stack of paper.

"My speech?"

"Yes, please read through it a few times; it needs to sound sincere."

"But why am I—"

"I'm sorry, Mr. President; but I'm afraid I need to tend

to some other things."

"But—"

Before McCoy could finish his sentence, Riley rushed by him, leaving the President alone.

As McCoy read 'his' speech, his stomach began to turn. For the hundredth time in the last five days, he wondered, "What have I gotten myself into?"

As McCoy sat with his head in his hands, Vice President Adair passed by and saw the President through the cracked door of Riley's office.

"Everything OK, Mr. President?" Adair asked.

"I'm not sure," McCoy mumbled, finally standing, and walking down the hallway back to the Oval Office. "I'm not even sure what OK is anymore."

As he had for the last four hours of the mostly pre-dawn trip, Ben Gossett checked the rearview mirror on his 2017 Camaro to ensure he wasn't being followed. Comfortable that he was alone on Virginia Highway 823 he made a final turn onto Crystal Shores Drive. Seeing the scarlet sign *Welcome to Crystal Shores Marina, Enjoy Yourself and Please Drive Safely*, he knew he was at the right place. Pulling into the parking lot, he looked again at Jeremy's text.

Slip number 46, boat name The Hammer.

Ben walked through the gravel parking lot, his shoes

crunching on the rocks made louder by the solitude of Smith Mountain Lake before 8 a.m. He entered the code on the security gate, then walked down the dock counting off slip numbers as he passed: 36, 38, 40. Peering ahead, he saw a large houseboat at the end of the dock that had to be Jeremy's. After a couple more steps, he could see the words *The Hammer* written in large letters.

The boat was larger than Ben had envisioned and much nicer.

"Any trouble finding me?" Jeremy shouted from the top of the houseboat.

"None!" Ben shouted back. "Google never fails."

"7:55 a.m. It's good to know the FBI is still punctual," Jeremy teased.

"If you can't be effective, at least be punctual. I'm sure someone taught us that at Quantico," Ben shot back.

"Door's open," Jeremy advised. "I'll meet you downstairs."

As Ben walked into the main level, he was taken aback by the luxury of the boat's interior. The kitchen cabinets were made of cherry. The living room featured plush leather furniture. The walls were a combination of gold trim and solid wood.

"So, this is your boat?"

"Well, it was my dad's; so yeah, I guess it belongs to our family."

Still looking around, Ben felt compelled to ask, "What did your dad do?"

"Owned a small hardware store and saved every penny

he made to pay for this."

"The boat's awesome."

"Thanks. Let's grab a seat. I don't have a lot of time. I told Savannah I'd be back early afternoon."

Jeremy waved Ben over to the living room area, and each took a seat in a leather chair.

Before the real meat of the conversation, Ben wanted to ensure that he and Jeremy shared similar concerns. "So, you're good with all of this secrecy and—"

"Let's see…," Jeremy interrupted, "they killed your boss, my dad, the Republican nominee for Vice President, and a few thousand more people you don't even know about. So yeah, I'm good with this secrecy." Jeremy's tone became sharp at the end of his rant.

"Good, I didn't mean to—"

"It's all good, Ben. We're definitely on the same page," Jeremy insisted.

For the past week, the two men had been sharing cryptic texts from burner cells, brief emails from random Gmail accounts, and even a short phone call. It was obvious each had accumulated new information that needed to be shared with the other. This clandestine meeting, suggested by Jeremy, gave the two men their first face-to-face meeting since Task Force Terracotta was disbanded.

"You want me to start?" Ben asked logging in to his iPad.

"Yeah, but hang on a second. I need to hook someone in with us."

Jeremy clicked the remote, and the large screen tv powered on. Another few clicks on a second remote, and the screen read *Connecting to Han Solo.*

"Han Solo?" Ben asked but received no response.

"Hey, Luke, can you hear me?" Leonard wondered squinting into the camera.

"Loud and clear Leonard...I mean, Han."

"Leonard?" Ben beamed. "*THE* Leonard? The IT genius still working at Mouse Trap?"

"That's the one," Jeremy confirmed.

"Is this the FBI guy?" Leonard quizzed.

"That's me," Ben declared, raising a hand at the screen.

"Now that we have the intros out of the way, let's get started. Ben, you want to go first."

"Sure, I'll start. You're not going to believe this, but I've become kind of good buddies with the Vice President."

Jeremy cocked his head. "The Vice President of *what?*"

"The Vice President of the United States," Ben announced proudly.

"*What?* How?"

"You remember, a week or so ago one of my old Navy contacts arranged for me to meet the Vice President at Annapolis. I told him all about the task force and everything that has happened over the last few months. He was really interested and asked me a ton of questions."

Jeremy shook his head. "So, this didn't all seem crazy to him?"

"Not at all. There's more. I've met with the Vice President twice since then. He said the President has been acting very strangely and keeps mentioning Victor."

"There's strange stuff happening here at Mouse Trap

too," Leonard chimed in. "Workers have been in Victor's office updating all his tech. I've been directed to refresh all his access information. We've heard he was coming back, but now his return seems imminent."

"Hey, Leonard. I need you to check something," Jeremy announced.

"What?"

"The Bombardier jet is back in operation, right?"

"That's right."

"Check the travel log and see if there's an itinerary for the next few days."

"Why?"

"Just check."

When Jeremy ascended to the top of the Mouse Trap organization, one of the perks he relished was having access to the organization's private jet. Although it was in high demand, he often checked the travel log and would reserve flights when there was an opening in the schedule. He knew any upcoming trip would be recorded in the log.

"OK, I got it," Leonard confirmed. "The plane is leaving...*wow*...in just a few hours out of College Park. The destination is Fremont County Airport in Colorado. What's in Colorado?"

Jeremy and Ben shot one another a knowing glance.

"Victor. Victor's in Colorado," Ben declared.

"But not for much longer," Jeremy added.

"The Vice President said there has been a lot of preparation for a big event and an important visitor tomorrow. You don't think—"

"Hey, Leonard. Check one more thing in the travel log. What's the plan for the #1 limo tomorrow?"

"Wow!" Leonard exclaimed.

"What?"

"The limo is going to the White House."

"So, today Victor Youngblood is in the highest security prison in the country, ADX Florence. But tomorrow, he's going to be meeting at the White House with the President of the United States. That's insane!" Ben exclaimed.

"That's Victor Youngblood," Jeremy replied.

"This dude is…scary," Ben moaned.

"And this is only the beginning," Jeremy warned.

"Mr. Youngblood, it has truly been an honor to meet you."

"Javier, the honor has been mine."

"I don't know how you pulled it off, but I am really happy that you are getting to go home. I knew you never belonged here. I could just tell."

"It is nice to have someone who believed me, Javier."

"It's not going to be the same without you." Javier removed his cap and extended a hand to Victor.

Victor shook Javier's hand, seeing true devotion and admiration in his eyes. As he released Javier's hand, he cocked his head in thought.

"Javier, do I recall correctly that you and your family live in Florence but that most of your siblings and extended family are in Denver?"

"Yes sir. I was born and raised in Denver. It's home."

"Would you ever consider moving back to Denver? I have business interests there, and I could sure use a good security director."

"What? My family would love to move back to Denver!" Just as he got excited, Javier hung his head in humility. "But you could find someone with more experience than me. I only have a GED. I—"

"Javier, consider it done." Victor reached into his suit jacket and handed him a card. "Call this number. Tell them that I said to call about the security position. OK?"

"OK. Thank you, sir. You don't know what this will mean to my family."

"I'm happy for you, Javier. It will be great for both of us."

As Zeke received word that Victor had been released and the limo had picked him up en route to the airport, he reached into his jacket pocket, pulled out the envelope, removed the list, and crossed off item #8.

52

Arise, avocado toast, quinoa, yogurt, kombucha, yoga, shower. On his way to the Oval Office, McCoy heard a familiar voice coming from the direction of Riley's office. He walked down the hallway to get a closer vantage point.

"Surely not?" McCoy thought. "Is he here already?"

Unable to quell his curiosity, McCoy pushed open Riley's office door to look inside.

"Mr. President, this is great timing. We were just going over the program for this afternoon's media event."

McCoy tried to form the words for a response, but questions were bombarding his mind faster than his mouth could process them. "*What* media event? I thought this was supposed to be a small gathering. *What are they all doing here? What's he doing here already?*"

Victor Youngblood stood, walked toward the President, and extended a hand. "Good morning, Mr. President, it is good to see you in person rather than on screen."

McCoy returned the handshake but looked at Riley, still confused. He took inventory of those around the table: Chief of Staff Riley Indigo; Attorney General Breland Fleming; FBI Director Gavin Thompson; and convicted felon, Victor Youngblood.

"Riley, would you mind joining me in the Oval Office for a brief meeting?"

"Yes sir, happy to."

As Riley got up from behind the desk, he whispered something to the Attorney General who nodded in understanding. Then Riley followed the President down the short hallway. The meeting began before the Oval Office door opened.

"What the hell is going on, Riley? What media event are you talking about? I thought this was just a small gathering."

Riley followed McCoy into the Oval Office as the President remained standing.

"I'm not sure why you thought that. This has been planned from inception as a significant media event. In fact, we want maximum coverage."

Moving on to his next sore subject, McCoy continued, "And what is Youngblood doing here so early? It's not even seven o'clock. The media thing—whatever you're calling it—doesn't start until 1."

"Just working out the details. We want this to be done properly."

McCoy then walked to the Resolute Desk and grabbed the speech Riley had given him the night before.

"And I have many edits to this speech. I wouldn't say—"

"I'm sorry; the speech is already finalized. We aren't so-liciting edits."

McCoy snarled at his Chief of Staff's response.

"What do you mean *not soliciting edits?* This is my speech, and I'll edit it if I want."

As McCoy was fuming, the door to the Oval Office opened. Attorney General Fleming entered with the other members of his entourage close behind.

Victor began to walk around the office admiring the fur-nishings.

"I've always enjoyed my visits to this office," Victor began. "You can feel history, authority, and power in these walls."

Trailing behind like a child, McCoy meekly attempted a protest.

"We need to get one thing straight early on—"

"Reagan had a picture of Nancy right here on the corner of his desk." Victor ignored McCoy's moans and continued strolling around the room.

"The first Bush had a picture of his father on this wall. Clinton had a razorback on this table you know for his love of the University of Arkansas."

"Now, just a minute—"

"Didn't have a single picture of Hillary. Can't say I blame him." Victor chuckled. "W had a picture one of his twins drew him hanging on that wall."

McCoy finally gave up trying to interject and turned his attention to Riley.

"Riley, we have a lot to discuss."

As McCoy spoke, Riley received a call on his cell and

turned 90 degrees away from the President.

"Oh, she's here? Great. Send her in."

"Who's here now?" McCoy shuddered.

"Liz Rosen, editor of the *Times*," Riley responded.

"What's *she* doing here?" McCoy whined, finally conceding he had no control in his own Oval Office.

Before Riley could respond, the Oval Office door swung open and in walked the 48-year-old editor of the most important newspaper in America, some would say the most important in the world.

Liz walked directly to McCoy.

"Mr. President, thank you for agreeing to meet me this morning."

"I didn't really agree to…," McCoy stammered before again yielding to another visitor.

"Can we sit down, Mr. President?"

Finally realizing he was no longer in charge, McCoy obliged. "Of course, please, take a seat."

McCoy sat on one sofa, Liz on the sofa across from him. The others remained standing while Victor continued his reminiscence tour around the office.

"Mr. President, the *Times* owes you an apology."

McCoy sat up in his chair. He could list a hundred topics for which he felt an apology was due. He couldn't wait to hear which one was the subject of this meeting.

"The story we ran on your father has proven to have significant flaws to the point we no longer believe it meets our high standards for veracity. In fact, we believe it is downright false."

McCoy's mouth flew open. This was the last thing he expected to hear from the *Times*.

"The story's primary writer and our assistant editor are meeting with your father as we speak to offer him a personal apology. I wanted to do the same for you."

"Well, that's very...kind of you." McCoy could barely speak because of a mixture of emotion and shock.

Liz continued, "I want to let you know what we're doing to address this breakdown in our verification process. First, we are printing a front-page retraction in tomorrow's paper. Second, those associated with the story are facing disciplinary action ranging from a written reprimand to 30 days' suspension. Lastly, we are reassessing our fact-checking protocols in order to do our best to avoid this situation in the future. Mr. President, I'm terribly sorry."

McCoy was still struggling to form a cogent response, so Liz continued.

"In fact, this retraction will have a story arc similar to the one for the media event you are hosting this afternoon, an honest attempt to correct an injustice." Liz looked in Victor's direction, prompting McCoy to look as well.

"But how did you know about—" McCoy began.

Riley interjected, "We gave some key media figures a summary of what to expect this afternoon in return for delaying the story until after the event is over."

"Mr. President, I know your time is limited; so, I won't take any more of it. Again, on behalf of everyone at the *Times*, please accept our most sincere apology."

Liz stood, extended a parting hand to McCoy, then

quickly exited the Oval Office.

Victor stepped into the void and patted McCoy on the back. "Congratulations, Mitch. Things seem to be looking up for you."

"Wait, did you…are *you* responsible for this?"

"Mitch, today marks the beginning of what will be a great partnership."

Sensing the need to move along, Riley jumped back into the conversation. "OK, gentlemen, let's go back to my office and finish planning the details for this afternoon."

As the four men prepared to leave the Oval Office, Riley turned back to McCoy. "Don't forget to read through your remarks." Riley grabbed the speech that he had prepared for McCoy. "And don't go off script. These words will be on the teleprompter. Say them just as they are written and say them like you mean them."

McCoy sat back down at his desk and again read the remarks. His nagging concern continuing, he wondered, "What have I gotten myself into?"

"OK, that's the last item of new business on the agenda. Given that we're two-and-a half hours into what was supposed to be a one-hour meeting and that we are keeping our esteemed guests way over their time, unless there's a strong objection I'm going to recommend that we adjourn. Keep up the good work and let us know what we can do to help. This meeting is adjourned."

As chair of the Mustangs, Minnie Carpenter presided over the monthly meeting with representatives from each of the 50 states. Minnie, Elijah, Vice President Adair, and various other staff and leadership originated the meeting from the Mustang headquarters in Knoxville, Tennessee, with other members participating virtually from around the country.

It was an exciting time to be a Mustang. In the month since Eric Mathis rebuilt his friend's treehouse, Mustang Projects, as they came to be known, had gone viral. Citizens from cities and towns throughout America were inspired to invest their time, talents, and treasures in making their communities better through projects of all shapes and sizes. Even movie and TV stars posted YouTube videos of their Mustang Projects. Sports stars rebuilt inner-city basketball courts. Of course, opportunistic politicians of both parties worked to get themselves associated with as many Mustang Projects as possible, thus the reason for this meeting's esteemed guests.

"That was superb. You folks have quite a movement going here." Bart Henninger, vice chairman of the Republican Party complimented. Henninger persistently pestered Vice President Adair until he finally relented to a visit by Henninger; Senator Maggie Beaufort, Republican from Louisiana; and Senator Rodney Chambers, Republican from Tennessee.

"Thank you. That's kind of you; but of course, it has little to do with us. We just fertilized the interest Americans have in improving their communities. They are doing all the work," Minnie Carpenter responded. At Adair's suggestion, only Minnie, Elijah, and Adair himself stayed after the monthly meeting for the discussion with the Republican visitors.

"Oh, you're being modest," Henninger declared. "It takes bold visionary leadership to start a movement like this, and this team clearly has that. For example, these Mustang Projects are sweeping the nation. Senator Chambers here worked on a shoreline cleanup project with Mr. Mustang."

"I certainly did, and it brought me a great sense of accomplishment in bringing service to the community." Chambers smiled.

Elijah just rolled his eyes.

Hoping to close the meeting, Minnie stood to shake hands with the visitors. "Thank you for coming today. We are honored to have you visit with us."

Holding up a hand, Henninger interrupted, "There was one topic we hoped to discuss with your team, Ms. Carpenter."

"Oh, I'm sorry. We were already way over our time, and I assumed you needed to get back to Washington."

"It's OK; we have some time, especially for meeting with fine folks like yourselves," Henninger schmoozed.

An awkward pause hung over the room as Elijah, Minnie, and Adair sat quietly waiting for one of the politicians to speak. Finally, Senator Chambers broke the silence.

"As a fellow Tennessean, I want to commend you for this brilliant movement you've started. As you know, Tennessee is known as the Volunteer State; and the work you are doing personifies that moniker. What we'd like to know is how we can help you take this good work to the next level. What assistance can we offer?"

The trio of Mustang leaders agreed in advance that Minnie would speak for the group should they receive a question like the one Senator Chambers posed.

"Senator, we tell everyone to grow where you're planted. Find a project in your hometown and get involved. Get your hands dirty. You won't believe how full your soul will feel when you invest time to help someone else."

Henninger decided it was time to advance the discussion to another gear. "Yes, we're all involved in projects at home; but we're thinking of something bigger. You see, six of our Congressmen are sponsoring a bill that would earmark $250 million for Mustang Projects. They plan to introduce the bill next month. We already have all of our side on board in the Senate, we just need to clear the House. We believe that Mustangs' formal endorsement of the bill will garner the necessary votes to pass. We just want to ensure we can count on your support."

Before Minnie could speak, Elijah decided it was time to engage. "I'm not in the mood for diplomacy, so I'm just going to cut through the bull and straight to the issue."

"I like that," Henninger affirmed.

"You won't," Elijah predicted. "A large group of people around the country have decided they are tired of waiting on someone else to improve their communities, so they are just doing it themselves. This effort has created a lot of goodwill around the nation, and now you want to swoop in and put this under the Republican umbrella and take that goodwill for yourselves. Do I have the situation about right?"

Both Minnie and Adair looked at one another, both in shock. They had never seen their normally mild-mannered Elijah so direct.

"No, Elijah, you got it all wrong." Senator Chambers protested. "We genuinely want to help. We—"

"You said six Congressmen are set to sponsor the bill. How many of those are Democrats?" Elijah demanded.

"Well...that's not how Washington works. We start everything in the party and then—"

"How Washington works?" Elijah chuckled. "You think Washington works? Let me make this clear. We don't need you to pass a bill, and we don't need $250 million of taxpayers' hard-earned money."

Henninger interjected, "In addition to the funding, the bill includes indemnification language for a variety of environmental and safety laws. That will likely prove to be important for your movement to continue on its current trajectory."

"What do you mean *indemnification*?" Minnie quizzed.

"We've noticed that many projects involved environmental hazards, safety hazards, and chemical hazards. Children are often working on these projects. It would only take one or two really bad events to damage the movement and derail all the good work and goodwill you've garnered."

"But we don't—" Minnie started.

"You're threatening us?!" Elijah fumed.

"Threatening? Oh no, Elijah, you misunderstood me." Henninger was now standing and walking toward Elijah. "We're just saying—"

"I understand exactly what you're saying. If we don't agree to allow the movement to be absorbed into the Republican Party, you're going to sic the federal government on us."

"Elijah, that's not—"

"Get out."

"Now, calm down…"

"I said, '*Get out*!'"

"But—"

"For the last time, GET OUT!"

With a big sigh, the Republican contingent gathered their belongs and walked toward the door. On the way, Senator Chambers approached Elijah. "Elijah, we didn't really mean to—"

"Just go."

With the 'esteemed visitors' gone, Adair, and Minnie sat in stunned silence as Elijah paced around the room trying to collect his thoughts.

"You guys did this on purpose, didn't you?" Elijah challenged.

Minnie cocked her head. "Did what, Elijah?"

"Invited these stuffed shirts to meet with us. I know you've been trying to get me to come on board with your plan, but maybe I've been too stubborn to listen," Elijah admitted, talking to the wall.

Adair stood and walked toward Elijah. "I assure you, Elijah, this meeting had nothing to do with convincing you of anything. They came to my office, assured me they wanted to discuss—"

Elijah raised a hand. "It's OK. I didn't mean to accuse you of anything. I'll admit that this conversation made me see things more clearly."

Elijah finally turned to face Minnie and Adair. He sighed in resignation.

"When I think back on the last couple of years, we were born as a political movement to challenge the two deeply entrenched parties. We had hoped we could get away from that and focus on just helping people, but they won't allow us to do that. We're becoming too much of a threat. It pains me to say it; but if we want to keep this movement going and help as many people as we can, you guys are right—we have to reengage politically. We have to give the people a choice."

Elijah couldn't have understood how this declaration would change the course of the movement in the months and years to come and how it would prove prophetic his prediction that the Mustangs were indeed becoming a threat not only to two political parties but also to the most powerful man in the world.

53

These types of events were usually well-orchestrated. Three days before an event, Secret Service would clear all guests. Two days before, all plans would be finalized and attendees confirmed. Twenty-four hours before, a general notice would be shared with the media at large. Twelve hours before, White House media relations personnel would leak the event's purpose to select trusted media members. Story outlines would be given to an even smaller media subset. Two hours before the meeting, a transcript of the prepared remarks would be sent to the entire White House press corps so they could adequately prepare to cover the event.

This afternoon's gathering was different. Six complete stories were pre-written and provided to six favored media representatives. Each story was unique, but all led to the same conclusion. This was going to be a historic day in U.S. justice. What the media wasn't told was that it was also going to be a historic day in terms of the way the White House, and by extension the entire country, would function for years to come.

"Ladies and gentlemen, the President of the United States."

As Mitch McCoy exited the West Wing and walked onto the Rose Garden stage, he was accompanied by Attorney General Breland Fleming; FBI Director Gavin Thompson; and the man of the hour, Victor Youngblood. Although McCoy had come to understand his eroding power behind the scenes, in this public forum he wanted to make a statement that he was still firmly the man in charge. To that end, he led the parade of dignitaries and was the first to approach the microphone. He paused for effect, struck his most presidential pose, and looked steely eyed directly at the assembled guests.

"Among the highest responsibilities our government shoulders is ensuring justice is fairly applied to all citizens of our great country, rich or poor, powerful or weak, young or old. The sacred words in the preamble to our Constitution remind us that in our pursuit of a more perfect union we must seek to establish justice. For our founding fathers, justice was…"

"You're watching this, right?" Vice President Adair had the unique vantage point of watching the President's speech on TV in the Cabinet Room while also viewing it live out the window.

"Yes sir, I'm watching every lying pompous word." In

lesser accommodations than Adair's, Ben Gossett was watching on his tablet in his 2013 Jeep Grand Cherokee in the parking lot of the Shawnee State Park Campground just outside of Bedford, Pennsylvania.

"Don't get distracted by the lies. There are many more still to come. Is everything still on track?" Adair asked.

"Yes sir, everything is on schedule. And Pittsburgh is on track from your end?"

"Pittsburgh is on track," Adair confirmed.

"Great. I'll make the next call," Ben agreed.

"Roger that."

"...and justice is exactly what we are here to discuss today. I'd like to welcome to the dais my Attorney General Breland Fleming."

McCoy stepped to the side as Fleming nodded his gratitude, paused for effect as he surveyed the press corps, and then began speaking.

"Last May, the U.S. Justice Department prosecuted Victor Youngblood for the murder of Senator Grant Wembley. Mr. Youngblood was found guilty of first-degree murder and was sentenced to life imprisonment without the possibility of parole. His sentence was to be served at The United States Penitentiary, Administrative Maximum Facility in Fremont County, Colorado, also known as ADX Florence. However, today we are announcing significant new evidence has come to light that raises concerning questions about Mr.

Youngblood's guilt. Here to discuss that new evidence is FBI Director, Gavin Thompson."

Fleming stepped aside as Thompson stepped to the mic.

"Thank you, General Breland. Working in cooperation with several other entities, the Bureau has obtained video evidence providing new context to a video that was the primary prosecutorial evidence in Mr. Youngblood's trial. I will direct your attention to this monitor. You can see a snippet of the video showing Senator Wembley's murder perpetrated by two men dressed in black. This video also appears to show Mr. Youngblood directing the two men's actions. The video we previously had stops here. We now have obtained this full video, which I will continue to play. As you can see, Mr. Youngblood was not the murderers' accomplice but instead a victim himself, who tried to intervene on Wembley's behalf. The video prompted us to review other evidence, which also points to Mr. Youngblood's innocence."

"Jeremy, I assume you are watching this?" Ben Gossett queried.

"Savannah and I are glued to the TV. Can you believe this crap?" Jeremy blurted.

"I just talked to the Admiral. Everything is good on his end, and Pittsburgh is a 'go.' How about you guys?"

"Yes, I'm all set. Ready for the next step. I'll call Leonard and let him know he can execute the plan on his end."

"…and as this video caused us to review other evidence, all of which we now call into question in light of this newly obtained information," FBI Director Thompson concluded. As had been rehearsed, he stepped aside as Attorney General Fleming again strode to the microphone.

"Based on the FBI's new information, the Justice Department has been reviewing this case over the past few weeks and has concluded that a mistake in prosecutorial judgment was made in Mr. Youngblood's case. If we had had the information at the time of prosecution that we now have, we would not have pursued a case against Mr. Youngblood.

"The next obvious question is what to do about this mistake. The Justice Department doesn't have the legal grounds to just wipe away a guilty verdict rendered by a jury and a sentence meted out by a judge. In a normal situation, we would be obligated to share this new evidence with Mr. Youngblood's legal counsel, who would then likely start the appeal process to seek a new trial. I won't bore you with the legal details; but this would be a protracted process that would take years all while Mr. Youngblood served a sentence in this country's most secure federal prison, spending 23 hours a day in a cell with no human contact…"

Hey, Han, you good to talk?

Yeah, Luke, I can talk.

With that confirmation, Jeremy called Leonard's cell phone.

"You watching this crap at the White House?" Jeremy asked.

"Yes, I am watching on the monitor in my office. Most everyone else here is watching in the Mouse Trap auditorium. I heard their cheers down the hall when they said Victor wasn't guilty."

"Kinda makes you want to hurl, doesn't it?" Jeremy blurted.

"Big chunks," Leonard confirmed.

"Wanted to let you know I talked with Ben, who talked with the Vice President. Everything is a go."

Leonard breathed deeply. "OK."

Jeremy could hear the concern in Leonard's voice. "You still OK with everything? I know this is huge for you."

"Yes, I'm OK. I know this is the right path. I'm just gonna—"

"Miss it there?" Jeremy interjected.

After a pause, Leonard responded, "No, I'm not gonna miss it." Speaking with a new resolve, he said, "I'm ready. There's one more thing, Jeremy. He's coming to see you."

"Who's coming to see me?"

"Victor. His plane is leaving D.C. this afternoon and coming back here to Bethesda, but it is leaving again tomorrow and landing in Abingdon."

"Wow, he's coming *here*? Any idea why?"

"No, the itinerary just says Abingdon, Virginia."

After a brief moment of reflection, Jeremy responded, "I'll be ready."

"...so, we have a different course of action that will better serve both the tenets of justice and the life of Mr. Youngblood."

Attorney General Fleming stepped away from the microphone as President McCoy stepped back into the center of the proceedings.

"As you have heard from Director Thompson and General Fleming, the United States Justice Department admits its mistakes in the prosecution of Mr. Youngblood. That's why earlier today I granted Mr. Youngblood a full pardon. He is now a free man and has agreed to join us today for this event. He has asked to make a few remarks and even field some questions from the media. Mr. Youngblood, you have the floor."

Watching on the large monitor in the Mouse Trap auditorium, Zeke reached into his jacket pocket, pulled out the envelope, removed the list, and crossed off item #9.

Victor stepped to the microphone and, always the showman, breathed deeply while wiping tears from both eyes.

"I'm not even sure where to begin," Victor professed. It was a speech he had written weeks ago and had refined it many times from his cell at ADX Florence. "I'm still stunned. Less than 24 hours ago, I was in a tiny concrete cell in the middle of nowhere, resigned to the fact that I would spend whatever years I had left in that very lonely existence. Now, I'm standing in the Rose Garden at the White House with the President of the United States. It's a lot to take in. I hope you'll understand if this is all still sinking in. First of all, I'd just like to thank everyone at the Justice Department who has been working on my case. I had no idea. And I want to express my most sincere gratitude for the President and the pardon he so graciously granted me."

Victor looked at McCoy.

"Thank you, Mr. President. Thank you from the bottom of my heart."

McCoy nodded in response.

"I think I'm supposed to answer a few questions," Victor commented in his most humble tone.

"Are you angry, Mr. Youngblood? Surely this all must be incredibly frustrating," the first reporter asked, perfectly reciting the question she'd been given.

"That's a great question." Victor looked aside as if pondering the depth of the question. "I can honestly say I do not feel any anger. Maybe that will come with more time to reflect on what I've been through over the past year; but for now, my only sentiment is gratitude."

"How much advance notice did you have about this? Had you heard from anyone that your case was being reviewed?" the next reporter asked, again a predetermined question.

"Completely in the dark, literally. I'm not sure how much you know about the facility where I was sent. As the Attorney General stated, I spent 23 hours a day in my cell with no human contact. The other hour was spent outside my cell, also with no human contact. I certainly had no access to news or outside information. This was a wonderful surprise."

"I know this is all new to you, but do you have any idea what's next?" the third assigned reporter asked.

With this question, McCoy stepped to the mic, just as he had been told.

"That's a great segue to the final news I'd like to share with you today," McCoy began. "Hearing about Mr. Youngblood's case has affected me greatly. As you will recall, a pillar of my campaign was justice reform. Too many innocent people have been the victim of our own justice system. The victims of this injustice are disproportionately people of color and those who don't have access to capable defense. This is something we must address and address soon. That's why today I am announcing a new initiative. I'm creating the Office of Justice Reform, or OJR, which will have broad responsibilities to investigate all federal cases involving even a hint of wrongful prosecution. OJR will also provide a framework for states to follow suit. I'm pleased to announce that Mr. Youngblood has agreed to serve as OJR's first director. He will report directly to me. Who better to lead this initiative than someone with the decades of executive experience

Mr. Youngblood has and who has also been personally victimized by our justice system. Much more will be discussed in the coming weeks about OJR. It will have my highest attention and focus. Thank you for coming today."

With the final remarks McCoy, Youngblood, Fleming, and Thompson stood side-by-side posing for pictures. After a few moments, the four walked away in unison, again with McCoy leading the way.

"Wait. Victor is going to work in the White House?" Savannah asked incredulously.

"Sounds like it," Jeremy gasped.

"How does this affect the plans?"

"It doesn't. This doesn't change anything. It just makes it more urgent," Jeremy warned.

"And Leonard said Victor is coming here tomorrow, right?" Savannah wondered.

"That's what he said," Jeremy confirmed.

"Are you still leaving tonight?"

"No, I think I'm going to stay. I want to see what he wants."

"Are you sure this is safe?" Savannah worried.

"Nope, not sure at all."

"I think that went well," McCoy proclaimed, walking back into the White House with Victor, Fleming, and Thompson, whom Riley Indigo met at the door.

"Let's step into the Roosevelt Room for a brief meeting." Riley gestured toward the meeting room door.

"What kind of meeting?" McCoy demanded.

He was ignored as the remaining members of the group followed Riley's lead and filed into the room. McCoy lagged behind and again queried Riley. "Riley, I didn't have a meeting on my schedule."

"No sir. It's just a quick follow-up meeting."

As he stepped into the room, the President saw the original group from the Rose Garden meeting; a few other members of his Cabinet; and three Democrat congressional leaders, including the House Speaker.

"Well done, Mr. President. Very well done." Victor had taken a position at the head of the table and was clearly in charge of this gathering.

Still unsure what was going on, McCoy joined Victor at the head of the table standing uneasily beside him and agreed, "Yes, I concur; the event went just as planned."

Victor looked at McCoy disapprovingly and whispered to him, "Sit down, Mitch."

At first offended, McCoy saw all eyes on him and mustered one last comment. "Yes, great job." He then looked for a seat and finally took the only one available near the end of the table.

Victor remained standing and spoke with authority. "I want to thank you all for joining us in this gathering. The purpose is to confirm that we understand the reset that just happened today. For my congressional friends in this meeting, we have several pieces of legislation for you to prioritize. I want you to status Riley weekly. He will be in direct contact with me. Going forward, every executive policy decision will also come from Riley. Understood?"

Before the lawmakers could respond, McCoy stood in protest. "Now just hang on a second. I'm not going to be a party to this. Victor, I know we have an understanding; but I just want to make this clear I am still the President of the United States. I'm—"

"Sit down, Mitch," Victor demanded, this time not whispering.

His mouth wide open, McCoy took a step away from his chair. "I *will not* sit down, and I will not be a party to this usurpation of my power. *I will not!*"

Behaving like a petulant child, McCoy tried to open the door but was unable to turn the knob on the first try. Finally, the door cooperated, and he stormed out of the room. He walked through the short corridor and into the Oval Office where he took a seat behind his desk.

It took him a moment to notice, but he saw two newspapers side-by-side on his desk. One had a large handwritten note that read, "RETURN TO THE MEETING." The newspaper beside it had a large headline that read, "McCoy Leads Historic Justice Initiative." The article praised his leadership and included him in the company of Presidents Lincoln, Kennedy, and Roosevelt. The second newspaper had a note that read, "STAY HERE." That paper's headline conveyed a vastly different message: "McCoy Administration Convicts Innocent Man." The article used words like *bungled* and *inept* to describe Victor Youngblood's conviction and said it was another example of Mitch McCoy's failed leadership.

McCoy studied the papers more closely and noticed both were dated with the following day's date. It was obviously Victor's handiwork and was meant to send a message. It was a message that was received loud and clear.

McCoy swallowed his pride—an enormous feat, put down the newspaper, walked back through the corridor, and opened the door to the meeting room. As he entered, all eyes turned to him, but no one said a word. After an awkward pause, he returned meekly to his seat.   Then all eyes returned to Victor.

"Any further questions from the group?" There were none. "Ladies and gentlemen, I look forward to this esteemed group making history together."

All nodded in agreement.

"Oh, Mitch, I'm going to need you to be out of the White House tomorrow evening."

"What do you mean *out of the White House*?" McCoy blurted.

Victor didn't answer, but instead put on his coat and walked toward the door.

"Don't worry; he'll be out," Riley promised as the group filed out of the room.

"But where am I supposed to go?" McCoy stammered before realizing he was alone.

54

"The fact that this room is packed wall-to-wall is a testament to your faith in leadership. Even when I, your leader, was sentenced to life in prison without the possibility of parole and Mouse Trap seemed to be fading into the dustbin of history, many of you helped to start rebuilding it. Some of you worked from your homes; some of you worked from remote cabins in the North Carolina mountains; others readied this place, our Bethesda headquarters, for today's implausible homecoming.

"You stood steadfast as you were told to focus on the task of rebuilding Mouse Trap. You didn't question that direction; you just followed it without hesitation. I want to believe that is due to your trust in me, but I know it is at least due in part to your respect for my #2 and closest of friends, Zeke Gibson. Zeke, come up here with me."

Zeke, who had been seated in the front row, reluctantly climbed the stairs to join Victor on stage. As he did, the

Mouse Trap team stood in unison cheering for their interim leader. They all knew Mouse Trap's rebuilding was largely due to Zeke's leadership over the past year.

"There are many chapters in my story of redemption and restoration that I can't share with you; but I *can* tell you Zeke was by my side, sometimes literally, sometimes figuratively, every step of the way. Zeke, my friend, I can't thank you enough."

Victor offered Zeke an uncharacteristic embrace, which again brought the crowd to its feet.

The hubbub was the perfect distraction for Leonard. He looked around the room, saw a few faces he would miss, reconciled that he wouldn't be able to say a proper goodbye, and walked out the back door of the auditorium.

Leonard had already packed a small box of mementos he wanted to take with him. He couldn't completely clear his desk for fear of revealing his absence too soon. He knew it wouldn't take long for them to find out, but he only needed a few hours. Sitting at his desk one last time, he logged in to Omnia and hit Control F8. Then he walked out the door. The clock was ticking.

"Beth, you have my itinerary. I will be leaving shortly. Is everything in place?" Adair quizzed.

"Yes sir, but I'm still not crazy about the idea," Beth McDonald, Director of the Secret Service, warned.

"I know, Beth, but I will be with my detail the entire time;

and they will be checking in regularly."

Adair was still astounded at Victor Youngblood's level of infiltration into the U.S. Government, which now included the President. One last bastion of relative independence was the Department of Homeland Security, through which the Secret Service reported. A former brigadier general, with whom Adair had served for over 20 years, served as Homeland Security Secretary. He was a man Adair could trust with the true story of what was happening with Victor Youngblood and with whom he could conduct the current operation.

"And tonight's still a go?" Adair queried.

"Yes sir," Beth confirmed. "Everything is set. Have your man go to the Treasury Building. Our agent will meet him there and lead him through the tunnel into the East Wing. Once he's there, we will have to improvise a rendezvous with your targets as we don't know exactly where they plan to be."

"But they will still be here tonight, right?"

"Yes, everything is set. The President has already left the White House, and they are scheduled to arrive early evening."

"This is going to be an important night, Beth. I can't thank you enough. Of course, I need you to keep this operation between us."

"Worthy of trust and confidence," Beth recited the Secret Service motto.

"Indeed, you are," Adair confirmed.

Cassidy had only been told to report to Victor's office, which she had never visited. Her heart was racing as she surveyed the spacious office. On one entire wall, she saw a bank of 20 large video screens that each played news from around the world. Another wall looked down to the floor below, where most Mouse Trap workspaces were located. Directly in front of her was Victor's modern desk and chair positioned perpendicular to a large glass conference table, where she was seated.

"I'm sorry to keep you waiting, Cassidy," Zeke greeted.

"Oh…it's uh…OK," she muttered, while standing.

"Cassidy, have you had the pleasure of meeting Victor?"

"Oh, yes, a couple of times; but I'm sure he doesn't remember me."

Victor smiled and extended a hand. "Of course, I remember you, Cassidy. I remember all of our high performers. Please, take a seat."

All three sat around Victor's table.

"I've been hearing good things about you from Zeke," Victor offered.

"Thank you, sir."

Usually brimming with confidence, Cassidy couldn't remember being more nervous. She wasn't sure why.

"Zeke has attempted to explain the setup you created with Leonard and Omnia. It sounds genius, but I'd like to hear you explain it yourself."

"Oh, of course." She looked to Zeke who nodded in agreement.

"Zeke shared with me the concern you both have about

Leonard's true loyalty. At first, Zeke assigned me just to watch Leonard, but that proved difficult. So instead, I rerouted his login protocols. For the last several weeks when he thought he was logging in to Omnia, he was really logging in to a mirror site I created that appears to be Omnia. I have been able to see exactly what Leonard has been working on. Each morning, I can see Leonard's work from the previous day and replicate it on the real Omnia rebuild. I can take advantage of Leonard's work without the threat of him having access to the actual system. Of course, I designed it in a way he will never know it is a mirror site."

"I was right; it is genius. So, Omnia is still on track for full recovery by when?" Victor pressed.

"Many connections have been fully recovered and a few new ones that weren't there before, but I'd say we're greater than 80% recovered. We're probably still a few weeks away from 100% recovery."

"Sounds great, Cassidy. Keep up the good work," Zeke approved. "Thank you for coming by."

Getting the message that she was being dismissed, Cassidy breathed for what seemed like the first time in 10 minutes and stood to leave. As she approached the office door, she felt compelled to offer one last thought. "There's one more thing. It seems that Leonard is working on something that's…" Cassidy struggled to find the right words before finally settling on "not quite right."

"What do you mean?" Zeke wondered.

"I'm not really sure; but I'll be keeping a close watch," Cassidy assured.

"You do that." Victor thanked Cassidy as she exited the office.

"I like her," Victor proclaimed.

He then searched his phone's contact list to find a number. "I need to call Gavin to make sure everything is on track for Pittsburgh."

"Is that supposed to happen tonight?" Zeke asked.

"That's what I need to confirm." Victor put his phone on speaker so Zeke could hear.

"Hello, Victor," Thompson answered foregoing the usual greeting of *FBI Director Thompson*.

"Gavin, I wanted to check on the status of Pittsburgh."

"All is well, Victor. The agent I mentioned to you who has been going rogue is meeting with the Pittsburgh office this afternoon. He thinks he's going around me to arrange an operation, but he will be detained when he arrives. Although he has been given strict orders to stay away from anything having to do with the case, he's been breaking those orders. This will result in criminal penalties."

"Very well, Gavin. I expect you to call me if anything changes."

"Will do, Victor."

Victor ended the call.

"OK, with that out of the way and Andrei in the clear, I have a list of operations I have authorized. I need you to get this list to Andrei before you leave today." Victor handed Zeke a two-page list of names.

Zeke understood "operations" was the code word for when Andrei Ovchenko's Blackforce was activated to eliminate an individual Victor deemed an impediment to progress. Operations would normally involve a single individual although on rare occasions might involve two or three. Therefore, Zeke was astonished to see a list of at least 50 names.

"They are prioritized," Victor pronounced.

Zeke nodded while reviewing the list.

"This is quite a list," Zeke observed.

"We have almost achieved our ultimate goal, but some threats have grown to unacceptable levels. We can't let anything get in our way when the finish line is in our sights."

"Some of these names I understand," Zeke confirmed. "However, several of our former Mouse Trap team members are on the list."

"Several of our managers didn't return when you worked to rebuild the team. We can't have disloyal people walking around knowing our secrets."

"You know, I didn't make returning to Mouse Trap mandatory. I gave each person the option to return or not."

Victor shook his head. "They knew leaving was never an option. They brought this on themselves."

"I see the Vice President is on the list. That will be challenging," Zeke observed.

"Andrei will figure out a way. Adair has to be out of the way for us to achieve our ultimate goal."

"Who is Javier Ramirez?"

"He was my guard in Colorado."

"I thought he treated you well." Zeke was perplexed.

"He did. He was wonderful. He did everything I asked."

"So then why—"

Victor held up a hand. "Don't tell me you are getting soft in your old age."

"Of course not, I just don't—"

"Javier knows everything that happened in that prison, and it is the opposite of what we want the public to know. I gave him an out by offering him a job with Mouse Trap. At first, he accepted; but after he talked it over with his wife, he changed his mind. That's unfortunate; he's a good man."

"And you have reason to think he'll talk?"

"Just can't have that risk," Victor blurted.

"And I see Jeremy Prince is on the list with a big question mark by his name."

"That's a great segue, my friend. My plane is waiting on me for a trip to Abingdon, Virginia, home of Prince's Hardware. My old apprentice and I are going to have a heart-to-heart. After that, we can either remove his name or remove the question mark."

Victor stood and put on his coat.

"Hmm. OK," Zeke mumbled.

"After Abingdon, I'm flying right back to D.C. You're meeting me at the airport at 5 and then we're driving to the White House, right?"

"That's right. See you then."

Victor left Zeke alone in his office. Perusing the list again, Zeke shook his head. He felt the unfamiliar tinge of doubt working to fight its way past 40 years of friendship and loyalty. The feeling left him bewildered.

"Hey, Jeremy, a fancy car just pulled up out front. I swear it looks like that dude who was on TV yesterday with the President." Chip, the front desk clerk, was growing accustomed to unexpected visitors to the hardware store.

"You mean Victor Youngblood?" Jeremy feigned surprise but was fully expecting the visit after Leonard's heads-up.

"Yeah! That's the guy! He's here!"

Jeremy walked out of the office and toward the front door, where Victor and a bodyguard had entered the store.

"Jeremy Prince, it is good to see you!" Victor proclaimed, extending a hand, which Jeremy accepted.

"It is good to see you too, Victor." It was an honest proclamation, but not for the reasons Victor assumed.

"Hello, Victor." As she and Jeremy had agreed, Savannah walked up to join the reunion.

"Savannah! Beautiful as ever. I heard that I might see you here. I'm glad that report was true."

"I saw you on TV yesterday. It sounds like things are going well," Jeremy observed.

"Very well, Jeremy." Looking around the store, Victor saw that he was attracting the attention of both customers and employees. "Is there somewhere we might have a short discussion?"

"Sure, we can meet in the office. Follow me. I assume it's OK for Savannah to join us."

"Certainly." Victor assured.

As Jeremy led Victor into the office, the bodyguard

remained outside.

"It's nothing like your office, of course," Jeremy confessed.

As the trio took their seats, Jeremy felt both pride and discomfort that he was in the boss's chair and that Victor was playing the role of visitor.

"I guess my first word should be *Congratulations*," Victor said.

Confused, Jeremy and Savannah looked at one another. "Congratulations?" Jeremy wondered.

"I see you have presented a ring to the young lady." Victor gestured toward Savannah's left hand. "Have you two set a date?"

Both Savannah and Jeremy managed a chuckle, but both were nauseated at the thought of Victor interjecting himself into their private lives.

"Oh, yeah, thank you. No, no date set yet. We'll be working on that."

"That's wonderful. I'm happy for you. You have great futures ahead of you."

After an awkward pause, Victor broke the silence.

"I would like to get a couple of things out of the way so that we can move ahead in our professional relationship."

Both Savannah and Jeremy squirmed in their chairs, curious about what was to come next.

"First of all, I want to clear the air about the unfortunate incident in Wyoming. I understand why you did what you did, Jeremy; and I want to assure you there are no hard feelings. In fact, I'm impressed that you were able to pull off such a feat. Men have been trying to get me behind bars for 40 years. You're the first one to succeed."

Unsure how to respond, Jeremy said, "Thank you."

"I also want to convey my most sincere condolences regarding your father and to assure you Andrei was working on his own and not as part of Mouse Trap. I know that won't bring back your father, but I am terribly sorry for your loss."

Now Jeremy was fuming but was trying hard to conceal his anger—not out of fear of Victor but because he was trying to focus on the larger picture and needed to see what Victor was really there to say. Again, he went with "Thank you."

Victor continued, "Jeremy, I know you were only with Mouse Trap for a short time, but you were among the most promising team members I've ever had. I'm here today to ask you to consider coming back into the fold. In my new position, I am able to offer you…" Realizing Savannah might be a source of additional enticement, Victor completed his comment, "…actually, offer both you and Savannah exciting new opportunities if you'd consider coming back. I have some things in mind for both of you, but you would also have wide latitude to design your own positions."

Jeremy cocked his head. "But I thought you were taking a new position in the White House to right all the wrongs of our justice system, or something like that."

"That's the official job. Unofficially, I will have substantially more responsibility. Jeremy, we are going to do great things; and I want you and Savannah to be part of that."

Jeremy nodded as if he understood.

"We have settled into a nice life here in Abingdon. I'm not sure we are interested in leaving," Jeremy offered.

"I understand, but Abingdon will always be here. I'm offering you the opportunity of a lifetime."

"When would you need to know?" Savannah asked, giving Victor hope that they were actually considering his offer.

"The offer will always stand; but to ensure you have the best opportunity, it would be optimal if we could work out something in the next week." Knowing he had pushed enough to at least plant a seed, Victor decided to pause.

"You two think about it for a few of days and get back with me with any questions you may have. Is that a deal?"

Jeremy looked at Savannah, who nodded in agreement.

"That's a deal, Victor. Thank you for coming all the way to Abingdon just for us."

Victor raised a hand. "Not a problem, Jeremy. You are two of the brightest minds I've ever encountered. I hope you come back to the team. We can accomplish great things together." Victor reached into his jacket pocket and handed business cards to both Jeremy and Savannah. "This has my direct line. Call me anytime."

The trio exchanged handshakes, and Victor left the store bound for the Virginia Highlands Airport for the return trip to D.C.

"That was...something," Savannah marveled. "You're not really considering this are you?"

"We gotta talk," Jeremy whispered.

He needed to talk quickly because he was also heading to the airport soon for a flight bound for Pittsburgh.

Ben Gossett took the Bates Street exit off I-376, circled back to Second Avenue, and crossed Hot Metal Bridge before turning onto South Water Street. He was fortunate to find a parking spot at the Steeler's training facility directly across the street from the Pittsburgh FBI office.

Located on the banks of the Monongahela River, the Pittsburgh FBI office is home to over 200 agents and support personnel, including a Special Agent in Charge and three Assistant Special Agents in Charge, one who met Ben at the door.

"Ben, it is good to see you, my friend. It has been too long." Anthony Grimaldi was a 25-year Bureau veteran. Among his five posts was a stint in D.C., where he worked with Ben Gossett on a variety of cases. Ben counted on this relationship when trying to find a familiar Pittsburgh-based agent.

"It has been too long Anthony. Your family doing well?"

"They are. Can you believe my oldest is graduating college in the spring?"

"You gotta be kidding me. That's crazy!"

"Come on up to my office and let's talk."

The two men passed through security and down the main hallway to the elevator bank. They rode up the fourth floor and found their way to Grimaldi's office.

"This is quite an interesting read you provided us," Grimaldi commented.

"Can you believe this is happening right here in your

district?" Ben cringed.

"In the FBI, we learn not to be shocked; but I'll be honest, this sounds like something out of a movie."

"Exactly!" Ben declared. "Is everything a go for tonight?"

"We have several agents here who were awaiting your arrival. They are just down the hallway. You ready to meet?"

"I am. Let's go."

"Here's the plan we've developed. Read through it and let me know what you think." Grimaldi handed Ben a document, but his expression let Ben know something wasn't right.

Ben looked down and read,

Ben, most likely my office is under surveillance. I'm really sorry, but tonight got scuttled by HQ. We have been told NOT to make a move on the warehouse. In fact, we've been instructed to detain you. HQ agents will return you to D.C. I'm really sorry about this. Before we go into the conference room, you might consider going to the bathroom, then turn left down the southwest hallway, which will lead to a service stairway and out the side door. Stay safe, my friend. There's definitely something strange happening in the Bureau.

"This looks great, Anthony. I think we can make this work. I'm excited to be a part of it. Hey, before we get started, I gotta hit the head. Did I see it down the hall?"

"Yes, just down the hallway."

"Great, be right back."

Ben gave Grimaldi a thankful nod, which Grimaldi subtly

returned.

Just as Grimaldi had suggested, Ben was out the back door and in his car in less than 10 minutes. The parking spot proved fortunate as it was an easy access back onto I-376 for the seven-hour drive south. The evening was just getting started.

55

"Hell of a view," Victor offered.

"And it's been a hell of a ride," Zeke confirmed.

"Be honest with me, Zeke. Did you really think we'd make it?"

"It is difficult to believe we're here!" Zeke marveled.

"Of course, there is much more work to do; but look at us. We have to stop along the way and appreciate what we've accomplished."

The two men were seated on the Truman Balcony on the White House second floor. Located off the Yellow Oval Room near the President's private residence, the balcony is normally used by the President and his private guests. On this evening, Victor Youngblood and Zeke Gibson were making themselves at home after dismissing McCoy from his own residence.

"Zeke, when we started this journey, I don't think either one of us envisioned this." Victor gestured around the house, down to the South Lawn and in the direction of the

Washington Monument.

"I know I didn't," Zeke confirmed.

In the 1970s, a young Victor Youngblood had established Youngblood and Associates, a public relations and marketing firm serving high-profile Washington D.C. clients. This exposure to the nation's most powerful decisionmakers, and their myriad indiscretions, opened doors for Victor to create the clandestine offshoot, Mouse Trap.

In the early years, Mouse Trap was fertile ground for the accumulation of money; property; and, most importantly, power. All were reaped in generous amounts. Mouse Trap, and by extension Victor, was thriving. Near the turn of the 21st century, Victor began refining his vision for a larger endgame, one that expanded beyond the walls of Mouse Trap, out of the shadows and into the light. That new vision involved the White House. He didn't need the formal title of president; he just craved the power that went with it, the power of the President.

"Zeke, my friend, I've brought us a bottle to celebrate this occasion. You know what this is?"

Victor held up a bottle of bourbon.

"Is that a Pappy Van Winkle?"

"None other. I retrieved these glasses from a cabinet in the Oval Office. The inscription said they belonged to Andrew Jackson. Let's have a toast."

Victor poured each man three fingers of the coveted drink.

"To 40 years of success, my friend." Victor raised a glass.

"To 40 years," Zeke repeated.

Both men sipped their drinks while looking out toward the South Lawn.

"Do you have the list?" Victor asked.

Reaching into his jacket pocket one last time, he handed the envelope to Victor.

"No, my friend. You've marked off the first nine; you can mark off #10."

Opening the envelope, Zeke unfolded the paper and marked off 'Private meeting with Zeke at the White House.'

"Feels good to complete a to-do list," Zeke announced.

"It certainly does."

As they emersed themselves in the scene, they heard a door in the Yellow Oval Room open. Dismayed, Victor shouted, "I asked to be left alone!"

"I'm sorry. Am I interrupting something?"

At first glance, Victor was angry, then confused, and then quickly released an involuntary chuckle.

"Zeke, am I dreaming or is the one and only hero of the common man, Elijah Mustang, gracing us with his presence?"

"Good evening, gentlemen."

Victor's mind quickly raced to explain Elijah's unexpected appearance.

"I see the good Vice President has been busy behind the scenes to facilitate this surprise visit."

"Ah, I was just in the neighborhood and thought I would drop by," Elijah mused.

"Can we interest you in a drink?" Victor enticed.

"No, thank you. I don't intend to stay that long."

"That's a shame," Victor mocked. "It must be difficult knowing how close you were to this all being yours."

Victor began to pace around the balcony.

"Who are we kidding? You got the most votes by far, way more than that imbecile McCoy. And yet somehow, he's the President of the United States; and the last I heard you're off in the jungles of Brazil saving lost souls. Come on, how is that fair?"

Elijah didn't respond but instead took a step toward the balcony railing and looked out over the perfectly manicured lawn glistening in the moonlight.

Victor raised both hands in surrender.

"OK, we give up. Are you going to make us ask why you are here?"

Turning around, Elijah placed his back against the railing and faced Victor and Zeke.

"I know you've had a rough year in that horrible, terrible prison, but it sounds like you've really landed on your feet," Elijah offered.

"God bless America, land of the free," Victor responded raising a glass.

Elijah nodded slightly, then looked Victor in the eye.

"I just want you to understand that we're all still here. We're all still here, and we're not done."

"Ah yes, the cry of the Mustangs, 'We're not done.' Kinda has a nice ring to it. I can almost hear the chants from the huddled masses even as we speak," Victor ridiculed.

Elijah allowed a slight grin to come upon his face. "You know, I can almost hear them too."

Victor again started pacing.

"You know this place where we're standing. It is called the Truman Balcony. Harry Truman saw an empty space here and had the vision for this balcony. He knew it would provide this wonderful vantage point we're enjoying this evening. He knew it would provide shade for the area below. But he encountered nothing but resistance. Everyone told him it was a bad idea and that he should abandon any thought of it. They couldn't see his vision; all they heard was that he wanted to make a change, and they were against it. It didn't stop Truman, who was a visionary. He persisted—no, he demanded that this balcony be built. Once it was completed, everyone saw it was a marvelous idea. They just needed someone to push until necessary change occurred.

"You see, Elijah, sometimes people need a visionary to push them to a place they didn't even know they wanted to go. That's what we're doing here, giving the people a little push. I'm sure you can understand that."

Elijah bobbed his head slightly as he put his hand on one of the columns.

"If memory serves, after Truman convinced the people to build this balcony, the construction process revealed serious structural defects in the foundation of the White House; and Truman had to move out for a number of years."

Elijah spun back to face Victor.

"You gotta be careful making changes; they may reveal foundational weaknesses you never knew existed."

"Now! Now we're finally getting somewhere!" Victor exclaimed. "Foundational weaknesses, like Andrei Ovchenko and Blackforce in Pittsburgh being raided by the Feds. Yeah, I know all about that. Or my own computer guy sabotaging my computer system, Omnia. Yeah, I know about that too. And the next thing, and the next thing, and the next thing, I'll know about them too. You think I got here, in this position in the White House, by letting neophytes like you get a step ahead of me?"

Elijah nodded in understanding. "I see. Sounds like you gentlemen have everything under control. Now that we have that settled, I'll leave you to your private celebration. It was great catching up. Have a wonderful rest of your evening."

Elijah smiled at the duo as he left the balcony and reentered the Yellow Oval Room, then disappeared into the White House.

Victor laughed as he sat in the chair taking a swig of Pappy Van Winkle as Zeke looked off into the distance unsure what had just happened or what might happen next.

Jeremy was surprised at how busy the Three Rivers Heritage Trail was at almost 11 p.m. Along the banks of the Ohio River at the trail's northernmost point, joggers, walkers, and bikers were milling about. As he approached the industrial area adjacent to the Westhall Street Trailhead, he saw the faded, rusty 'Quality Manufacturing' sign and knew he was in the right place. He snaked around the building and found the closest thing to a main entrance where he stood looking up into a crumbling brick façade.

Inside the building's central control room, the two men on evening assignment perked up when they saw Jeremy on the security camera. Looking at each other, they wondered if the man on the screen had taken a wrong turn on the trail. They quickly had their answer.

Jeremy saw the camera, waved, and then shouted, "This is Jeremy Prince! Tell Andrei I'm here to see him!"

The two guards again looked at one another, and one uttered, "Crazy man."

Jeremy again shouted at the building, "I know you can hear me! I'm sure Andrei has already gone beddy-bye and you nice fellas don't want to wake the little booger, but just tell him it's Jeremy. Trust me, he'll be glad you did! I'll just wait here."

The guards flipped a coin with the loser getting the chore of waking Andrei. The guard was surprised to find Jeremy was telling the truth. Andrei didn't even bother putting on shoes before heading out the warehouse door to meet Jeremy.

Upon seeing Ovchenko coming out the door, Jeremy exclaimed, "Andrei! It is great to see you!"

Ovchenko walked to Jeremy without saying a word, grabbed him by his shirt, drug him back into the warehouse, and threw him into the center of the dirty floor.

"You are fool for coming here."

Not bothering to stand but instead spinning to a seated position, Jeremy conceded, "You're probably right."

"Why are you here?" Ovchenko demanded.

"I just wanted to see you one more time, Andrei—you

know, for old time's sake."

The commotion had brought most of Ovchenko's men out of their rooms to see what was happening. Most had heard of Jeremy Prince as both Victor's protégé and the man who disbanded Mouse Trap and, by extension, tried to disband Blackforce. Most of Ovchenko's men were underwhelmed, expecting someone older, bigger, and stronger.

"What you mean, *one more time?*" Ovchenko queried, again grabbing Jeremy by his shirt.

"You're a legend Andrei. Everyone wants to see a legend when they say goodbye. Everyone wanted to be there in Jordan's last game, Tyson's last fight, Usain Bolt's last race. You see in just a moment; federal agents are going to rush through that door and put an end to all of this. I wanted to be here to see it."

Ovchenko dropped Jeremy back on the ground and emitted a hearty laugh. "Federal agents coming?" Ovchenko repeated once in English and again in Russian, each time eliciting hearty laughs from the now huddling Blackforce operators.

"Jeremy, you don't know; Victor now runs FBI. They are not coming to save you."

Again, the room burst into laughter.

"Oh, I didn't say the FBI was coming. I just said FEDERAL AGENTS are coming." Jeremy ensured the words *federal agents* were at full volume.

"End of games," Ovchenko declared.

"I said FEDERAL AGENTS!" Jeremy was now screaming. Just as he again reached for Jeremy, Ovchenko was startled by an abrupt sound quickly followed by bright lights. As Ovchenko and his men worked to understand what was happening, armored vehicles burst through four different entrances; and three dozen agents, guns drawn, encircled them.

The lead agent announced, "Andrei Ovchenko, we are with Immigration and Customs Enforcement, Enforcement and Removal Operations. You and your men are in this country illegally. We have a warrant to for your detention, and we are authorized to execute immediate deportation."

"Deportation?" Ovchenko managed to utter.

It was a moment Jeremy had dreamt of for over six months since laying his father to rest. He didn't know exactly how it would happen, but he knew the opportunity would arise for him to avenge his father's death. When the FBI asked him to review Mouse Trap's information, Jeremy found that although many of the Blackforce operators had been in the United States for over 20 years, they had never bothered to become citizens or register for green cards. This provided the perfect opportunity for a surprise attack that Ovchenko would never see coming.

Before the Blackforce operators could muster resistance, ICE agents ordered the men face down on the floor. The confused horde complied, unsure what to do next. Agents quickly zip-tied the men's hands and began loading the men in waiting buses. Ovchenko was the last man in the warehouse accompanied by four agents and Jeremy Prince. Jeremy stepped to Ovchenko and stood nose to nose.

"You killed my father, you son of a bitch. Then you

walked away, just like you have thousands of other times, thinking you'd gotten away with murder. I'm glad I'm here to see the end of Andrei Ovchenko and Blackforce. I have the satisfaction of knowing exactly where you are going, and I've been promised that you will suffer the same fate as my father."

Jeremy did his best to grab the barrel-chested man by the shirt and punch him as hard as he could, bringing blood from his mouth. However, Ovchenko barely flinched.

"I hope they make it slow and painful. I've heard they're really good at that."

As the agents led Ovchenko away, the lead agent shook Jeremy's hand and thanked him for the tip.

"Do you have a way to get back to wherever you're going?" the agent asked.

"Yeah, I'm good. I have a car just down the street. You guys have a good trip to the airport."

The agent left Jeremy alone in the warehouse, where he looked up at one of the surveillance cameras mounted on the railing above. He smiled at the camera and waved. "See you in a few hours," he shouted. Then he walked out the door.

"Did he have to make that so dramatic?" Savannah shrilled.

"You know we're talking about Jeremy, right?" Leonard remarked.

"So, he's always been that way?" Ben Gossett joked.

Savannah just shook her head.

At the back of the boat, Vice President Adair was on the phone.

"Excellent. You are authorized for full deportation. The destination country is expecting you. Great job. Let your men know they saved many lives by their actions tonight. ... Yes, I am safe. Good evening."

Leonard was first to arrive at The Hammer, the Prince family's Smith Mountain Lake houseboat. He left the Mouse Trap headquarters in Bethesda, Maryland, as Victor was concluding his 'I'm back' speech. He arrived at The Hammer around 2 p.m. Two prior trips in the last month had provided Leonard the opportunity to fully equip the vessel for this eventful gathering. The Hammer had become the most technologically advanced houseboat on the planet, now fully tethered to Omnia. That afternoon he was testing its extensive surveillance infrastructure, ensuring he could connect to Ovchenko's security system.

Savannah arrived around 5 p.m. with more questions than answers. Before she left Abingdon, Jeremy spent an hour with her doing his best to bring her up to speed on the recent weeks' events and the most unbelievable scheme she'd ever heard. Jeremy explained that Thomas Hanover, his FBI contact, had been murdered by Victor's men, the same men who had started the hardware store fire that killed his father. Jeremy shared that he had been working with FBI Agent Ben Gossett, who was working with the Vice President of the United States, who was working with Elijah Mustang. He explained that he had to make a quick trip to Pittsburgh to help ICE apprehend Ovchenko and that Savannah needed to go to the houseboat, which until then she didn't know existed, to meet Leonard and that he would be there soon. And he mentioned the Vice President was also going to be at the boat.

Ben Gossett was the third to arrive, shortly after Savannah. He drove straight from Pittsburgh, receiving many calls and texts along the way from the FBI trying to ascertain his whereabouts. He had the foresight to turn off all location services on his phone so he couldn't be tracked.

Around 8 p.m., Adair was the fourth to arrive at the boat. Per agreement with Beth McDonald, Director of the Secret Service, Adair would be disguised as a fisherman on a trip with two buddies, Adair's Secret Service detail. Before leaving Washington, Adair finalized plans with the Department of Homeland Security (to whom ICE reports) for Ovchenko and his men's deportation, a plan that had been in the works for over a month. As a final action, Adair also arranged the pass for Elijah to crash Victor's White House celebration in order to send the message that Victor wouldn't have free reign at the White House without a battle.

"Where exactly are Ovchenko and his men going?" Savannah asked, still not believing she was having a conversation with the Vice President of the United States.

"If I understand correctly, you worked for Victor at Mouse Trap, along with Mr. Prince, correct?" Adair asked.

"Not exactly something I'm proud of—but yeah, we worked there."

"So, you know some of Ovchenko's background," Adair

surmised.

"I know he was a Soviet general and that he was as bad a guy there as he was here in the States."

"Exactly. Beyond being a general, Ovchenko worked for the KGB and was a brutal enforcer in Ukraine. As the Soviet Union staggered toward dissolution in the late '80s, an independence movement arose in Ukraine seeing a hopeful future as a sovereign nation. However, Ovchenko's job was to tamp down that independence, something he did in a most brutal way. Now, a nation for almost 30 years, many of Ukraine's current leaders remember Ovchenko's actions and were more than pleased when we offered the prospect of his, and many of his ruthless henchmen's, return. A C130 transport plane should be somewhere over the Atlantic right about now taking those men to justice."

"You know, it's almost midnight; and I'm wiped out. Is anyone else tired? I'm ready for bed," Leonard proclaimed.

"I'm going to wait up for a couple more to arrive at the boat; then I'll call it a night too. We have a big day ahead of us," Adair agreed.

"Wait, we're doing more stuff tomorrow?" Savannah protested. "Jeremy didn't say anything about tomorrow."

56

SEPTEMBER 21, 2017

"Hey, Babe! You made it!"

"What time did you get here?" Savannah asked, wiping her eyes as she ascended to the third level, greeting Jeremy with a kiss at the captain's bridge.

"A little after 6. I was able to drive around 90 until I got off I-64, so I made great time," Jeremy recalled.

"So, we're actually on a boat...apparently your boat... with the Vice President of the United States? I'm not dreaming, right?"

"Not dreaming," Jeremy confirmed.

Watching the sun rise over the horizon in the east, Savannah asked, "So, you really own this boat?"

"Yeah, she's pretty sweet, isn't she?"

Before Savannah could respond, Adair joined them on the bridge.

"Nice vessel, Jeremy."

"Thank you, sir. It is great to see you again." Jeremy

shook the Vice President's hand.

"Quite a show you put on last night in Pittsburgh."

"I'm not gonna lie; the ICE guys could have come a little sooner. I was getting worried."

"Hey, you guys want to come down to the meeting area. Things are about to get interesting at Mouse Trap," Leonard shouted to the bridge.

"Sure, be right there," Jeremy yelled down to the lower level.

The crew began to take seats around the large living room. Leonard sat in a chair behind a desk; Jeremy and Savannah shared a love seat; Adair was in a recliner with his fishing buddies/Secret Service detail positioned by two doors; and Ben Gossett sat in a recliner next to Adair.

As Leonard was readying the large screen, the group was joined by two more guests who had arrived during the night and caught a few hours of sleep in cabins on the lower level.

"Good morning!" Elijah Mustang greeted. "Some of you don't know my colleague, Minnie Carpenter. Minnie is the leader of our movement.

As Minnie walked around the room shaking hands, she observed, "He's still too humble to call it what everyone else calls it, the Mustang movement; and we all know he's the real leader."

Elijah shared with the group the story of his Truman Balcony encounter with Victor and Zeke. Leonard had hoped to find a way to livestream that meeting via a lapel camera; but everyone agreed it was too high a risk, so Elijah went solo.

"OK, things are going to get interesting in less than five minutes. Let's all watch the screen." Leonard split the 85-inch screen into quadrants, each showing a livestream video inside Mouse Trap.

"Has anyone seen Zeke?" Victor asked poking his head out of his office.

"No, sir," his assistant replied.

"This isn't like him to be late. I need an update on Blackforce operations. They should have already taken several actions."

As he spoke, a phone rang in the background. "Sir, FBI Director Thompson wants to speak with you."

"OK. I will take it in my office."

Victor returned to his office, shut the door, and turned on the speakerphone.

"Yes, Gavin."

"Victor, I'm afraid there's been a development in Pittsburgh."

"What kind of development?"

"I'm still working through the details, but it seems there was an ICE raid on your asset's location."

"I thought you said you had it covered."

"I had the FBI covered. ICE isn't in the Justice Department. They don't report to us."

"Enough with the civics lesson. What's their status?"

"Sir...I'm afraid it's not good. They appear to have been

deported."

"*Deported*? How is that possible? Deported to where?"

"Still working on that, sir."

"Well, work faster!"

"I'm not sure we are able to—"

Before Thompson could finish his thought, Victor hung up on him. He moved behind his desk to log in to Omnia to send Ovchenko a message. As he completed his login credentials, the screen went blue. He clicked on his mouse, tapped on his keyboard, and then pounded on his desk.

"My screen is dead! Get Cassidy in here!"

"Did you really go with the blue screen of death?" Jeremy asked Leonard.

"Seemed like the right thing to do," Leonard confirmed.

"Strong," Jeremy chuckled.

"Cassidy! Get in here!" Victor screamed.

"My computer won't log in to Omnia. Fix it!"

"Yes sir, there...uh...seems to be a problem."

"What kind of problem!"

"It appears that Omnia is...*gone*."

"Gone? How is it gone?"

"It seems that Leonard—"

"Leonard!?" Victor interrupted. "I thought you said

Leonard wasn't working on the real Omnia, that he was working on a copy."

"Well…"

"So, they knew you were working against them?" Jeremy asked.

"I had my suspicions as soon as I returned; but when they sent that Cassidy gal—I didn't like her; I knew something was up. You're not going to believe this; they tried to pass a fake Omnia off on me."

"They *what?*" Savannah asked.

"They made a fake Omnia and had me work on that while Cassidy (did I mention I didn't like her?) worked on the real Omnia."

"How did you know it was fake?"

Leonard drooped his shoulders. "Really? Are you serious? If I went down the street, found a blonde about the same size and height as Savannah, brought her to you, and said, 'Hey, Jeremy, here's Savannah'—you'd know the difference, right?"

Jeremy cocked his head. "So, you're saying Omnia is… your girlfriend?"

"Fiancé," Savanna corrected.

"You make it sound weird," Leonard blubbered.

"Because it *is* weird," Jeremy blurted.

"So, what did you do to Omnia?" Savannah wondered.

"First, I switched around Cassidy's program so that they'd

be working on the fake site, which is much smaller than the real Omnia. For the past six hours, I've been wiping the real Omnia off all Mouse Trap's servers. Then, when that finished just a few minutes ago, I ran a routine that wiped the fake Omnia too. Now, they have nothing."

"So, Omnia's gone?" Jeremy asked.

"No! Omnia's here. That's how we're watching."

"Leonard, I remember the last time you were supposed to destroy Omnia and didn't, a lot of really bad things happened," Jeremy warned.

"I remember, but this time will be different. I promise." Leonard assured.

Sensing a need to change the conversation's tone, Elijah interjected, "Leonard, you should be proud of yourself. Well done."

Elijah looked around the room. "This is quite a group. The FBI. Three former members of this thing called Mouse Trap. The leader of—OK, I'll say it, the Mustang Movement. The Vice President of the United States."

"And the guy who should be the president," Leonard blurted, pointing at Elijah. As the group applauded, Elijah acknowledged them with a nod.

"Let's get back to this group of heroes because that's what you are—heroes." Elijah again gestured around the room.

"This group, many of whom barely knew one another, managed to work together to strike a serious blow to the most dangerous man I've ever encountered. Looking into his eyes last night, I know that man is a cancer that must be removed from this country; otherwise, it will result in our country's demise. We've managed to slow the growth of that cancer, but be confident, it is still alive and will metastasize. Although his capacity is temporarily diminished, Victor still has many assets at his disposal. He has the media. He still has the Mouse Trap organization, which I'm just beginning to understand; but I know enough to realize it is lethal. And he has the power of the President.

"So, what now? What do we do about this wounded animal?" Elijah gestured to the screen as Victor was seen flailing about in the Mouse Trap office. "We must get to work with the end goal of completely eradicating this man. It will take every one of us and millions more working together. It won't be quick; in fact, it will take years. We'll lose battles, and we'll take steps backwards; but we must remain fixed on the goal of the complete defeat of Victor Youngblood. We must all agree, here in this room, that we'll devote our remaining days to this cause."

Elijah began walking around the room looking each person in the eye.

"Do you agree?" Ben nodded.

"Do you agree?" Adair nodded.

"Do you agree?" Minnie nodded.

"Do you agree?" Leonard nodded.

"Do you agree?" Jeremy and Savannah nodded.

"Then this is a powerful start and a formidable team, but we'll need more. In fact, there's one more member who's ready to join our cause." Elijah walked to the stairs leading from the lower level to the second level where the group was assembled.

"I'd like to welcome Zeke Gibson to the team."

Jeremy's, Leonard's, and Savannah's mouths all dropped. Adair looked at Elijah incredulously. Zeke walked toward the group.

"You gotta be kidding me!" Jeremy cringed.

"I understand this is quite a shock, and I recognize there's a thick air of skepticism in the room; but I'd like to take the first step to assure you that I'm on your side," Zeke avowed.

"This is bull," Jeremy roared.

"During our balcony encounter, Zeke slipped me a note telling me to call him. We spoke shortly thereafter, and he explained that he wanted a way out."

Zeke spent the next 15 minutes explaining how his time away from Victor made him see Mouse Trap's deeds more clearly. Things had changed. He wasn't sure if they had changed with Victor, changed with him, or maybe some of both. He shared that the final straw was the kill order Victor gave to the faithful jailor, Javier. He couldn't explain what was different about that order other than the thousands of similar orders Victor had made over the last 40 years, but he was certain it was time for Zeke to step away. As he had predicted, skepticism lingered in the room.

Jeremy stood to speak. "OK, so I'm not totally on board with this whole Zeke thing, but I'm at least willing to see where it may lead." He took a couple of steps toward Zeke and offered his hand, which Zeke shook firmly.

"Thank you, Jeremy."

"Anyone else?" Jeremy asked.

The group stood and shook Zeke's hand—albeit with varying degrees of reluctance

Elijah regained the floor. "OK, it's settled. This is the group. This is the group that's going to take on Victor Youngblood. Let's talk about next steps."

Jeremy stood again. "I have a next step. Hey, Leonard, unmute the screen."

On the screen, Victor could be seen uncharacteristically screaming at his team, "Where's Zeke! Someone get me Zeke!"

"OK, everyone be quiet for just a second," Jeremy said while dialing his phone.

In the midst of the chaos, Victor felt his phone vibrate. He peeked to see who was calling. Surprised to see the caller, he answered, "Jeremy?"

"Victor! It is great to hear your voice. Hope you are doing well."

"Well, actually, I'm—"

Ignoring Victor, Jeremy continued, "I wanted to get back with you about our discussion yesterday. I've given a lot of thought to your offer of rejoining the team, and well…I'm in!"

THE END

I hope you enjoyed Presidential Power. To stay in touch with John Ford Clayton visit www.johnfordclayton.com, www.twitter.com/johnfordclayton or www.facebook.com/johnfordclayton.